MARVEL-VERSE
SHANG-CHI

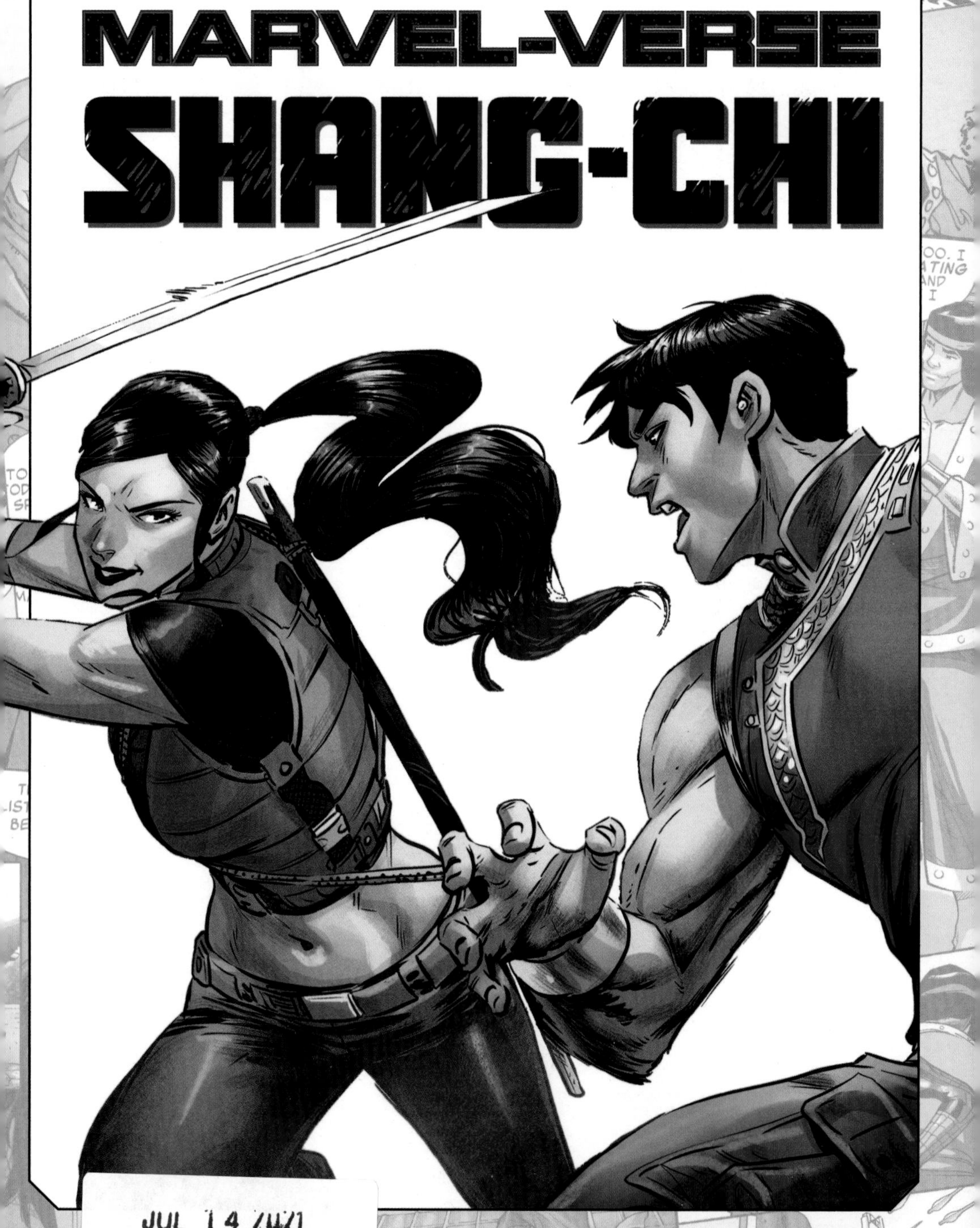

MARVEL-VERSE
SHANG-CHI

MARVEL ADVENTURES SPIDER-MAN #2

WRITER: **PAUL TOBIN**
PENCILER: **MATTEO LOLLI**
INKERS: **CHRISTIAN DALLA VECCHIA,
TERRY PALLOT & SCOTT KOBLISH**
COLORIST: **SOTOCOLOR**
LETTERER: **DAVE SHARPE**
COVER ART: **KARL KERSCHL,
SERGE LAPOINTE & NADINE THOMAS**
ASSISTANT EDITOR: **MICHAEL HORWITZ**
EDITOR: **NATHAN COSBY**

WOLVERINE: FIRST CLASS #9

WRITER: **FRED VAN LENTE**
ARTIST: **FRANCIS PORTELA**
COLORIST: **ULISES ARREOLA**
LETTERER: **VC'S JOE CARAMAGNA**
COVER ART: **SALVA ESPIN,
KARL KESEL & WIL QUINTANA**
ASSISTANT EDITOR: **JORDAN D. WHITE**
CONSULTING EDITOR: **RALPH MACCHIO**
EDITORS: **MARK PANICCIA &
NATHAN COSBY**

MARVEL-VERSE: SHANG-CHI. Contains material originally published in magazine form as WOLVERINE: FIRST CLASS (2008) #9, MARVEL ADVENTURES SPIDER-MAN (2010) #2, FREE COMIC BOOK DAY 2011 (SPIDER-MAN) #1, MASTER OF KUNG FU (2017) #126 and THE LEGEND OF SHANG-CHI (2021) #1. First printing 2021. ISBN 978-1-302-92777-6. Published by MARVEL WORLDWIDE, INC., a subsidiary of MARVEL ENTERTAINMENT, LLC. OFFICE OF PUBLICATION: 1290 Avenue of the Americas, New York, NY 10104. © 2021 MARVEL No similarity between any of the names, characters, persons, and/or institutions in this magazine with those of any living or dead person or institution is intended, and any such similarity which may exist is purely coincidental. **Printed in Canada.** KEVIN FEIGE, Chief Creative Officer; DAN BUCKLEY, President, Marvel Entertainment; JOE QUESADA, EVP & Creative Director; DAVID BOGART, Associate Publisher & SVP of Talent Affairs; TOM BREVOORT, VP, Executive Editor; NICK LOWE, Executive Editor, VP of Content, Digital Publishing; DAVID GABRIEL, VP of Print & Digital Publishing; JEFF YOUNGQUIST, VP of Production & Special Projects; ALEX MORALES, Director of Publishing Operations; DAN EDINGTON, Managing Editor; RICKEY PURDIN, Director of Talent Relations; JENNIFER GRÜNWALD, Senior Editor, Special Projects; SUSAN CRESPI, Production Manager; STAN LEE, Chairman Emeritus. For information regarding advertising in Marvel Comics or on Marvel.com, please contact Vit DeBellis, Custom Solutions & Integrated Advertising Manager, at vdebellis@marvel.com. For Marvel subscription inquiries, please call 888-511-5480. **Manufactured between 4/2/2021 and 5/4/2021 by SOLISCO PRINTERS, SCOTT, QC, CANADA.**

10 9 8 7 6 5 4 3 2 1

FREE COMIC BOOK DAY 2011 (SPIDER-MAN)

WRITER: **DAN SLOTT**
PENCILER: **HUMBERTO RAMOS**
INKERS: **CARLOS CUEVAS & VICTOR OLAZABA**
COLORIST: **EDGAR DELGADO**
LETTERER: **VC'S JOE CARAMAGNA**
COVER ART: **HUMBERTO RAMOS &
EDGAR DELGADO**
ASSISTANT EDITOR: **ELLIE PYLE**
EDITOR: **STEPHEN WACKER**

THE LEGEND OF SHANG-CHI #1

WRITER: **ALYSSA WONG**
ARTIST: **ANDIE TONG**
COLORIST: **RACHELLE ROSENBERG**
LETTERER: **VC'S TRAVIS LANHAM**
COVER ART: **ANDIE TONG & RACHELLE
ROSENBERG**
ASSISTANT EDITOR: **KAT GREGOROWICZ**
EDITOR: **DARREN SHAN**

MASTER OF KUNG FU #126

WRITER: **CM PUNK**
ARTIST: **DALIBOR TALAJIĆ**
COLORIST: **ERICK ARCINIEGA**
LETTERER: **VC'S TRAVIS LANHAM**
COVER ART: **JAVIER RODRÍGUEZ**
EDITOR: **KATHLEEN WISNESKI**
SUPERVISING EDITOR: **NICK LOWE**

COLLECTION EDITOR: **JENNIFER GRÜNWALD** ASSISTANT EDITOR: **DANIEL KIRCHHOFFER**
ASSISTANT MANAGING EDITOR: **MAIA LOY** ASSISTANT MANAGING EDITOR: **LISA MONTALBANO**
ASSOCIATE MANAGER, DIGITAL ASSETS: **JOE HOCHSTEIN** VP PRODUCTION & SPECIAL PROJECTS: **JEFF YOUNGQUIST**
RESEARCH: **JESS HARROLD** BOOK DESIGNERS: **STACIE ZUCKER & ADAM DEL RE** with **JAY BOWEN**
SVP PRINT, SALES & MARKETING: **DAVID GABRIEL** EDITOR IN CHIEF: **C.B. CEBULSKI**

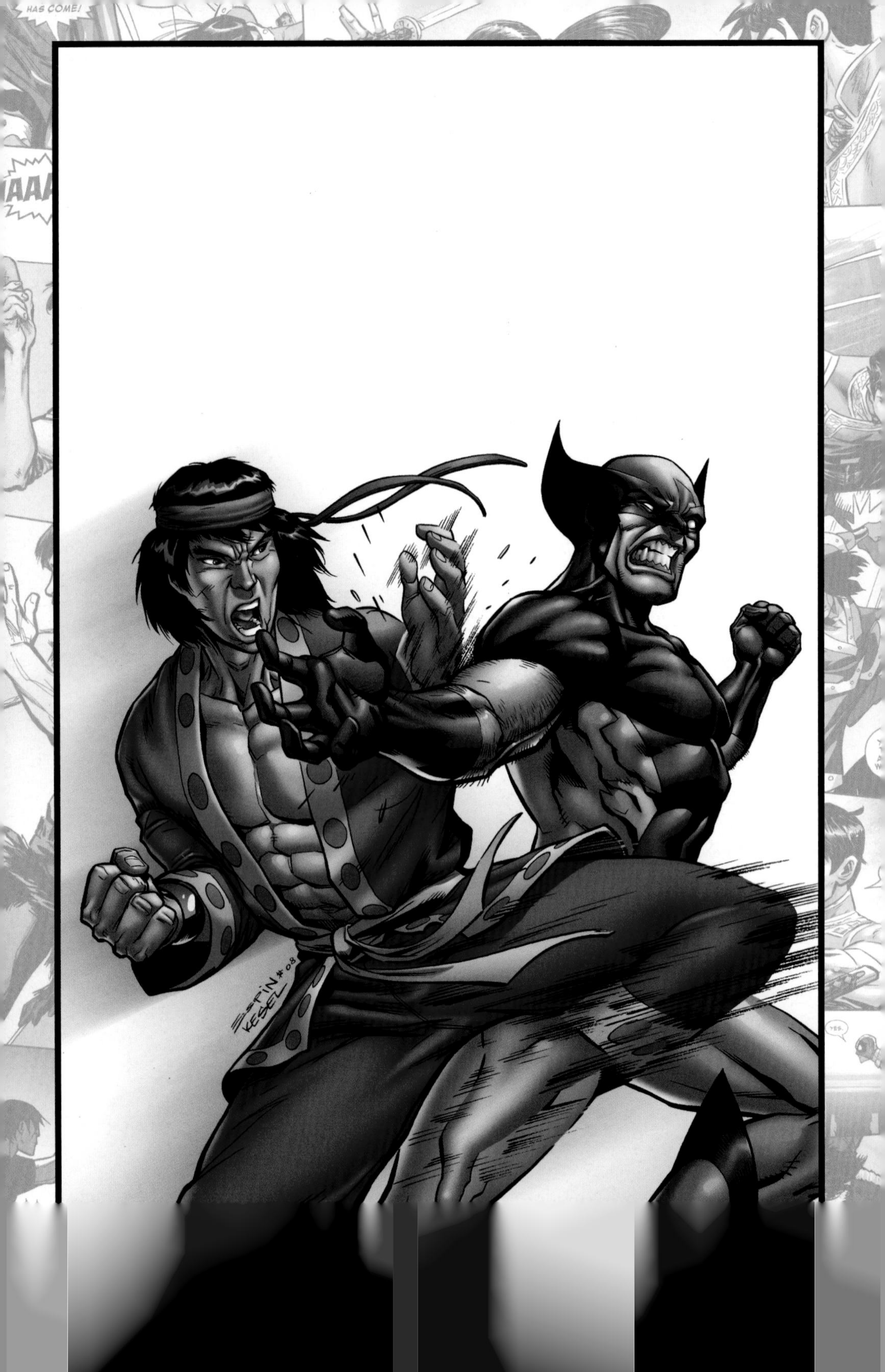
HAS COME!
YES.

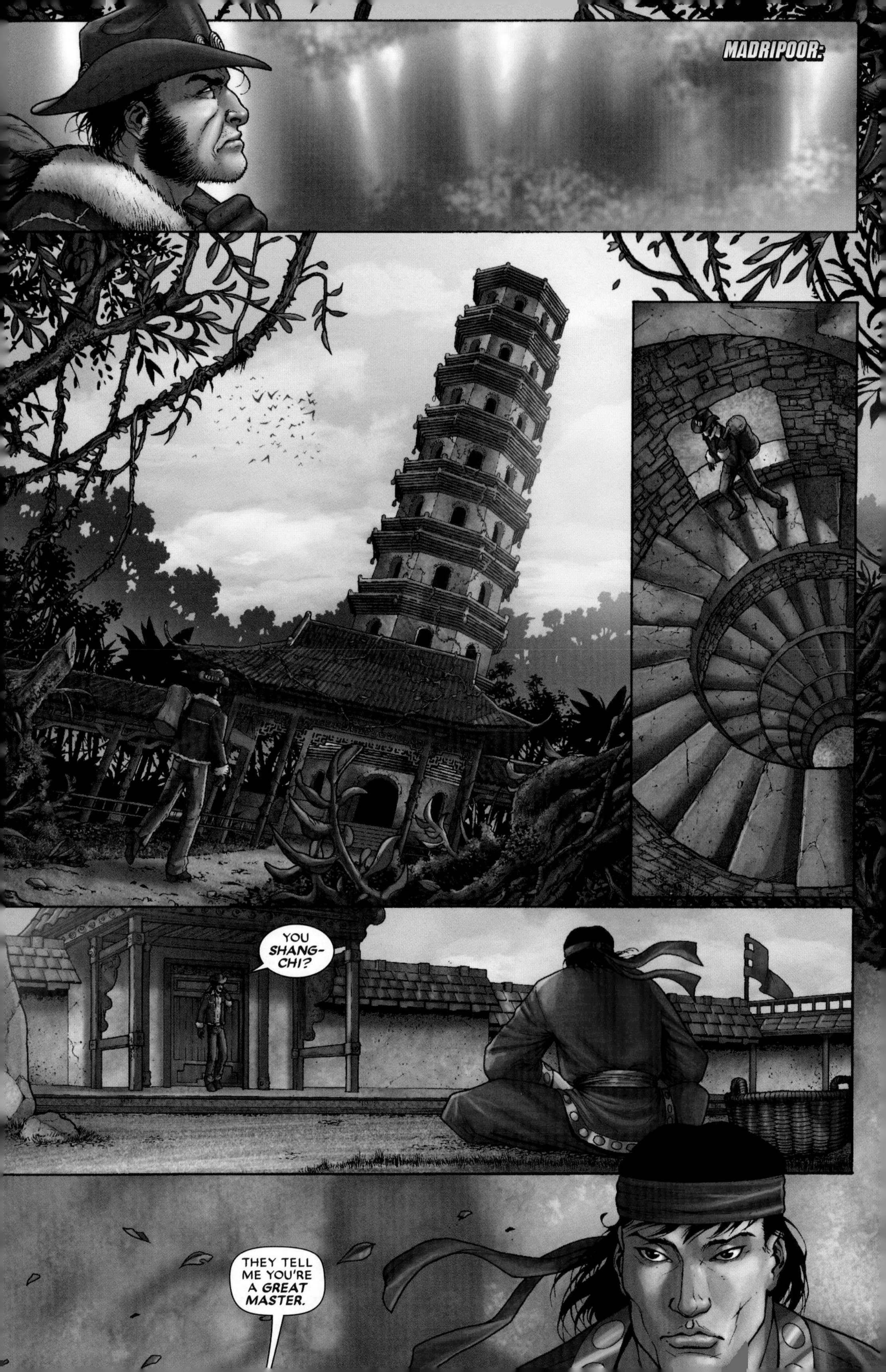
MADRIPOOR:
YOU SHANG-CHI?
THEY TELL ME YOU'RE A GREAT MASTER.

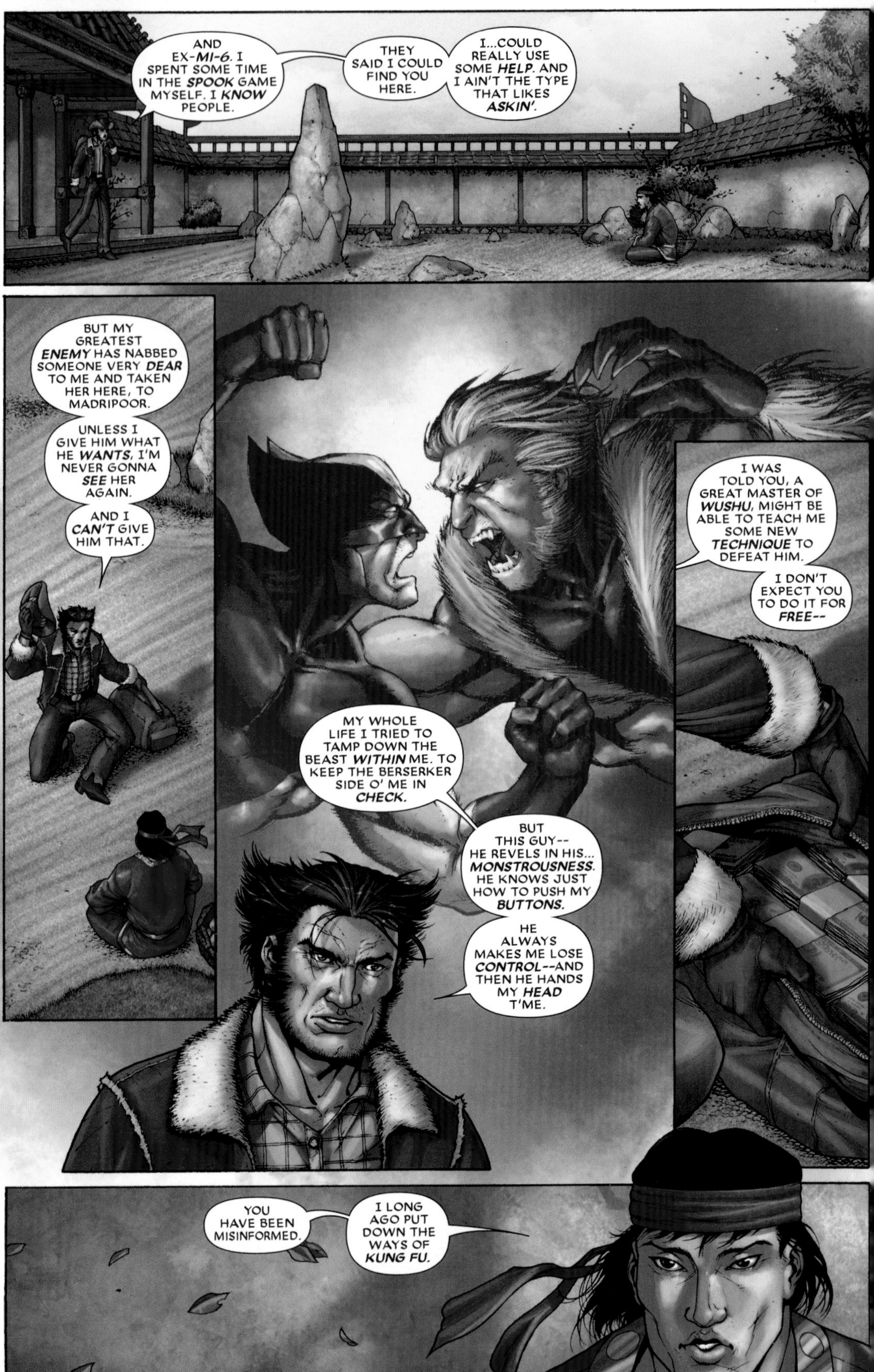
AND EX-MI-6. I SPENT SOME TIME IN THE SPOOK GAME MYSELF. I KNOW PEOPLE.
THEY SAID I COULD FIND YOU HERE.
I...COULD REALLY USE SOME HELP. AND I AIN'T THE TYPE THAT LIKES ASKIN'.
BUT MY GREATEST ENEMY HAS NABBED SOMEONE VERY DEAR TO ME AND TAKEN HER HERE, TO MADRIPOOR.
UNLESS I GIVE HIM WHAT HE WANTS, I'M NEVER GONNA SEE HER AGAIN.
AND I CAN'T GIVE HIM THAT.
I WAS TOLD YOU, A GREAT MASTER OF WUSHU, MIGHT BE ABLE TO TEACH ME SOME NEW TECHNIQUE TO DEFEAT HIM.
I DON'T EXPECT YOU TO DO IT FOR FREE--
MY WHOLE LIFE I TRIED TO TAMP DOWN THE BEAST WITHIN ME. TO KEEP THE BERSERKER SIDE O' ME IN CHECK.
BUT THIS GUY-- HE REVELS IN HIS... MONSTROUSNESS. HE KNOWS JUST HOW TO PUSH MY BUTTONS.
HE ALWAYS MAKES ME LOSE CONTROL--AND THEN HE HANDS MY HEAD T'ME.
YOU HAVE BEEN MISINFORMED.
I LONG AGO PUT DOWN THE WAYS OF KUNG FU.

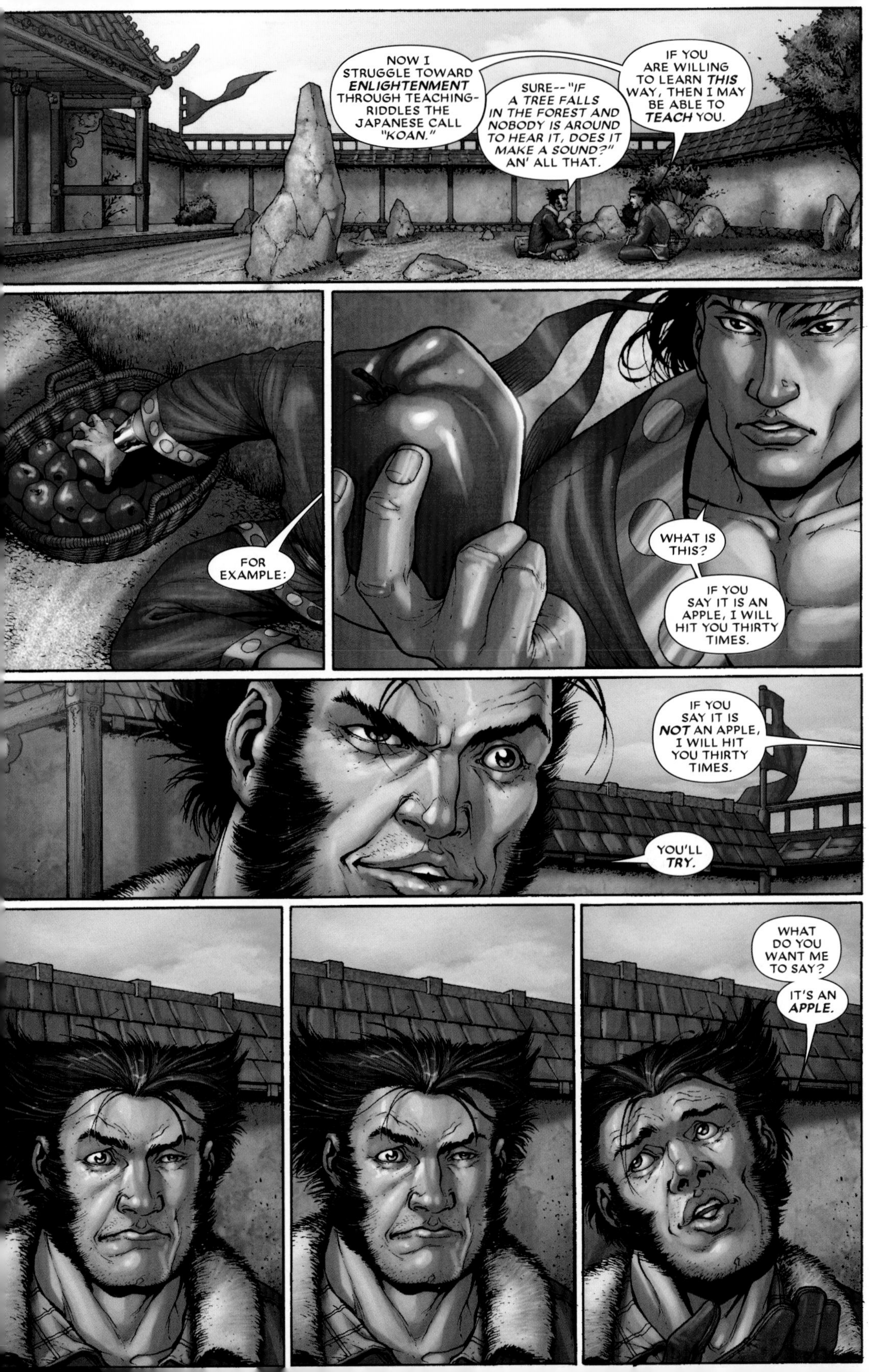
NOW I STRUGGLE TOWARD ENLIGHTENMENT THROUGH TEACHING-RIDDLES THE JAPANESE CALL "KOAN."
SURE--"IF A TREE FALLS IN THE FOREST AND NOBODY IS AROUND TO HEAR IT, DOES IT MAKE A SOUND?" AN' ALL THAT.
IF YOU ARE WILLING TO LEARN THIS WAY, THEN I MAY BE ABLE TO TEACH YOU.
FOR EXAMPLE:
WHAT IS THIS?
IF YOU SAY IT IS AN APPLE, I WILL HIT YOU THIRTY TIMES.
IF YOU SAY IT IS NOT AN APPLE, I WILL HIT YOU THIRTY TIMES.
YOU'LL TRY.
WHAT DO YOU WANT ME TO SAY?
IT'S AN APPLE.

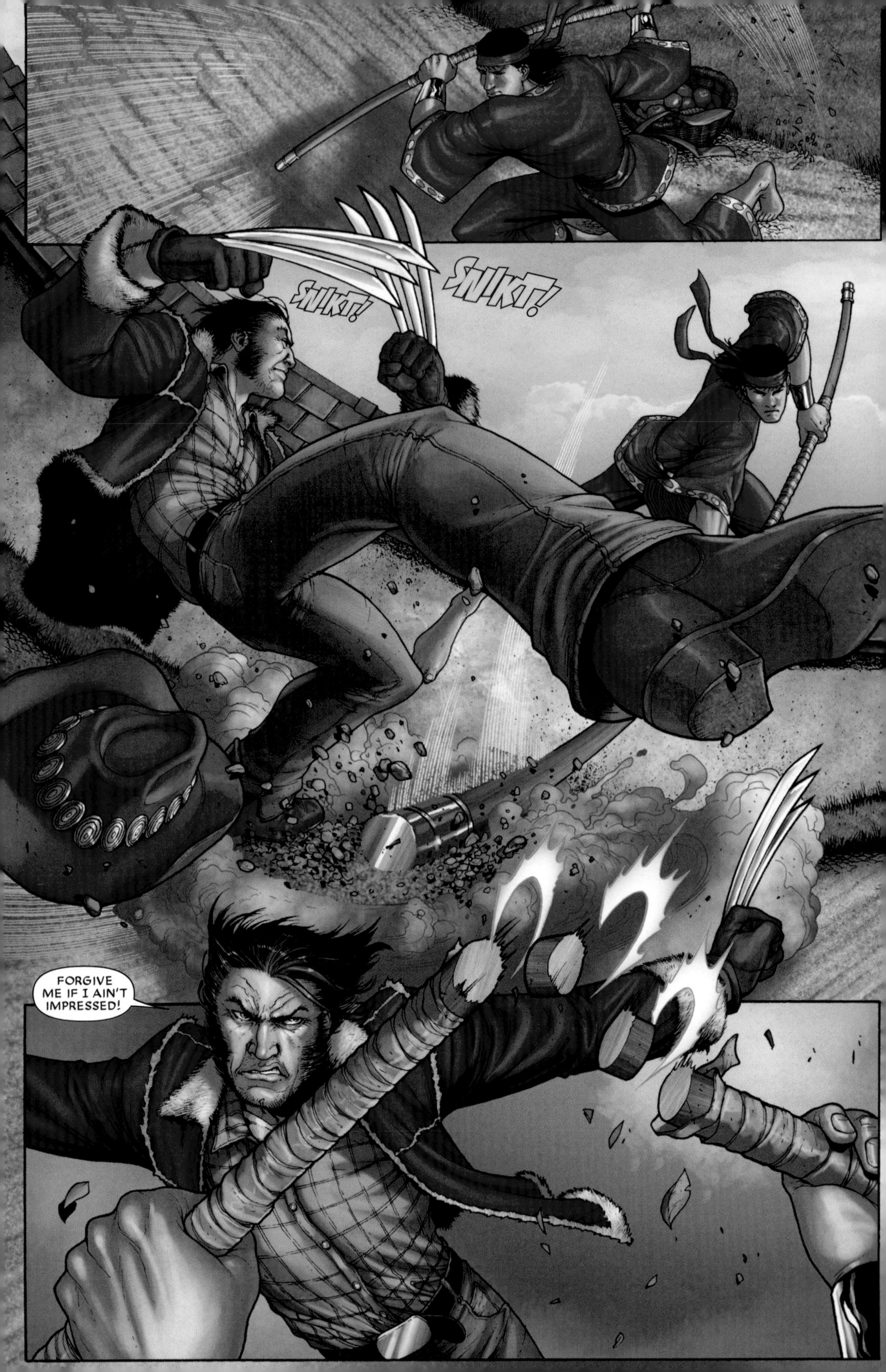
SNIKT!
SNIKT!
FORGIVE ME IF I AIN'T IMPRESSED!

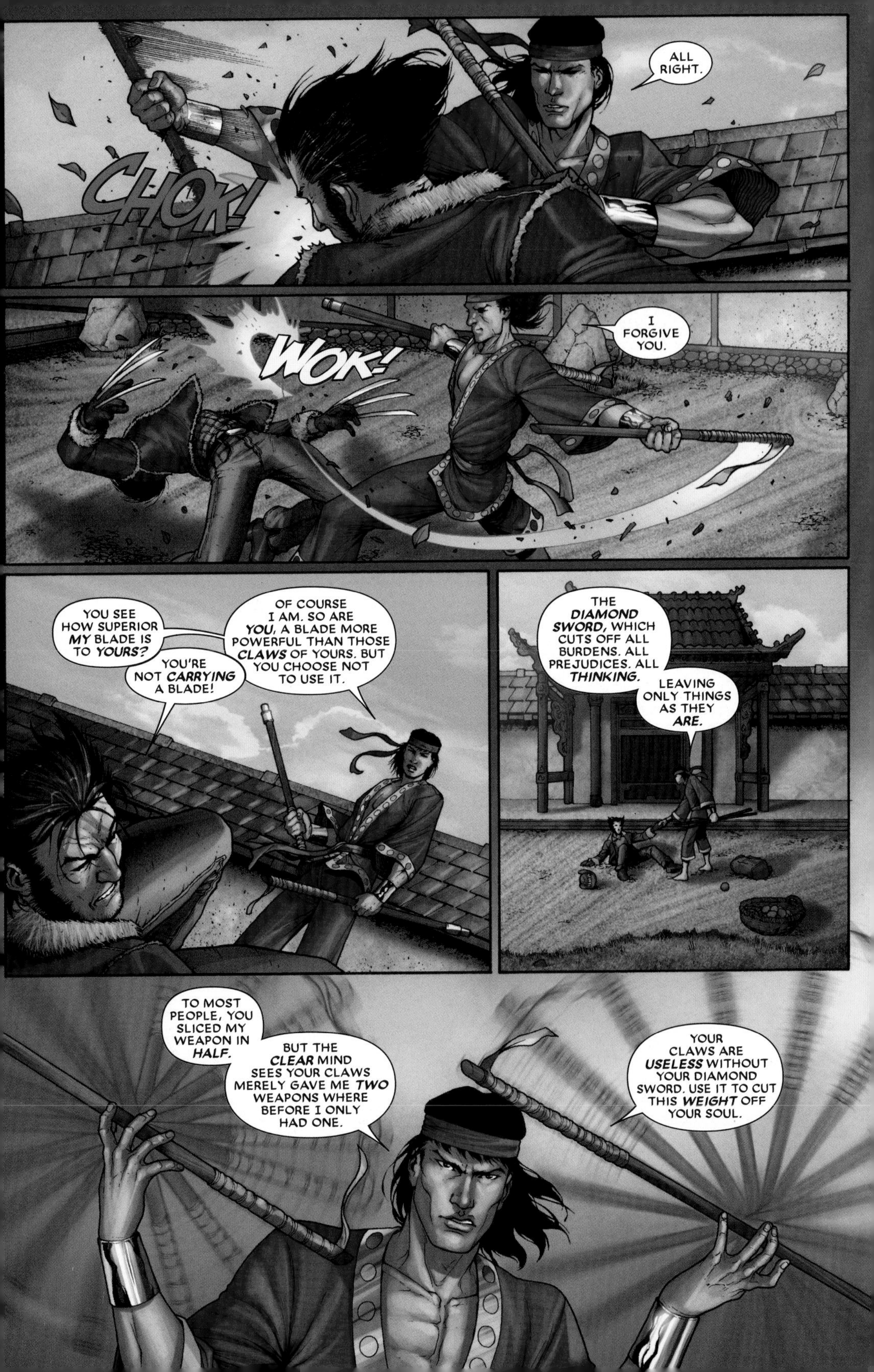

CHOK!
ALL RIGHT.
WOK!
I FORGIVE YOU.
YOU SEE HOW SUPERIOR *MY* BLADE IS TO *YOURS?*
OF COURSE I AM. SO ARE *YOU*, A BLADE MORE POWERFUL THAN THOSE *CLAWS* OF YOURS. BUT YOU CHOOSE NOT TO USE IT.
YOU'RE NOT *CARRYING* A BLADE!
THE *DIAMOND SWORD,* WHICH CUTS OFF ALL BURDENS. ALL PREJUDICES. ALL *THINKING.*
LEAVING ONLY THINGS AS THEY *ARE.*
TO MOST PEOPLE, YOU SLICED MY WEAPON IN *HALF.*
BUT THE *CLEAR* MIND SEES YOUR CLAWS MERELY GAVE ME *TWO* WEAPONS WHERE BEFORE I ONLY HAD ONE.
YOUR CLAWS ARE *USELESS* WITHOUT YOUR DIAMOND SWORD. USE IT TO CUT THIS *WEIGHT* OFF YOUR SOUL.

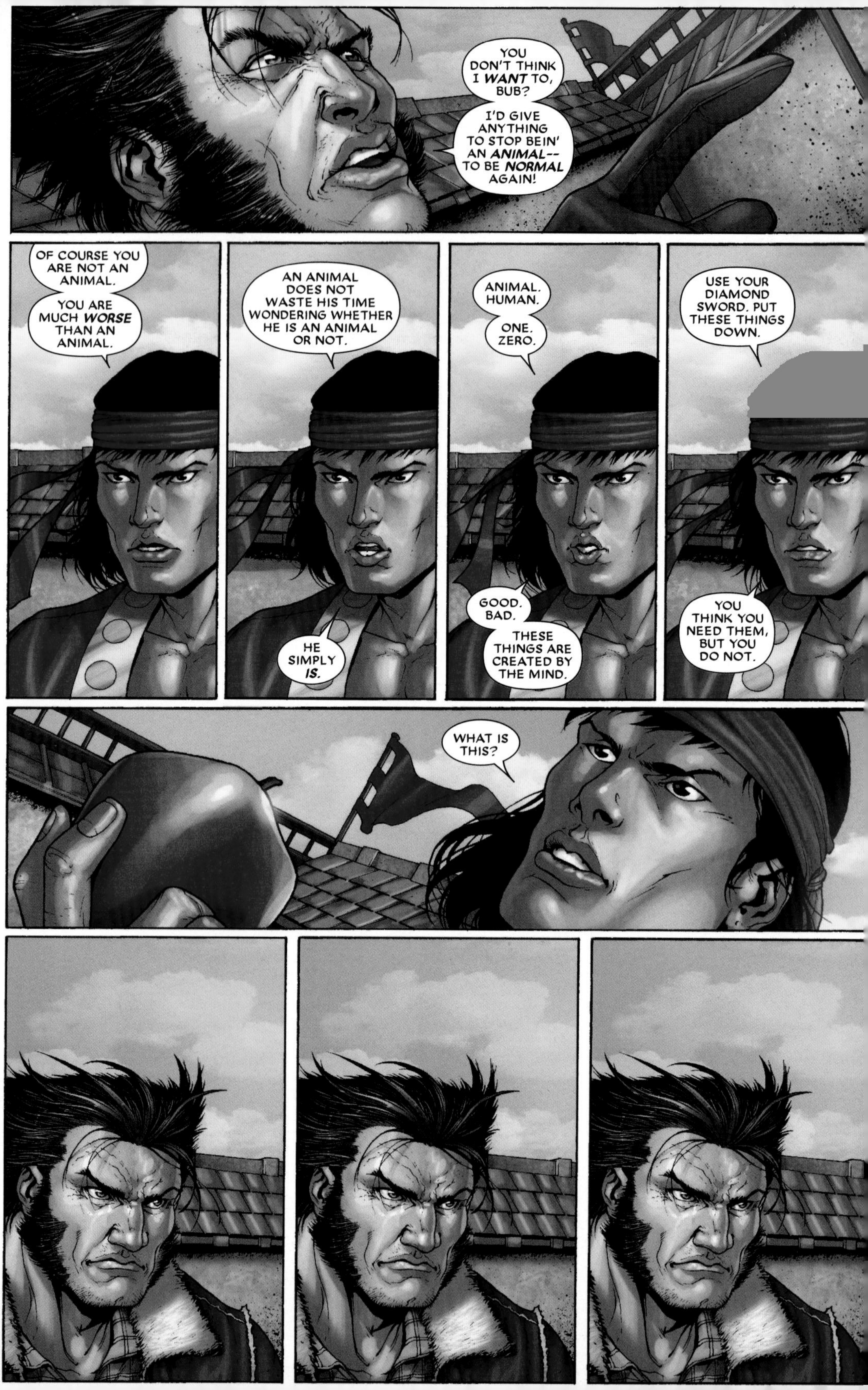
YOU DON'T THINK I *WANT* TO, BUB?
I'D GIVE ANYTHING TO STOP BEIN' AN *ANIMAL*-- TO BE *NORMAL* AGAIN!
OF COURSE YOU ARE NOT AN ANIMAL.
YOU ARE MUCH *WORSE* THAN AN ANIMAL.
AN ANIMAL DOES NOT WASTE HIS TIME WONDERING WHETHER HE IS AN ANIMAL OR NOT.
HE SIMPLY *IS.*
ANIMAL. HUMAN.
ONE. ZERO.
GOOD. BAD.
THESE THINGS ARE CREATED BY THE MIND.
USE YOUR DIAMOND SWORD. PUT THESE THINGS DOWN.
YOU THINK YOU NEED THEM, BUT YOU DO NOT.
WHAT IS THIS?

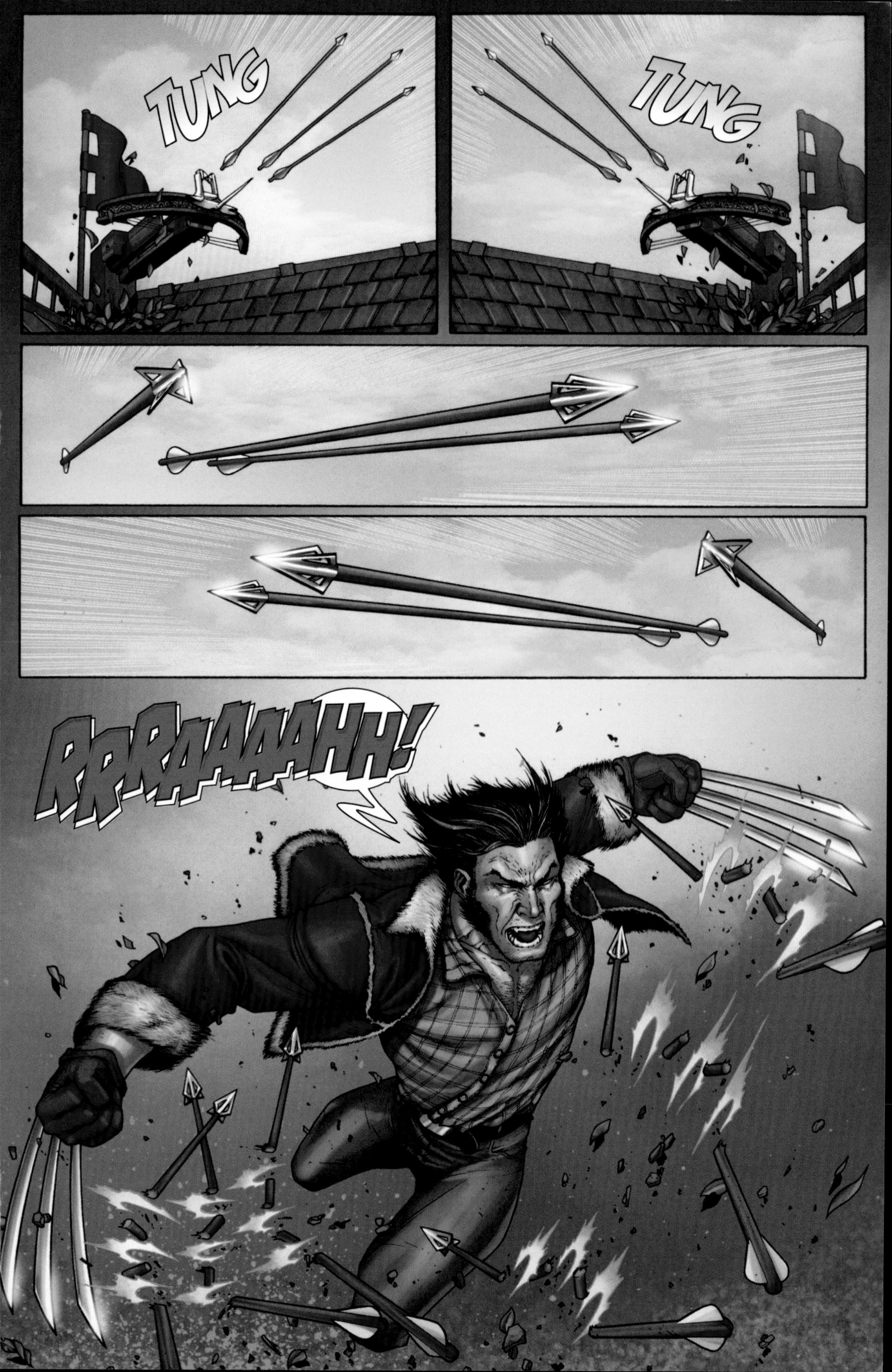
TUNG
TUNG
RRRAAAAAHH!

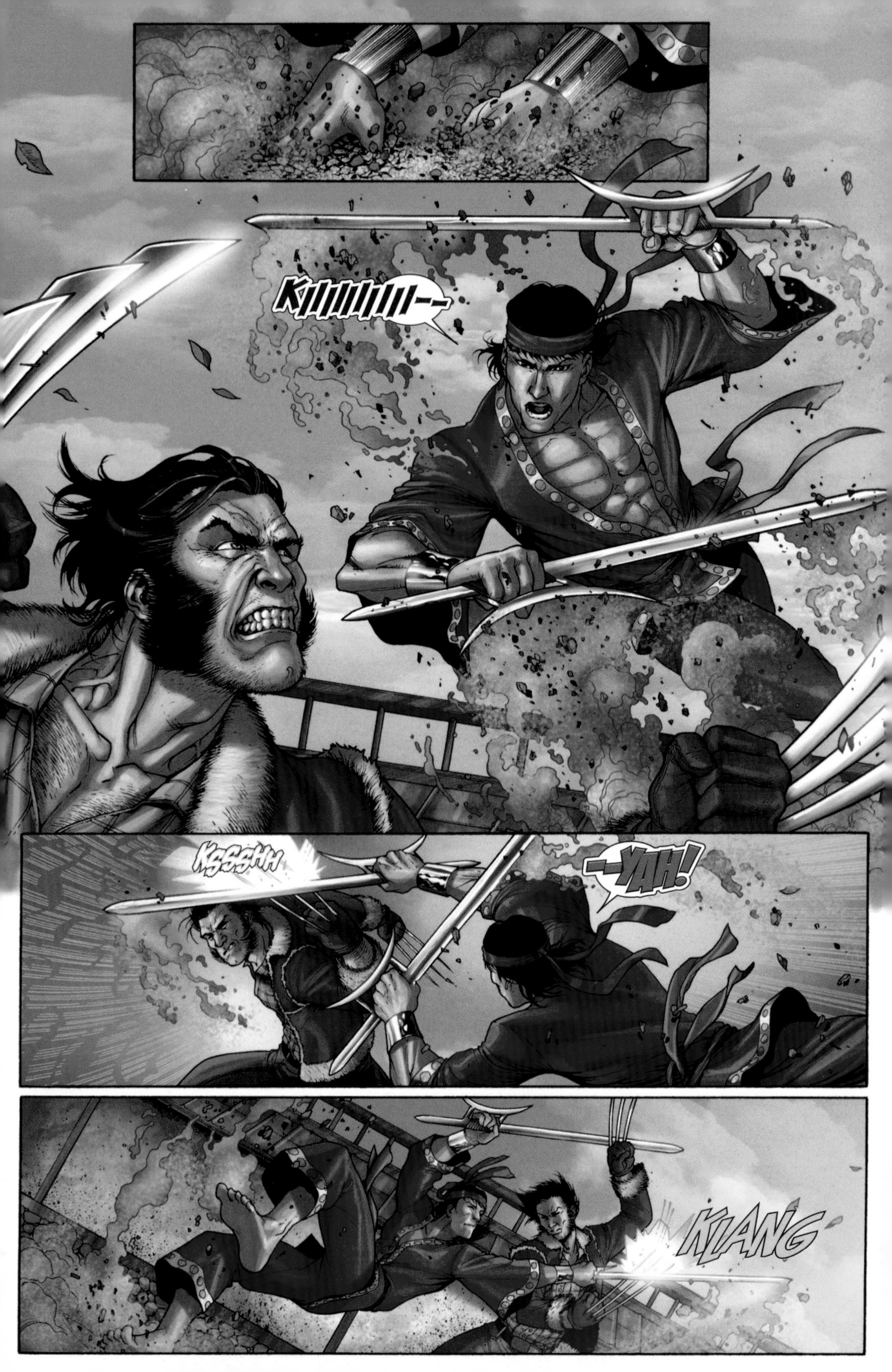
KIIIIIIIII--
KSSSHH
--YAH!
KLANG

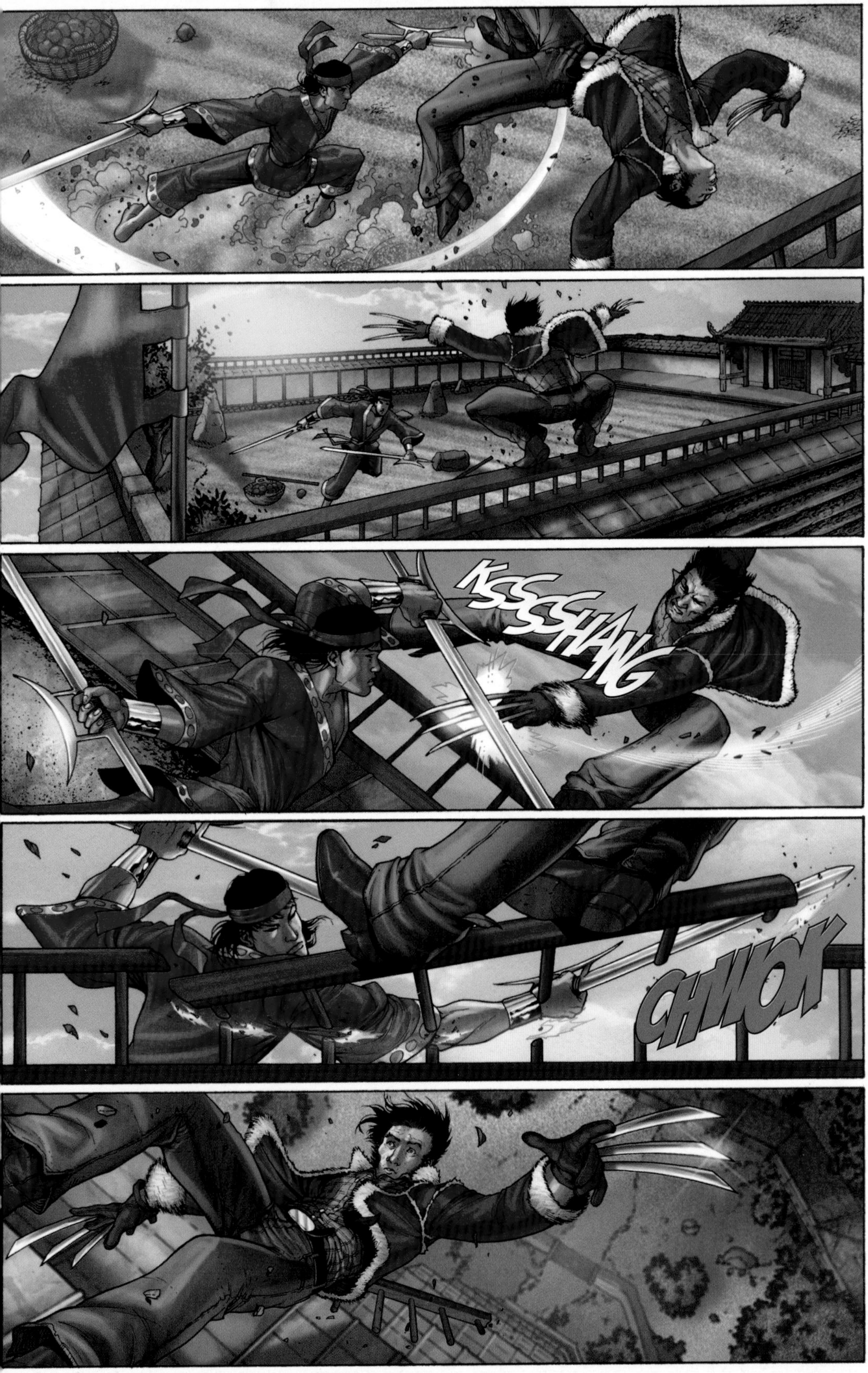
KSSSHANG
CHWOK

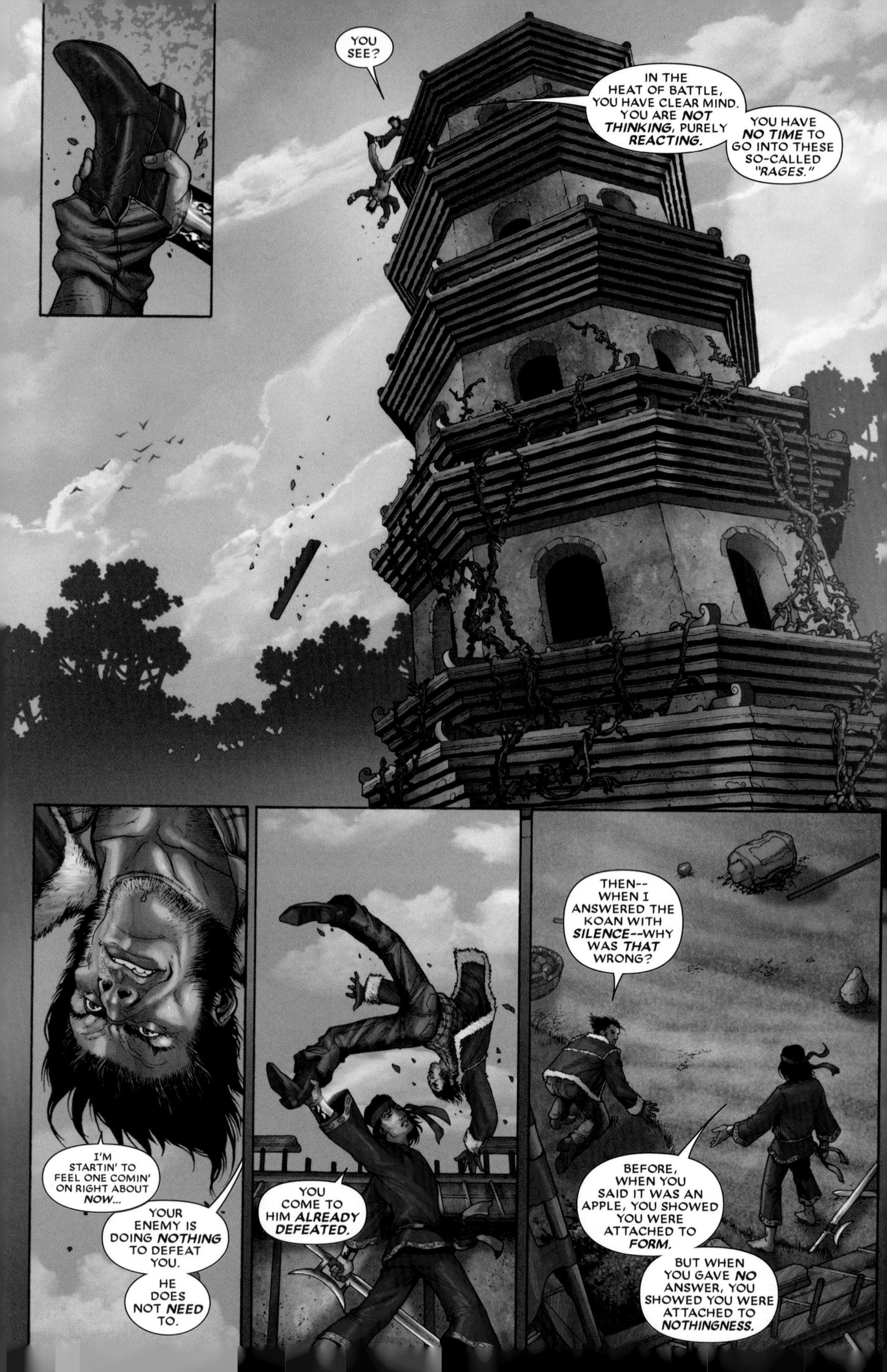
YOU SEE?
IN THE HEAT OF BATTLE, YOU HAVE CLEAR MIND. YOU ARE NOT THINKING, PURELY REACTING.
YOU HAVE NO TIME TO GO INTO THESE SO-CALLED "RAGES."
I'M STARTIN' TO FEEL ONE COMIN' ON RIGHT ABOUT NOW...
YOUR ENEMY IS DOING NOTHING TO DEFEAT YOU.
HE DOES NOT NEED TO.
YOU COME TO HIM ALREADY DEFEATED.
THEN-- WHEN I ANSWERED THE KOAN WITH SILENCE--WHY WAS THAT WRONG?
BEFORE, WHEN YOU SAID IT WAS AN APPLE, YOU SHOWED YOU WERE ATTACHED TO FORM.
BUT WHEN YOU GAVE NO ANSWER, YOU SHOWED YOU WERE ATTACHED TO NOTHINGNESS.

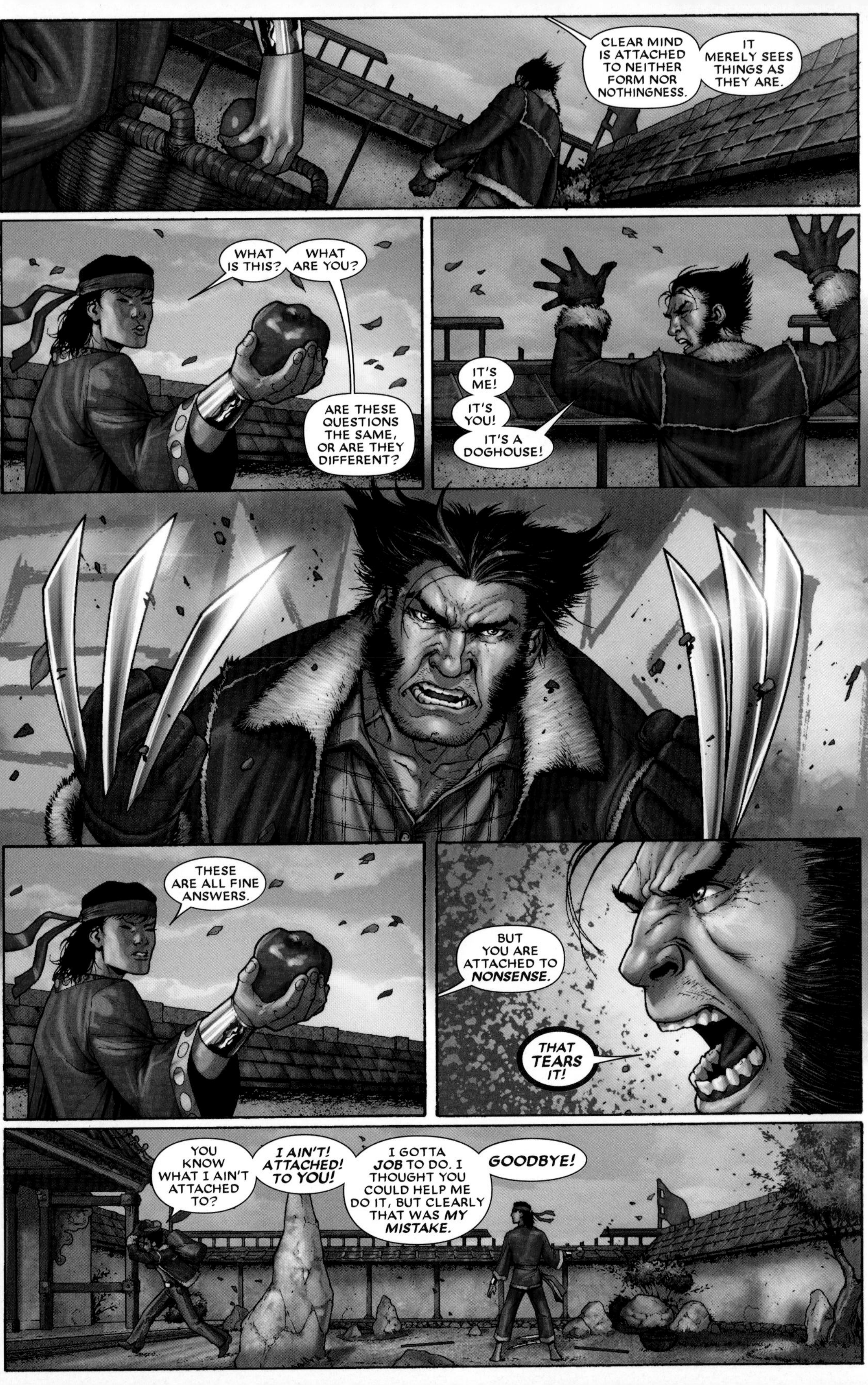
CLEAR MIND IS ATTACHED TO NEITHER FORM NOR NOTHINGNESS.
IT MERELY SEES THINGS AS THEY ARE.
WHAT IS THIS?
WHAT ARE YOU?
ARE THESE QUESTIONS THE SAME, OR ARE THEY DIFFERENT?
IT'S ME!
IT'S YOU!
IT'S A DOGHOUSE!
THESE ARE ALL FINE ANSWERS.
BUT YOU ARE ATTACHED TO NONSENSE.
THAT TEARS IT!
YOU KNOW WHAT I AIN'T ATTACHED TO?
I AIN'T! ATTACHED! TO YOU!
I GOTTA JOB TO DO. I THOUGHT YOU COULD HELP ME DO IT, BUT CLEARLY THAT WAS MY MISTAKE.
GOODBYE!

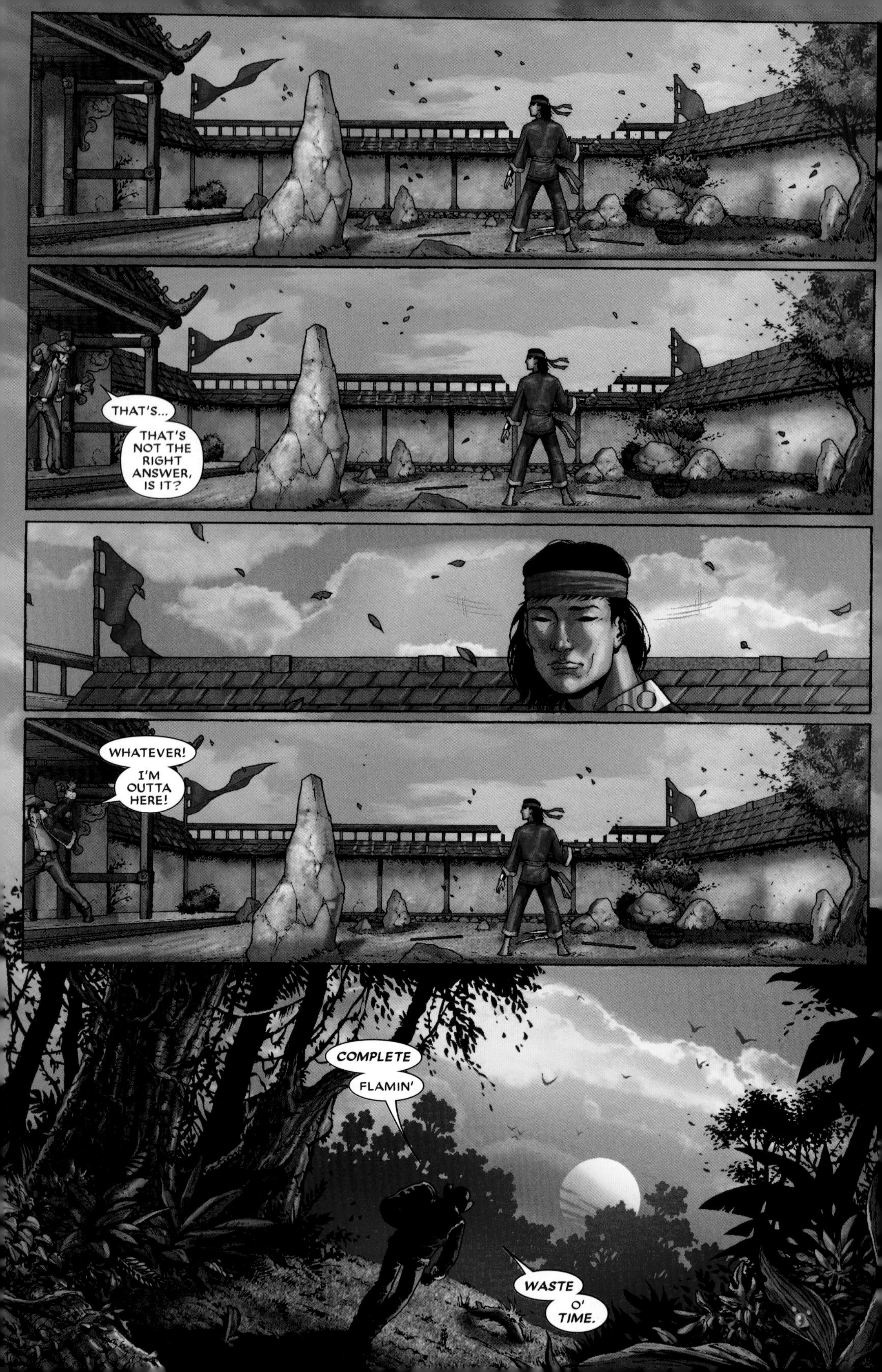
THAT'S... THAT'S NOT THE RIGHT ANSWER, IS IT?
WHATEVER! I'M OUTTA HERE!
COMPLETE
FLAMIN'
WASTE O' TIME.

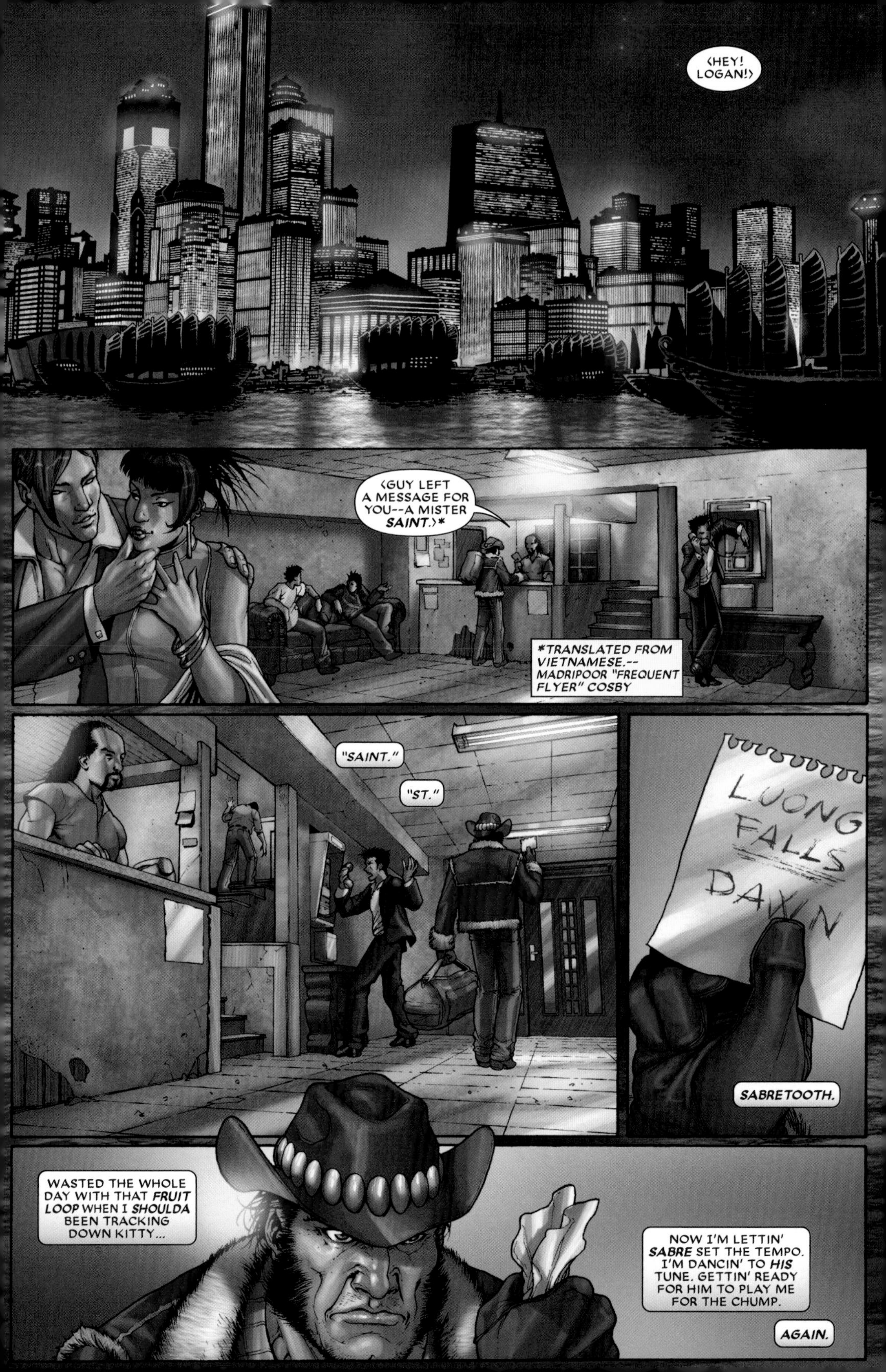
⟨HEY! LOGAN!⟩
⟨GUY LEFT A MESSAGE FOR YOU--A MISTER SAINT.⟩*
*TRANSLATED FROM VIETNAMESE.-- MADRIPOOR "FREQUENT FLYER" COSBY
"SAINT."
"ST."
LUONG FALLS DAWN
SABRETOOTH.
WASTED THE WHOLE DAY WITH THAT FRUIT LOOP WHEN I SHOULDA BEEN TRACKING DOWN KITTY...
NOW I'M LETTIN' SABRE SET THE TEMPO. I'M DANCIN' TO HIS TUNE. GETTIN' READY FOR HIM TO PLAY ME FOR THE CHUMP.
AGAIN.

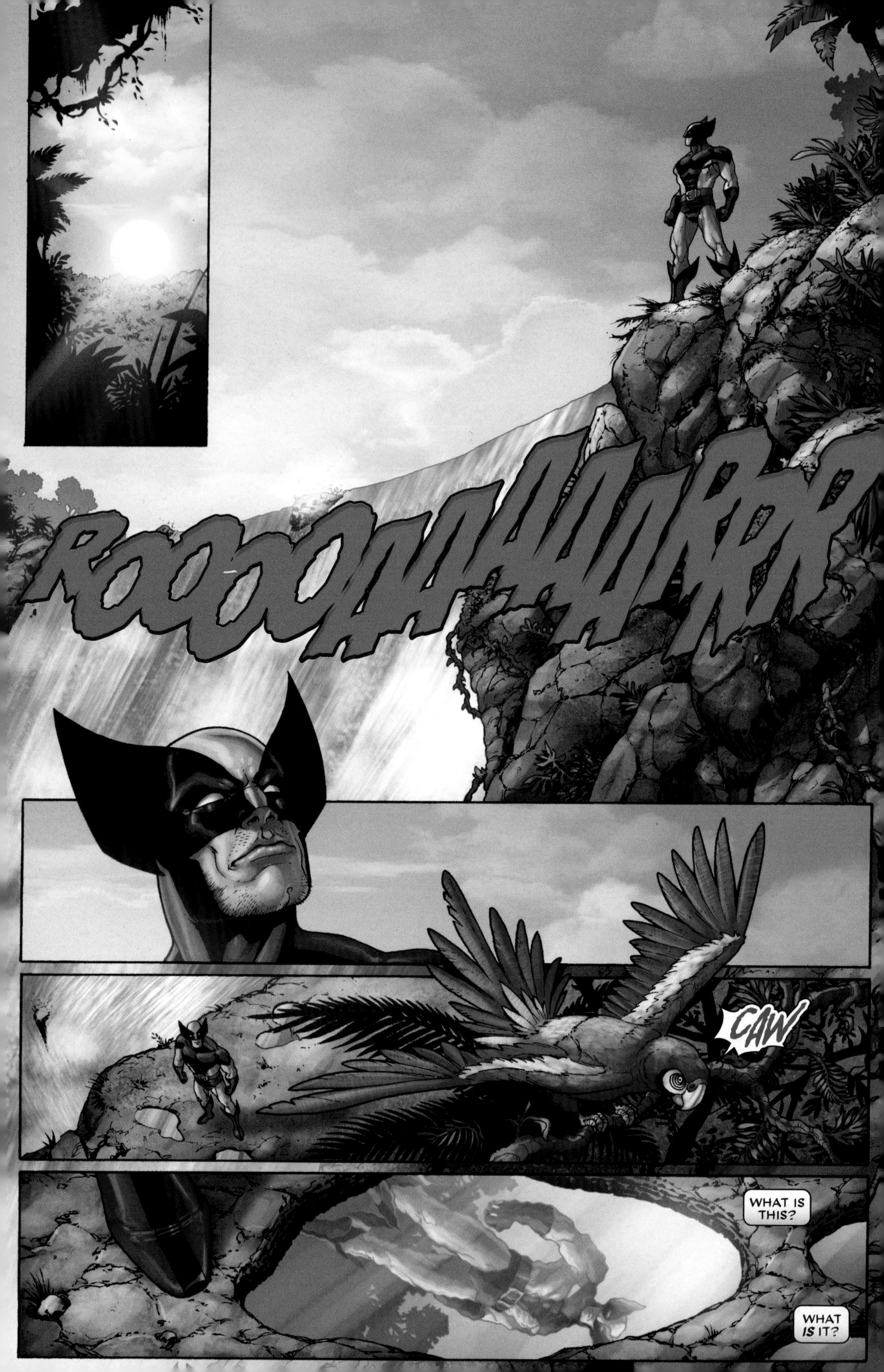
ROOOOAAAARRR
CAW
WHAT IS THIS?
WHAT *IS* IT?

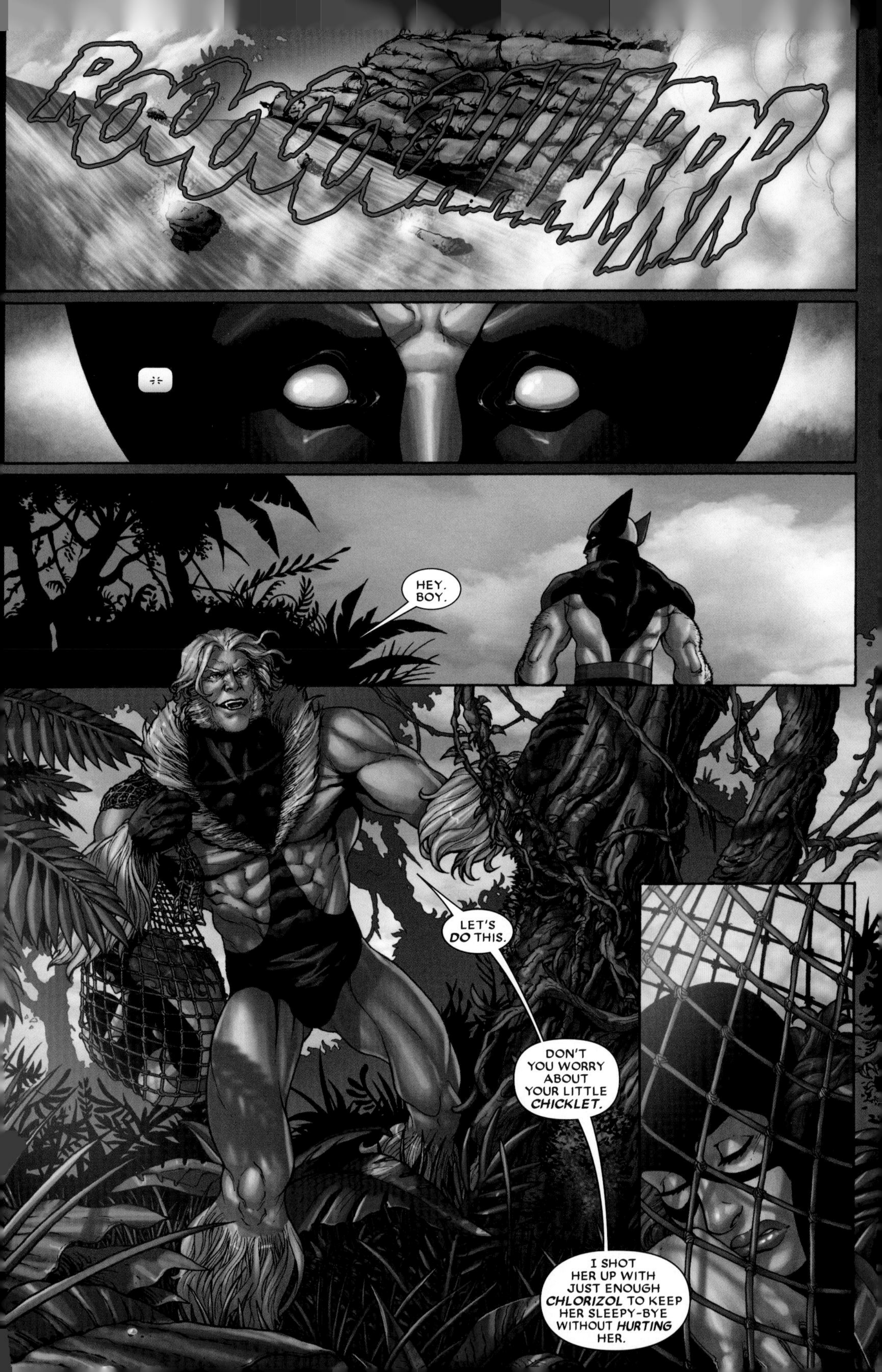

ROOOOOOOAAAAAAARRRR
HEY. BOY.
LET'S DO THIS.
DON'T YOU WORRY ABOUT YOUR LITTLE CHICKLET.
I SHOT HER UP WITH JUST ENOUGH CHLORIZOL TO KEEP HER SLEEPY-BYE WITHOUT HURTING HER.

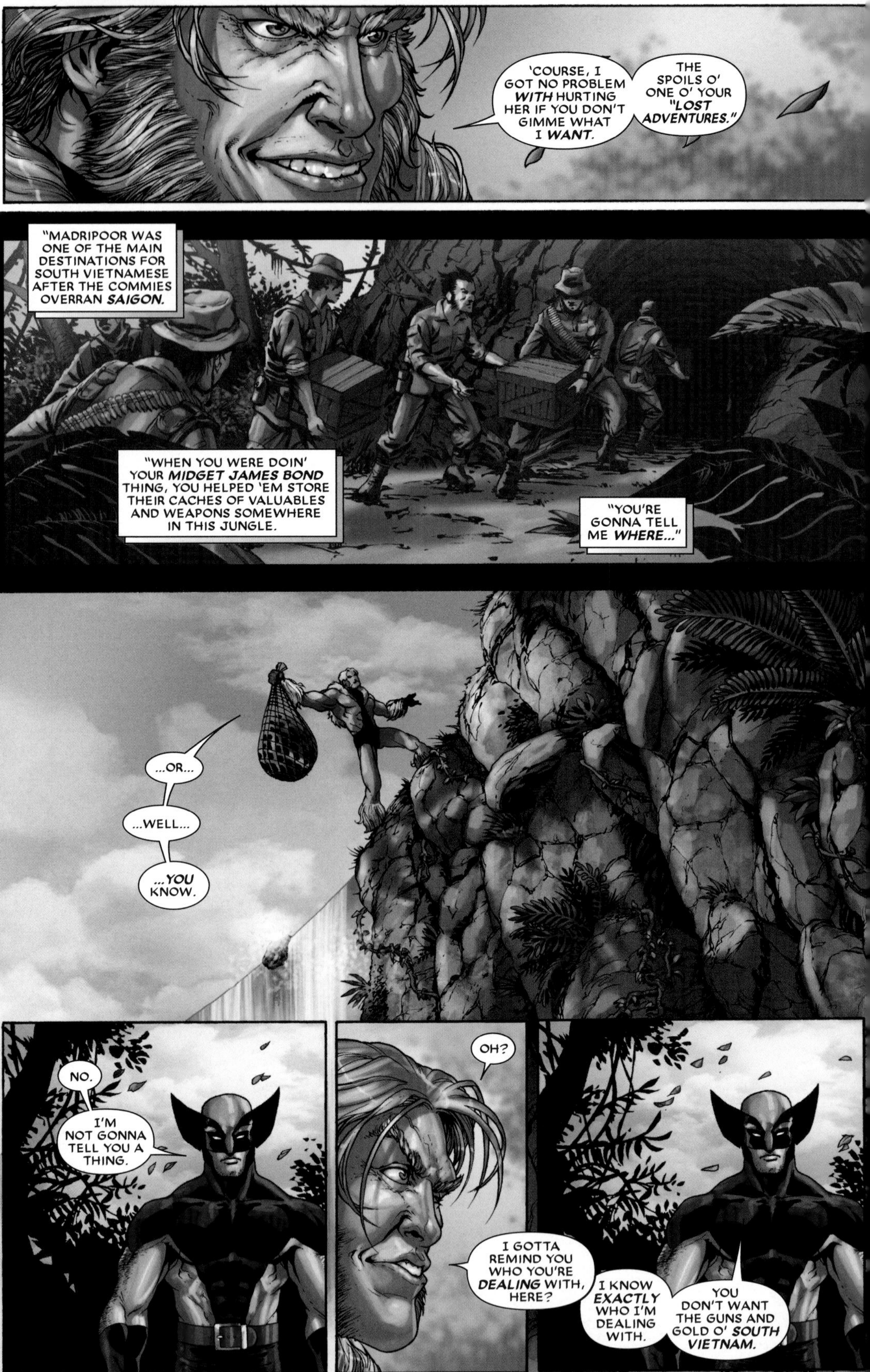
'COURSE, I GOT NO PROBLEM *WITH* HURTING HER IF YOU DON'T GIMME WHAT I *WANT*.
THE SPOILS O' ONE O' YOUR *"LOST ADVENTURES."*
"MADRIPOOR WAS ONE OF THE MAIN DESTINATIONS FOR SOUTH VIETNAMESE AFTER THE COMMIES OVERRAN *SAIGON*.
"WHEN YOU WERE DOIN' YOUR *MIDGET JAMES BOND* THING, YOU HELPED 'EM STORE THEIR CACHES OF VALUABLES AND WEAPONS SOMEWHERE IN THIS JUNGLE.
"YOU'RE GONNA TELL ME *WHERE...*"
...OR...
...WELL...
...YOU KNOW.
NO.
I'M NOT GONNA TELL YOU A THING.
OH?
I GOTTA REMIND YOU WHO YOU'RE *DEALING* WITH, HERE?
I KNOW *EXACTLY* WHO I'M DEALING WITH.
YOU DON'T WANT THE GUNS AND GOLD O' *SOUTH VIETNAM*.

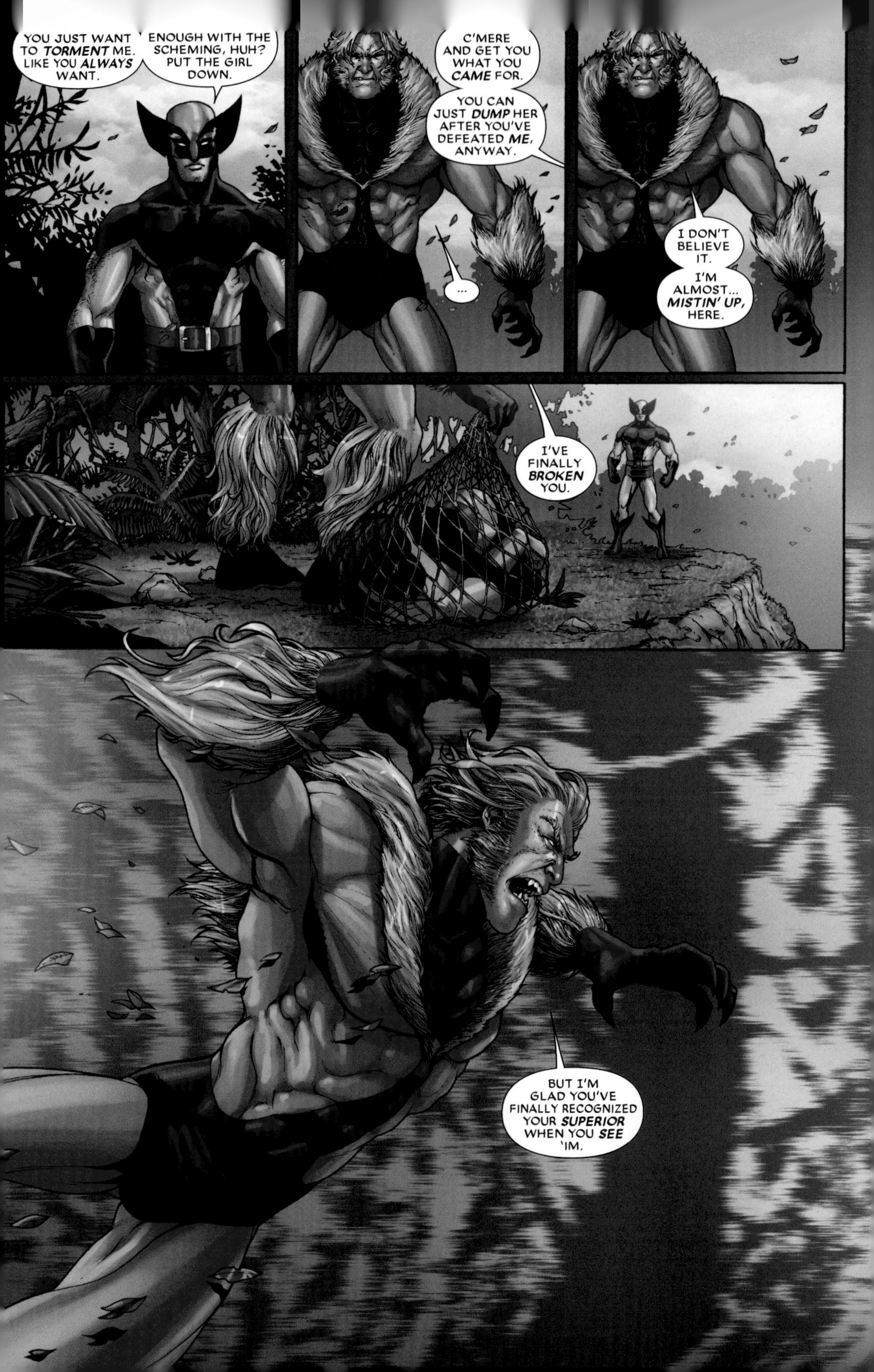
YOU JUST WANT TO TORMENT ME. LIKE YOU ALWAYS WANT.
ENOUGH WITH THE SCHEMING, HUH? PUT THE GIRL DOWN.
C'MERE AND GET YOU WHAT YOU CAME FOR.
YOU CAN JUST DUMP HER AFTER YOU'VE DEFEATED ME, ANYWAY.
...
I DON'T BELIEVE IT.
I'M ALMOST... MISTIN' UP, HERE.
I'VE FINALLY BROKEN YOU.
BUT I'M GLAD YOU'VE FINALLY RECOGNIZED YOUR SUPERIOR WHEN YOU SEE 'IM.

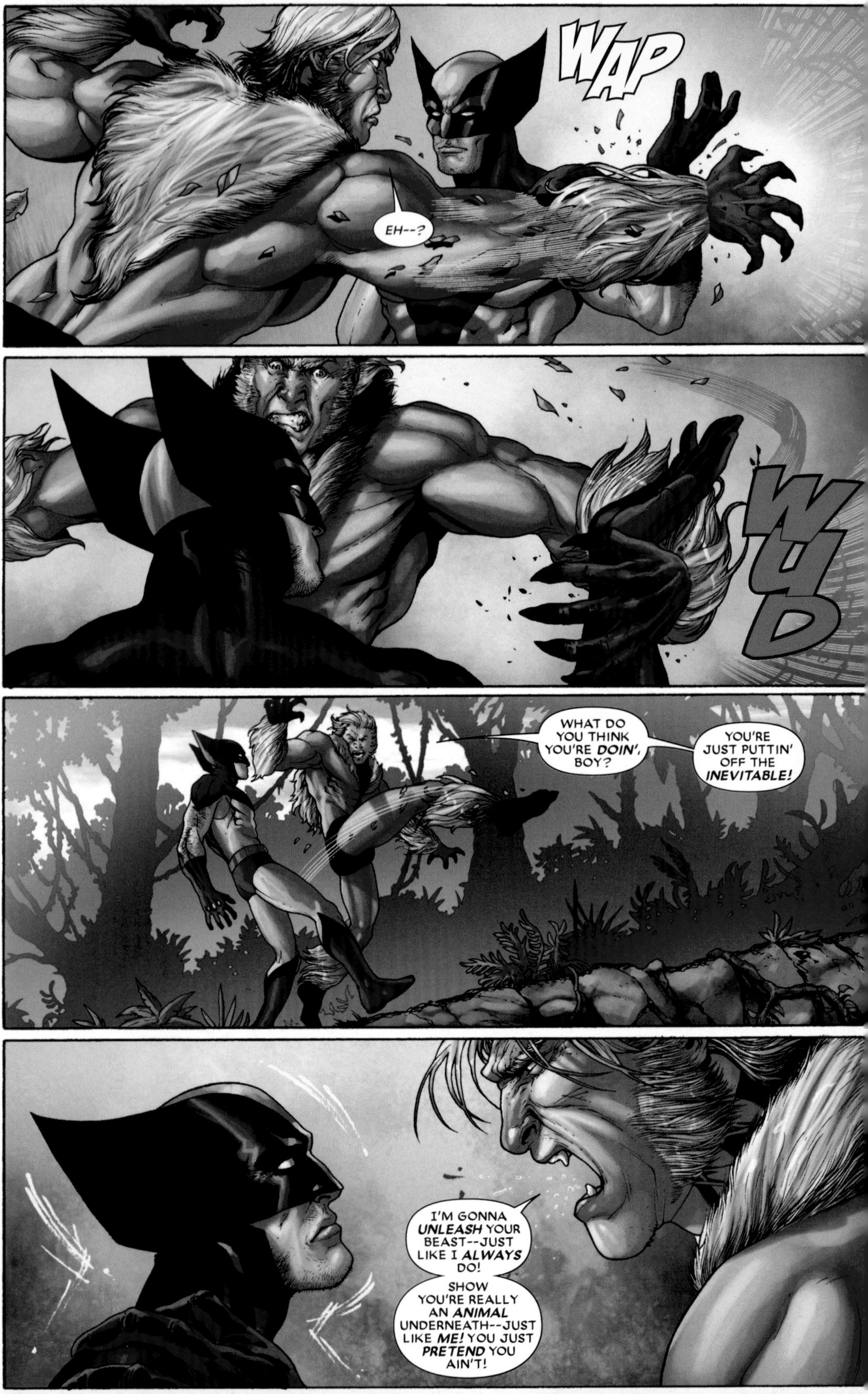
WAP
EH--?
WUD
WHAT DO YOU THINK YOU'RE DOIN', BOY?
YOU'RE JUST PUTTIN' OFF THE INEVITABLE!
I'M GONNA UNLEASH YOUR BEAST--JUST LIKE I ALWAYS DO!
SHOW YOU'RE REALLY AN ANIMAL UNDERNEATH--JUST LIKE ME! YOU JUST PRETEND YOU AIN'T!

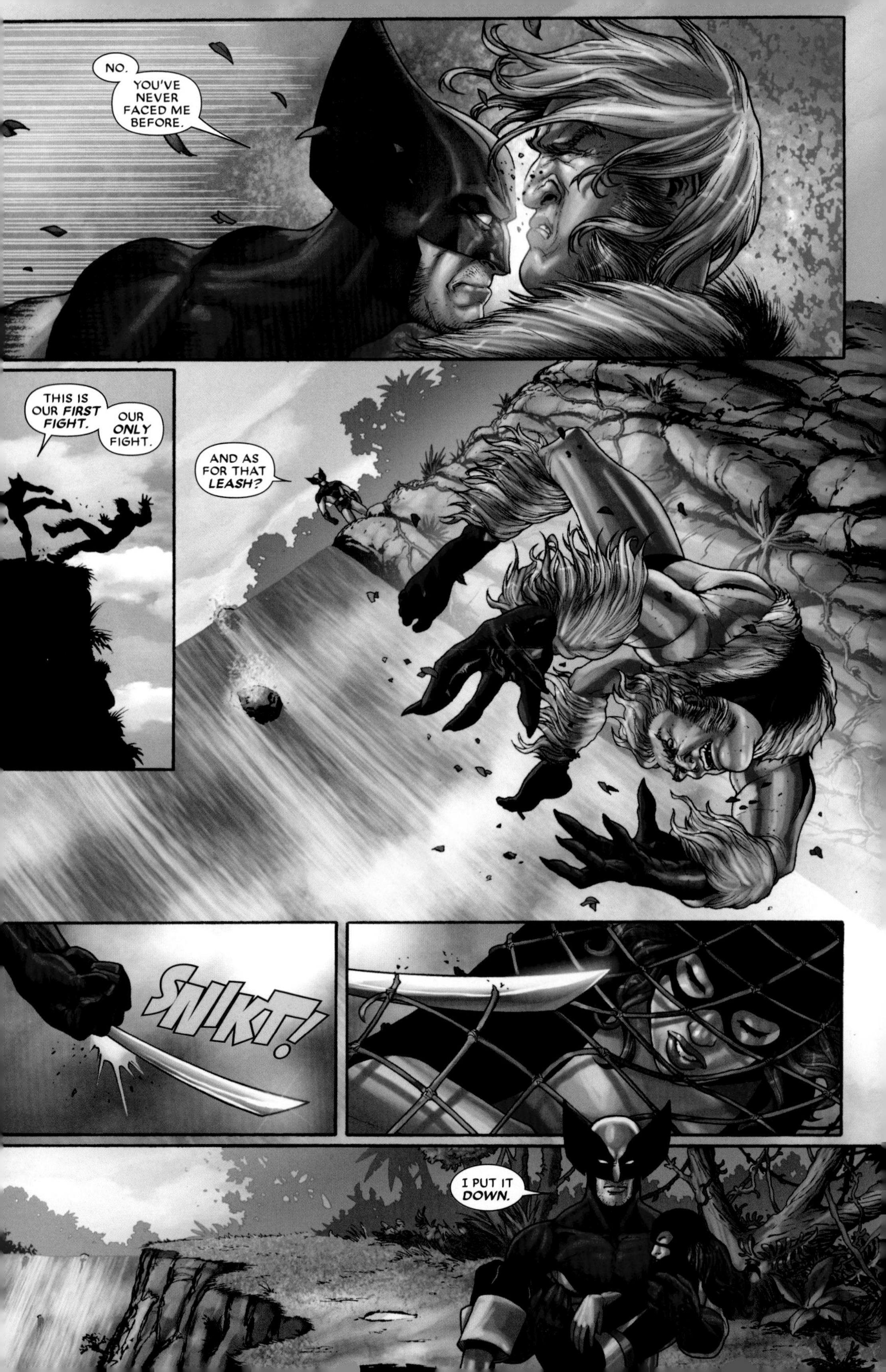
NO.
YOU'VE NEVER FACED ME BEFORE.
THIS IS OUR *FIRST* *FIGHT.*
OUR *ONLY* FIGHT.
AND AS FOR THAT *LEASH?*
SNIKT!
I PUT IT *DOWN.*

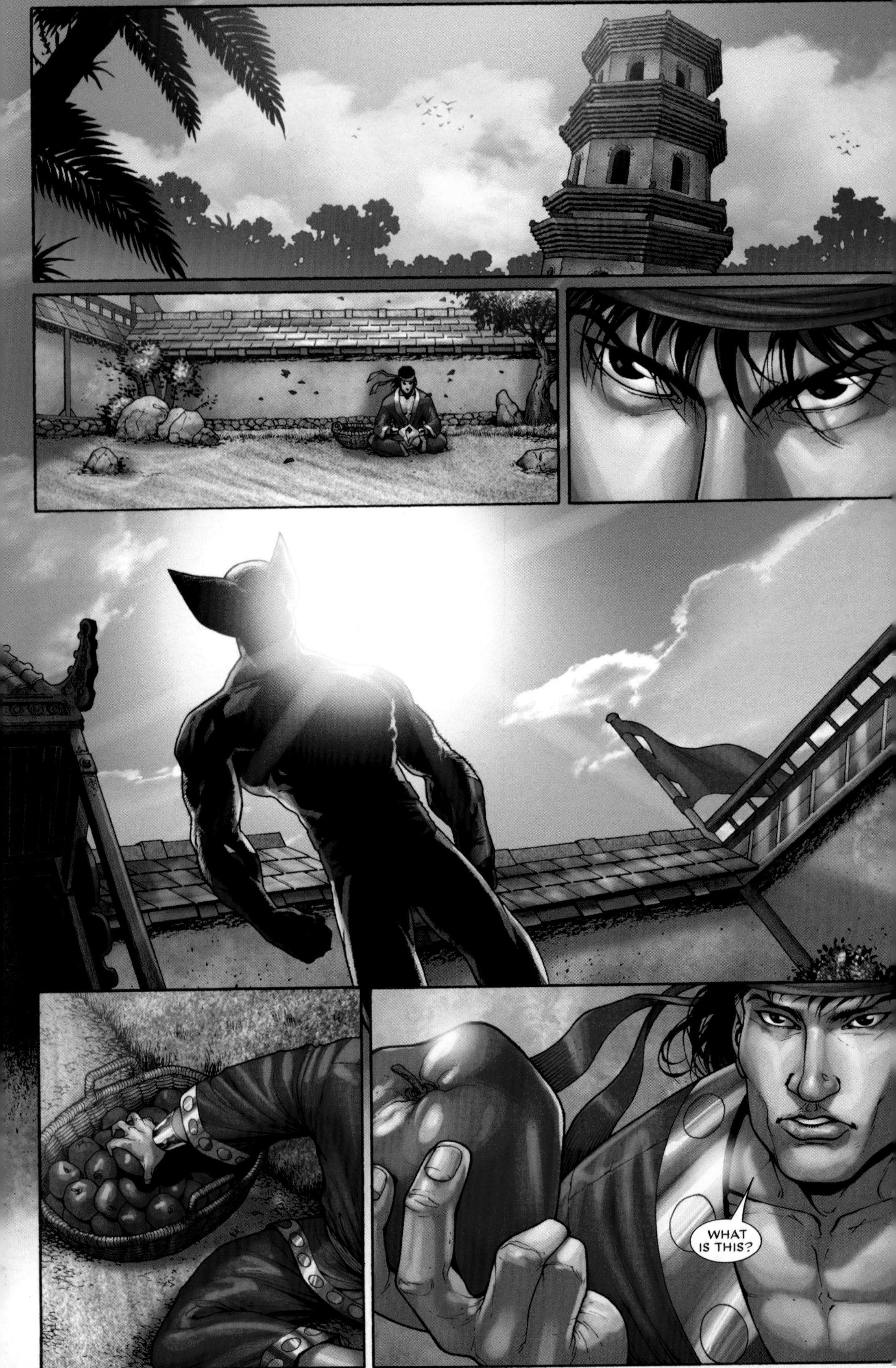
WHAT IS THIS?

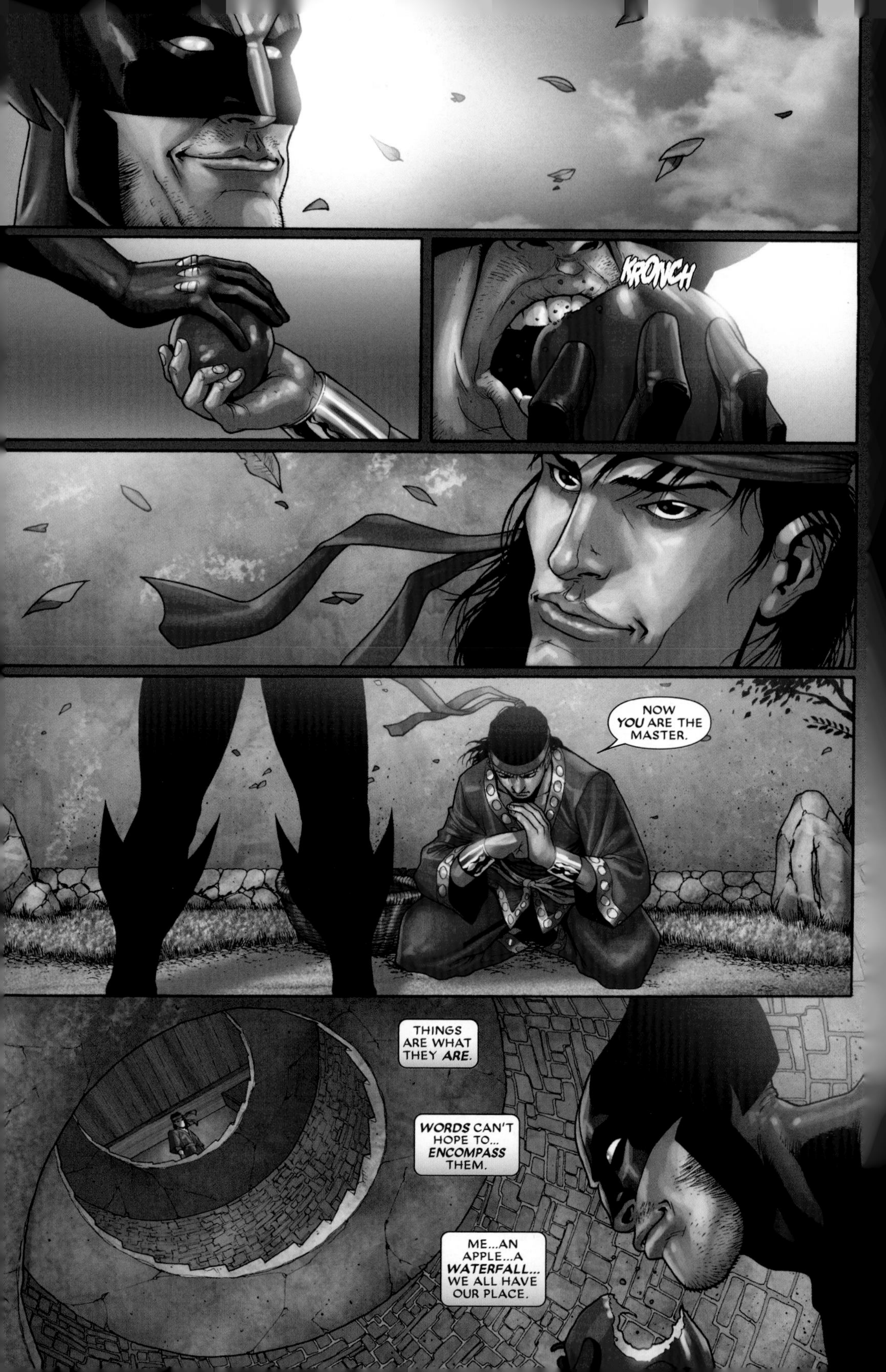
KRONCH
NOW YOU ARE THE MASTER.
THINGS ARE WHAT THEY ARE.
WORDS CAN'T HOPE TO... ENCOMPASS THEM.
ME...AN APPLE...A WATERFALL... WE ALL HAVE OUR PLACE.

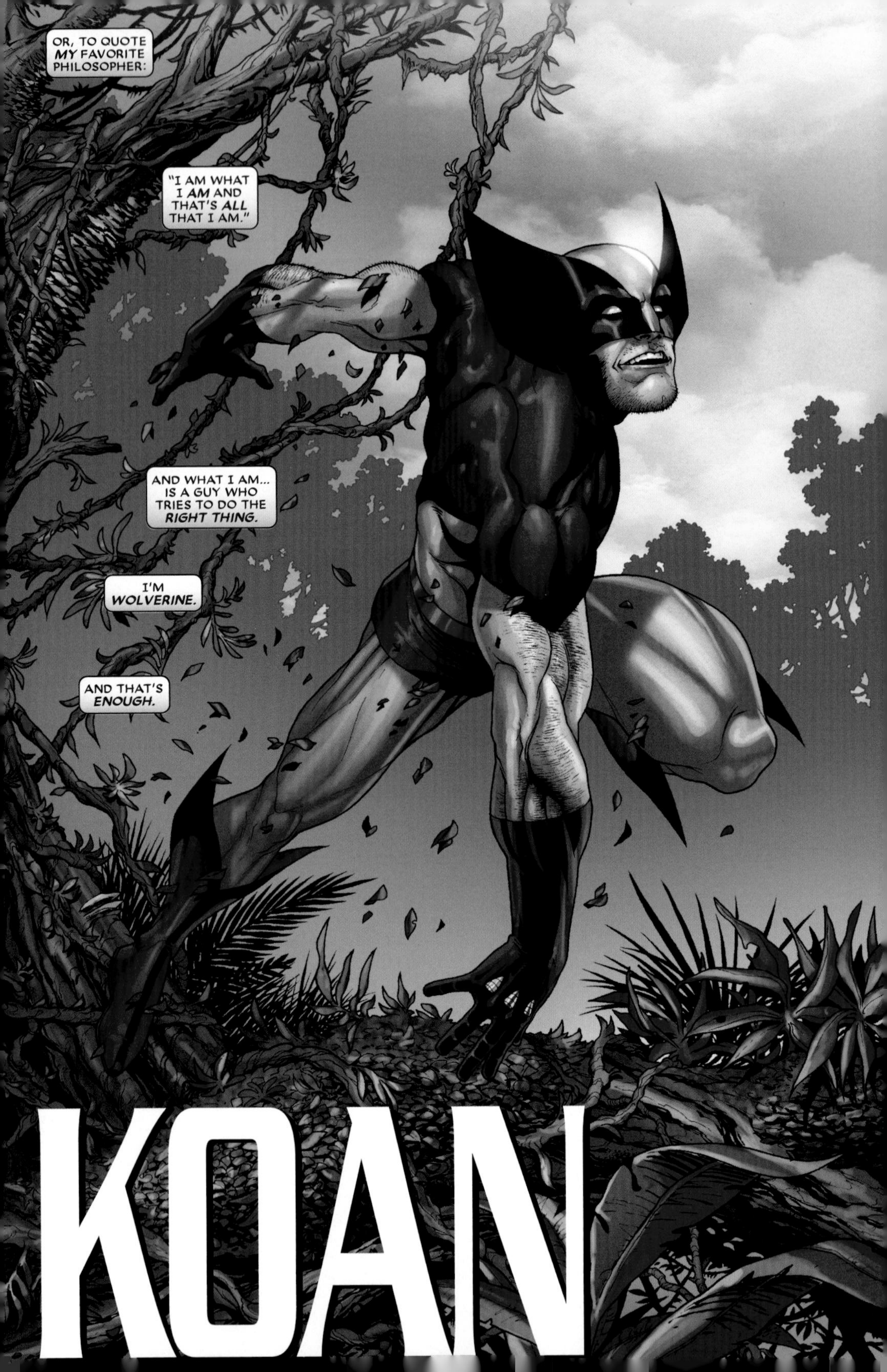
OR, TO QUOTE MY FAVORITE PHILOSOPHER:
"I AM WHAT I AM AND THAT'S ALL THAT I AM."
AND WHAT I AM... IS A GUY WHO TRIES TO DO THE RIGHT THING.
I'M WOLVERINE.
AND THAT'S ENOUGH.
KOAN

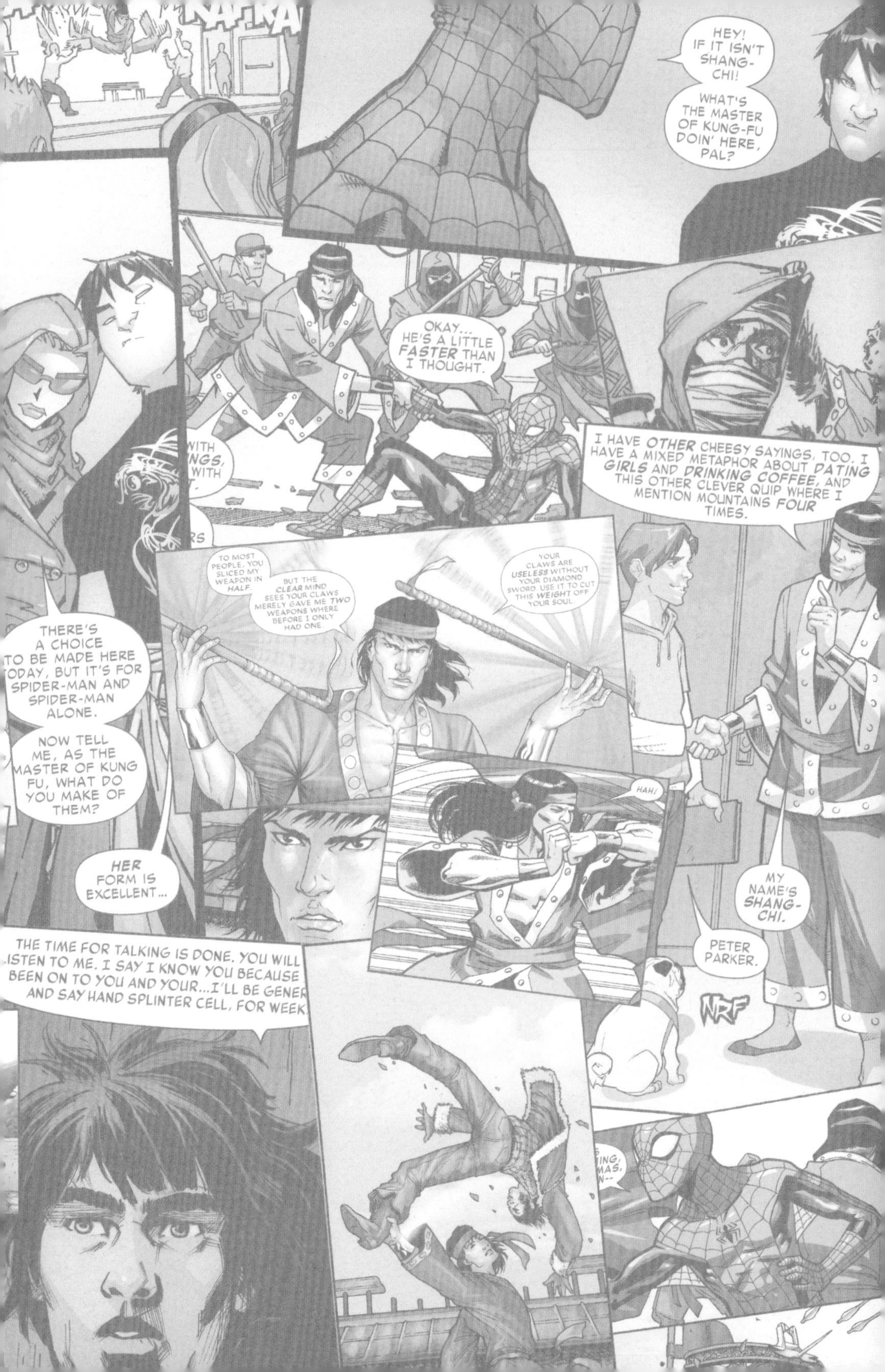
HEY! IF IT ISN'T SHANG-CHI!
WHAT'S THE MASTER OF KUNG-FU DOIN' HERE, PAL?
OKAY... HE'S A LITTLE FASTER THAN I THOUGHT.
I HAVE OTHER CHEESY SAYINGS, TOO. I HAVE A MIXED METAPHOR ABOUT DATING GIRLS AND DRINKING COFFEE, AND THIS OTHER CLEVER QUIP WHERE I MENTION MOUNTAINS FOUR TIMES.
TO MOST PEOPLE, YOU SLICED MY WEAPON IN HALF.
BUT THE CLEAR MIND SEES YOUR CLAWS MERELY GAVE ME TWO WEAPONS WHERE BEFORE I ONLY HAD ONE.
YOUR CLAWS ARE USELESS WITHOUT YOUR DIAMOND SWORD. USE IT TO CUT THIS WEIGHT OFF YOUR SOUL.
THERE'S A CHOICE TO BE MADE HERE TODAY, BUT IT'S FOR SPIDER-MAN AND SPIDER-MAN ALONE.
NOW TELL ME, AS THE MASTER OF KUNG FU, WHAT DO YOU MAKE OF THEM?
HER FORM IS EXCELLENT...
HAH!
MY NAME'S SHANG-CHI.
PETER PARKER.
NRF
THE TIME FOR TALKING IS DONE. YOU WILL LISTEN TO ME. I SAY I KNOW YOU BECAUSE BEEN ON TO YOU AND YOUR...I'LL BE GENER AND SAY HAND SPLINTER CELL, FOR WEEK

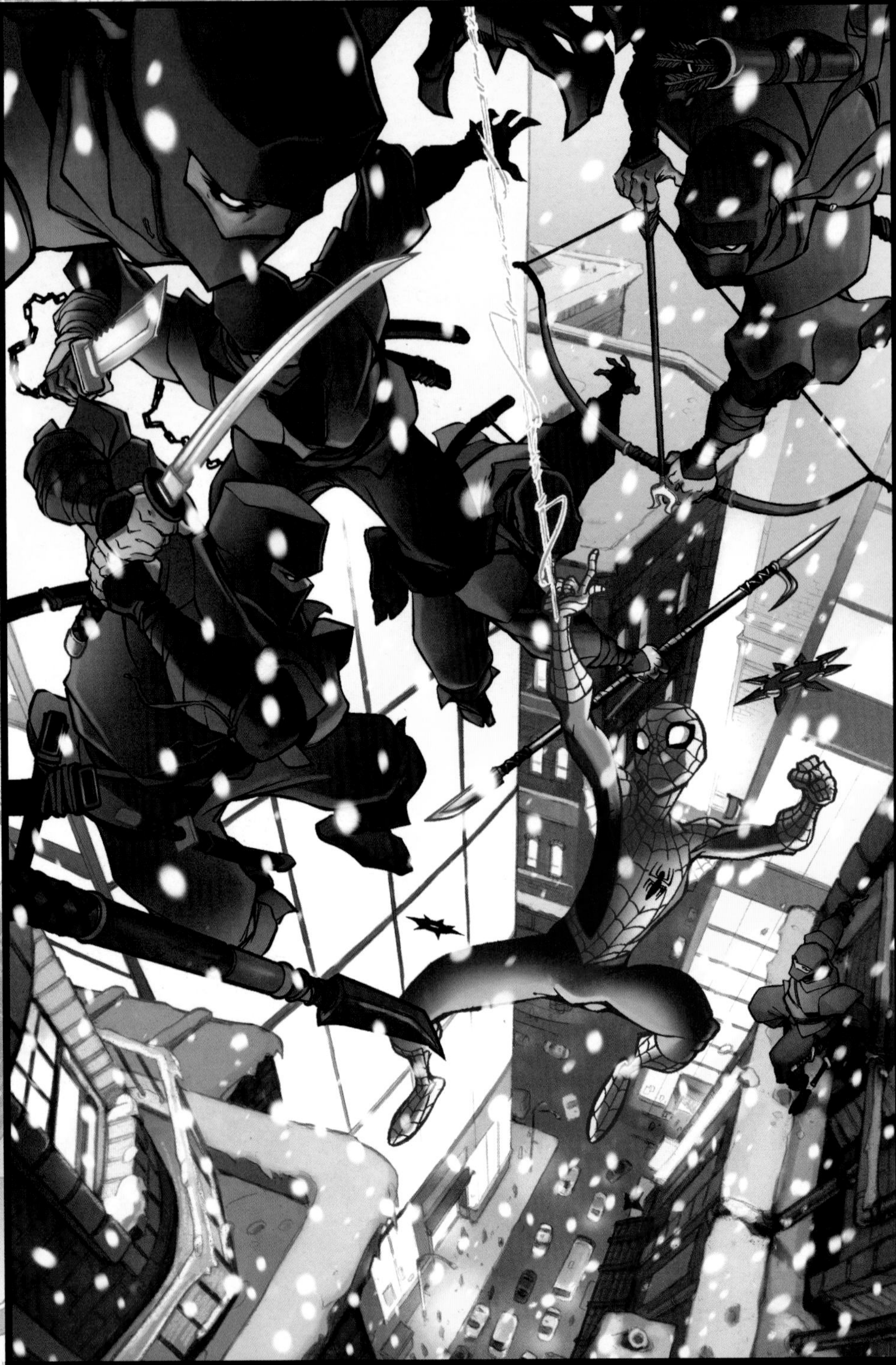

MARVEL ADVENTURES SPIDER-MAN #2

WHEN SHANG-CHI VISITS MIDTOWN HIGH, PETER PARKER
MUST DEAL WITH FEUDING FRIENDS, A NEW CLASSMATE

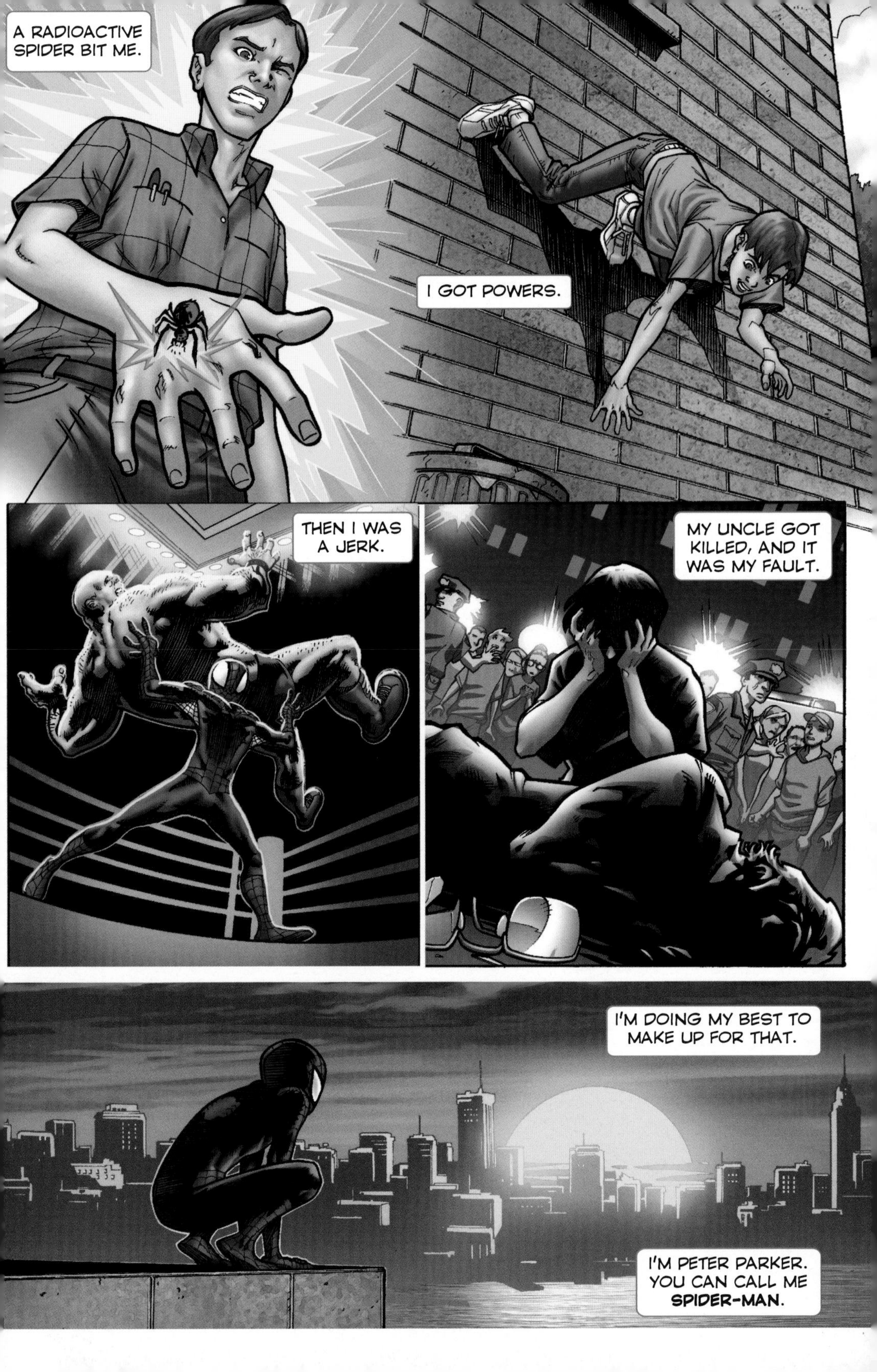
A RADIOACTIVE SPIDER BIT ME.
I GOT POWERS.
THEN I WAS A JERK.
MY UNCLE GOT KILLED, AND IT WAS MY FAULT.
I'M DOING MY BEST TO MAKE UP FOR THAT.
I'M PETER PARKER. YOU CAN CALL ME **SPIDER-MAN**.

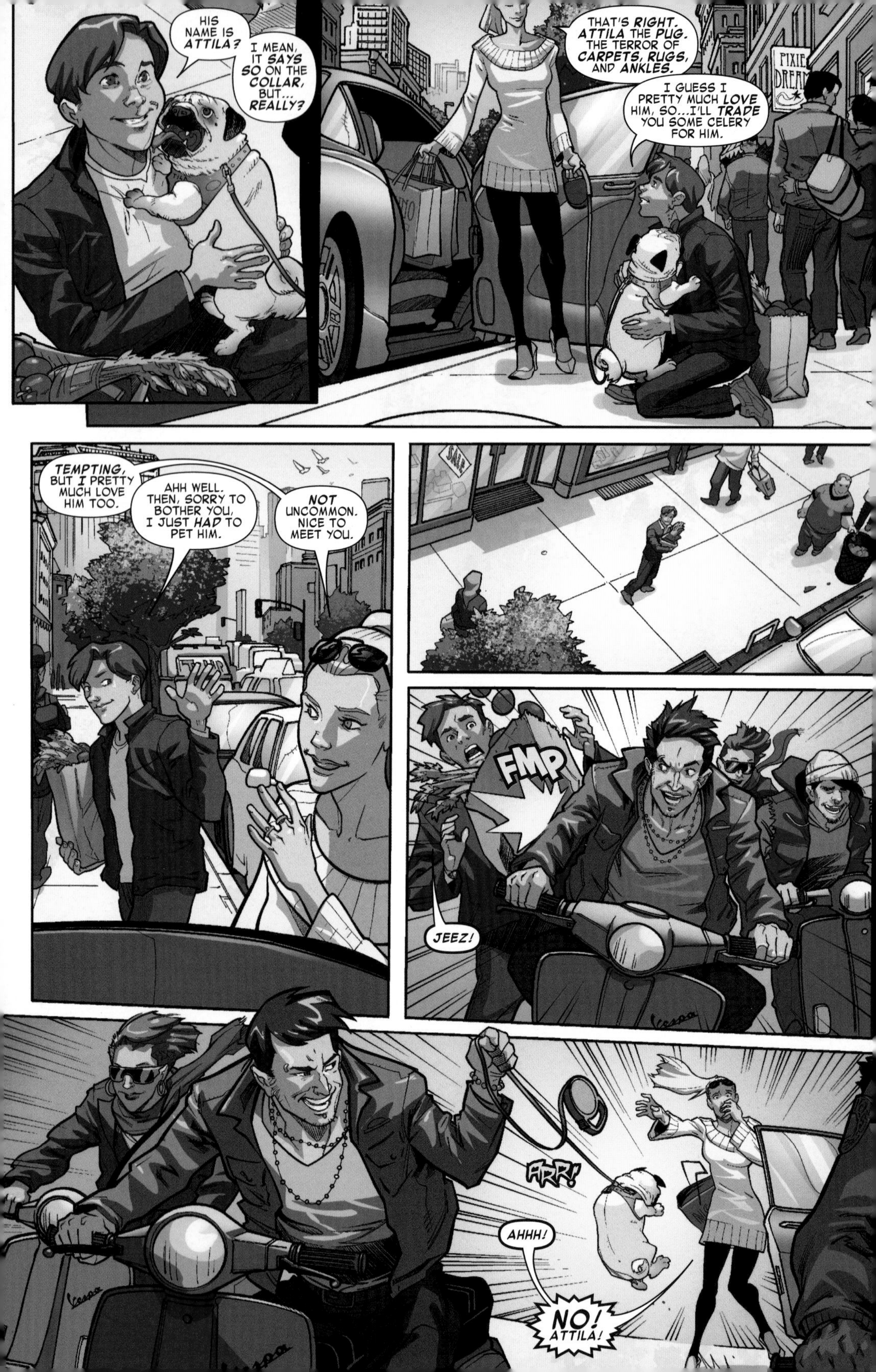

HIS NAME IS ATTILA?
I MEAN, IT SAYS SO ON THE COLLAR, BUT... REALLY?
THAT'S RIGHT. ATTILA THE PUG. THE TERROR OF CARPETS, RUGS, AND ANKLES.
I GUESS I PRETTY MUCH LOVE HIM, SO...I'LL TRADE YOU SOME CELERY FOR HIM.
PIXIE DREAM
TEMPTING, BUT I PRETTY MUCH LOVE HIM TOO.
AHH WELL. THEN, SORRY TO BOTHER YOU, I JUST HAD TO PET HIM.
NOT UNCOMMON. NICE TO MEET YOU.
FMP
JEEZ!
ARR!
AHHH!
NO! ATTILA!

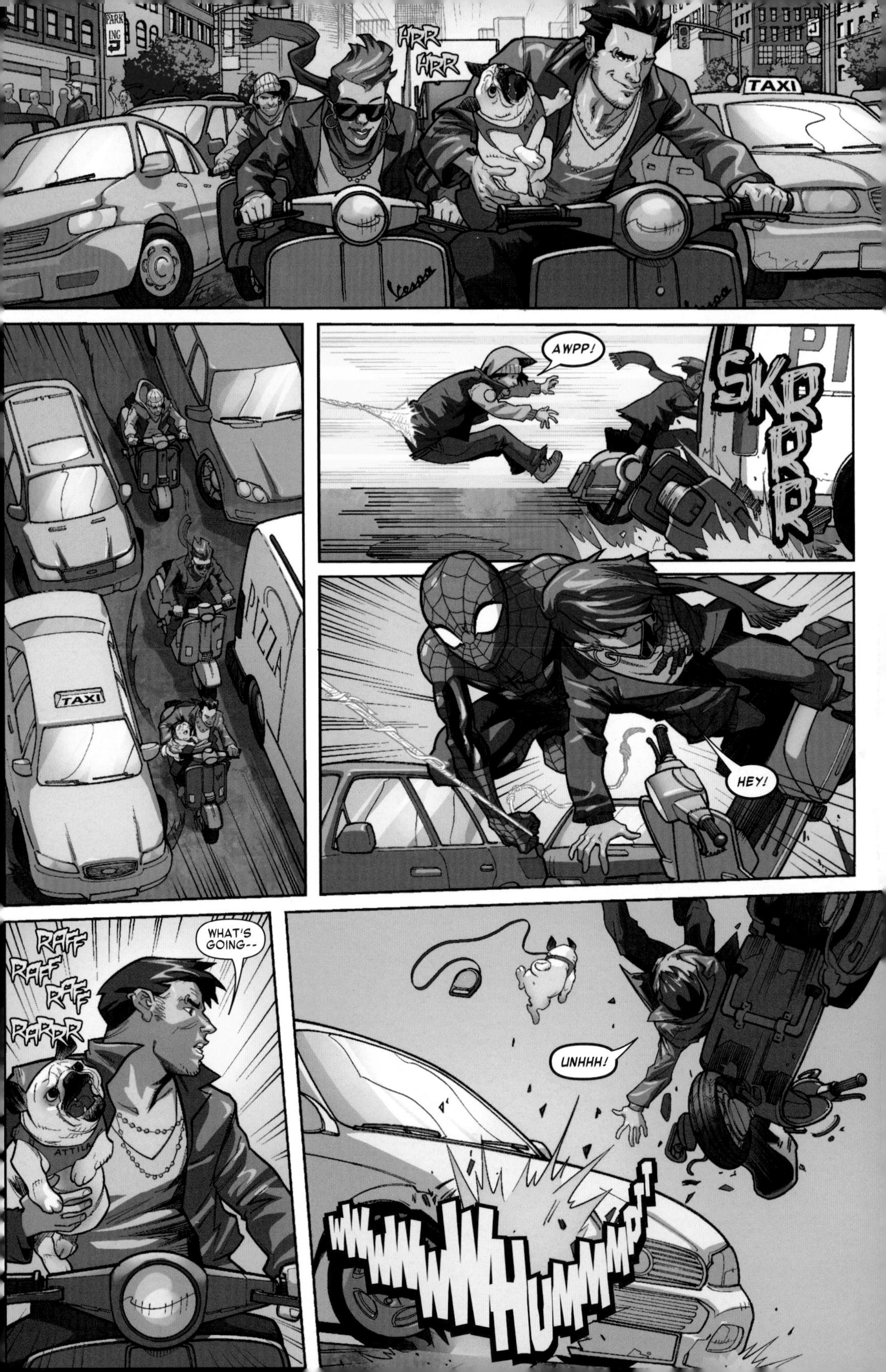
HRR
HRR
TAXI
AWPP!
SKRRRR
HEY!
RAFF
RAFF
RAFF
RARRR
WHAT'S GOING--
UNHHH!
WWWWWHUMMMPT

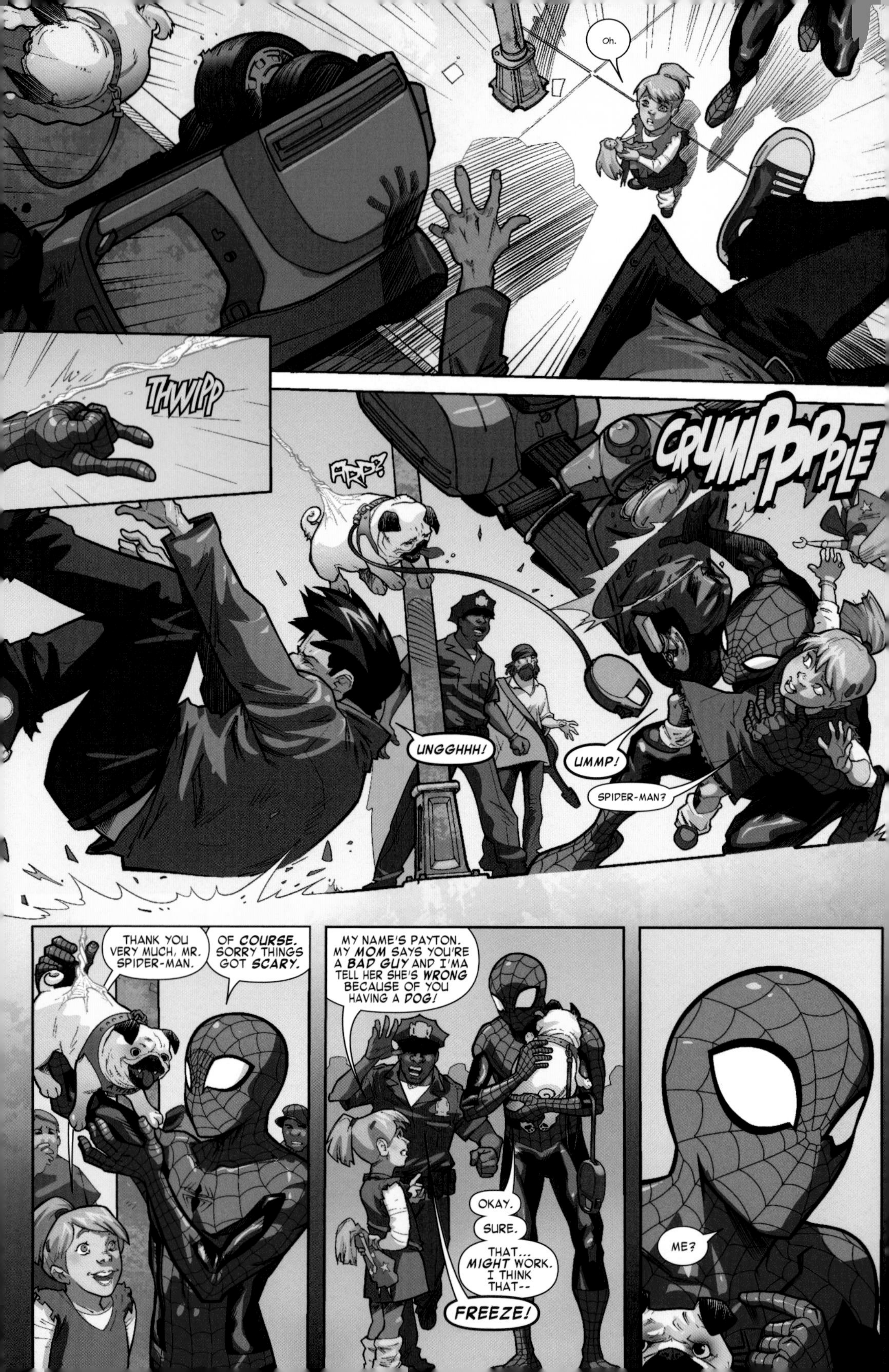

Oh.
THWIPP
CRUMPPPPLE
UNGGHHH!
UMMP!
SPIDER-MAN?
THANK YOU VERY MUCH, MR. SPIDER-MAN.
OF COURSE. SORRY THINGS GOT SCARY.
MY NAME'S PAYTON. MY MOM SAYS YOU'RE A BAD GUY AND I'MA TELL HER SHE'S WRONG BECAUSE OF YOU HAVING A DOG!
OKAY.
SURE.
THAT... MIGHT WORK. I THINK THAT--
FREEZE!
ME?

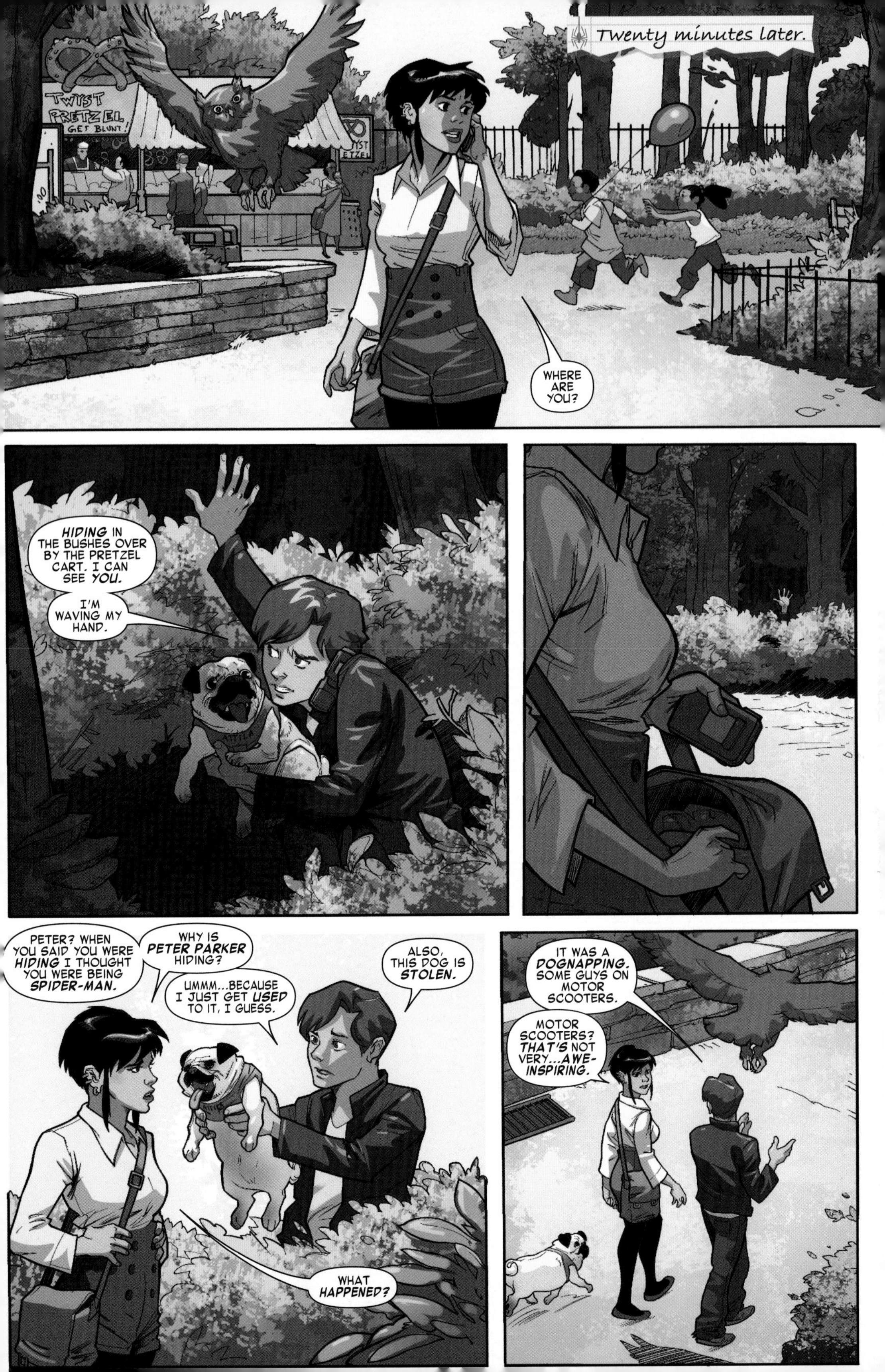
Twenty minutes later.
TWIST PRETZEL GET BLUNT!
WHERE ARE YOU?
HIDING IN THE BUSHES OVER BY THE PRETZEL CART. I CAN SEE YOU.
I'M WAVING MY HAND.
PETER? WHEN YOU SAID YOU WERE HIDING I THOUGHT YOU WERE BEING SPIDER-MAN.
WHY IS PETER PARKER HIDING?
UMMM...BECAUSE I JUST GET USED TO IT, I GUESS.
ALSO, THIS DOG IS STOLEN.
WHAT HAPPENED?
IT WAS A DOGNAPPING. SOME GUYS ON MOTOR SCOOTERS.
MOTOR SCOOTERS? THAT'S NOT VERY...AWE-INSPIRING.

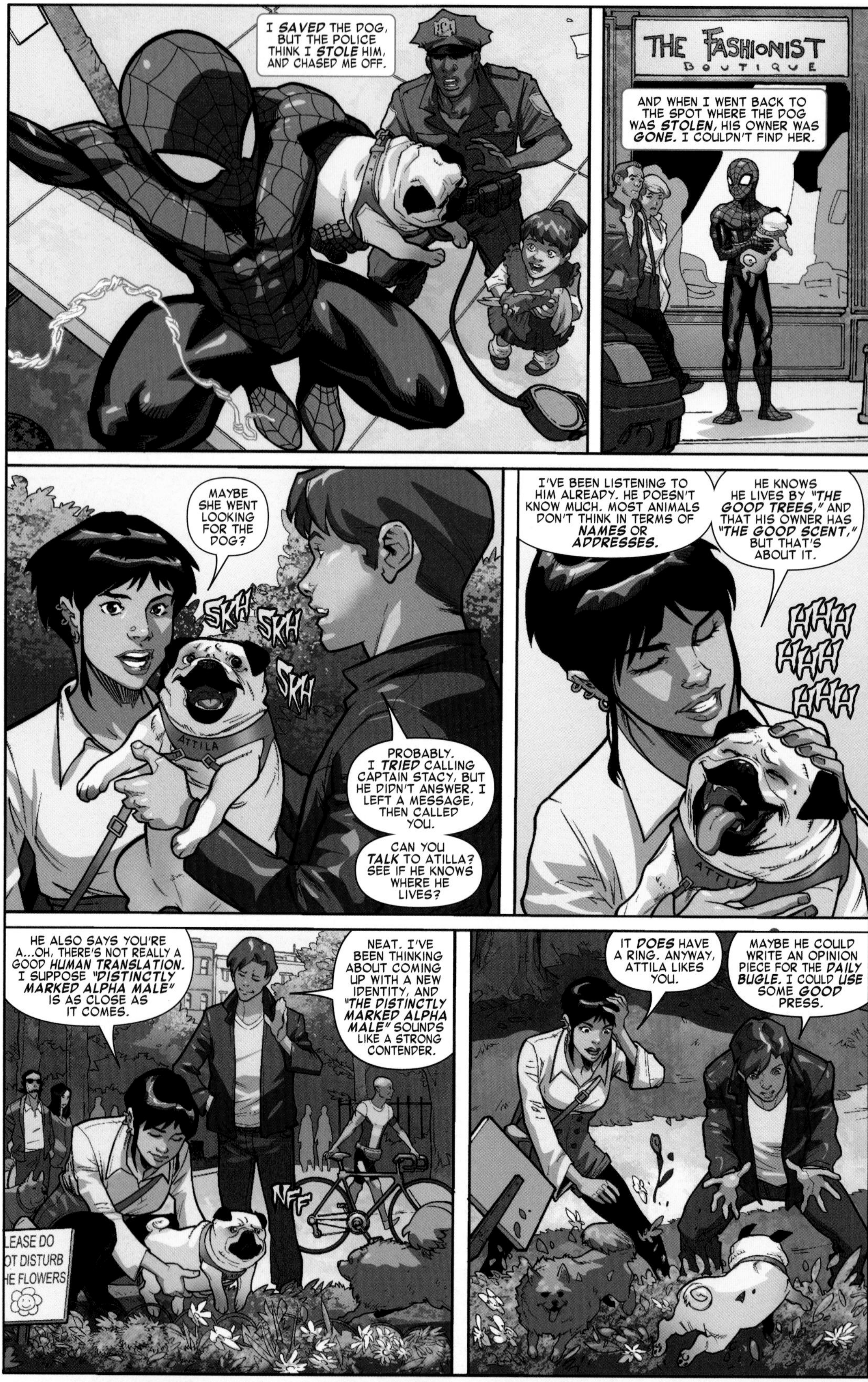
I SAVED THE DOG, BUT THE POLICE THINK I STOLE HIM, AND CHASED ME OFF.
THE FASHIONIST BOUTIQUE
AND WHEN I WENT BACK TO THE SPOT WHERE THE DOG WAS STOLEN, HIS OWNER WAS GONE. I COULDN'T FIND HER.
MAYBE SHE WENT LOOKING FOR THE DOG?
SKH SKH SKH
ATTILA
PROBABLY. I TRIED CALLING CAPTAIN STACY, BUT HE DIDN'T ANSWER. I LEFT A MESSAGE, THEN CALLED YOU.
CAN YOU TALK TO ATILLA? SEE IF HE KNOWS WHERE HE LIVES?
I'VE BEEN LISTENING TO HIM ALREADY. HE DOESN'T KNOW MUCH. MOST ANIMALS DON'T THINK IN TERMS OF NAMES OR ADDRESSES.
HE KNOWS HE LIVES BY "THE GOOD TREES," AND THAT HIS OWNER HAS "THE GOOD SCENT," BUT THAT'S ABOUT IT.
HHH HHH HHH
HE ALSO SAYS YOU'RE A...OH, THERE'S NOT REALLY A GOOD HUMAN TRANSLATION. I SUPPOSE "DISTINCTLY MARKED ALPHA MALE" IS AS CLOSE AS IT COMES.
NEAT. I'VE BEEN THINKING ABOUT COMING UP WITH A NEW IDENTITY, AND "THE DISTINCTLY MARKED ALPHA MALE" SOUNDS LIKE A STRONG CONTENDER.
NFF
LEASE DO OT DISTURB HE FLOWERS
IT DOES HAVE A RING. ANYWAY, ATTILA LIKES YOU.
MAYBE HE COULD WRITE AN OPINION PIECE FOR THE DAILY BUGLE. I COULD USE SOME GOOD PRESS.

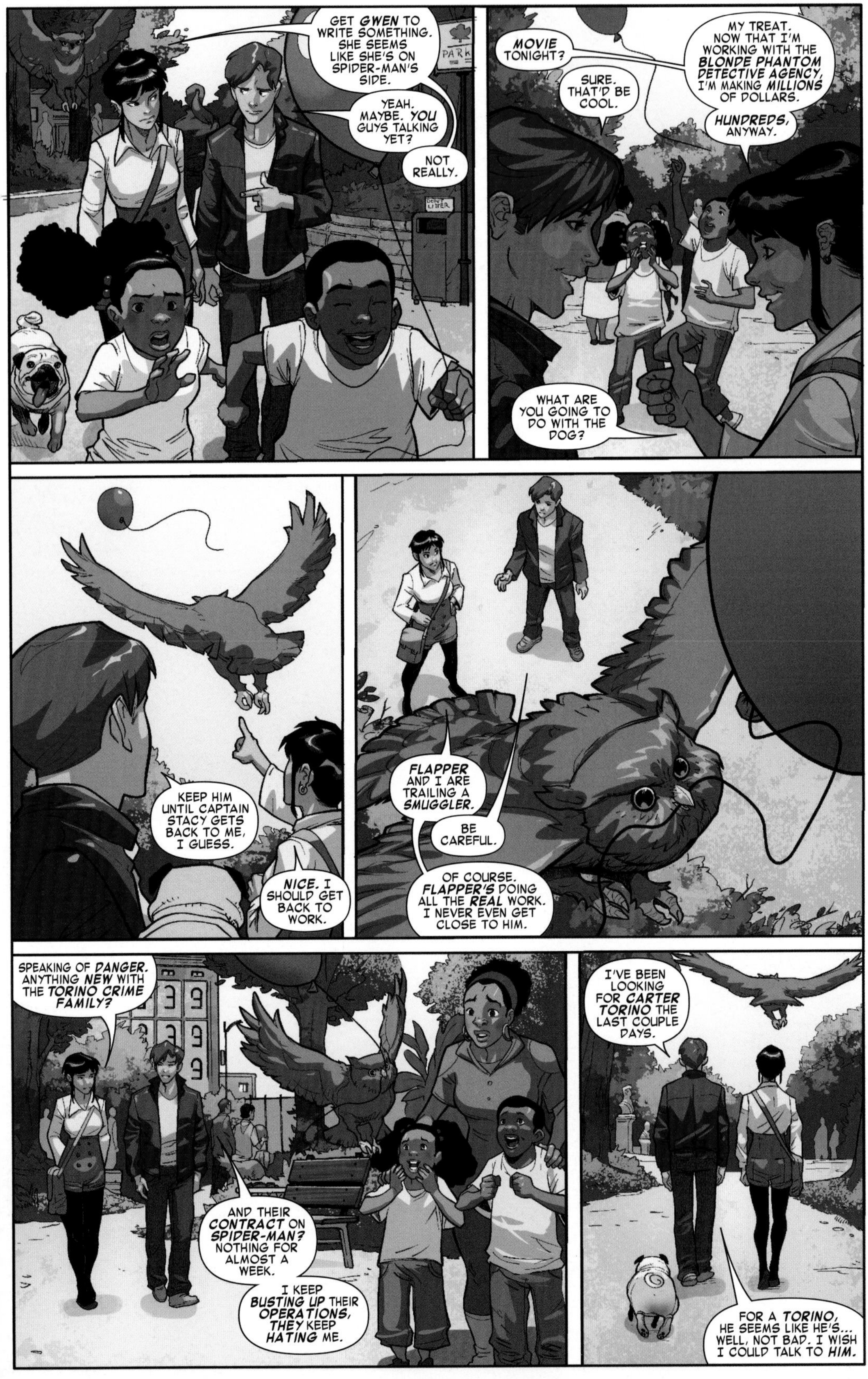
PARK
GET GWEN TO WRITE SOMETHING. SHE SEEMS LIKE SHE'S ON SPIDER-MAN'S SIDE.
YEAH. MAYBE. YOU GUYS TALKING YET?
NOT REALLY.
DON'T LITTER
MOVIE TONIGHT?
SURE. THAT'D BE COOL.
MY TREAT. NOW THAT I'M WORKING WITH THE BLONDE PHANTOM DETECTIVE AGENCY, I'M MAKING MILLIONS OF DOLLARS.
HUNDREDS, ANYWAY.
WHAT ARE YOU GOING TO DO WITH THE DOG?
KEEP HIM UNTIL CAPTAIN STACY GETS BACK TO ME, I GUESS.
NICE. I SHOULD GET BACK TO WORK.
FLAPPER AND I ARE TRAILING A SMUGGLER.
BE CAREFUL.
OF COURSE. FLAPPER'S DOING ALL THE REAL WORK. I NEVER EVEN GET CLOSE TO HIM.
SPEAKING OF DANGER. ANYTHING NEW WITH THE TORINO CRIME FAMILY?
AND THEIR CONTRACT ON SPIDER-MAN? NOTHING FOR ALMOST A WEEK.
I KEEP BUSTING UP THEIR OPERATIONS, THEY KEEP HATING ME.
I'VE BEEN LOOKING FOR CARTER TORINO THE LAST COUPLE DAYS.
FOR A TORINO, HE SEEMS LIKE HE'S... WELL, NOT BAD. I WISH I COULD TALK TO HIM.

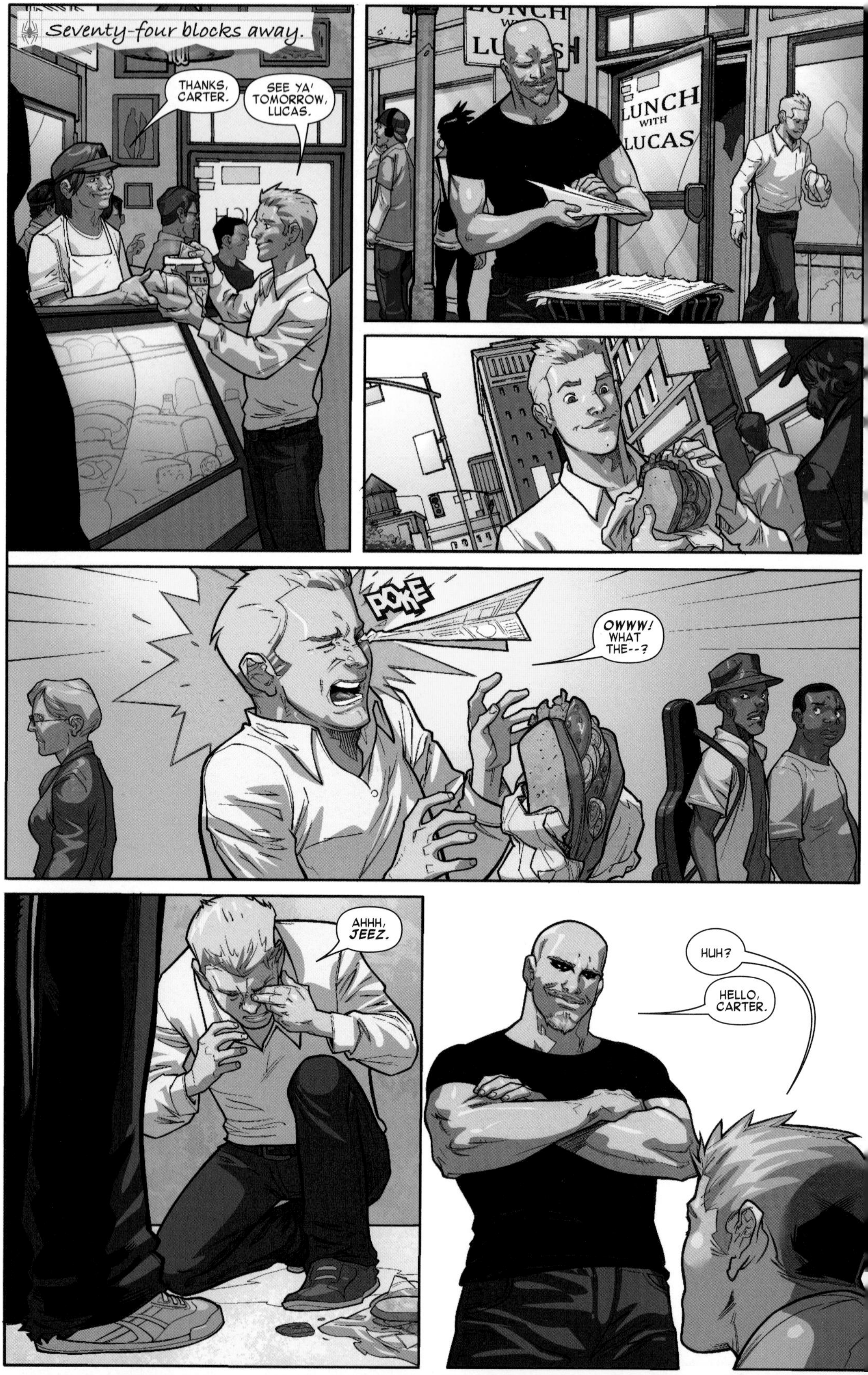
Seventy-four blocks away.
THANKS, CARTER.
SEE YA' TOMORROW, LUCAS.
LUNCH WITH LUCAS
POKE
OWWW! WHAT THE--?
AHHH, JEEZ.
HUH?
HELLO, CARTER.

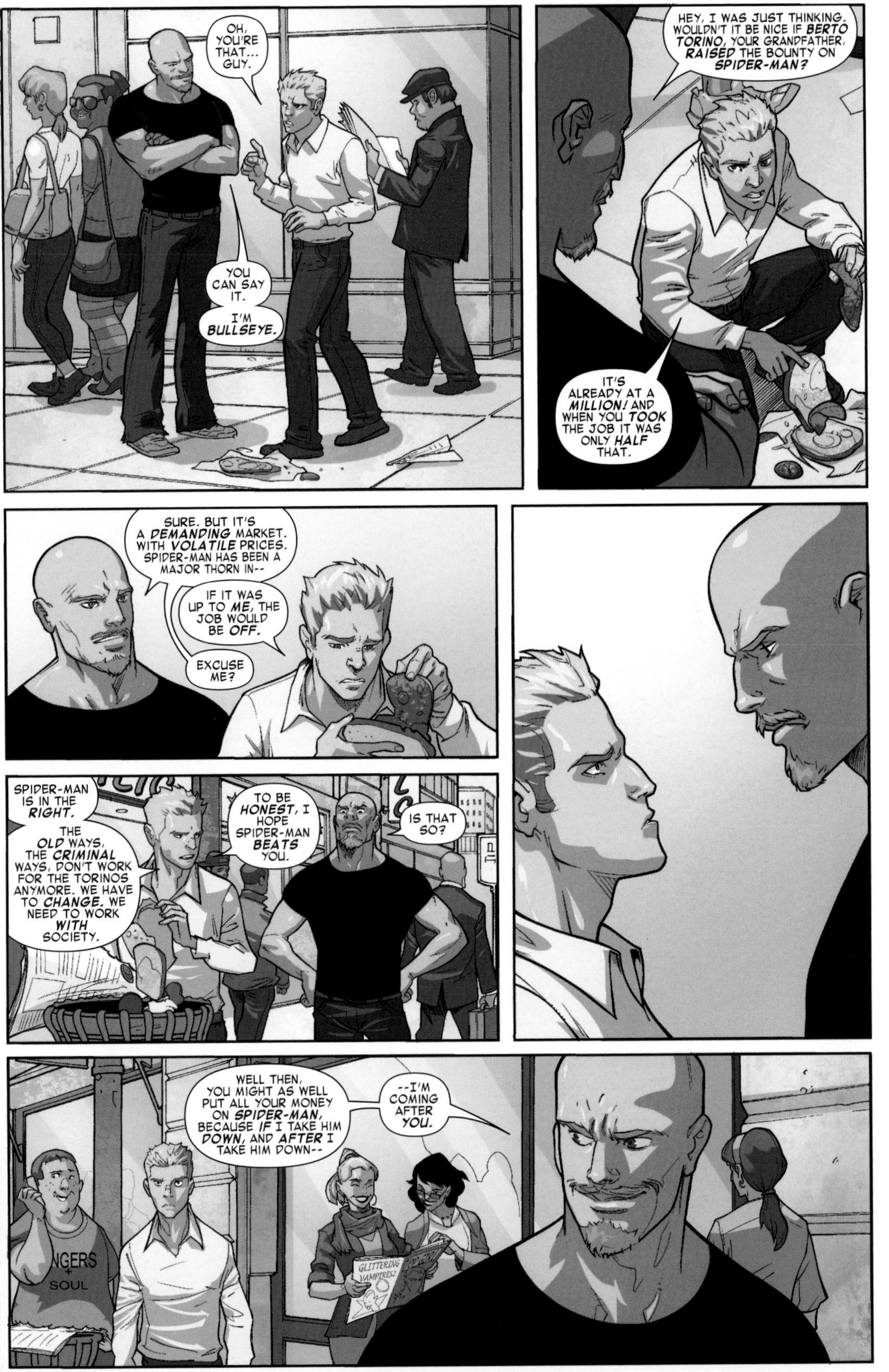

OH, YOU'RE THAT... GUY.
YOU CAN SAY IT.
I'M BULLSEYE.
HEY, I WAS JUST THINKING. WOULDN'T IT BE NICE IF BERTO TORINO, YOUR GRANDFATHER, RAISED THE BOUNTY ON SPIDER-MAN?
IT'S ALREADY AT A MILLION! AND WHEN YOU TOOK THE JOB IT WAS ONLY HALF THAT.
SURE. BUT IT'S A DEMANDING MARKET. WITH VOLATILE PRICES. SPIDER-MAN HAS BEEN A MAJOR THORN IN--
IF IT WAS UP TO ME, THE JOB WOULD BE OFF.
EXCUSE ME?
SPIDER-MAN IS IN THE RIGHT.
THE OLD WAYS, THE CRIMINAL WAYS, DON'T WORK FOR THE TORINOS ANYMORE. WE HAVE TO CHANGE. WE NEED TO WORK WITH SOCIETY.
TO BE HONEST, I HOPE SPIDER-MAN BEATS YOU.
IS THAT SO?
WELL THEN, YOU MIGHT AS WELL PUT ALL YOUR MONEY ON SPIDER-MAN, BECAUSE IF I TAKE HIM DOWN, AND AFTER I TAKE HIM DOWN--
--I'M COMING AFTER YOU.
NGERS + SOUL
GLITTERING VAMPIRES 2

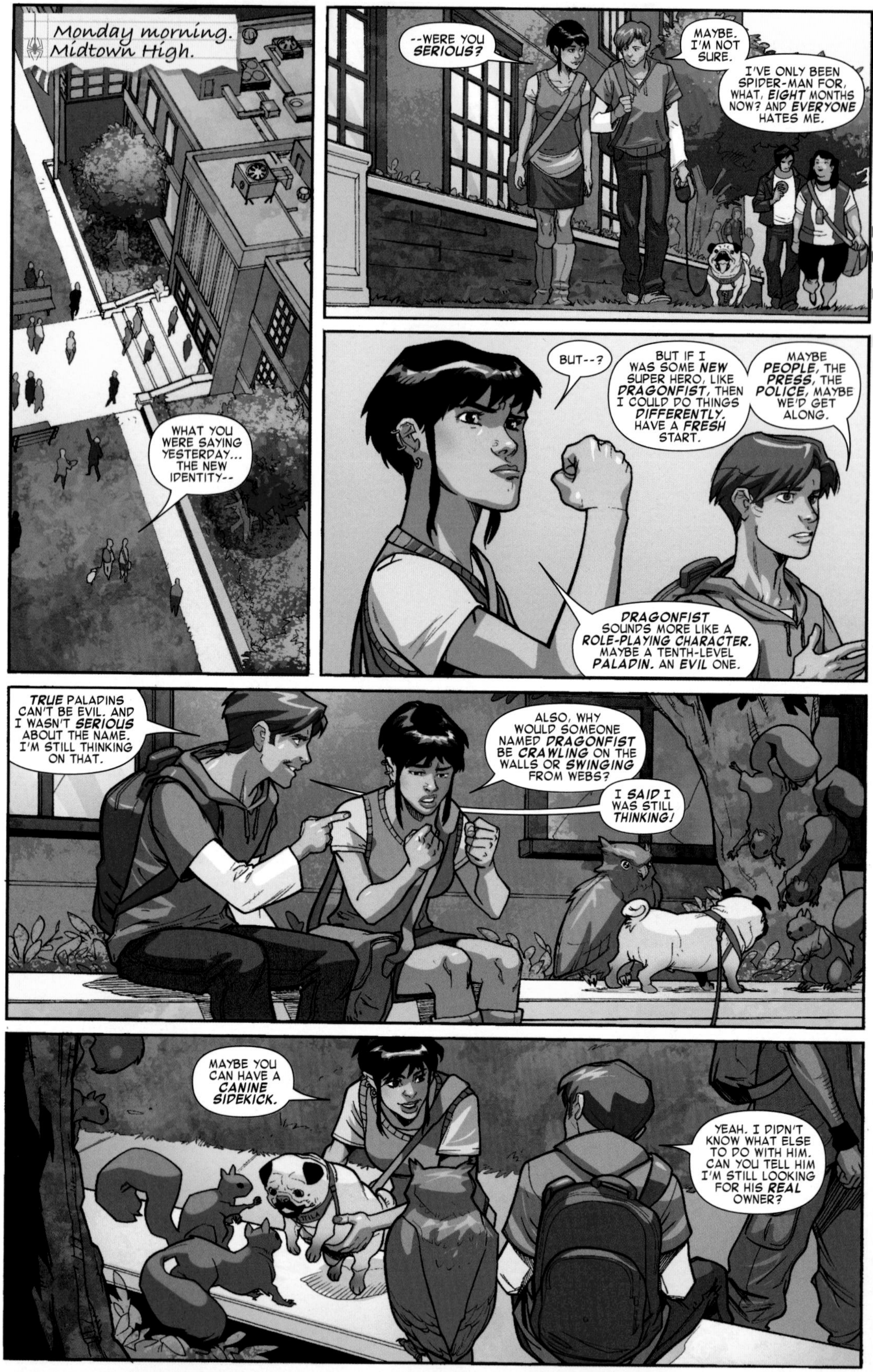

Monday morning. Midtown High.
WHAT YOU WERE SAYING YESTERDAY... THE NEW IDENTITY--
--WERE YOU SERIOUS?
MAYBE. I'M NOT SURE.
I'VE ONLY BEEN SPIDER-MAN FOR, WHAT, EIGHT MONTHS NOW? AND EVERYONE HATES ME.
BUT--?
BUT IF I WAS SOME NEW SUPER HERO, LIKE DRAGONFIST, THEN I COULD DO THINGS DIFFERENTLY. HAVE A FRESH START.
MAYBE PEOPLE, THE PRESS, THE POLICE, MAYBE WE'D GET ALONG.
DRAGONFIST SOUNDS MORE LIKE A ROLE-PLAYING CHARACTER. MAYBE A TENTH-LEVEL PALADIN. AN EVIL ONE.
TRUE PALADINS CAN'T BE EVIL. AND I WASN'T SERIOUS ABOUT THE NAME. I'M STILL THINKING ON THAT.
ALSO, WHY WOULD SOMEONE NAMED DRAGONFIST BE CRAWLING ON THE WALLS OR SWINGING FROM WEBS?
I SAID I WAS STILL THINKING!
MAYBE YOU CAN HAVE A CANINE SIDEKICK.
YEAH. I DIDN'T KNOW WHAT ELSE TO DO WITH HIM. CAN YOU TELL HIM I'M STILL LOOKING FOR HIS REAL OWNER?

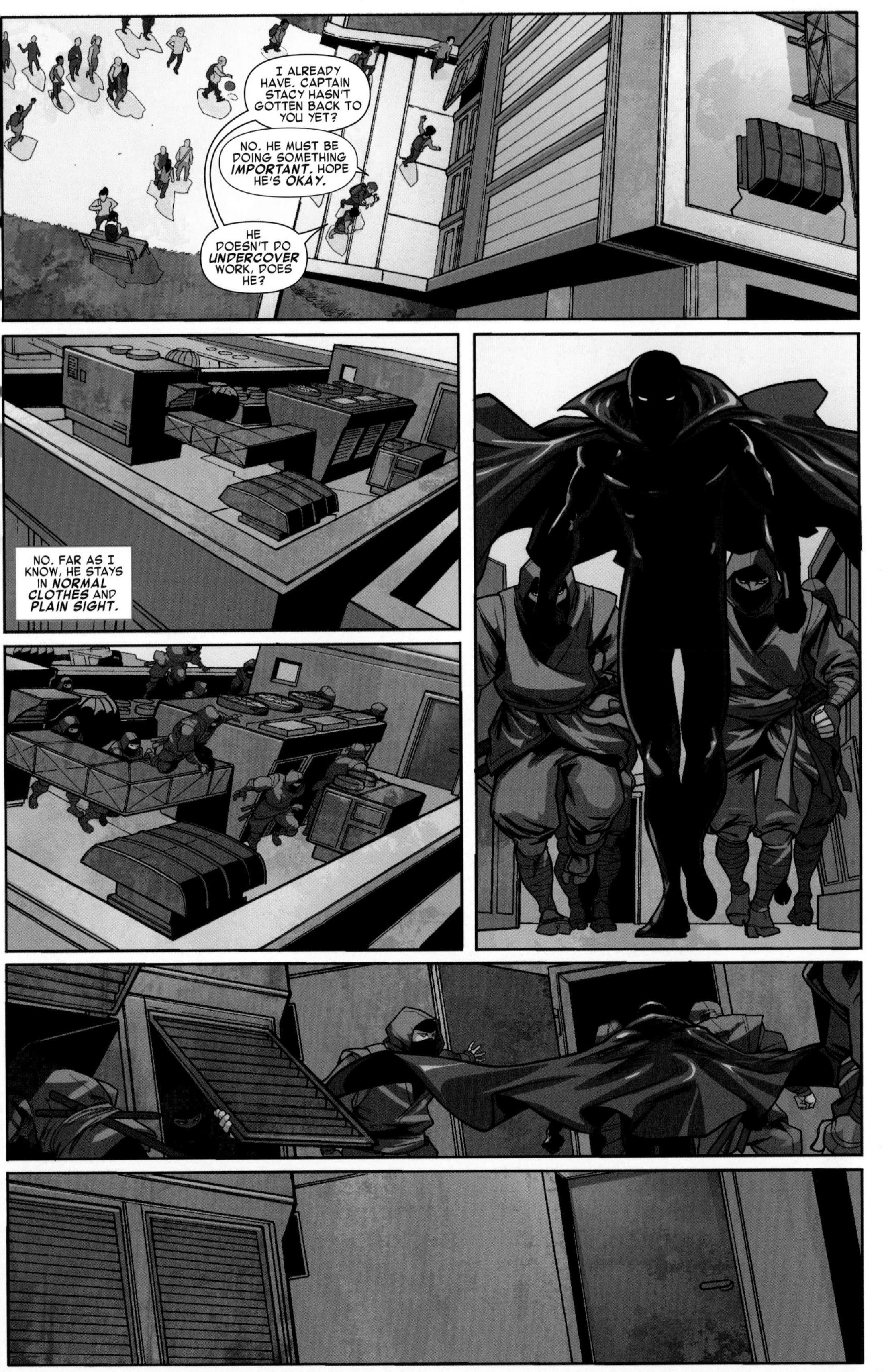
I ALREADY HAVE. CAPTAIN STACY HASN'T GOTTEN BACK TO YOU YET?
NO. HE MUST BE DOING SOMETHING IMPORTANT. HOPE HE'S OKAY.
HE DOESN'T DO UNDERCOVER WORK, DOES HE?
NO. FAR AS I KNOW, HE STAYS IN NORMAL CLOTHES AND PLAIN SIGHT.

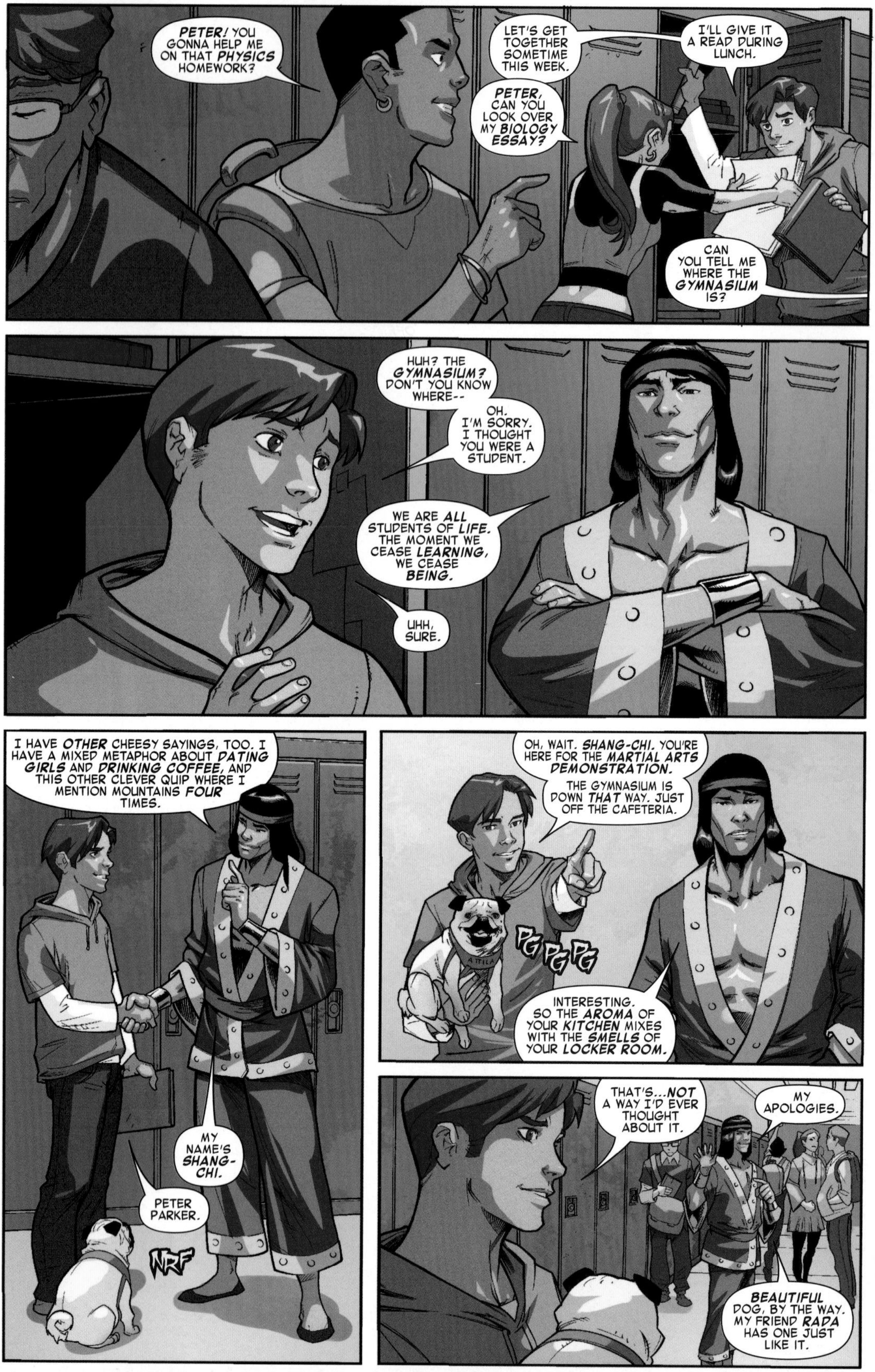
PETER! YOU GONNA HELP ME ON THAT PHYSICS HOMEWORK?
LET'S GET TOGETHER SOMETIME THIS WEEK.
PETER, CAN YOU LOOK OVER MY BIOLOGY ESSAY?
I'LL GIVE IT A READ DURING LUNCH.
CAN YOU TELL ME WHERE THE GYMNASIUM IS?
HUH? THE GYMNASIUM? DON'T YOU KNOW WHERE--
OH. I'M SORRY. I THOUGHT YOU WERE A STUDENT.
WE ARE ALL STUDENTS OF LIFE. THE MOMENT WE CEASE LEARNING, WE CEASE BEING.
UHH, SURE.
I HAVE OTHER CHEESY SAYINGS, TOO. I HAVE A MIXED METAPHOR ABOUT DATING GIRLS AND DRINKING COFFEE, AND THIS OTHER CLEVER QUIP WHERE I MENTION MOUNTAINS FOUR TIMES.
MY NAME'S SHANG-CHI.
PETER PARKER.
NRF
OH, WAIT. SHANG-CHI. YOU'RE HERE FOR THE MARTIAL ARTS DEMONSTRATION.
THE GYMNASIUM IS DOWN THAT WAY. JUST OFF THE CAFETERIA.
PG PG PG
INTERESTING. SO THE AROMA OF YOUR KITCHEN MIXES WITH THE SMELLS OF YOUR LOCKER ROOM.
THAT'S...NOT A WAY I'D EVER THOUGHT ABOUT IT.
MY APOLOGIES.
BEAUTIFUL DOG, BY THE WAY. MY FRIEND RADA HAS ONE JUST LIKE IT.

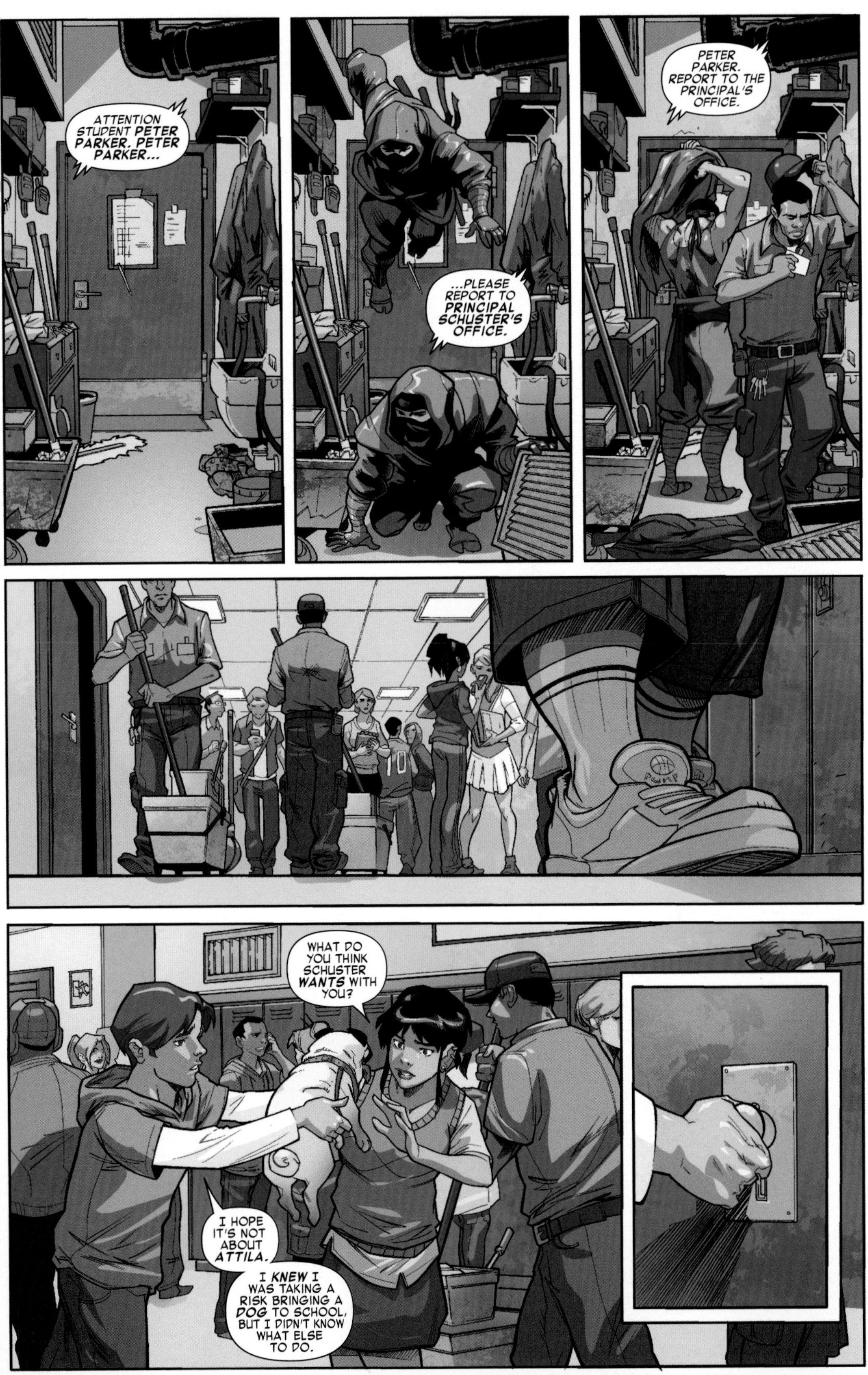
ATTENTION STUDENT PETER PARKER. PETER PARKER...
...PLEASE REPORT TO PRINCIPAL SCHUSTER'S OFFICE.
PETER PARKER. REPORT TO THE PRINCIPAL'S OFFICE.
WHAT DO YOU THINK SCHUSTER WANTS WITH YOU?
I HOPE IT'S NOT ABOUT ATTILA.
I KNEW I WAS TAKING A RISK BRINGING A DOG TO SCHOOL, BUT I DIDN'T KNOW WHAT ELSE TO DO.

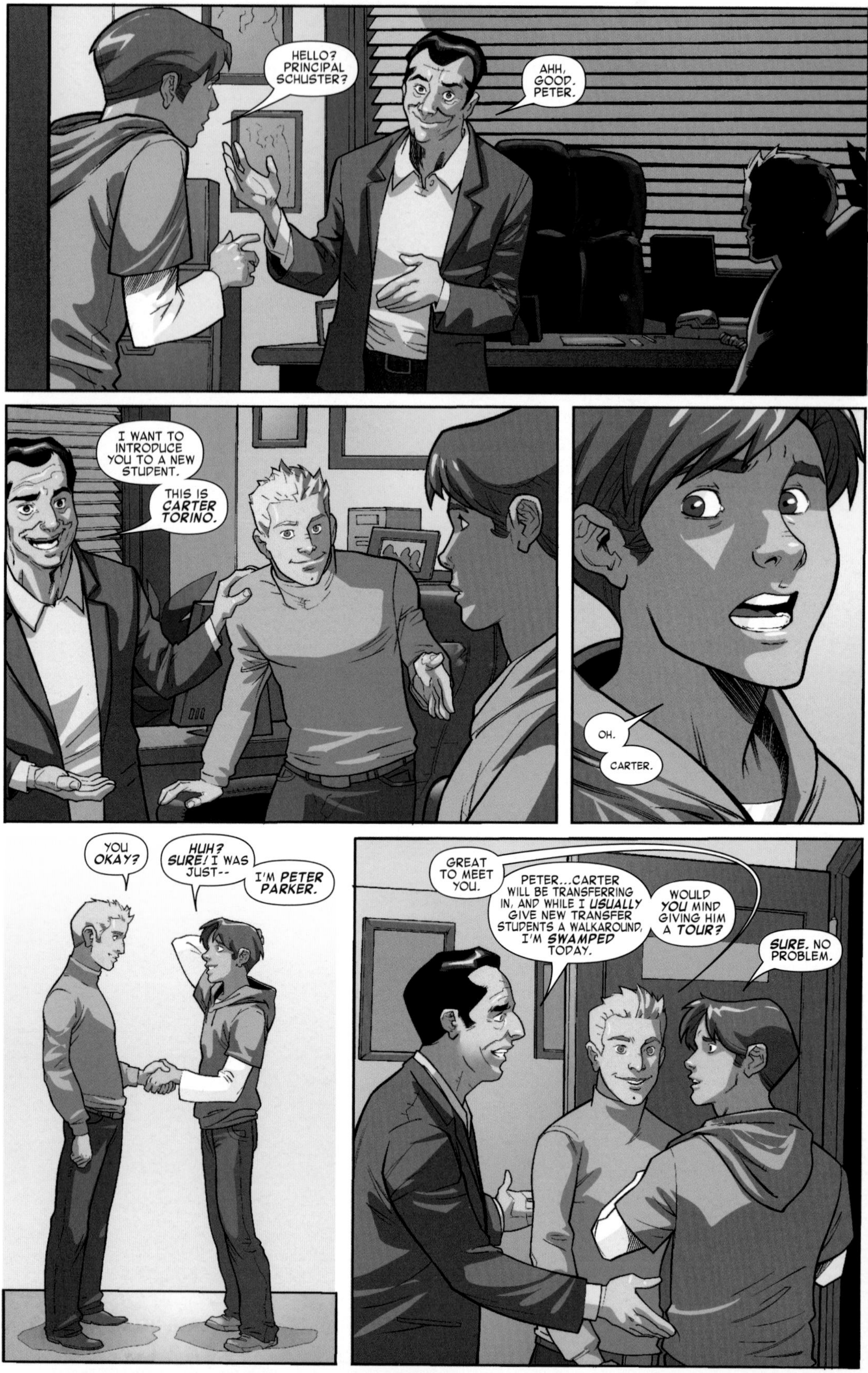

HELLO? PRINCIPAL SCHUSTER?
AHH, GOOD. PETER.
I WANT TO INTRODUCE YOU TO A NEW STUDENT.
THIS IS CARTER TORINO.
OH.
CARTER.
YOU OKAY?
HUH? SURE! I WAS JUST--
I'M PETER PARKER.
GREAT TO MEET YOU.
PETER...CARTER WILL BE TRANSFERRING IN, AND WHILE I USUALLY GIVE NEW TRANSFER STUDENTS A WALKAROUND, I'M SWAMPED TODAY.
WOULD YOU MIND GIVING HIM A TOUR?
SURE. NO PROBLEM.

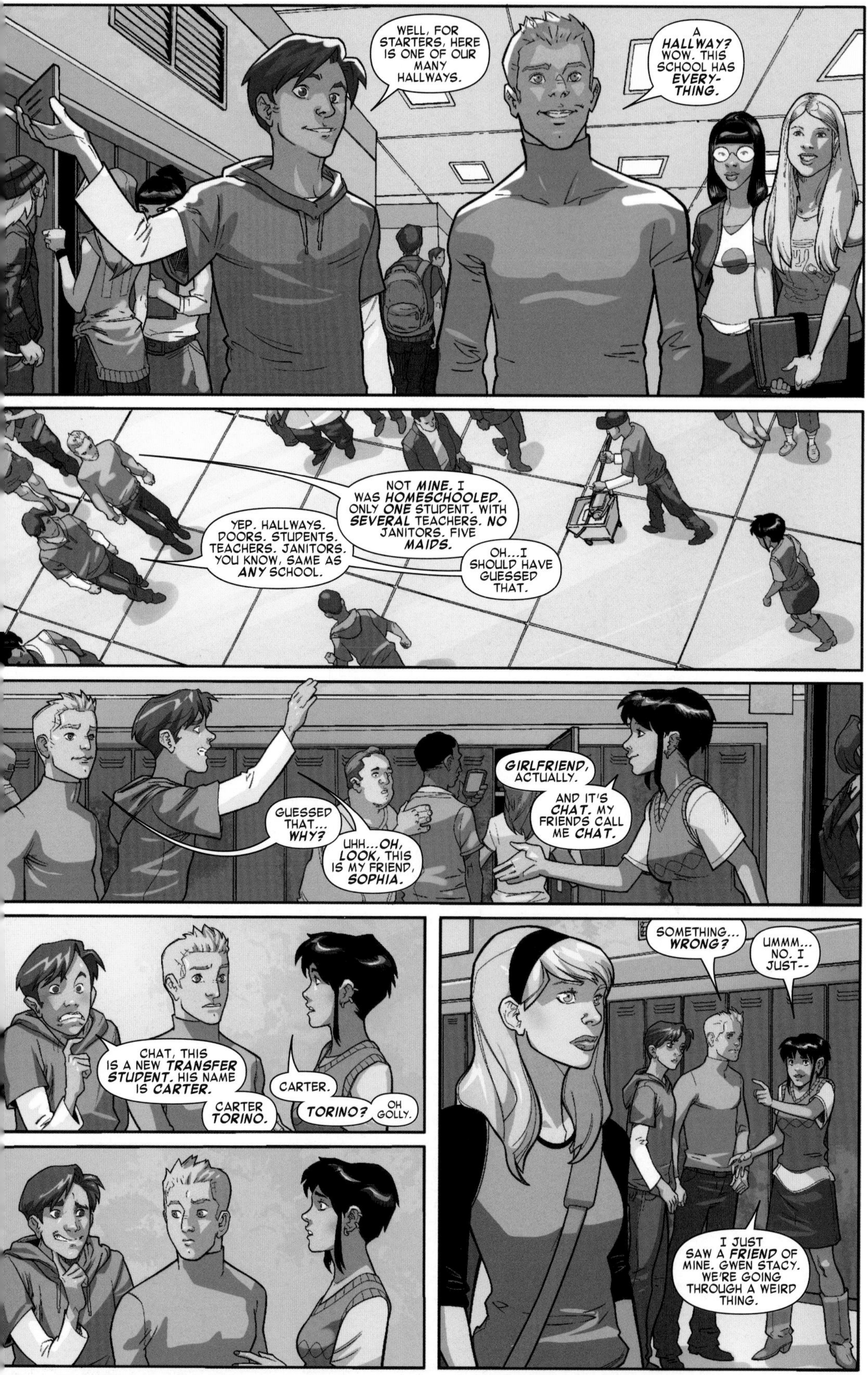
WELL, FOR STARTERS, HERE IS ONE OF OUR MANY HALLWAYS.
A *HALLWAY?* WOW. THIS SCHOOL HAS *EVERY-THING.*
YEP. HALLWAYS. DOORS. STUDENTS. TEACHERS. JANITORS. YOU KNOW, SAME AS *ANY* SCHOOL.
NOT *MINE.* I WAS *HOMESCHOOLED.* ONLY *ONE* STUDENT. WITH *SEVERAL* TEACHERS. *NO* JANITORS. FIVE *MAIDS.*
OH...I SHOULD HAVE GUESSED THAT.
GUESSED THAT... *WHY?*
UHH...*OH, LOOK,* THIS IS MY FRIEND, *SOPHIA.*
GIRLFRIEND, ACTUALLY.
AND IT'S *CHAT.* MY FRIENDS CALL ME *CHAT.*
CHAT, THIS IS A NEW *TRANSFER STUDENT.* HIS NAME IS *CARTER.*
CARTER *TORINO.*
CARTER.
TORINO?
OH GOLLY.
SOMETHING... *WRONG?*
UMMM... NO. I JUST--
I JUST SAW A *FRIEND* OF MINE. GWEN STACY. WE'RE GOING THROUGH A WEIRD THING.

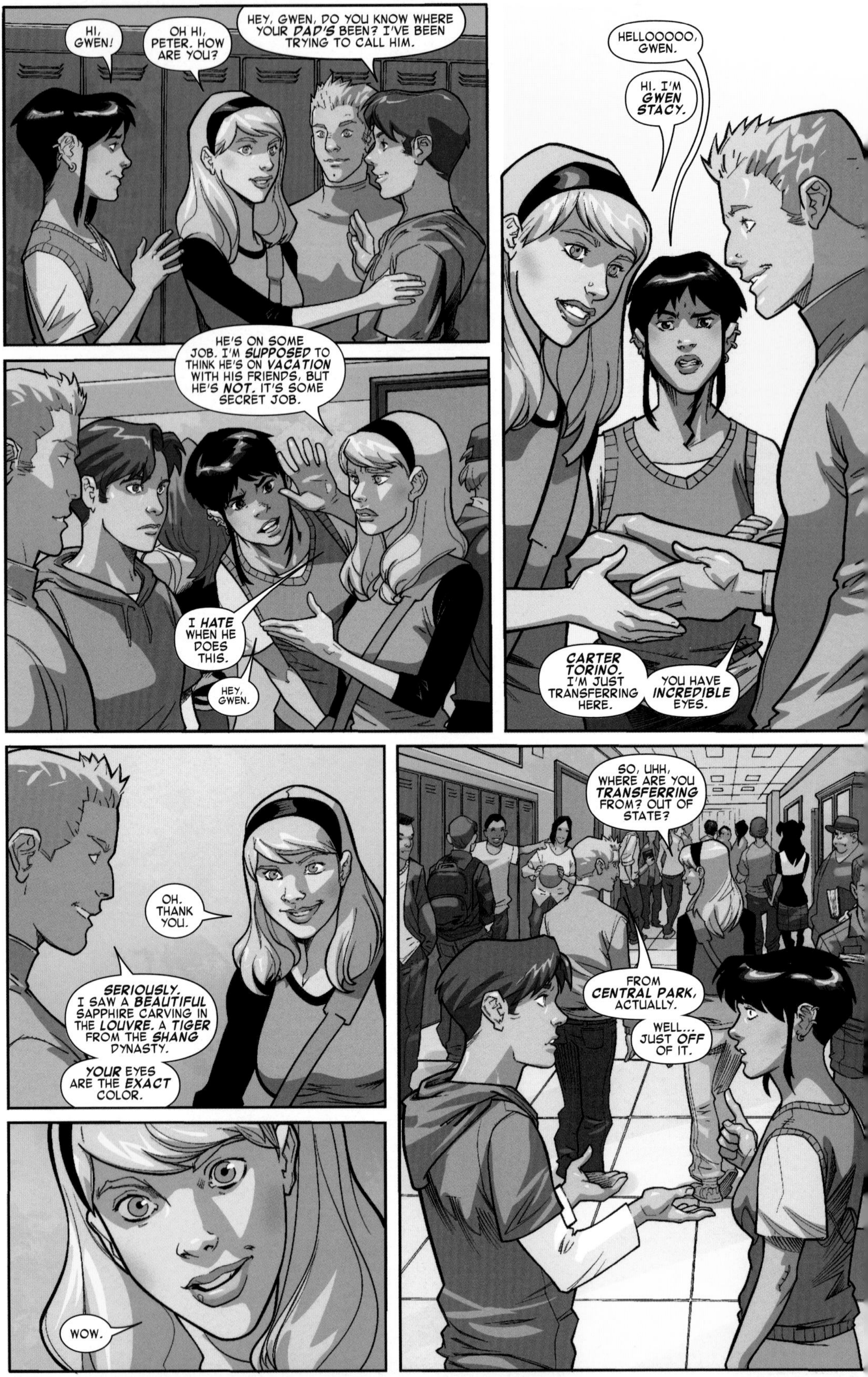
HI, GWEN!
OH HI, PETER. HOW ARE YOU?
HEY, GWEN, DO YOU KNOW WHERE YOUR DAD'S BEEN? I'VE BEEN TRYING TO CALL HIM.
HE'S ON SOME JOB. I'M SUPPOSED TO THINK HE'S ON VACATION WITH HIS FRIENDS, BUT HE'S NOT. IT'S SOME SECRET JOB.
I HATE WHEN HE DOES THIS.
HEY, GWEN.
HELLOOOOO, GWEN.
HI. I'M GWEN STACY.
CARTER TORINO. I'M JUST TRANSFERRING HERE.
YOU HAVE INCREDIBLE EYES.
OH. THANK YOU.
SERIOUSLY. I SAW A BEAUTIFUL SAPPHIRE CARVING IN THE LOUVRE. A TIGER FROM THE SHANG DYNASTY.
YOUR EYES ARE THE EXACT COLOR.
WOW.
SO, UHH, WHERE ARE YOU TRANSFERRING FROM? OUT OF STATE?
FROM CENTRAL PARK, ACTUALLY.
WELL... JUST OFF OF IT.

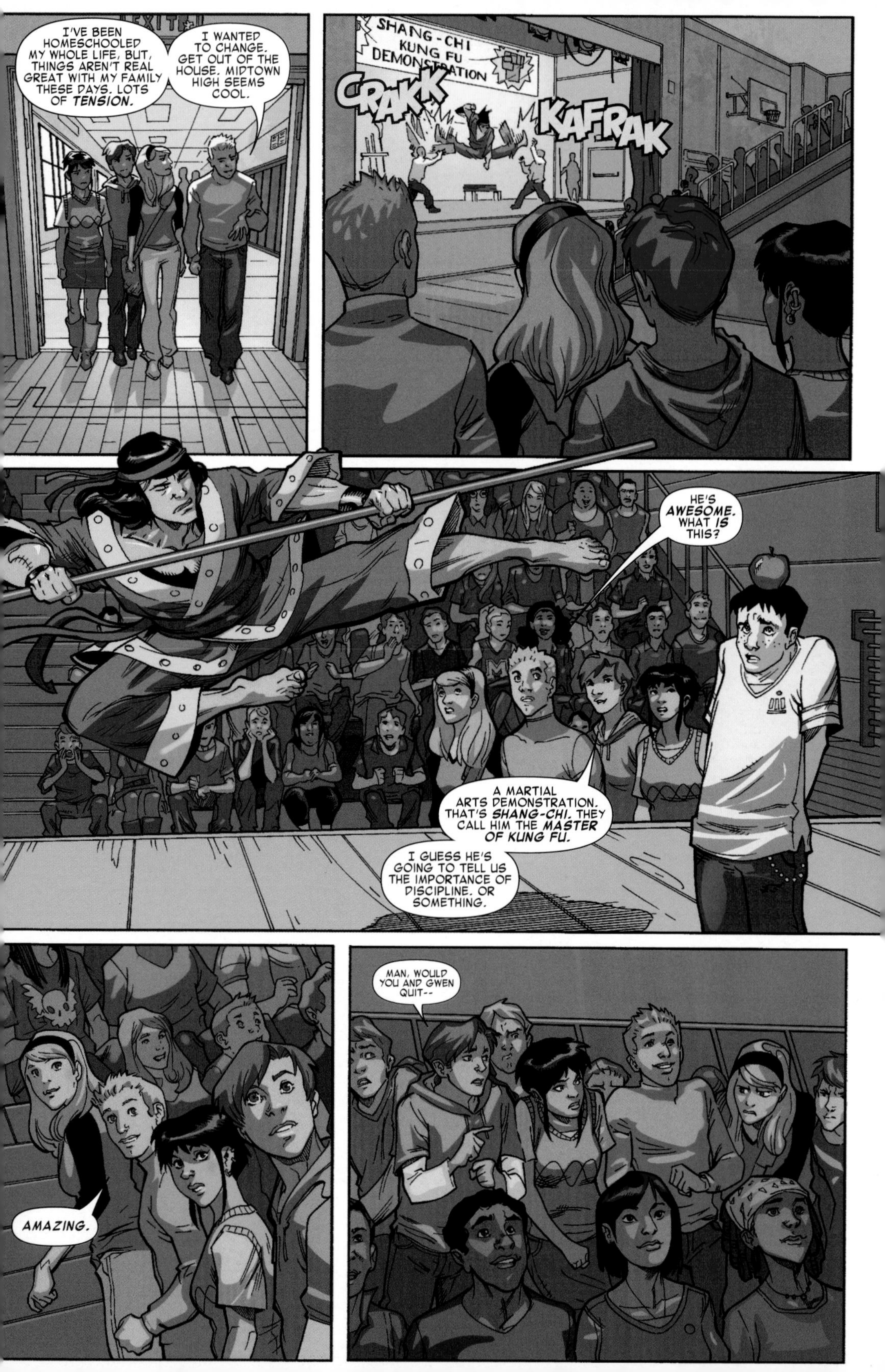
EXIT
I'VE BEEN HOMESCHOOLED MY WHOLE LIFE, BUT, THINGS AREN'T REAL GREAT WITH MY FAMILY THESE DAYS. LOTS OF TENSION.
I WANTED TO CHANGE. GET OUT OF THE HOUSE. MIDTOWN HIGH SEEMS COOL.
SHANG-CHI KUNG FU DEMONSTRATION
CRAKK
KAFRAK
HE'S AWESOME. WHAT IS THIS?
A MARTIAL ARTS DEMONSTRATION. THAT'S SHANG-CHI. THEY CALL HIM THE MASTER OF KUNG FU.
I GUESS HE'S GOING TO TELL US THE IMPORTANCE OF DISCIPLINE. OR SOMETHING.
AMAZING.
MAN, WOULD YOU AND GWEN QUIT--

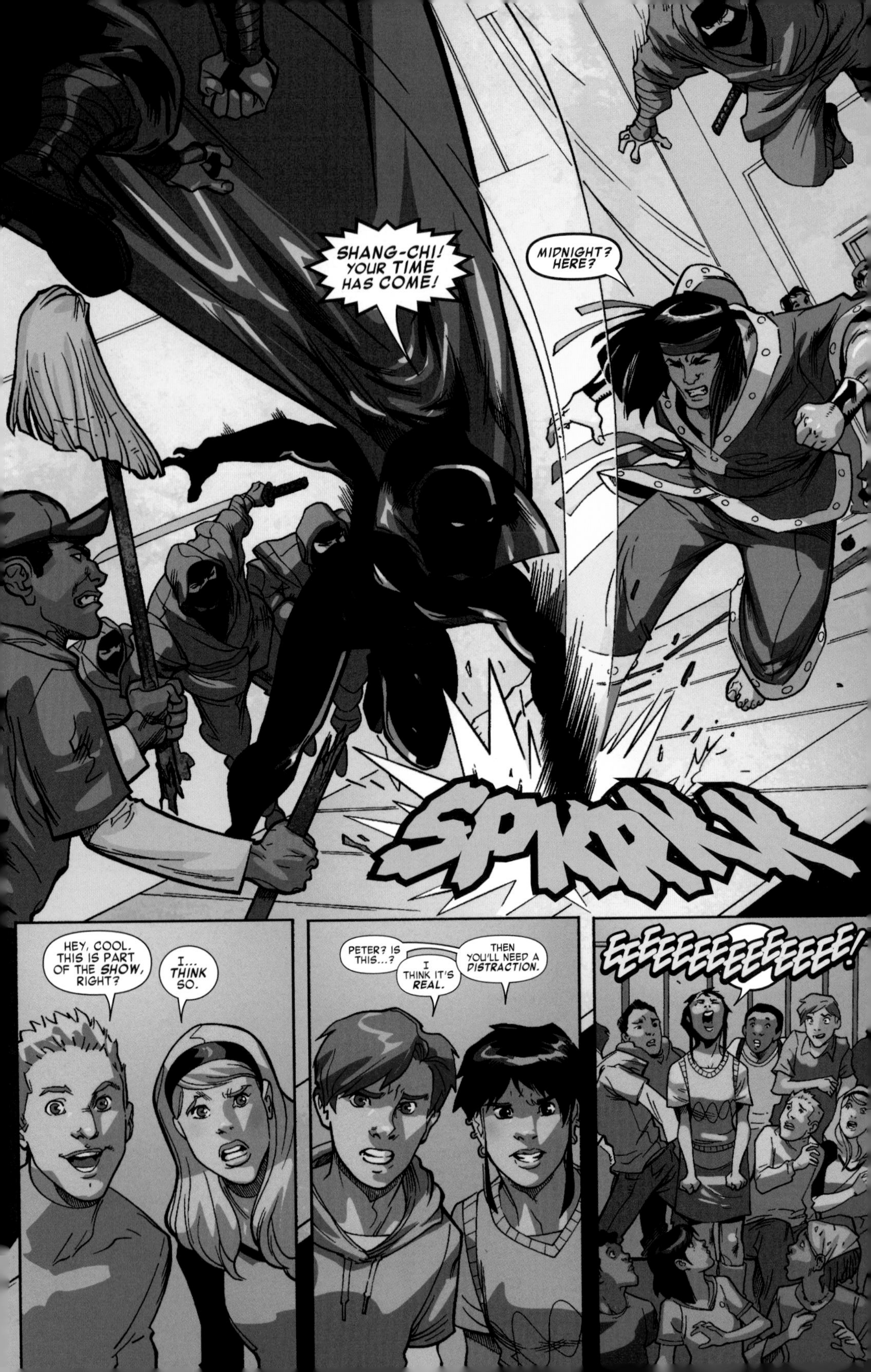
SHANG-CHI! YOUR TIME HAS COME!
MIDNIGHT? HERE?
HEY, COOL. THIS IS PART OF THE SHOW, RIGHT?
I... THINK SO.
PETER? IS THIS...?
I THINK IT'S REAL.
THEN YOU'LL NEED A DISTRACTION.
EEEEEEEEEEEEEEE!

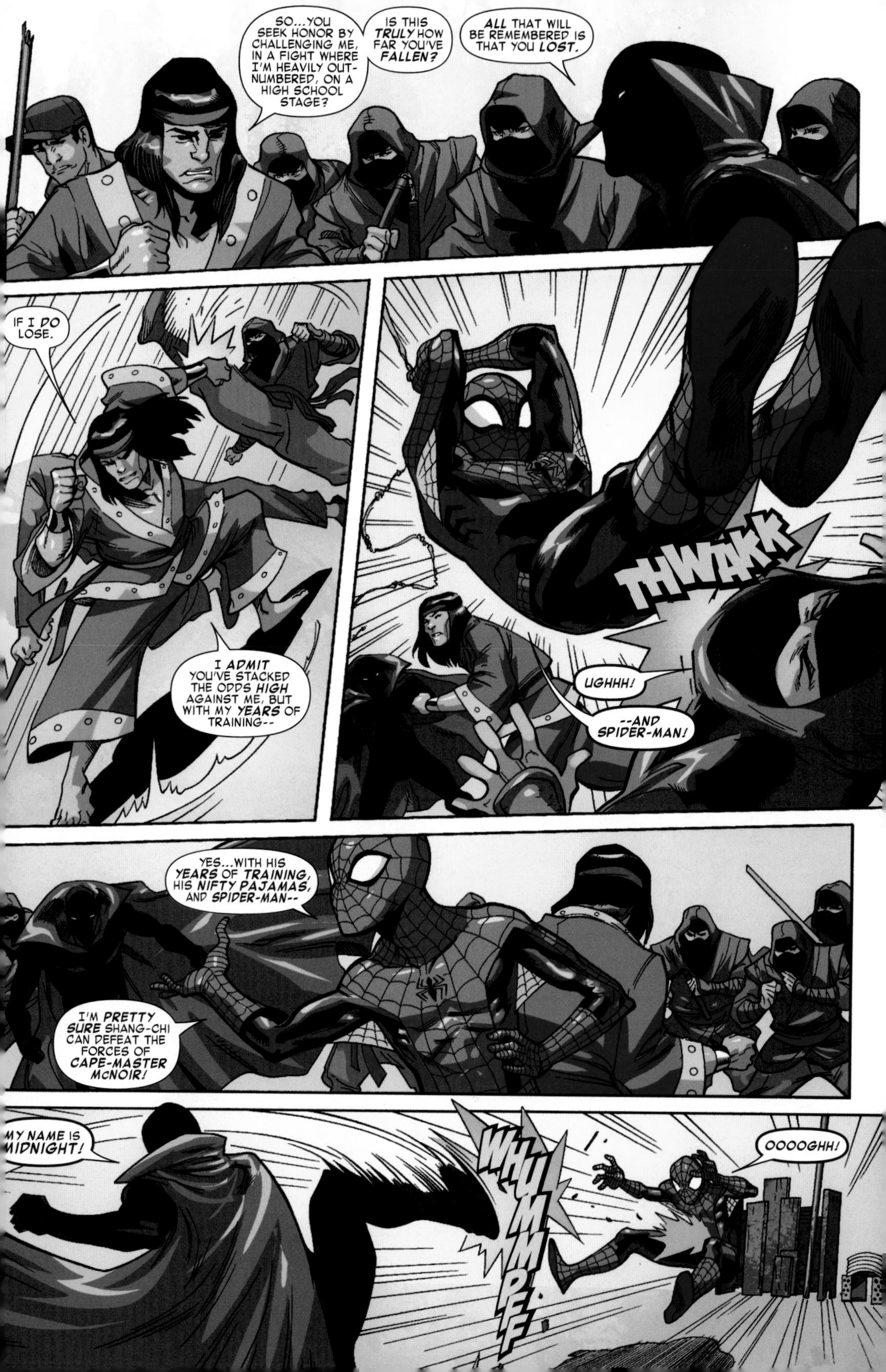

SO...YOU SEEK HONOR BY CHALLENGING ME, IN A FIGHT WHERE I'M HEAVILY OUT-NUMBERED, ON A HIGH SCHOOL STAGE?
IS THIS TRULY HOW FAR YOU'VE FALLEN?
ALL THAT WILL BE REMEMBERED IS THAT YOU LOST.
IF I DO LOSE.
I ADMIT YOU'VE STACKED THE ODDS HIGH AGAINST ME, BUT WITH MY YEARS OF TRAINING--
THWAKK
UGHHH!
--AND SPIDER-MAN!
YES...WITH HIS YEARS OF TRAINING, HIS NIFTY PAJAMAS, AND SPIDER-MAN--
I'M PRETTY SURE SHANG-CHI CAN DEFEAT THE FORCES OF CAPE-MASTER McNOIR!
MY NAME IS MIDNIGHT!
WHUMMMPFF
OOOOGHH!

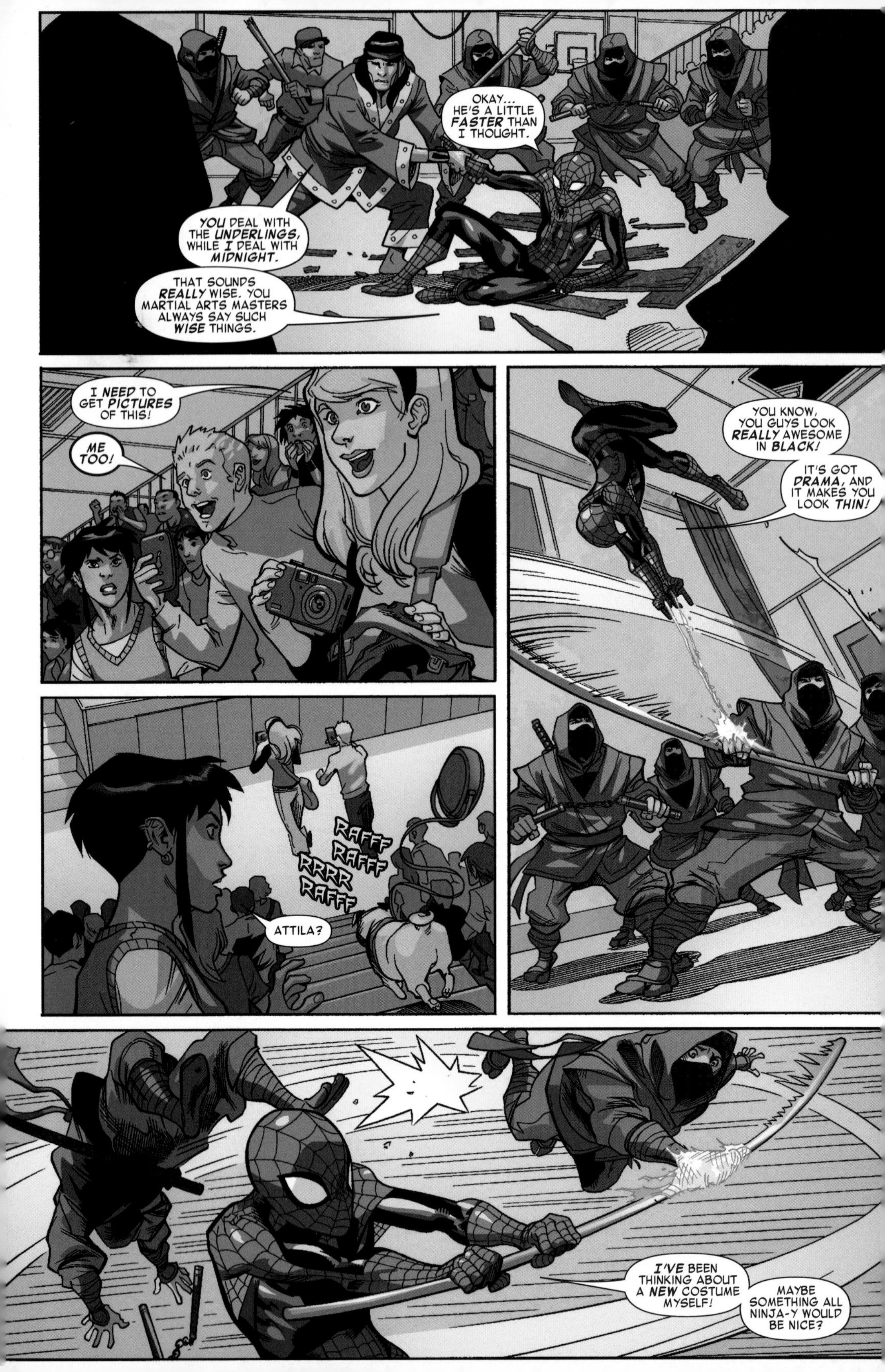
OKAY... HE'S A LITTLE FASTER THAN I THOUGHT.
YOU DEAL WITH THE UNDERLINGS, WHILE I DEAL WITH MIDNIGHT.
THAT SOUNDS REALLY WISE. YOU MARTIAL ARTS MASTERS ALWAYS SAY SUCH WISE THINGS.
I NEED TO GET PICTURES OF THIS!
ME TOO!
RAFFF
RAFFF
RRRR
RAFFF
ATTILA?
YOU KNOW, YOU GUYS LOOK REALLY AWESOME IN BLACK!
IT'S GOT DRAMA, AND IT MAKES YOU LOOK THIN!
I'VE BEEN THINKING ABOUT A NEW COSTUME MYSELF!
MAYBE SOMETHING ALL NINJA-Y WOULD BE NICE?

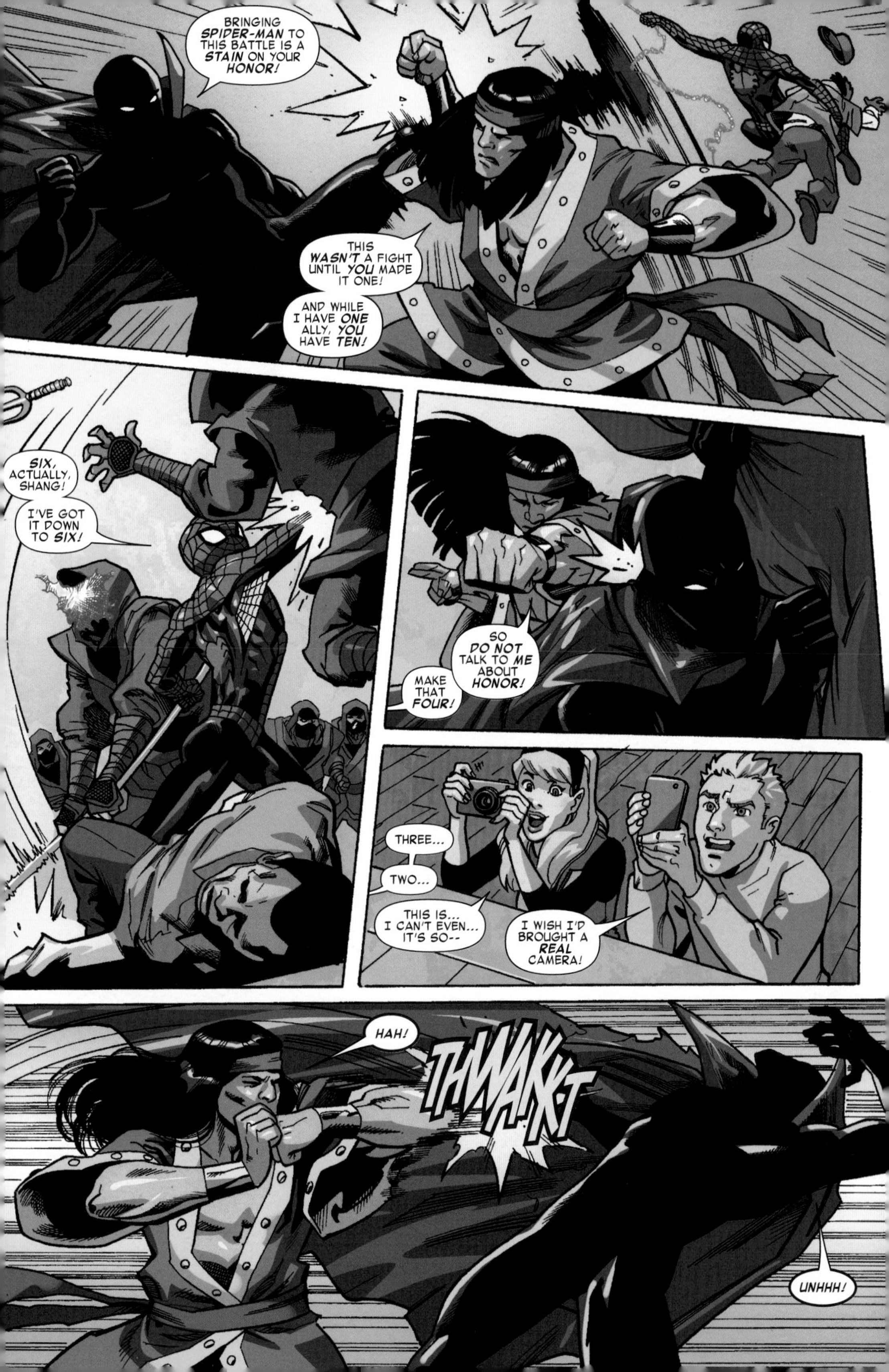
BRINGING SPIDER-MAN TO THIS BATTLE IS A STAIN ON YOUR HONOR!
THIS WASN'T A FIGHT UNTIL YOU MADE IT ONE!
AND WHILE I HAVE ONE ALLY, YOU HAVE TEN!
SIX, ACTUALLY, SHANG!
I'VE GOT IT DOWN TO SIX!
SO DO NOT TALK TO ME ABOUT HONOR!
MAKE THAT FOUR!
THREE...
TWO...
THIS IS... I CAN'T EVEN... IT'S SO--
I WISH I'D BROUGHT A REAL CAMERA!
HAH!
THWAKK-T
UNHHH!

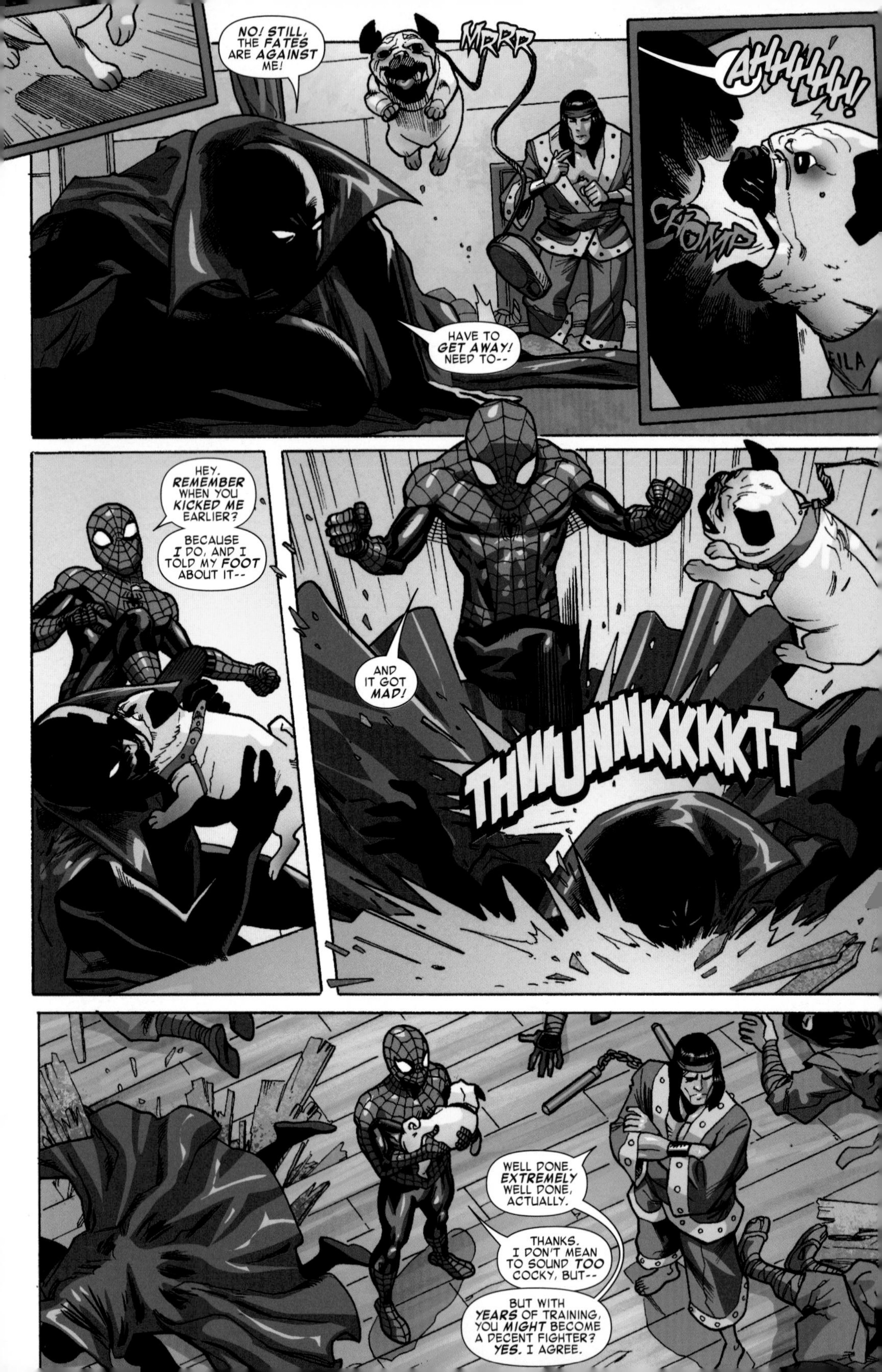
NO! STILL, THE FATES ARE AGAINST ME!
MRRR
HAVE TO GET AWAY! NEED TO--
AHHHHH!
CHOMP
HEY. REMEMBER WHEN YOU KICKED ME EARLIER?
BECAUSE I DO, AND I TOLD MY FOOT ABOUT IT--
AND IT GOT MAD!
THWUNNKKKKTT
WELL DONE. EXTREMELY WELL DONE, ACTUALLY.
THANKS. I DON'T MEAN TO SOUND TOO COCKY, BUT--
BUT WITH YEARS OF TRAINING, YOU MIGHT BECOME A DECENT FIGHTER? YES. I AGREE.

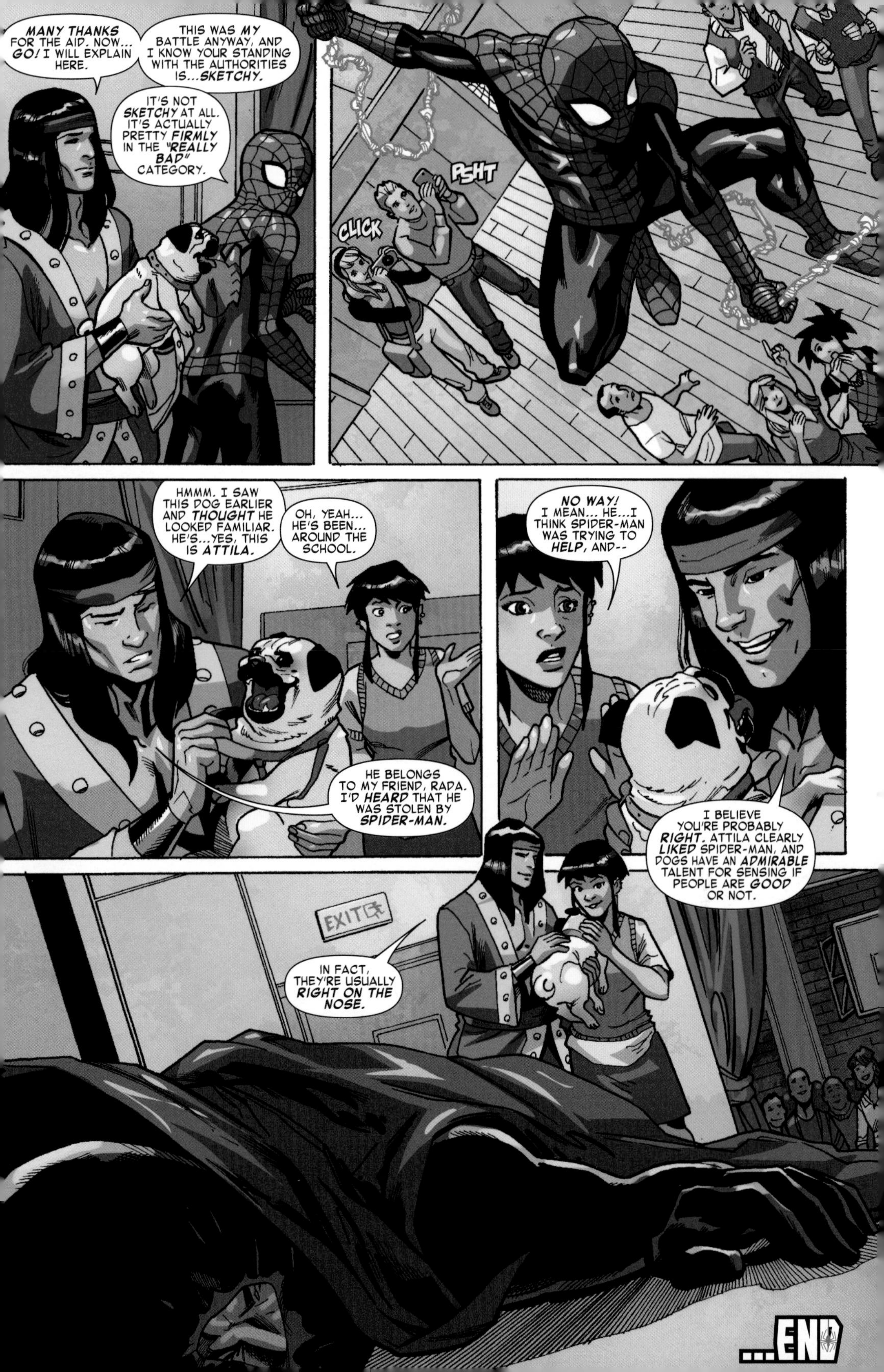
MANY THANKS FOR THE AID. NOW... GO! I WILL EXPLAIN HERE.
THIS WAS MY BATTLE ANYWAY, AND I KNOW YOUR STANDING WITH THE AUTHORITIES IS...SKETCHY.
IT'S NOT SKETCHY AT ALL. IT'S ACTUALLY PRETTY FIRMLY IN THE "REALLY BAD" CATEGORY.
PSHT
CLICK
HMMM. I SAW THIS DOG EARLIER AND THOUGHT HE LOOKED FAMILIAR. HE'S...YES, THIS IS ATTILA.
OH, YEAH... HE'S BEEN... AROUND THE SCHOOL.
HE BELONGS TO MY FRIEND, RADA. I'D HEARD THAT HE WAS STOLEN BY SPIDER-MAN.
NO WAY! I MEAN... HE...I THINK SPIDER-MAN WAS TRYING TO HELP, AND--
I BELIEVE YOU'RE PROBABLY RIGHT. ATTILA CLEARLY LIKED SPIDER-MAN, AND DOGS HAVE AN ADMIRABLE TALENT FOR SENSING IF PEOPLE ARE GOOD OR NOT.
EXIT
IN FACT, THEY'RE USUALLY RIGHT ON THE NOSE.
...END

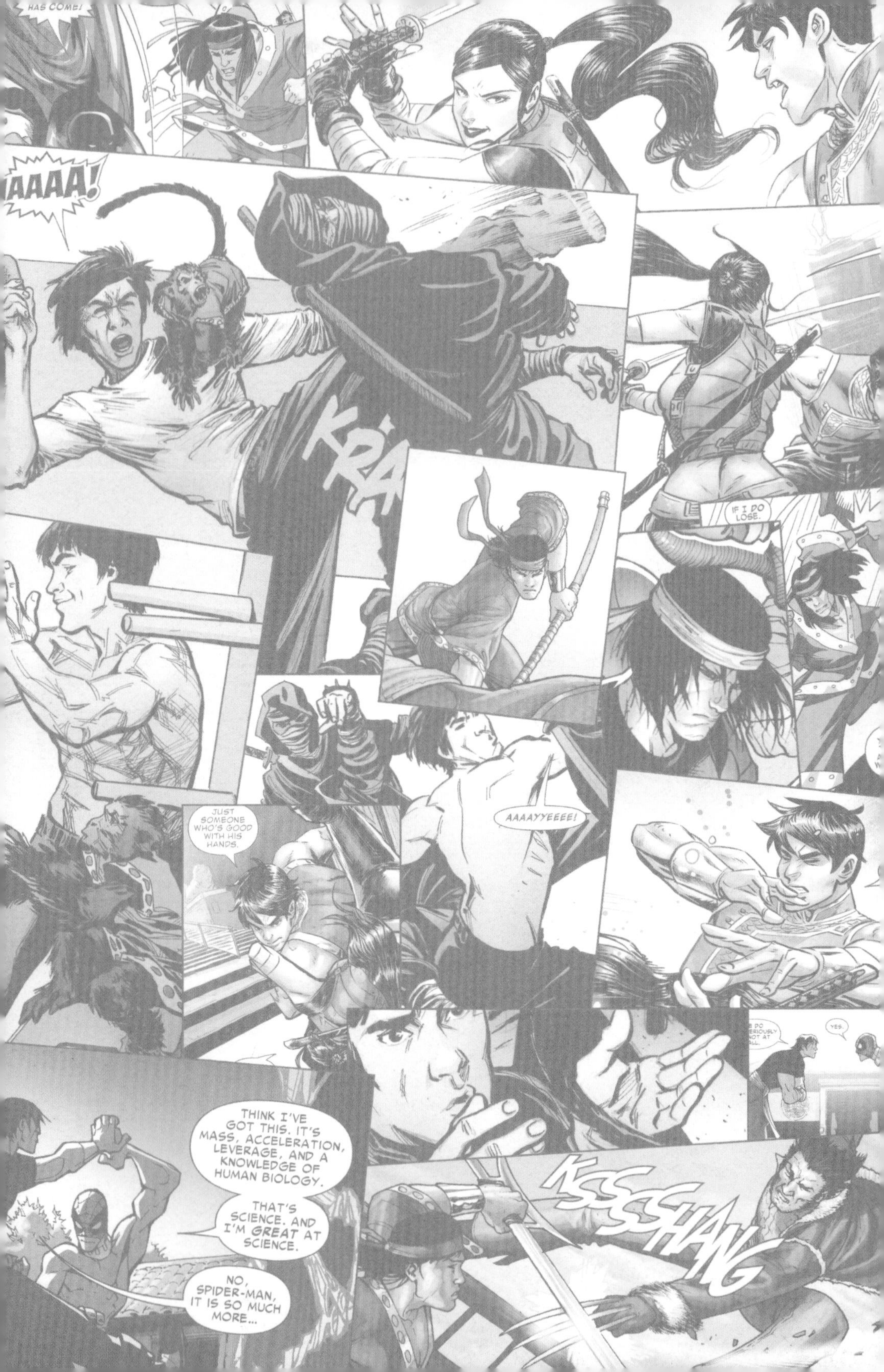
HAS COME!
AAAA!
KRA
IF I DO LOSE.
JUST SOMEONE WHO'S GOOD WITH HIS HANDS.
AAAAYYEEEE!
YES.
THINK I'VE GOT THIS. IT'S MASS, ACCELERATION, LEVERAGE, AND A KNOWLEDGE OF HUMAN BIOLOGY.
THAT'S SCIENCE. AND I'M GREAT AT SCIENCE.
NO, SPIDER-MAN, IT IS SO MUCH MORE...
KSSSHANG

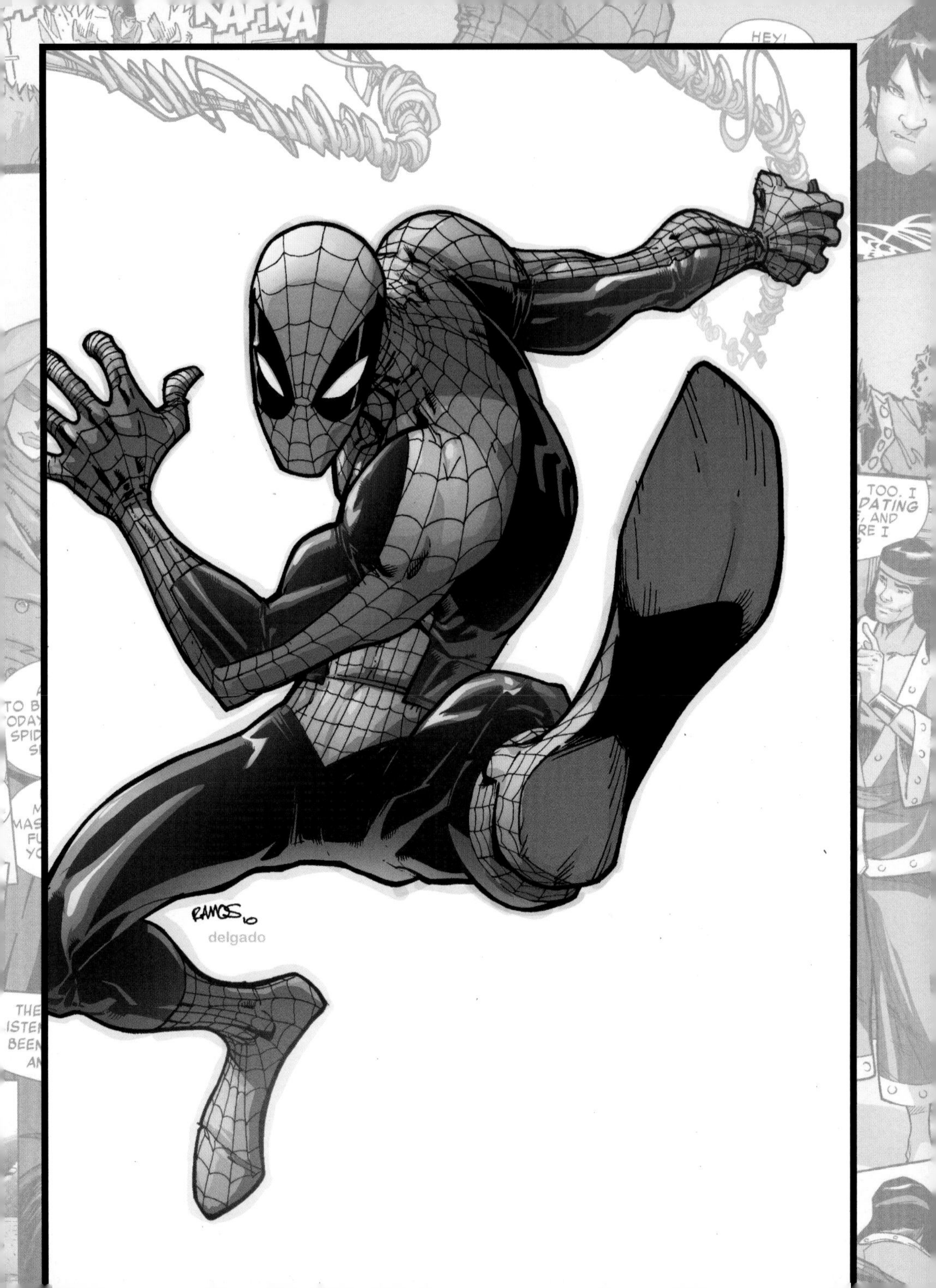

HEY!
RAMOS 10
delgado

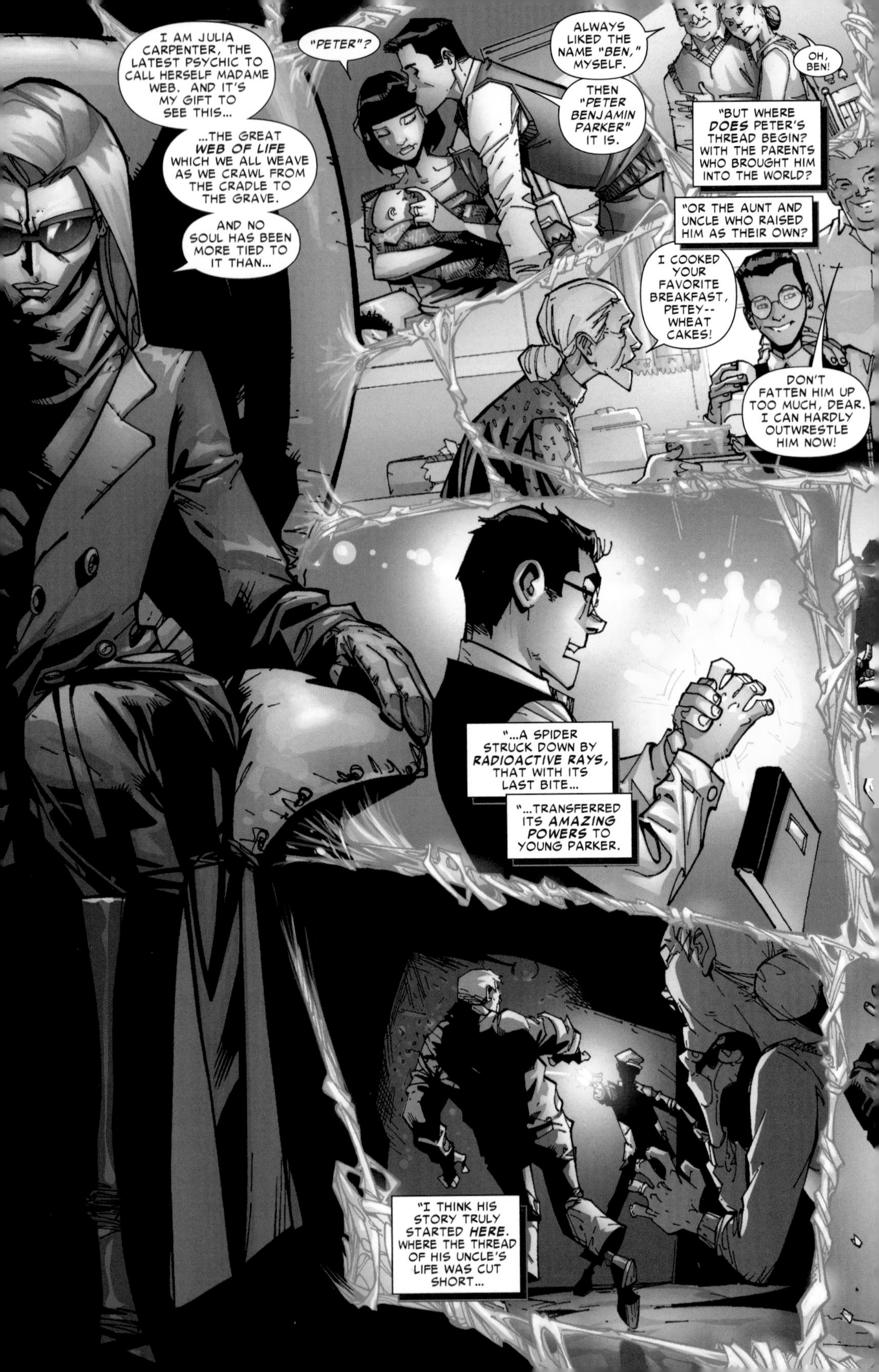
I AM JULIA CARPENTER, THE LATEST PSYCHIC TO CALL HERSELF MADAME WEB. AND IT'S MY GIFT TO SEE THIS...
...THE GREAT WEB OF LIFE WHICH WE ALL WEAVE AS WE CRAWL FROM THE CRADLE TO THE GRAVE.
AND NO SOUL HAS BEEN MORE TIED TO IT THAN...
"PETER"?
ALWAYS LIKED THE NAME "BEN," MYSELF.
THEN "PETER BENJAMIN PARKER" IT IS.
OH, BEN!
"BUT WHERE DOES PETER'S THREAD BEGIN? WITH THE PARENTS WHO BROUGHT HIM INTO THE WORLD?
"OR THE AUNT AND UNCLE WHO RAISED HIM AS THEIR OWN?
I COOKED YOUR FAVORITE BREAKFAST, PETEY-- WHEAT CAKES!
DON'T FATTEN HIM UP TOO MUCH, DEAR. I CAN HARDLY OUTWRESTLE HIM NOW!
"...A SPIDER STRUCK DOWN BY RADIOACTIVE RAYS, THAT WITH ITS LAST BITE...
"...TRANSFERRED ITS AMAZING POWERS TO YOUNG PARKER.
"I THINK HIS STORY TRULY STARTED HERE. WHERE THE THREAD OF HIS UNCLE'S LIFE WAS CUT SHORT...

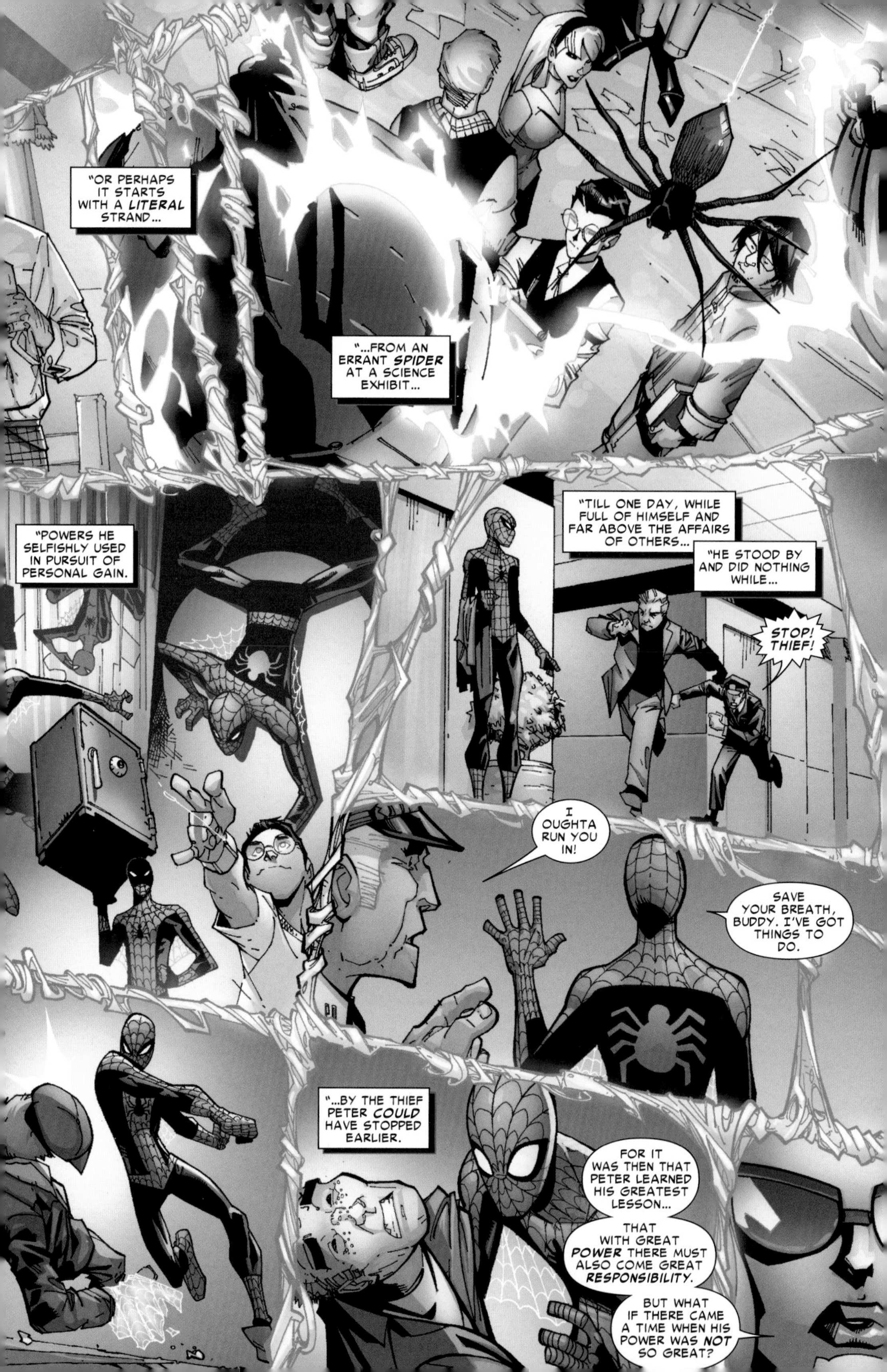
"OR PERHAPS IT STARTS WITH A *LITERAL* STRAND...
"...FROM AN ERRANT *SPIDER* AT A SCIENCE EXHIBIT...
"POWERS HE SELFISHLY USED IN PURSUIT OF PERSONAL GAIN.
"TILL ONE DAY, WHILE FULL OF HIMSELF AND FAR ABOVE THE AFFAIRS OF OTHERS...
"HE STOOD BY AND DID NOTHING WHILE...
STOP! THIEF!
I OUGHTA RUN YOU IN!
SAVE YOUR BREATH, BUDDY. I'VE GOT THINGS TO DO.
"...BY THE THIEF PETER *COULD* HAVE STOPPED EARLIER.
FOR IT WAS THEN THAT PETER LEARNED HIS GREATEST LESSON...
THAT WITH GREAT *POWER* THERE MUST ALSO COME GREAT *RESPONSIBILITY*.
BUT WHAT IF THERE CAME A TIME WHEN HIS POWER WAS *NOT* SO GREAT?

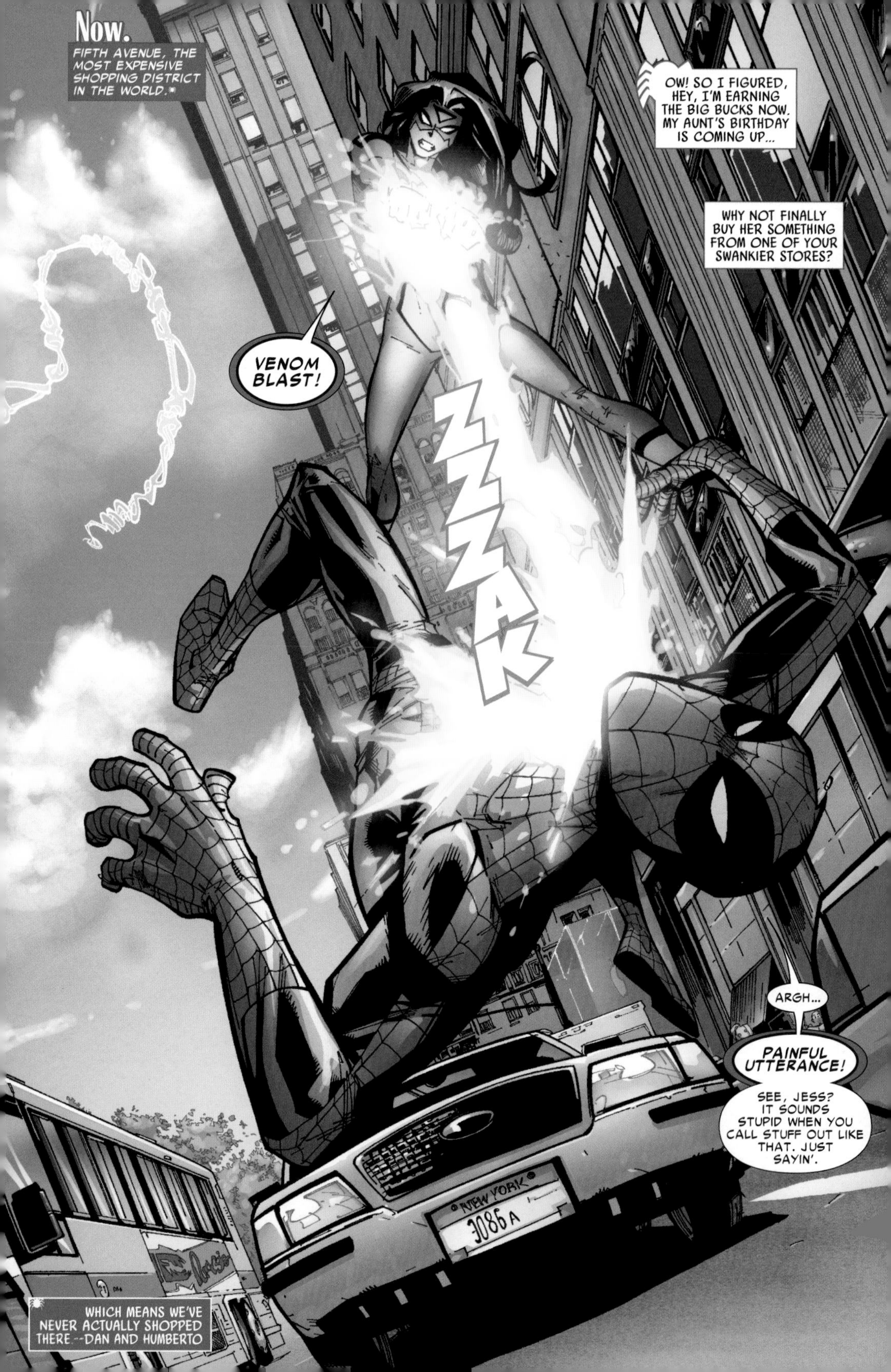
Now.
FIFTH AVENUE, THE MOST EXPENSIVE SHOPPING DISTRICT IN THE WORLD.*
OW! SO I FIGURED, HEY, I'M EARNING THE BIG BUCKS NOW. MY AUNT'S BIRTHDAY IS COMING UP...
WHY NOT FINALLY BUY HER SOMETHING FROM ONE OF YOUR SWANKIER STORES?
VENOM BLAST!
ZZZAK
ARGH...
PAINFUL UTTERANCE!
SEE, JESS? IT SOUNDS STUPID WHEN YOU CALL STUFF OUT LIKE THAT. JUST SAYIN'.
NEW YORK
3086 A
*WHICH MEANS WE'VE NEVER ACTUALLY SHOPPED THERE.--DAN AND HUMBERTO

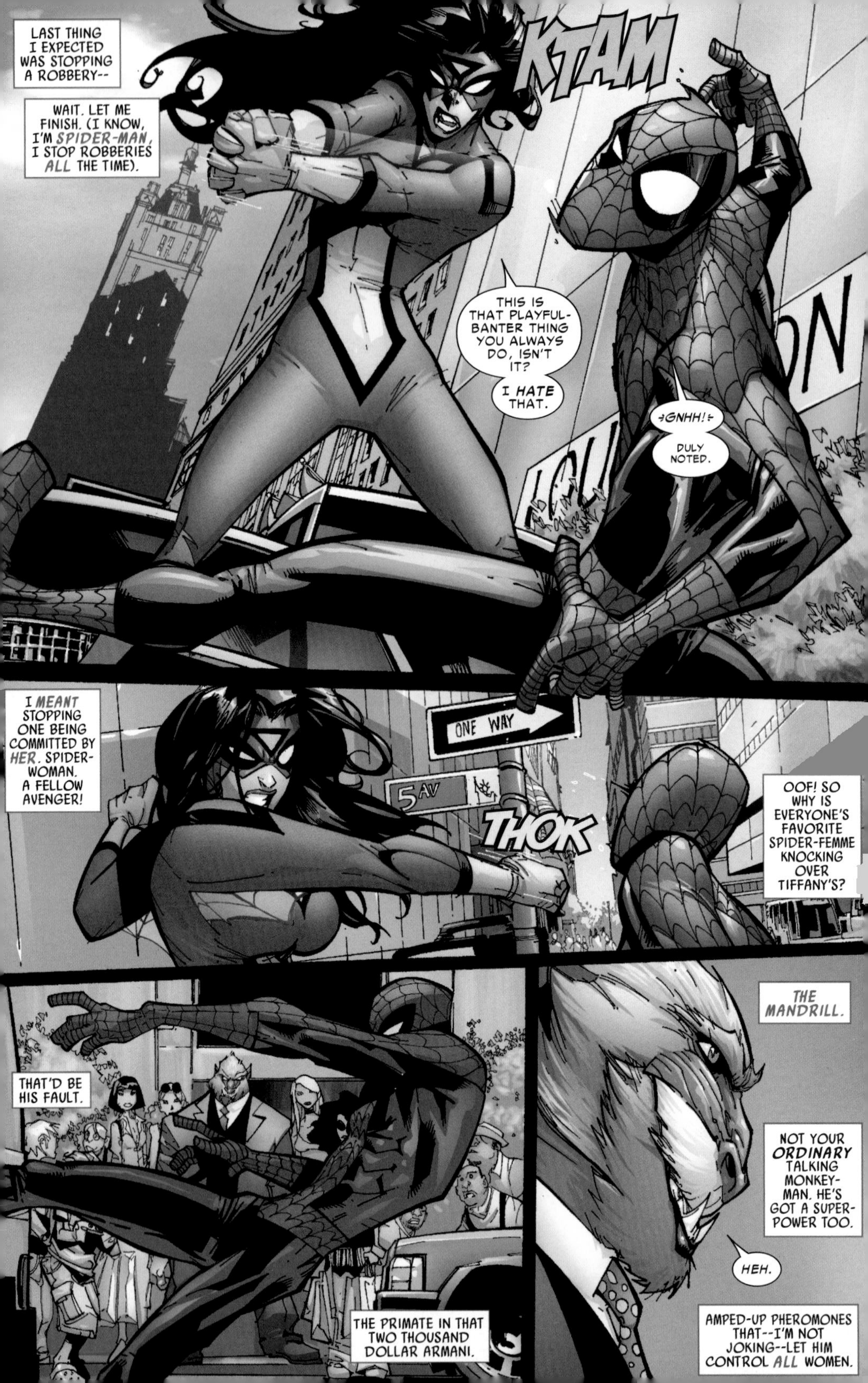
LAST THING I EXPECTED WAS STOPPING A ROBBERY--
WAIT. LET ME FINISH. (I KNOW, I'M SPIDER-MAN, I STOP ROBBERIES ALL THE TIME).
KTAM
THIS IS THAT PLAYFUL-BANTER THING YOU ALWAYS DO, ISN'T IT?
I HATE THAT.
=GNHH!=
DULY NOTED.
I MEANT STOPPING ONE BEING COMMITTED BY HER. SPIDER-WOMAN. A FELLOW AVENGER!
ONE WAY
5 AV
THOK
OOF! SO WHY IS EVERYONE'S FAVORITE SPIDER-FEMME KNOCKING OVER TIFFANY'S?
THAT'D BE HIS FAULT.
THE PRIMATE IN THAT TWO THOUSAND DOLLAR ARMANI.
THE MANDRILL.
NOT YOUR ORDINARY TALKING MONKEY-MAN. HE'S GOT A SUPER-POWER TOO.
HEH.
AMPED-UP PHEROMONES THAT--I'M NOT JOKING--LET HIM CONTROL ALL WOMEN.

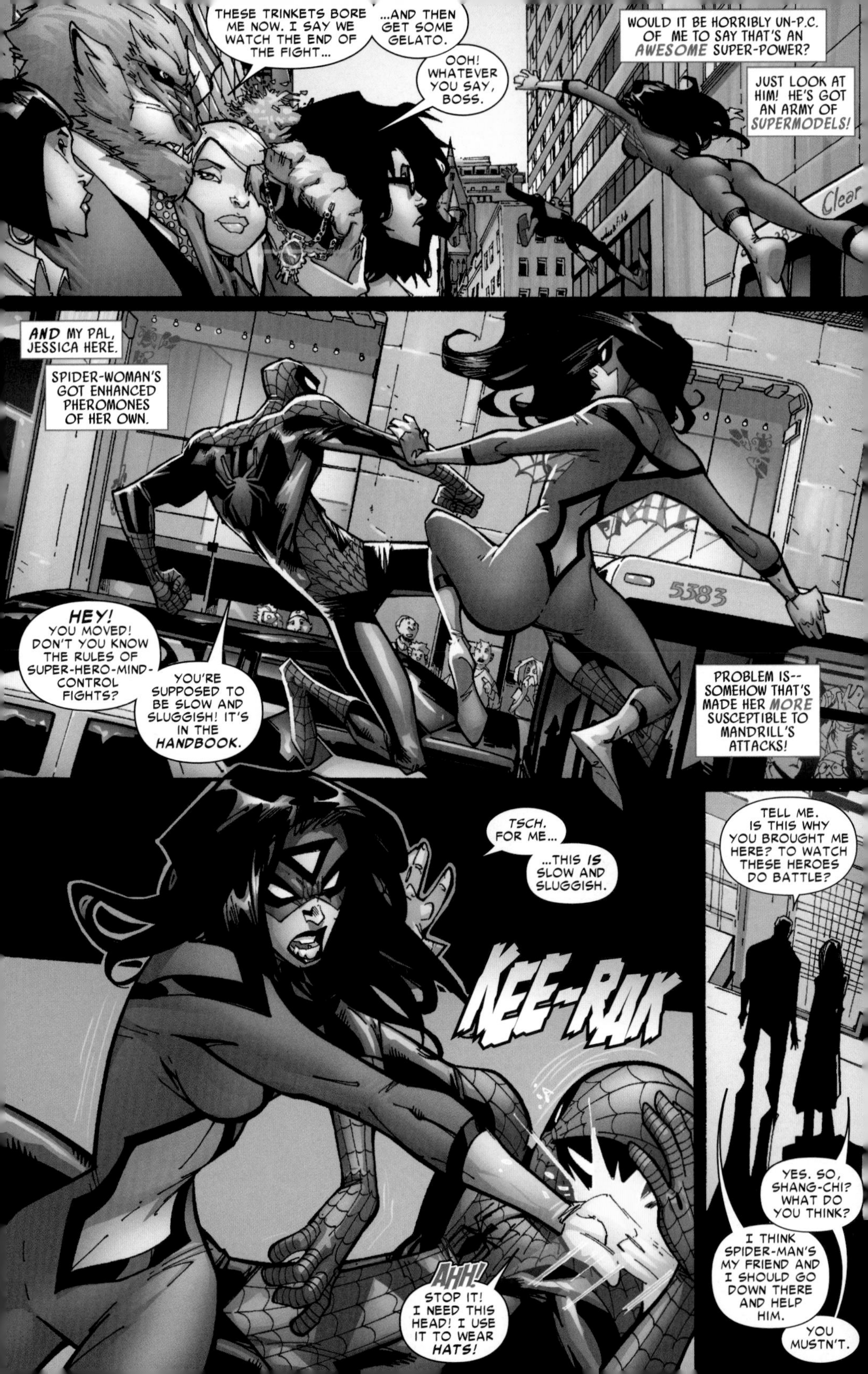
THESE TRINKETS BORE ME NOW. I SAY WE WATCH THE END OF THE FIGHT...
...AND THEN GET SOME GELATO.
OOH! WHATEVER YOU SAY, BOSS.
WOULD IT BE HORRIBLY UN-P.C. OF ME TO SAY THAT'S AN AWESOME SUPER-POWER?
JUST LOOK AT HIM! HE'S GOT AN ARMY OF SUPERMODELS!
Clear
AND MY PAL, JESSICA HERE.
SPIDER-WOMAN'S GOT ENHANCED PHEROMONES OF HER OWN.
5383
HEY! YOU MOVED! DON'T YOU KNOW THE RULES OF SUPER-HERO-MIND-CONTROL FIGHTS?
YOU'RE SUPPOSED TO BE SLOW AND SLUGGISH! IT'S IN THE HANDBOOK.
PROBLEM IS-- SOMEHOW THAT'S MADE HER MORE SUSCEPTIBLE TO MANDRILL'S ATTACKS!
TSCH. FOR ME...
...THIS IS SLOW AND SLUGGISH.
KEE-RAK
AHH! STOP IT! I NEED THIS HEAD! I USE IT TO WEAR HATS!
TELL ME. IS THIS WHY YOU BROUGHT ME HERE? TO WATCH THESE HEROES DO BATTLE?
YES. SO, SHANG-CHI? WHAT DO YOU THINK?
I THINK SPIDER-MAN'S MY FRIEND AND I SHOULD GO DOWN THERE AND HELP HIM.
YOU MUSTN'T.

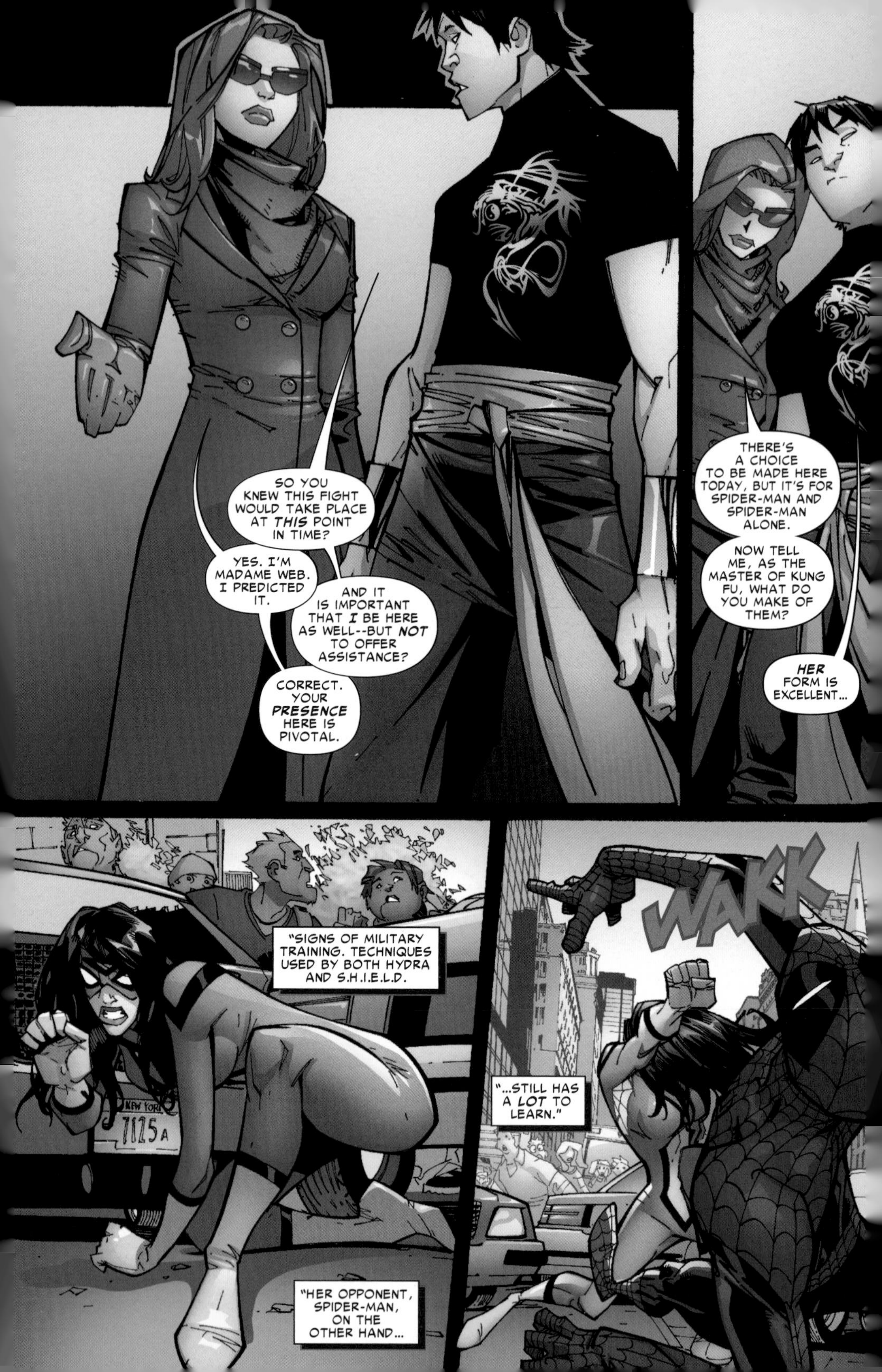
SO YOU KNEW THIS FIGHT WOULD TAKE PLACE AT *THIS* POINT IN TIME?
YES. I'M MADAME WEB. I PREDICTED IT.
AND IT IS IMPORTANT THAT *I* BE HERE AS WELL--BUT *NOT* TO OFFER ASSISTANCE?
CORRECT. YOUR *PRESENCE* HERE IS PIVOTAL.
THERE'S A CHOICE TO BE MADE HERE TODAY, BUT IT'S FOR SPIDER-MAN AND SPIDER-MAN ALONE.
NOW TELL ME, AS THE MASTER OF KUNG FU, WHAT DO YOU MAKE OF THEM?
HER FORM IS EXCELLENT...
"SIGNS OF MILITARY TRAINING. TECHNIQUES USED BY BOTH HYDRA AND S.H.I.E.L.D.
NEW YORK
7125 A
"HER OPPONENT, SPIDER-MAN, ON THE OTHER HAND...
WAKK
"...STILL HAS A *LOT* TO LEARN."

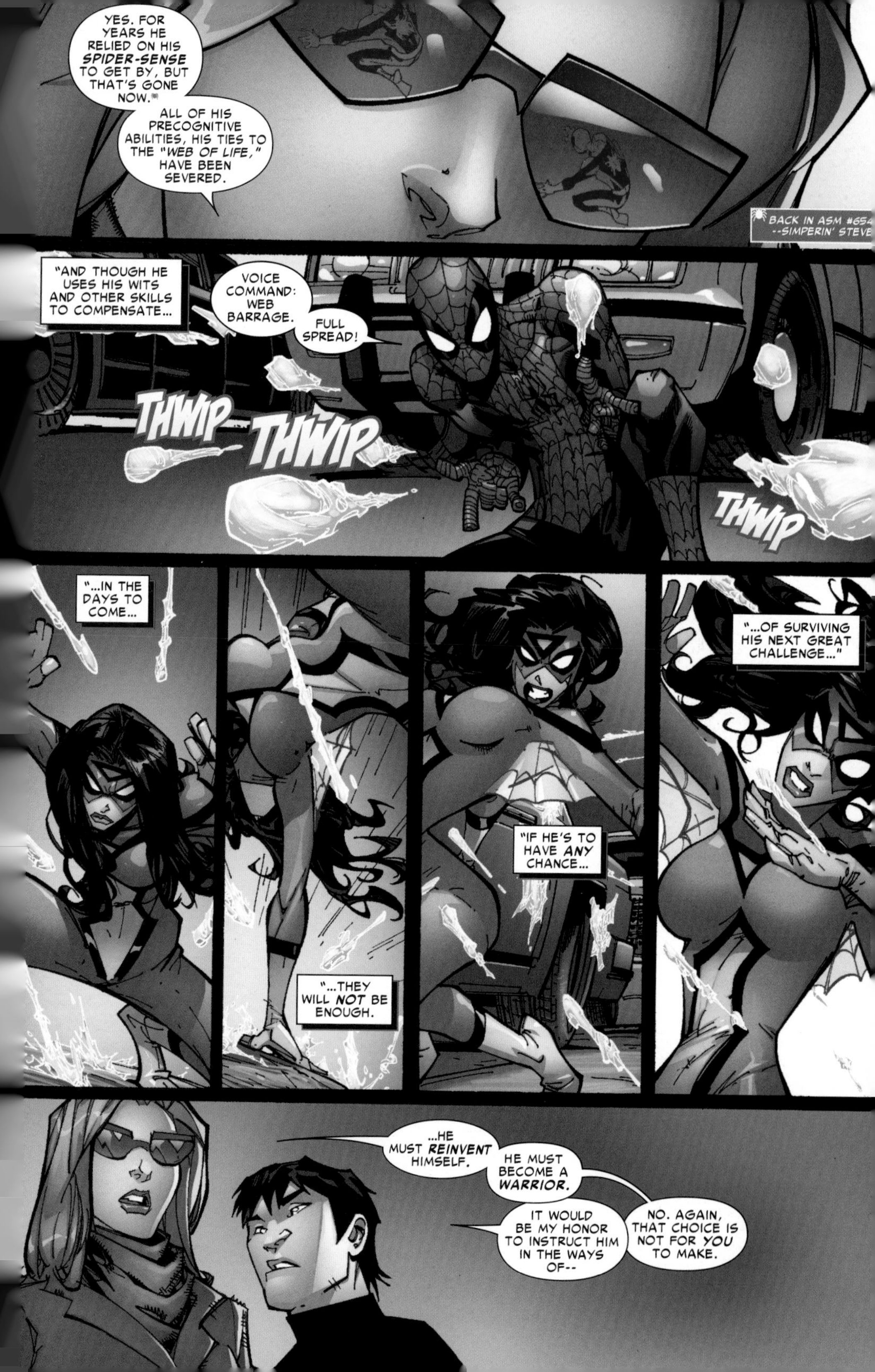
YES. FOR YEARS HE RELIED ON HIS SPIDER-SENSE TO GET BY, BUT THAT'S GONE NOW.*
ALL OF HIS PRECOGNITIVE ABILITIES, HIS TIES TO THE "WEB OF LIFE," HAVE BEEN SEVERED.
*BACK IN ASM #654 --SIMPERIN' STEVE
"AND THOUGH HE USES HIS WITS AND OTHER SKILLS TO COMPENSATE...
VOICE COMMAND: WEB BARRAGE.
FULL SPREAD!
THWIP
THWIP
THWIP
"...IN THE DAYS TO COME...
"...THEY WILL NOT BE ENOUGH.
"IF HE'S TO HAVE ANY CHANCE...
"...OF SURVIVING HIS NEXT GREAT CHALLENGE..."
...HE MUST REINVENT HIMSELF.
HE MUST BECOME A WARRIOR.
IT WOULD BE MY HONOR TO INSTRUCT HIM IN THE WAYS OF--
NO. AGAIN, THAT CHOICE IS NOT FOR YOU TO MAKE.

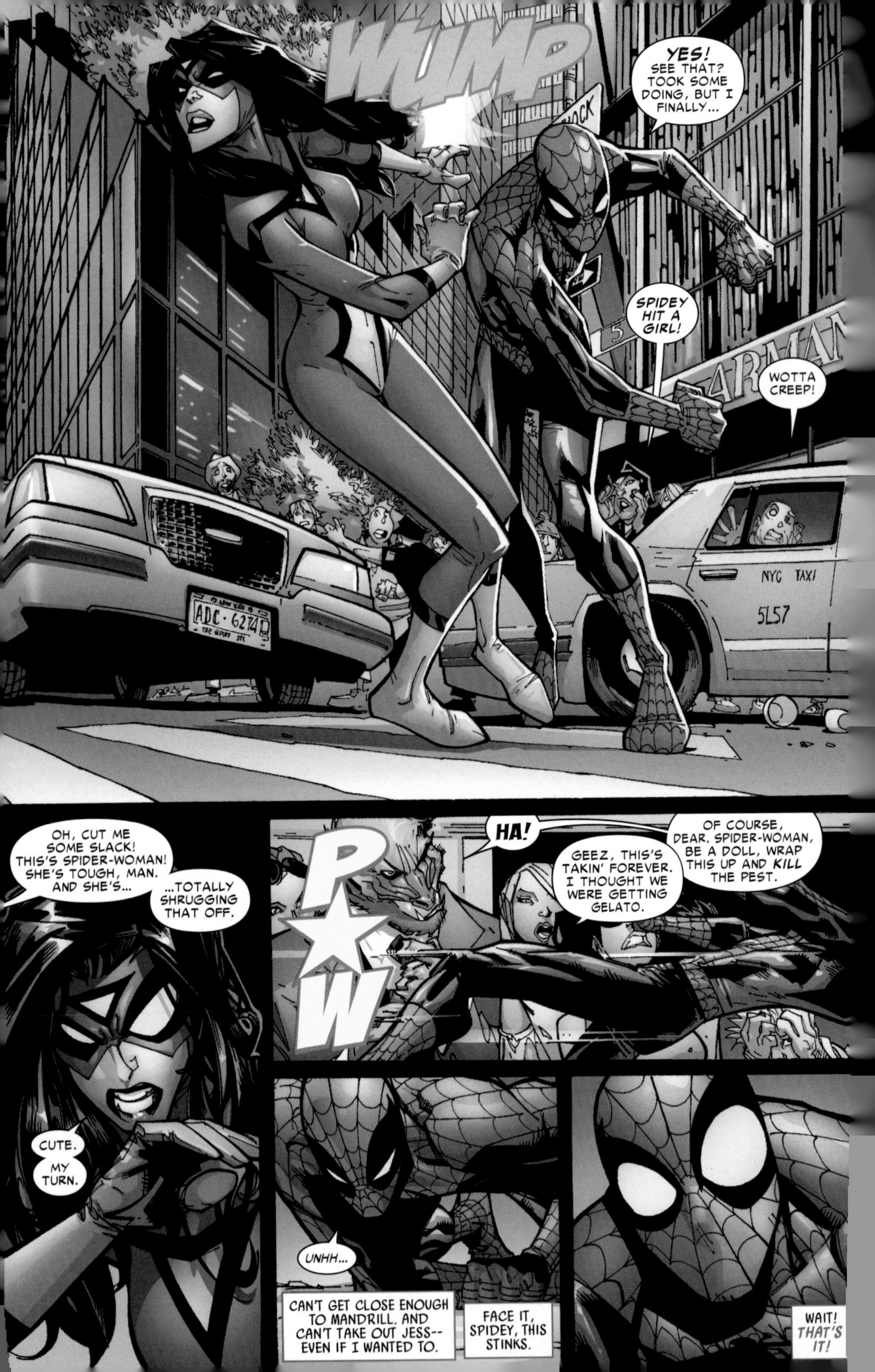

WUMP
YES! SEE THAT? TOOK SOME DOING, BUT I FINALLY...
SPIDEY HIT A GIRL!
WOTTA CREEP!
NYC TAXI
5L57
OH, CUT ME SOME SLACK! THIS'S SPIDER-WOMAN! SHE'S TOUGH, MAN. AND SHE'S...
...TOTALLY SHRUGGING THAT OFF.
CUTE. MY TURN.
POW
HA!
GEEZ, THIS'S TAKIN' FOREVER. I THOUGHT WE WERE GETTING GELATO.
OF COURSE, DEAR. SPIDER-WOMAN, BE A DOLL, WRAP THIS UP AND KILL THE PEST.
UNHH...
CAN'T GET CLOSE ENOUGH TO MANDRILL. AND CAN'T TAKE OUT JESS-- EVEN IF I WANTED TO.
FACE IT, SPIDEY, THIS STINKS.
WAIT! THAT'S IT!

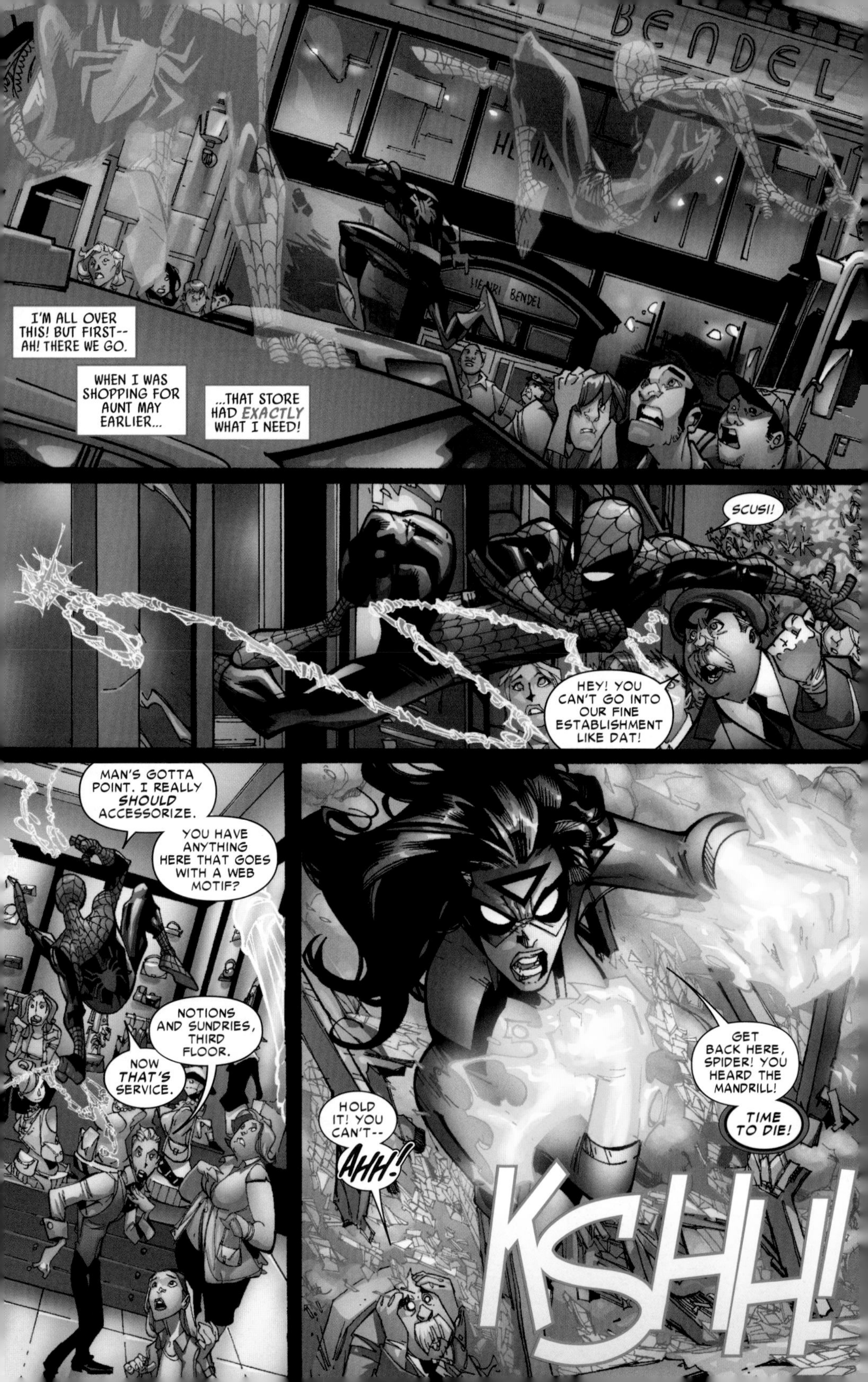
BENDEL
HENRI BENDEL
I'M ALL OVER THIS! BUT FIRST-- AH! THERE WE GO.
WHEN I WAS SHOPPING FOR AUNT MAY EARLIER...
...THAT STORE HAD EXACTLY WHAT I NEED!
SCUSI!
HEY! YOU CAN'T GO INTO OUR FINE ESTABLISHMENT LIKE DAT!
MAN'S GOTTA POINT. I REALLY SHOULD ACCESSORIZE.
YOU HAVE ANYTHING HERE THAT GOES WITH A WEB MOTIF?
NOTIONS AND SUNDRIES, THIRD FLOOR.
NOW THAT'S SERVICE.
GET BACK HERE, SPIDER! YOU HEARD THE MANDRILL!
TIME TO DIE!
HOLD IT! YOU CAN'T--
AHH!
KSHH!

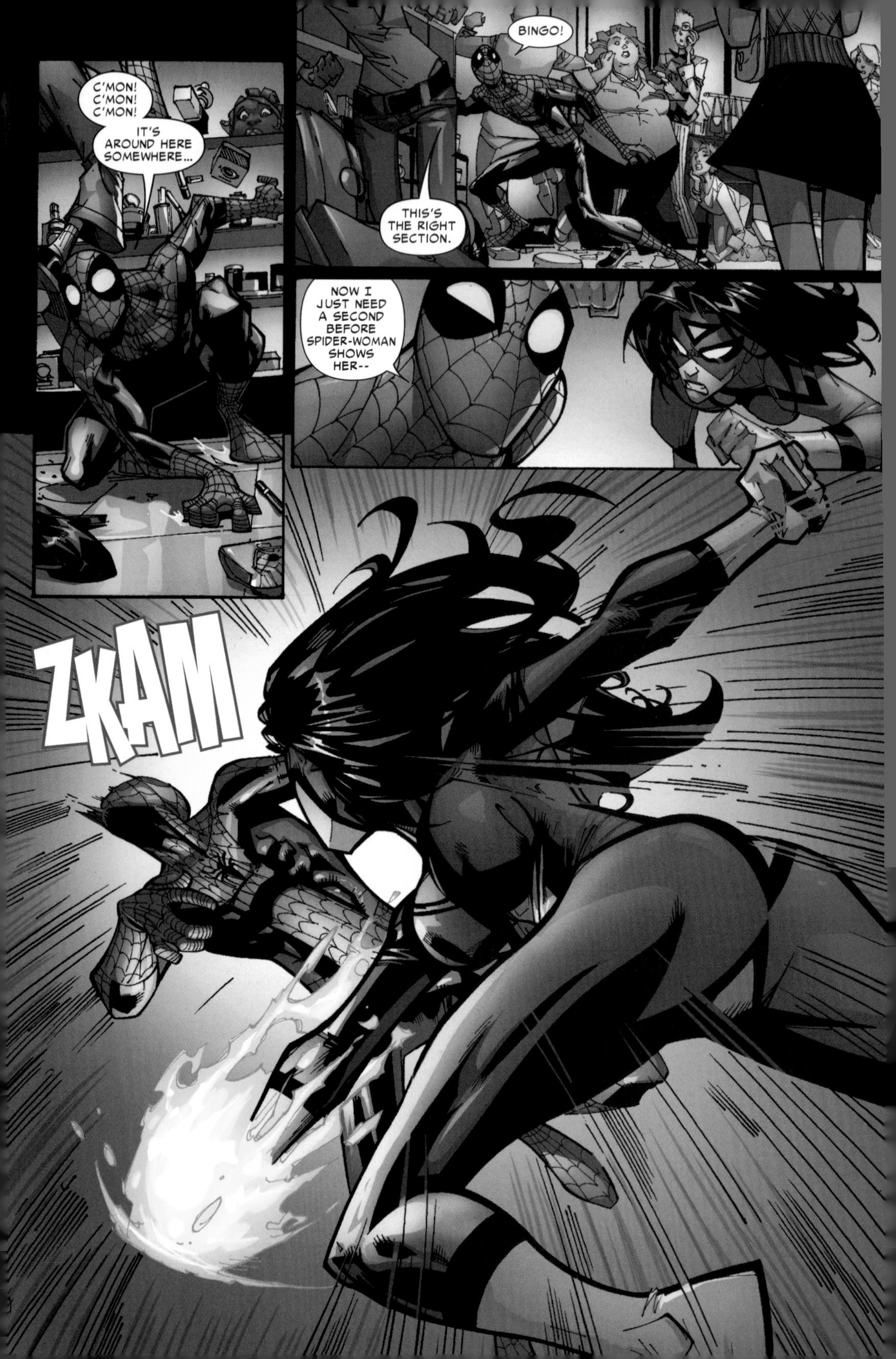
C'MON! C'MON! C'MON!
IT'S AROUND HERE SOMEWHERE...
BINGO!
THIS'S THE RIGHT SECTION.
NOW I JUST NEED A SECOND BEFORE SPIDER-WOMAN SHOWS HER--
ZKAM

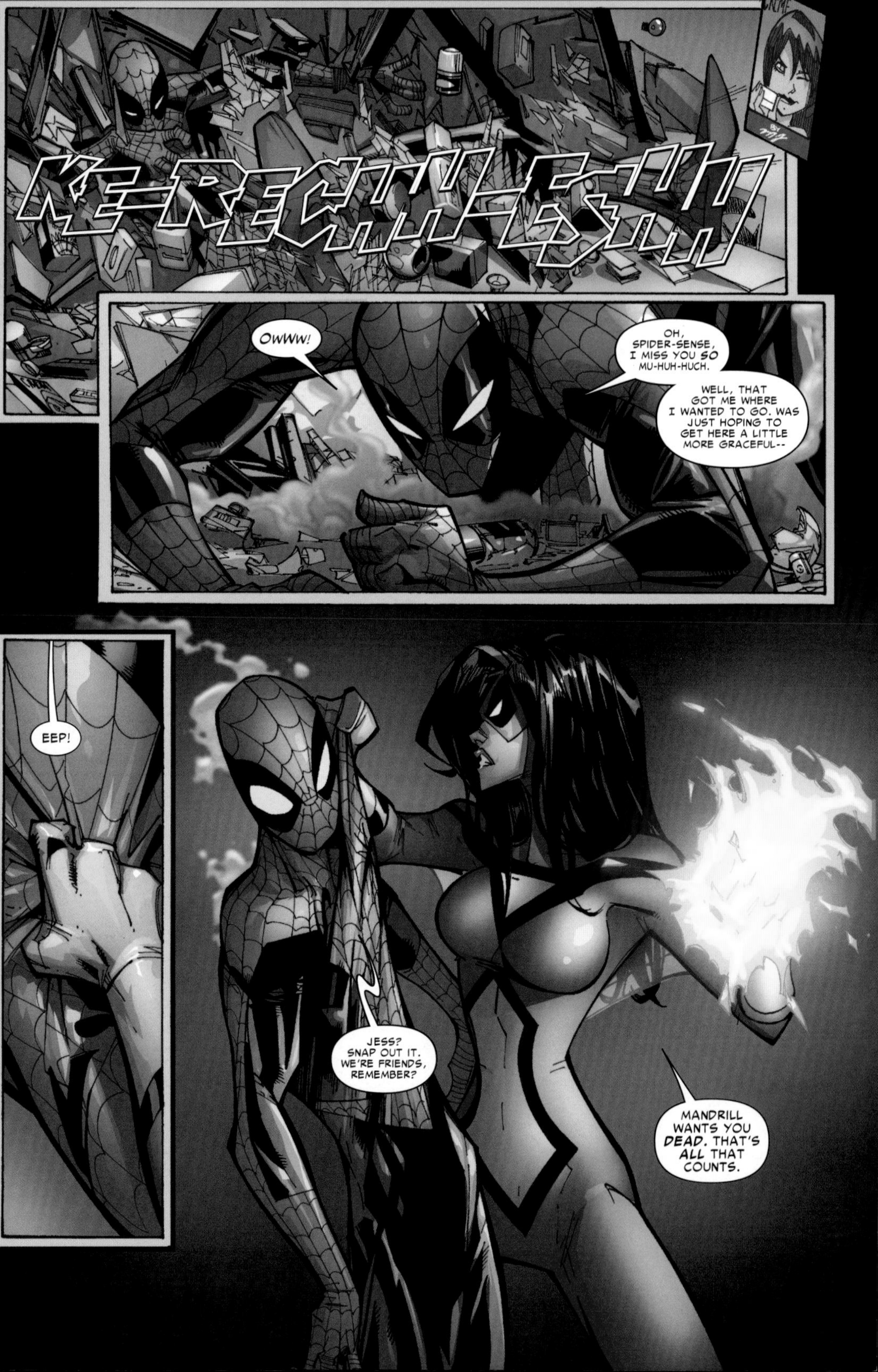
KE-RECHHH-ESHH
OWWW!
OH, SPIDER-SENSE, I MISS YOU SO MU-HUH-HUCH.
WELL, THAT GOT ME WHERE I WANTED TO GO. WAS JUST HOPING TO GET HERE A LITTLE MORE GRACEFUL--
EEP!
JESS? SNAP OUT IT. WE'RE FRIENDS, REMEMBER?
MANDRILL WANTS YOU DEAD. THAT'S ALL THAT COUNTS.

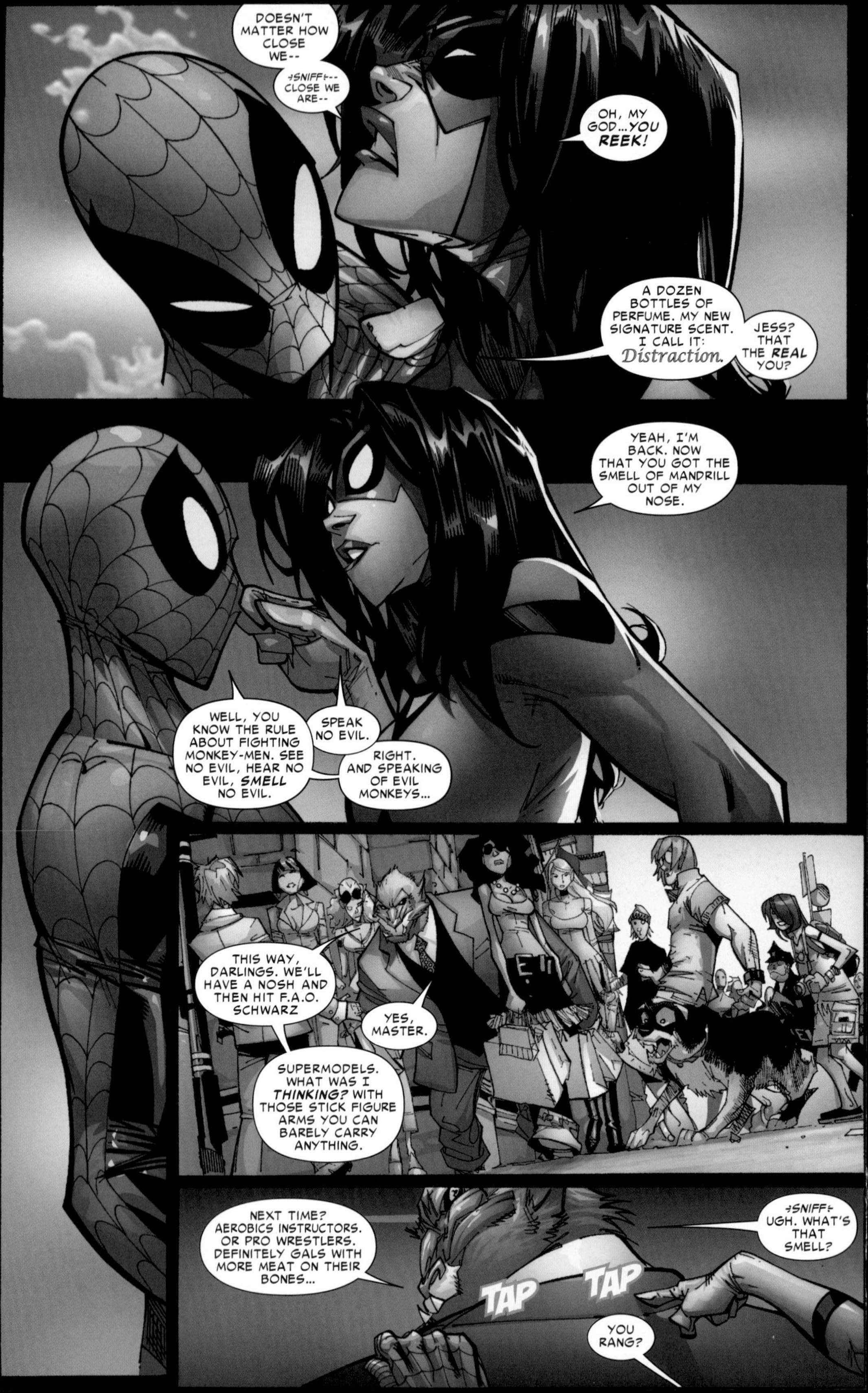
DOESN'T MATTER HOW CLOSE WE--
⸗SNIFF⸗-- CLOSE WE ARE--
OH, MY GOD...YOU REEK!
A DOZEN BOTTLES OF PERFUME. MY NEW SIGNATURE SCENT. I CALL IT: Distraction.
JESS? THAT THE REAL YOU?
YEAH, I'M BACK. NOW THAT YOU GOT THE SMELL OF MANDRILL OUT OF MY NOSE.
WELL, YOU KNOW THE RULE ABOUT FIGHTING MONKEY-MEN. SEE NO EVIL, HEAR NO EVIL, SMELL NO EVIL.
SPEAK NO EVIL.
RIGHT. AND SPEAKING OF EVIL MONKEYS...
THIS WAY, DARLINGS. WE'LL HAVE A NOSH AND THEN HIT F.A.O. SCHWARZ
YES, MASTER.
SUPERMODELS. WHAT WAS I THINKING? WITH THOSE STICK FIGURE ARMS YOU CAN BARELY CARRY ANYTHING.
NEXT TIME? AEROBICS INSTRUCTORS. OR PRO WRESTLERS. DEFINITELY GALS WITH MORE MEAT ON THEIR BONES...
⸗SNIFF⸗ UGH. WHAT'S THAT SMELL?
TAP TAP
YOU RANG?

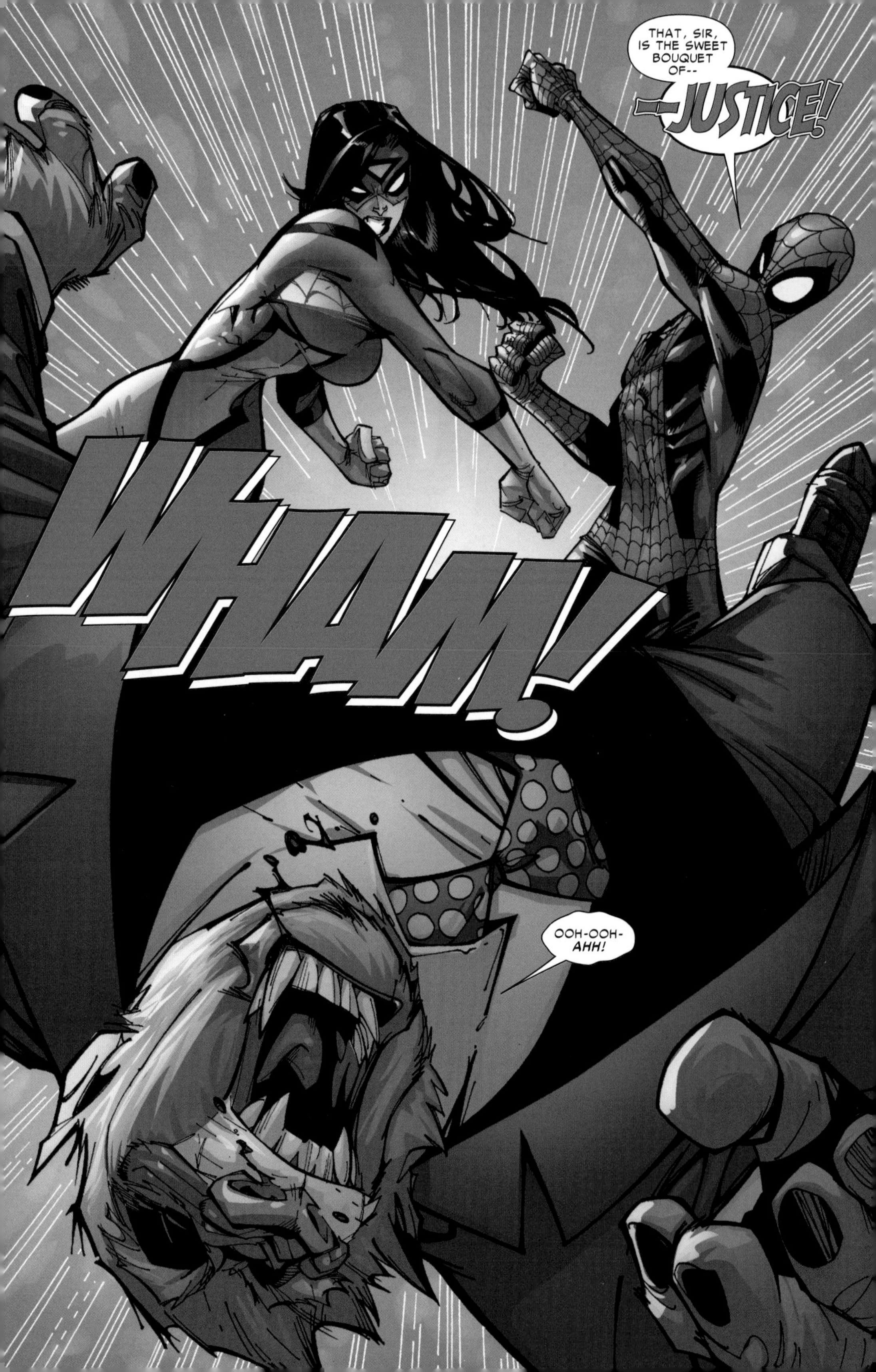
THAT, SIR, IS THE SWEET BOUQUET OF--
--JUSTICE!
WHAM!
OOH-OOH-AHH!

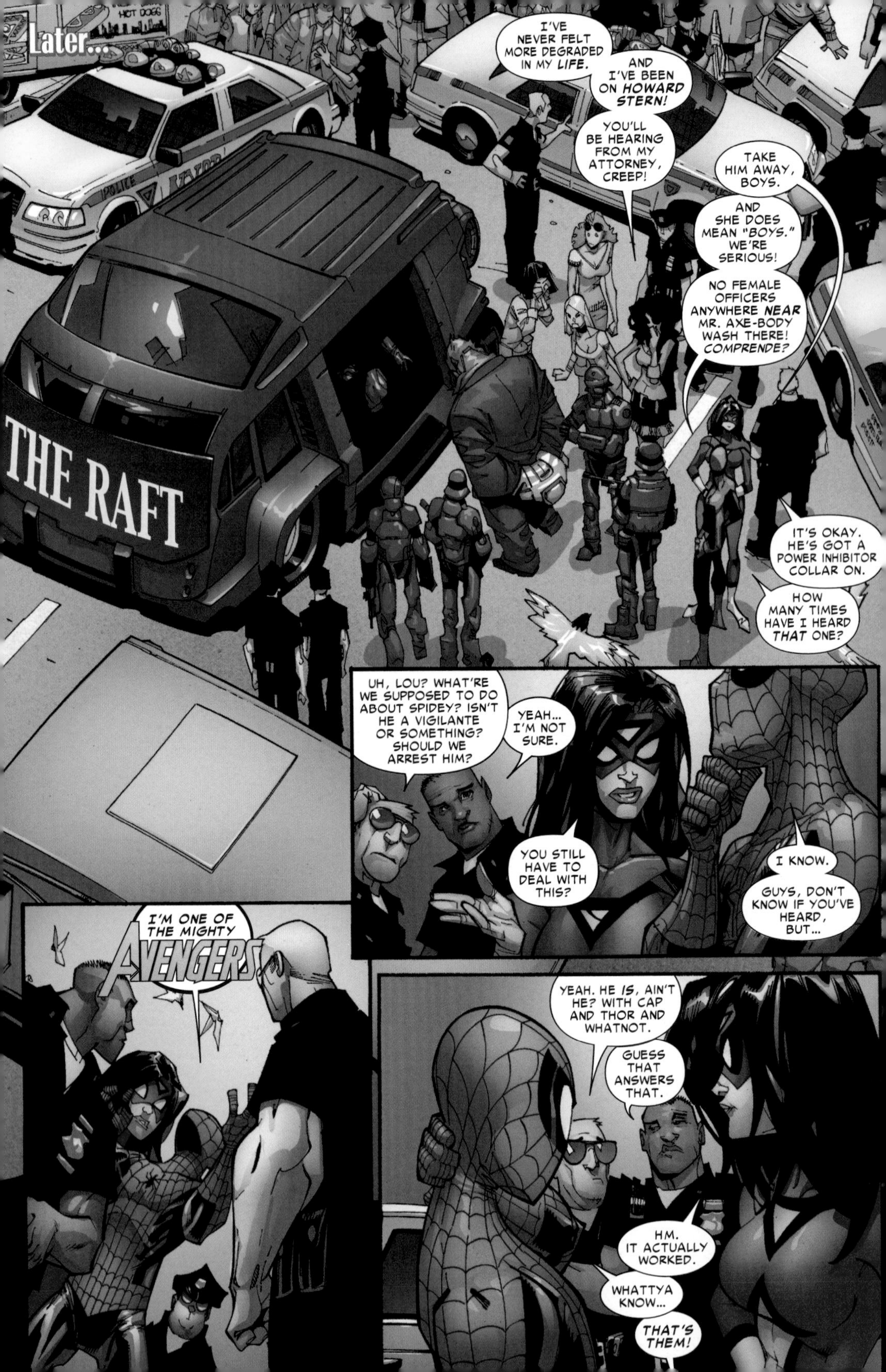

Later...
HOT DOGG
I'VE NEVER FELT MORE DEGRADED IN MY LIFE.
AND I'VE BEEN ON HOWARD STERN!
YOU'LL BE HEARING FROM MY ATTORNEY, CREEP!
TAKE HIM AWAY, BOYS.
AND SHE DOES MEAN "BOYS." WE'RE SERIOUS!
NO FEMALE OFFICERS ANYWHERE NEAR MR. AXE-BODY WASH THERE! COMPRENDE?
THE RAFT
IT'S OKAY. HE'S GOT A POWER INHIBITOR COLLAR ON.
HOW MANY TIMES HAVE I HEARD THAT ONE?
UH, LOU? WHAT'RE WE SUPPOSED TO DO ABOUT SPIDEY? ISN'T HE A VIGILANTE OR SOMETHING? SHOULD WE ARREST HIM?
YEAH... I'M NOT SURE.
YOU STILL HAVE TO DEAL WITH THIS?
I KNOW.
GUYS, DON'T KNOW IF YOU'VE HEARD, BUT...
I'M ONE OF THE MIGHTY AVENGERS
YEAH. HE IS, AIN'T HE? WITH CAP AND THOR AND WHATNOT.
GUESS THAT ANSWERS THAT.
HM. IT ACTUALLY WORKED.
WHATTYA KNOW...
THAT'S THEM!

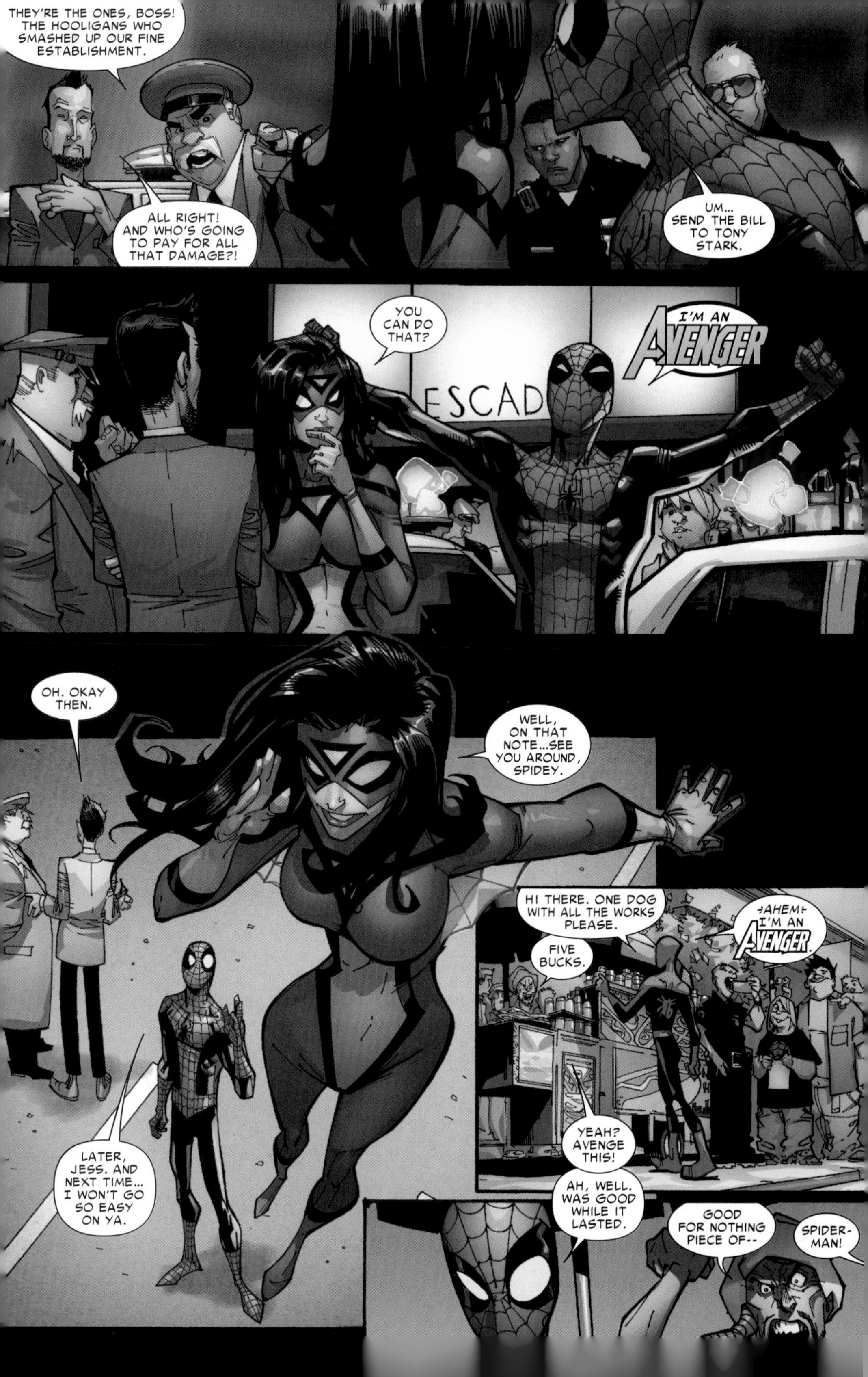
THEY'RE THE ONES, BOSS! THE HOOLIGANS WHO SMASHED UP OUR FINE ESTABLISHMENT.
ALL RIGHT! AND WHO'S GOING TO PAY FOR ALL THAT DAMAGE?!
UM... SEND THE BILL TO TONY STARK.
YOU CAN DO THAT?
I'M AN AVENGER
ESCAD
OH. OKAY THEN.
WELL, ON THAT NOTE...SEE YOU AROUND, SPIDEY.
LATER, JESS. AND NEXT TIME... I WON'T GO SO EASY ON YA.
HI THERE. ONE DOG WITH ALL THE WORKS PLEASE.
FIVE BUCKS.
AHEM I'M AN AVENGER.
YEAH? AVENGE THIS!
AH, WELL. WAS GOOD WHILE IT LASTED.
GOOD FOR NOTHING PIECE OF--
SPIDER-MAN!

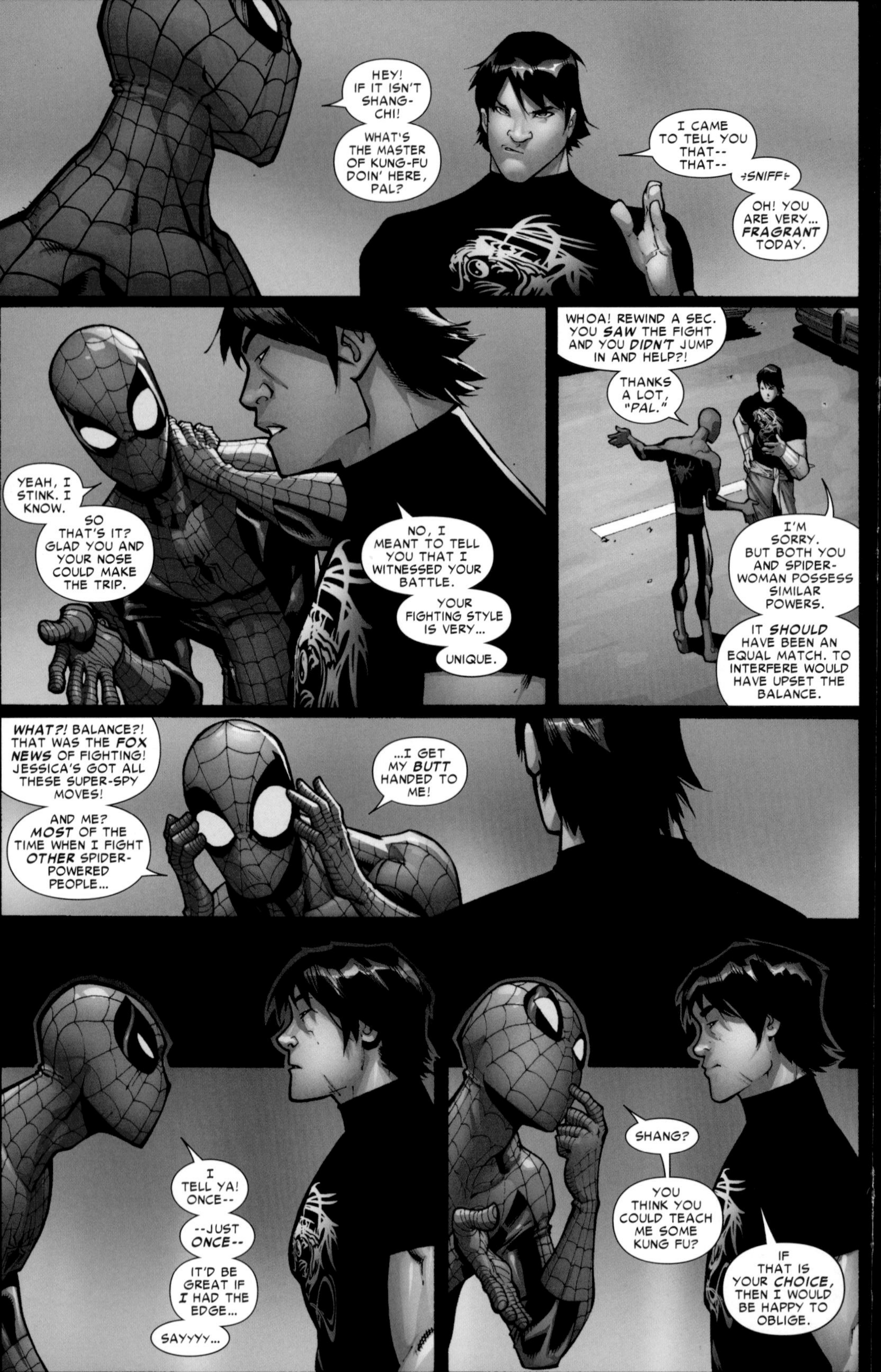
HEY! IF IT ISN'T SHANG-CHI!
WHAT'S THE MASTER OF KUNG-FU DOIN' HERE, PAL?
I CAME TO TELL YOU THAT-- THAT--
SNIFF
OH! YOU ARE VERY... FRAGRANT TODAY.
YEAH, I STINK. I KNOW.
SO THAT'S IT? GLAD YOU AND YOUR NOSE COULD MAKE THE TRIP.
NO, I MEANT TO TELL YOU THAT I WITNESSED YOUR BATTLE.
YOUR FIGHTING STYLE IS VERY...
UNIQUE.
WHOA! REWIND A SEC. YOU SAW THE FIGHT AND YOU DIDN'T JUMP IN AND HELP?!
THANKS A LOT, "PAL."
I'M SORRY. BUT BOTH YOU AND SPIDER-WOMAN POSSESS SIMILAR POWERS.
IT SHOULD HAVE BEEN AN EQUAL MATCH. TO INTERFERE WOULD HAVE UPSET THE BALANCE.
WHAT?! BALANCE?! THAT WAS THE FOX NEWS OF FIGHTING! JESSICA'S GOT ALL THESE SUPER-SPY MOVES!
AND ME? MOST OF THE TIME WHEN I FIGHT OTHER SPIDER-POWERED PEOPLE...
...I GET MY BUTT HANDED TO ME!
I TELL YA! ONCE--
--JUST ONCE--
IT'D BE GREAT IF I HAD THE EDGE...
SAYYYY...
SHANG?
YOU THINK YOU COULD TEACH ME SOME KUNG FU?
IF THAT IS YOUR CHOICE, THEN I WOULD BE HAPPY TO OBLIGE.

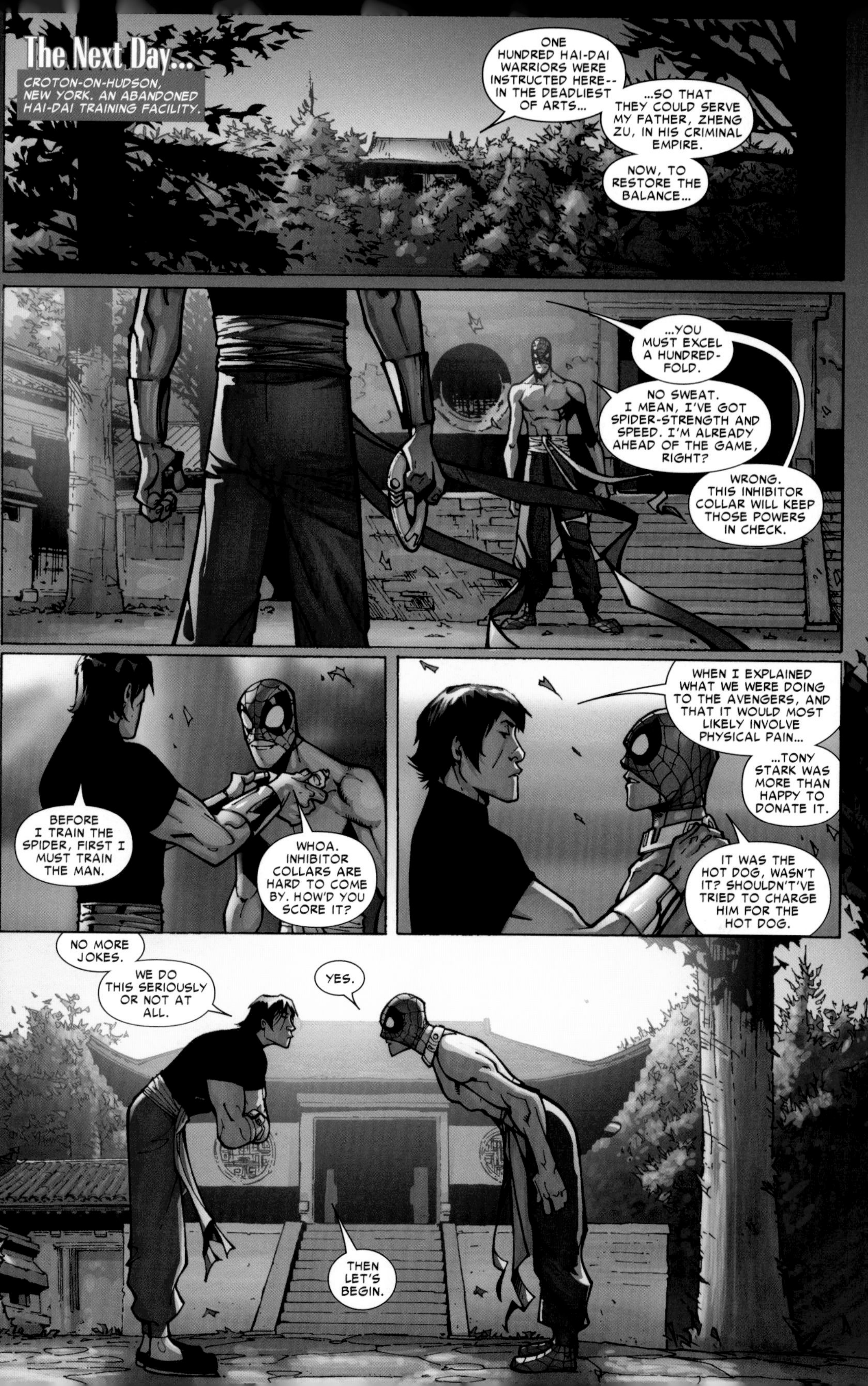
The Next Day...
CROTON-ON-HUDSON, NEW YORK. AN ABANDONED HAI-DAI TRAINING FACILITY.
ONE HUNDRED HAI-DAI WARRIORS WERE INSTRUCTED HERE-- IN THE DEADLIEST OF ARTS...
...SO THAT THEY COULD SERVE MY FATHER, ZHENG ZU, IN HIS CRIMINAL EMPIRE.
NOW, TO RESTORE THE BALANCE...
...YOU MUST EXCEL A HUNDRED-FOLD.
NO SWEAT. I MEAN, I'VE GOT SPIDER-STRENGTH AND SPEED. I'M ALREADY AHEAD OF THE GAME, RIGHT?
WRONG. THIS INHIBITOR COLLAR WILL KEEP THOSE POWERS IN CHECK.
BEFORE I TRAIN THE SPIDER, FIRST I MUST TRAIN THE MAN.
WHOA. INHIBITOR COLLARS ARE HARD TO COME BY. HOW'D YOU SCORE IT?
WHEN I EXPLAINED WHAT WE WERE DOING TO THE AVENGERS, AND THAT IT WOULD MOST LIKELY INVOLVE PHYSICAL PAIN...
...TONY STARK WAS MORE THAN HAPPY TO DONATE IT.
IT WAS THE HOT DOG, WASN'T IT? SHOULDN'T'VE TRIED TO CHARGE HIM FOR THE HOT DOG.
NO MORE JOKES.
WE DO THIS SERIOUSLY OR NOT AT ALL.
YES.
THEN LET'S BEGIN.

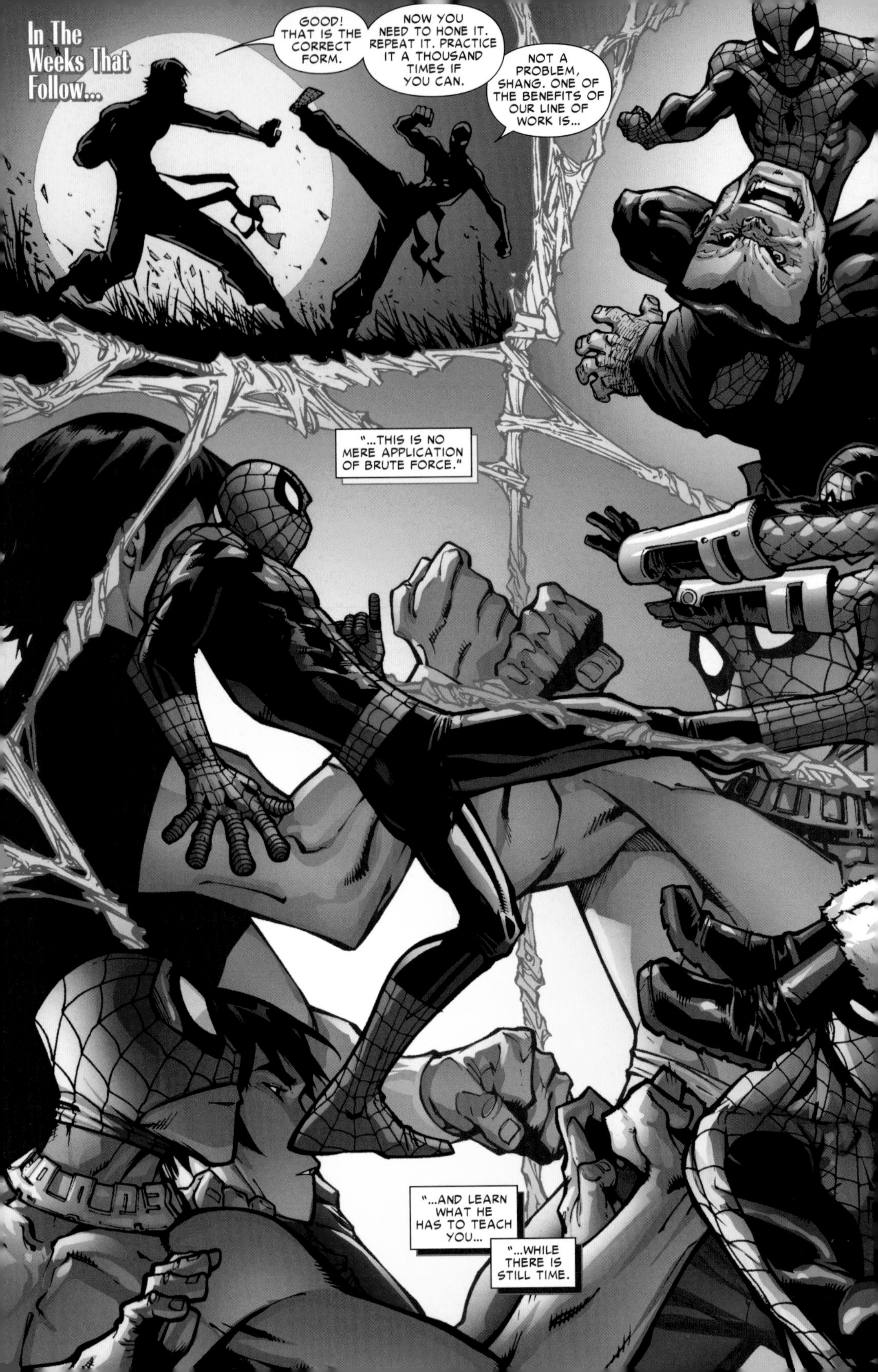

In The Weeks That Follow...
GOOD! THAT IS THE CORRECT FORM.
NOW YOU NEED TO HONE IT. REPEAT IT. PRACTICE IT A THOUSAND TIMES IF YOU CAN.
NOT A PROBLEM, SHANG. ONE OF THE BENEFITS OF OUR LINE OF WORK IS...
"...THIS IS NO MERE APPLICATION OF BRUTE FORCE."
"...AND LEARN WHAT HE HAS TO TEACH YOU...
"...WHILE THERE IS STILL TIME.

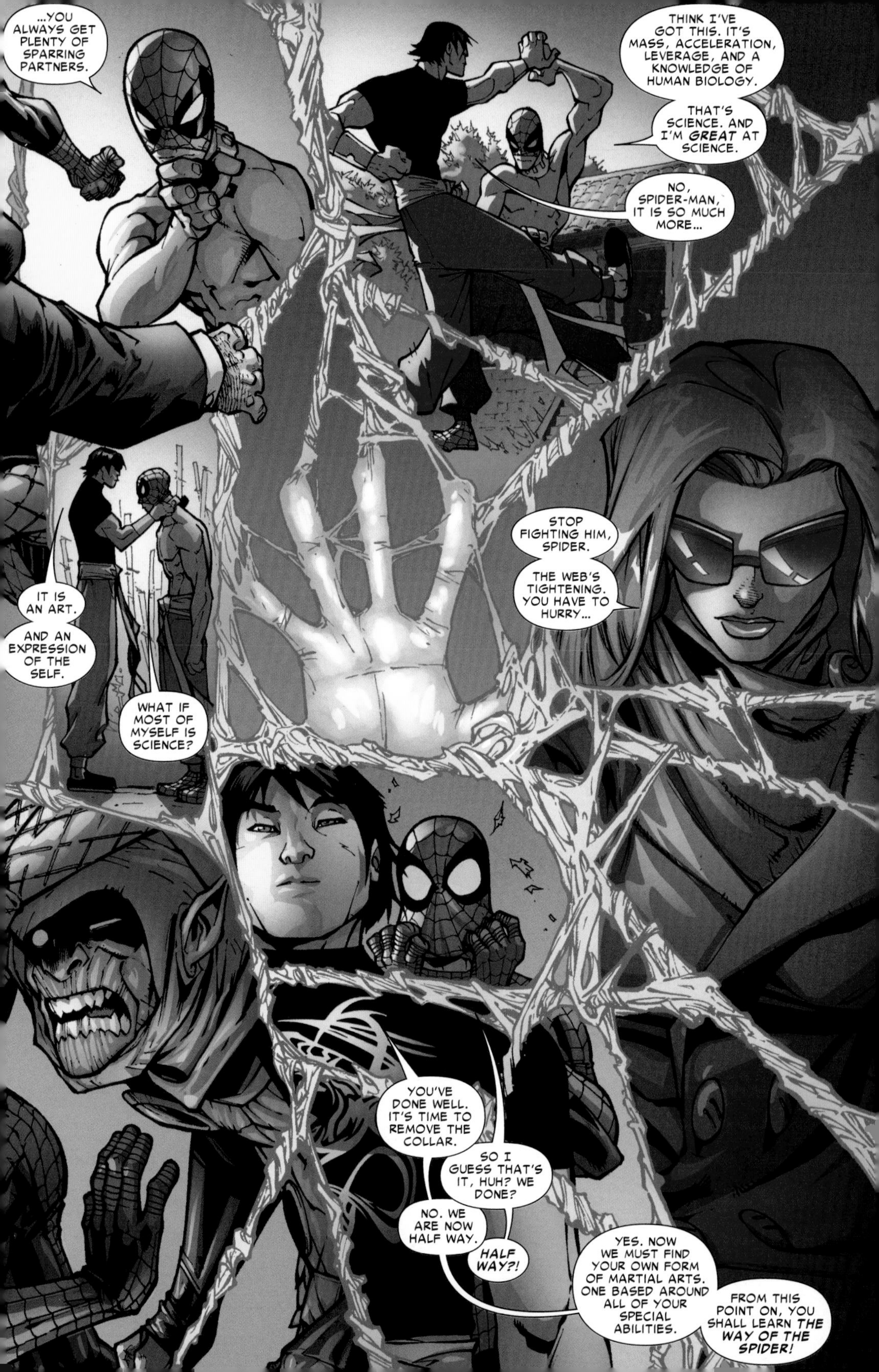
...YOU ALWAYS GET PLENTY OF SPARRING PARTNERS.
THINK I'VE GOT THIS. IT'S MASS, ACCELERATION, LEVERAGE, AND A KNOWLEDGE OF HUMAN BIOLOGY.
THAT'S SCIENCE. AND I'M GREAT AT SCIENCE.
NO, SPIDER-MAN, IT IS SO MUCH MORE...
IT IS AN ART.
AND AN EXPRESSION OF THE SELF.
WHAT IF MOST OF MYSELF IS SCIENCE?
STOP FIGHTING HIM, SPIDER.
THE WEB'S TIGHTENING. YOU HAVE TO HURRY...
YOU'VE DONE WELL. IT'S TIME TO REMOVE THE COLLAR.
SO I GUESS THAT'S IT, HUH? WE DONE?
NO. WE ARE NOW HALF WAY.
HALF WAY?!
YES. NOW WE MUST FIND YOUR OWN FORM OF MARTIAL ARTS. ONE BASED AROUND ALL OF YOUR SPECIAL ABILITIES.
FROM THIS POINT ON, YOU SHALL LEARN THE WAY OF THE SPIDER!

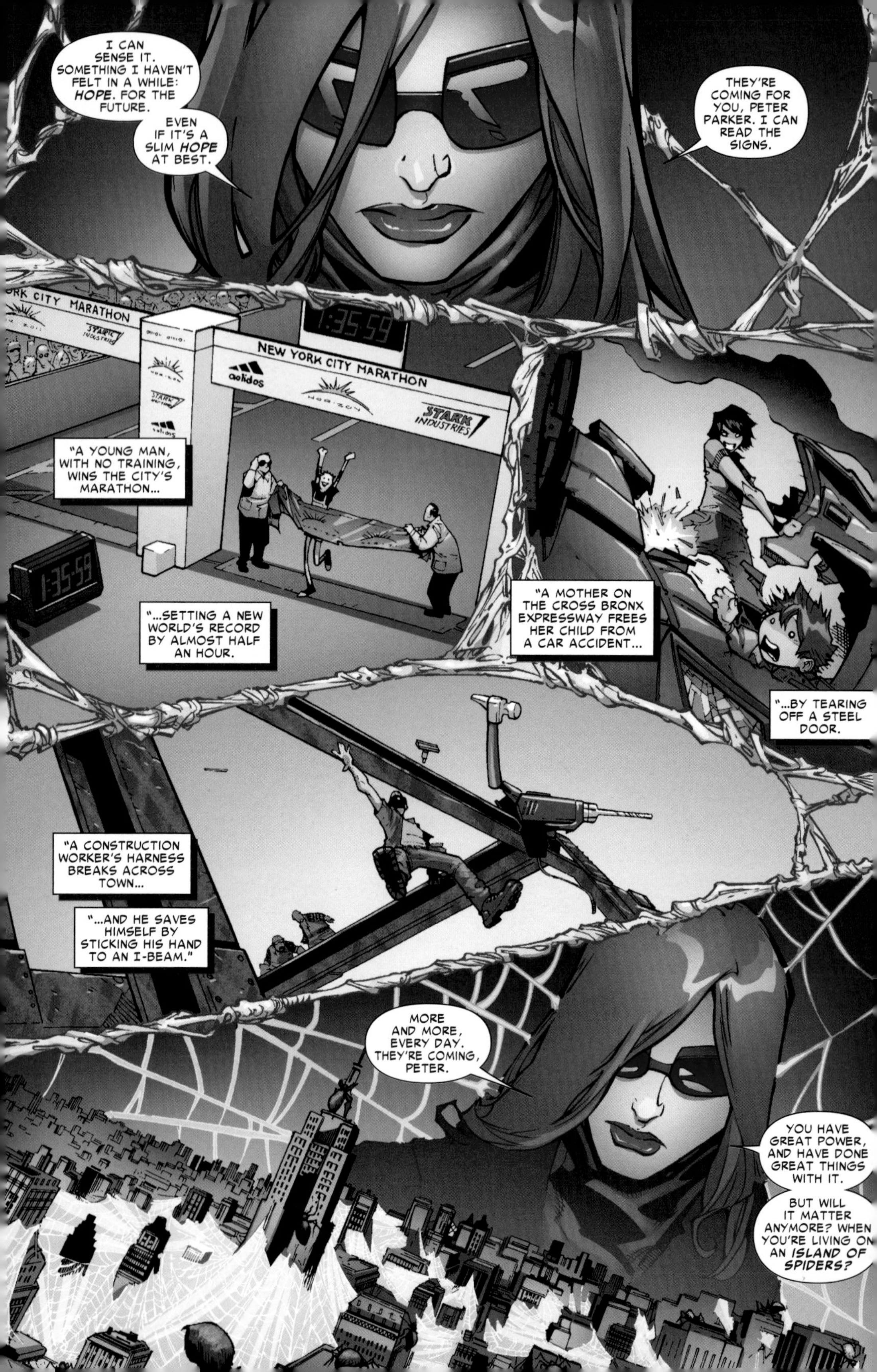

I CAN SENSE IT. SOMETHING I HAVEN'T FELT IN A WHILE: HOPE. FOR THE FUTURE.
EVEN IF IT'S A SLIM HOPE AT BEST.
THEY'RE COMING FOR YOU, PETER PARKER. I CAN READ THE SIGNS.
NEW YORK CITY MARATHON
STARK INDUSTRIES
1:35:59
"A YOUNG MAN, WITH NO TRAINING, WINS THE CITY'S MARATHON...
"...SETTING A NEW WORLD'S RECORD BY ALMOST HALF AN HOUR.
"A MOTHER ON THE CROSS BRONX EXPRESSWAY FREES HER CHILD FROM A CAR ACCIDENT...
"...BY TEARING OFF A STEEL DOOR.
"A CONSTRUCTION WORKER'S HARNESS BREAKS ACROSS TOWN...
"...AND HE SAVES HIMSELF BY STICKING HIS HAND TO AN I-BEAM."
MORE AND MORE, EVERY DAY. THEY'RE COMING, PETER.
YOU HAVE GREAT POWER, AND HAVE DONE GREAT THINGS WITH IT.
BUT WILL IT MATTER ANYMORE? WHEN YOU'RE LIVING ON AN ISLAND OF SPIDERS?

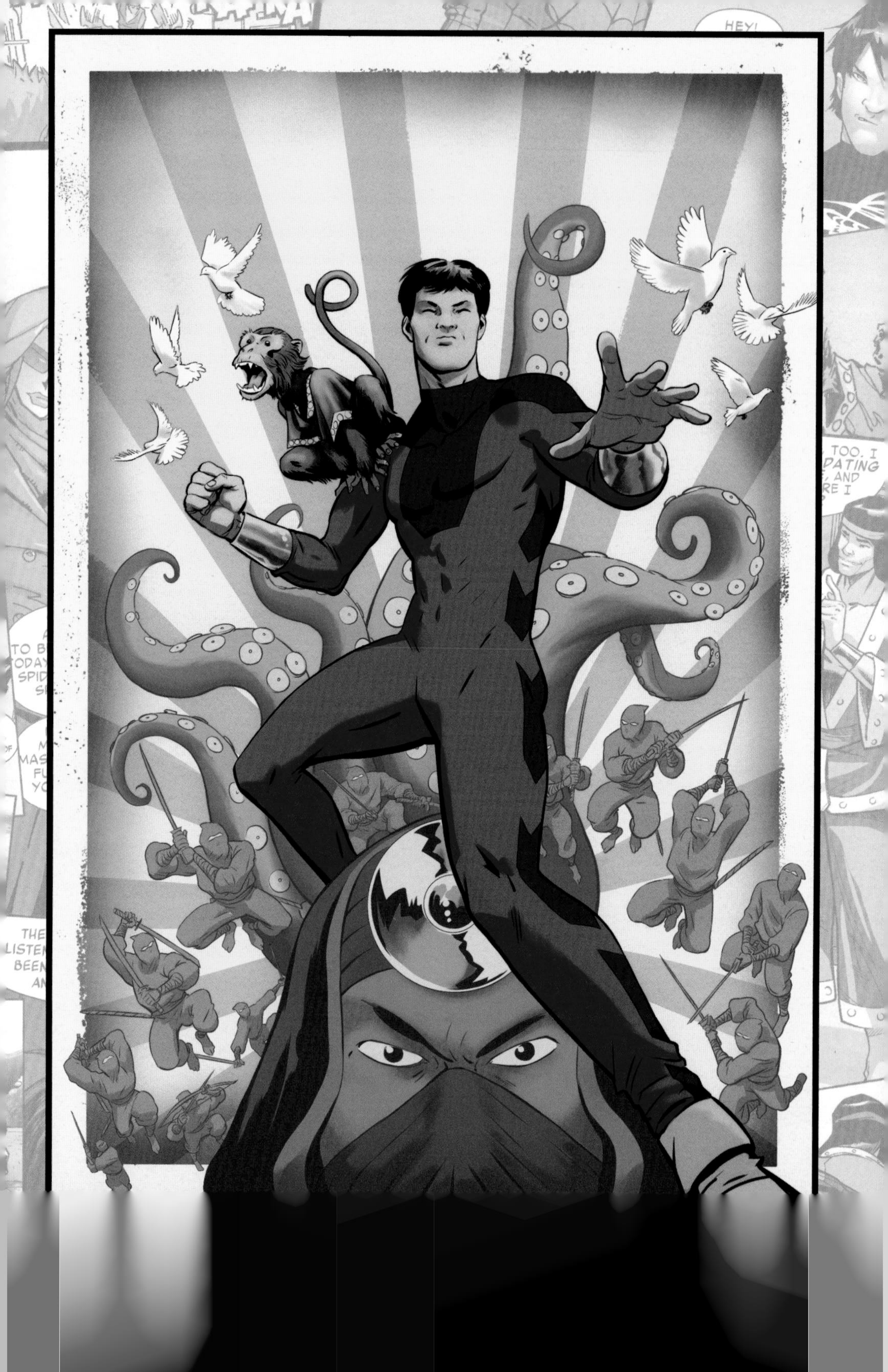
HEY!

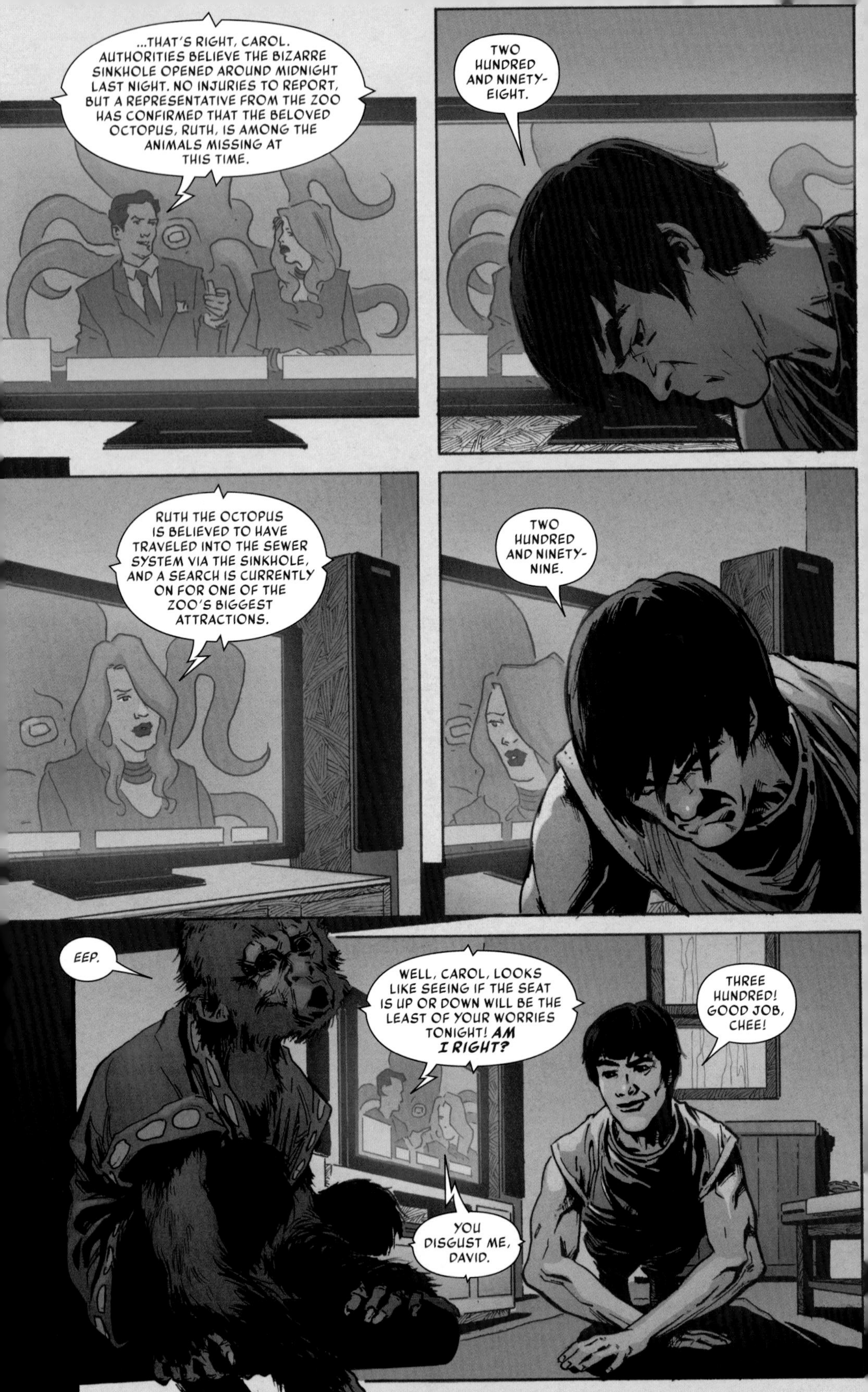
...THAT'S RIGHT, CAROL. AUTHORITIES BELIEVE THE BIZARRE SINKHOLE OPENED AROUND MIDNIGHT LAST NIGHT. NO INJURIES TO REPORT, BUT A REPRESENTATIVE FROM THE ZOO HAS CONFIRMED THAT THE BELOVED OCTOPUS, RUTH, IS AMONG THE ANIMALS MISSING AT THIS TIME.
TWO HUNDRED AND NINETY-EIGHT.
RUTH THE OCTOPUS IS BELIEVED TO HAVE TRAVELED INTO THE SEWER SYSTEM VIA THE SINKHOLE, AND A SEARCH IS CURRENTLY ON FOR ONE OF THE ZOO'S BIGGEST ATTRACTIONS.
TWO HUNDRED AND NINETY-NINE.
EEP.
WELL, CAROL, LOOKS LIKE SEEING IF THE SEAT IS UP OR DOWN WILL BE THE LEAST OF YOUR WORRIES TONIGHT! ***AM I RIGHT?***
YOU DISGUST ME, DAVID.
THREE HUNDRED! GOOD JOB, CHEE!

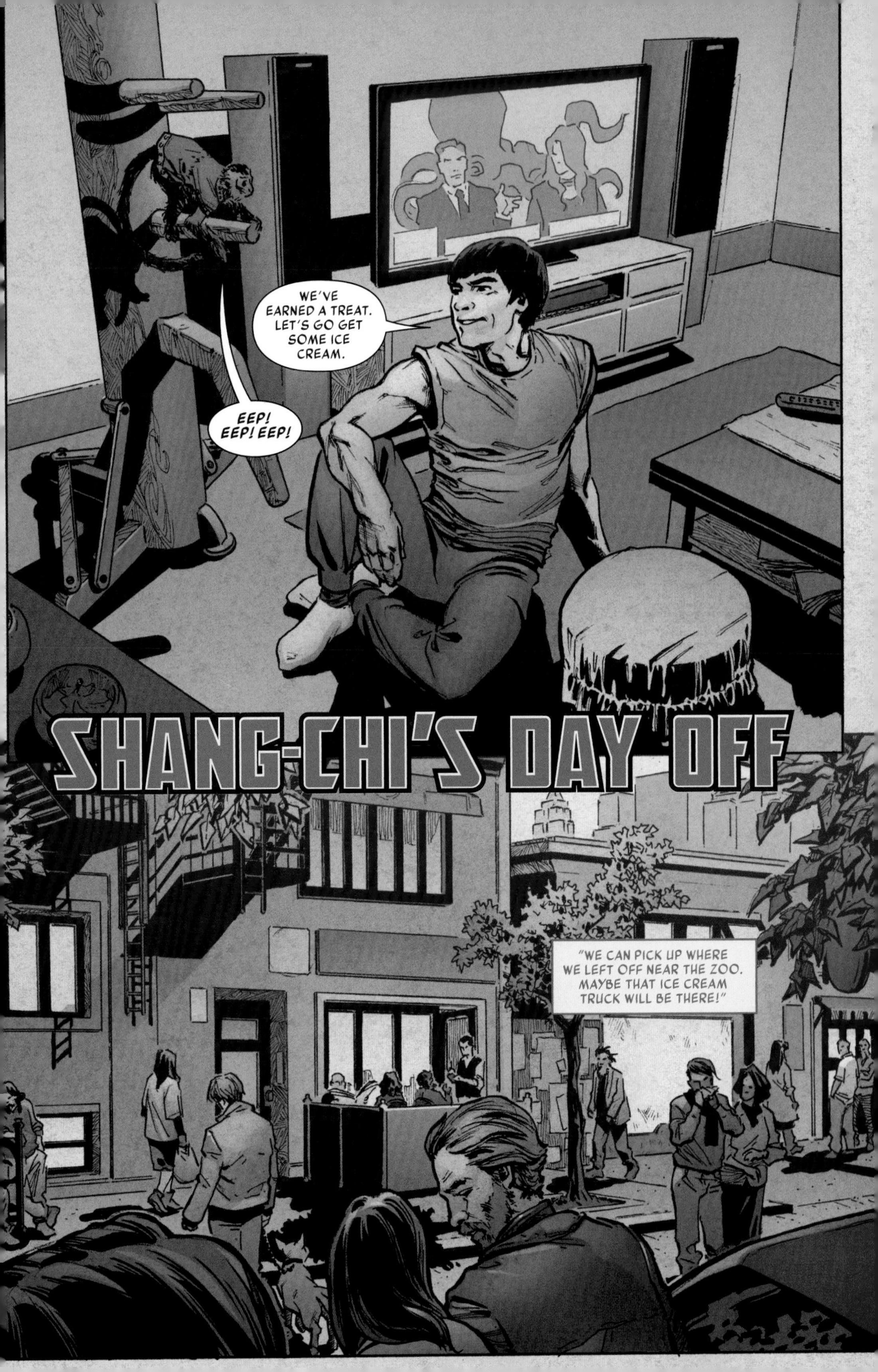
WE'VE EARNED A TREAT. LET'S GO GET SOME ICE CREAM.
EEP! EEP! EEP!
SHANG-CHI'S DAY OFF
"WE CAN PICK UP WHERE WE LEFT OFF NEAR THE ZOO. MAYBE THAT ICE CREAM TRUCK WILL BE THERE!"

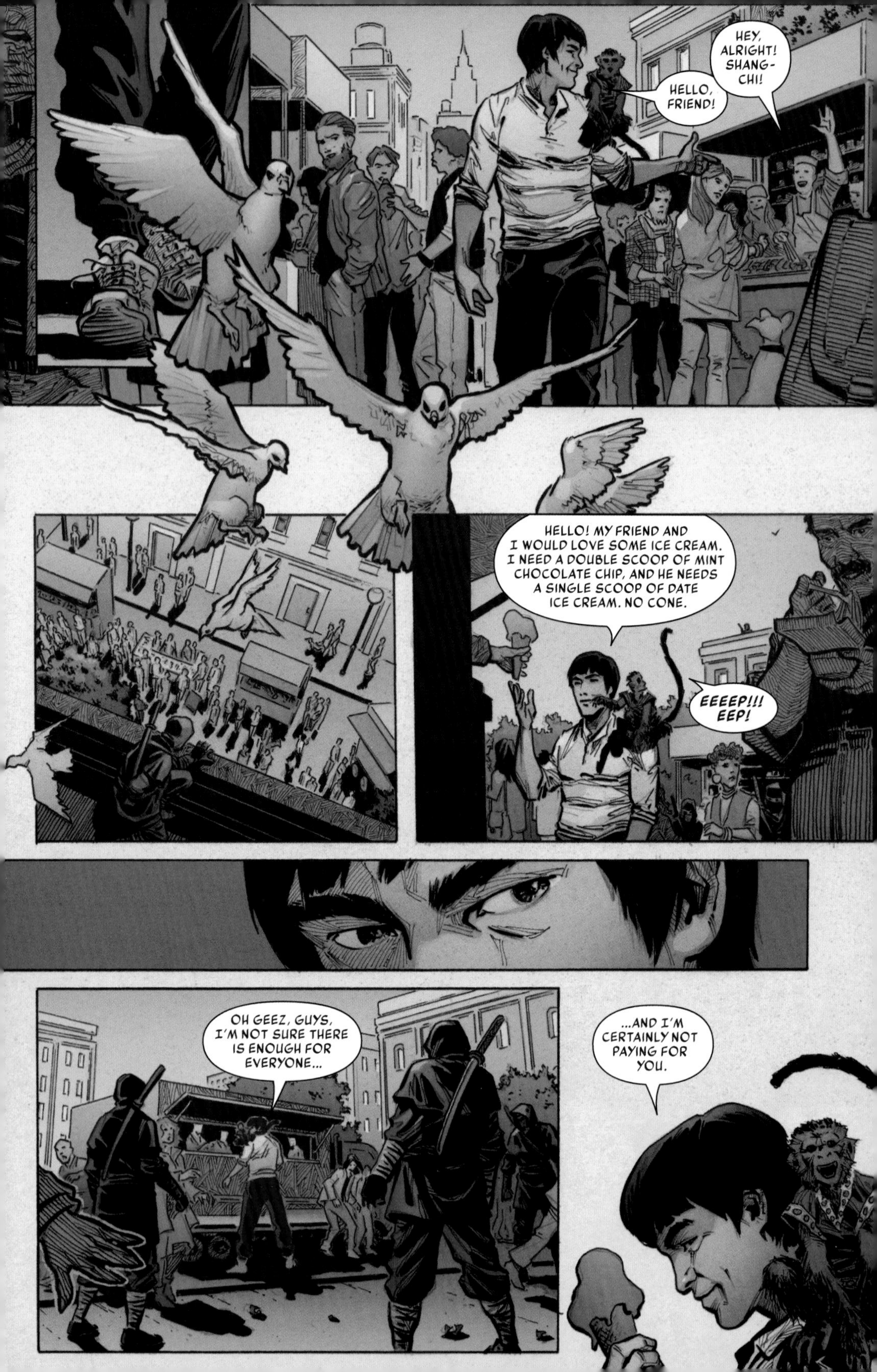
HELLO, FRIEND!
HEY, ALRIGHT! SHANG-CHI!
HELLO! MY FRIEND AND I WOULD LOVE SOME ICE CREAM. I NEED A DOUBLE SCOOP OF MINT CHOCOLATE CHIP, AND HE NEEDS A SINGLE SCOOP OF DATE ICE CREAM. NO CONE.
EEEEP!!! EEP!
OH GEEZ, GUYS, I'M NOT SURE THERE IS ENOUGH FOR EVERYONE...
...AND I'M CERTAINLY NOT PAYING FOR YOU.

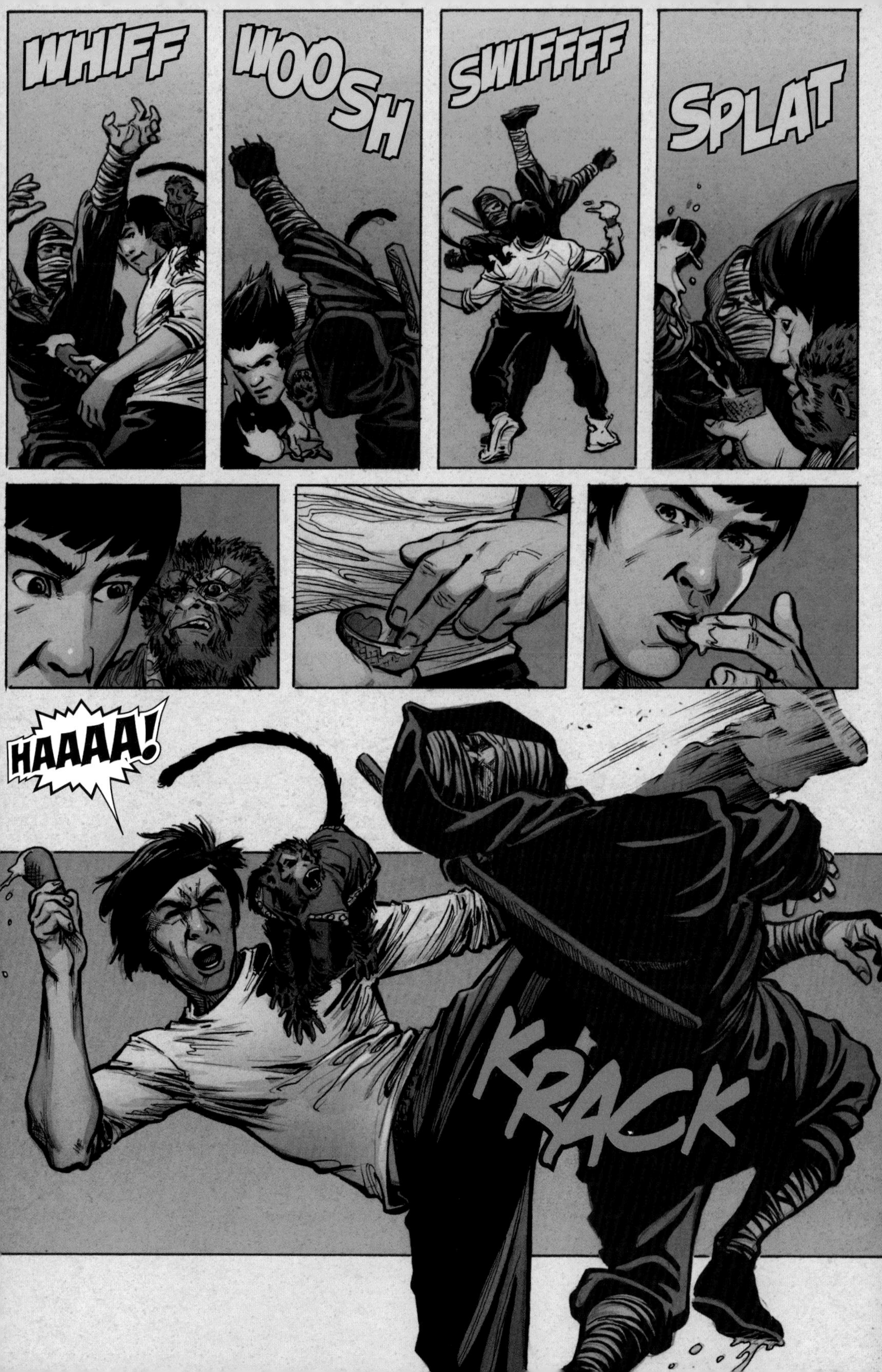
WHIFF
WOOSH
SWIFFFF
SPLAT
HAAAA!
KRACK

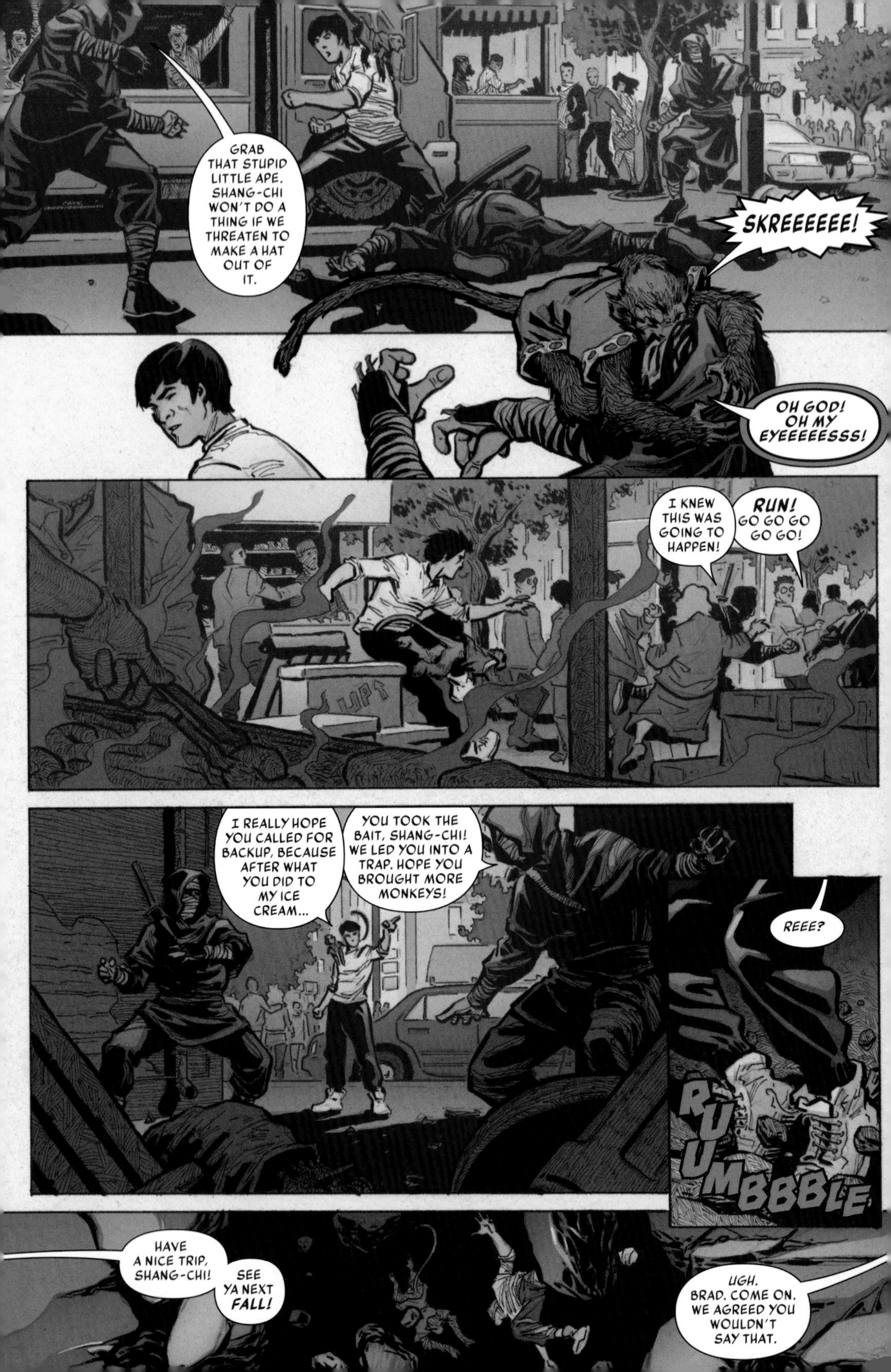

GRAB THAT STUPID LITTLE APE. SHANG-CHI WON'T DO A THING IF WE THREATEN TO MAKE A HAT OUT OF IT.
SKREEEEEE!
OH GOD! OH MY EYEEEEESSS!
I KNEW THIS WAS GOING TO HAPPEN!
RUN! GO GO GO GO GO!
I REALLY HOPE YOU CALLED FOR BACKUP, BECAUSE AFTER WHAT YOU DID TO MY ICE CREAM...
YOU TOOK THE BAIT, SHANG-CHI! WE LED YOU INTO A TRAP. HOPE YOU BROUGHT MORE MONKEYS!
REEE?
RUUMBBBLE
HAVE A NICE TRIP, SHANG-CHI!
SEE YA NEXT FALL!
UGH. BRAD. COME ON. WE AGREED YOU WOULDN'T SAY THAT.

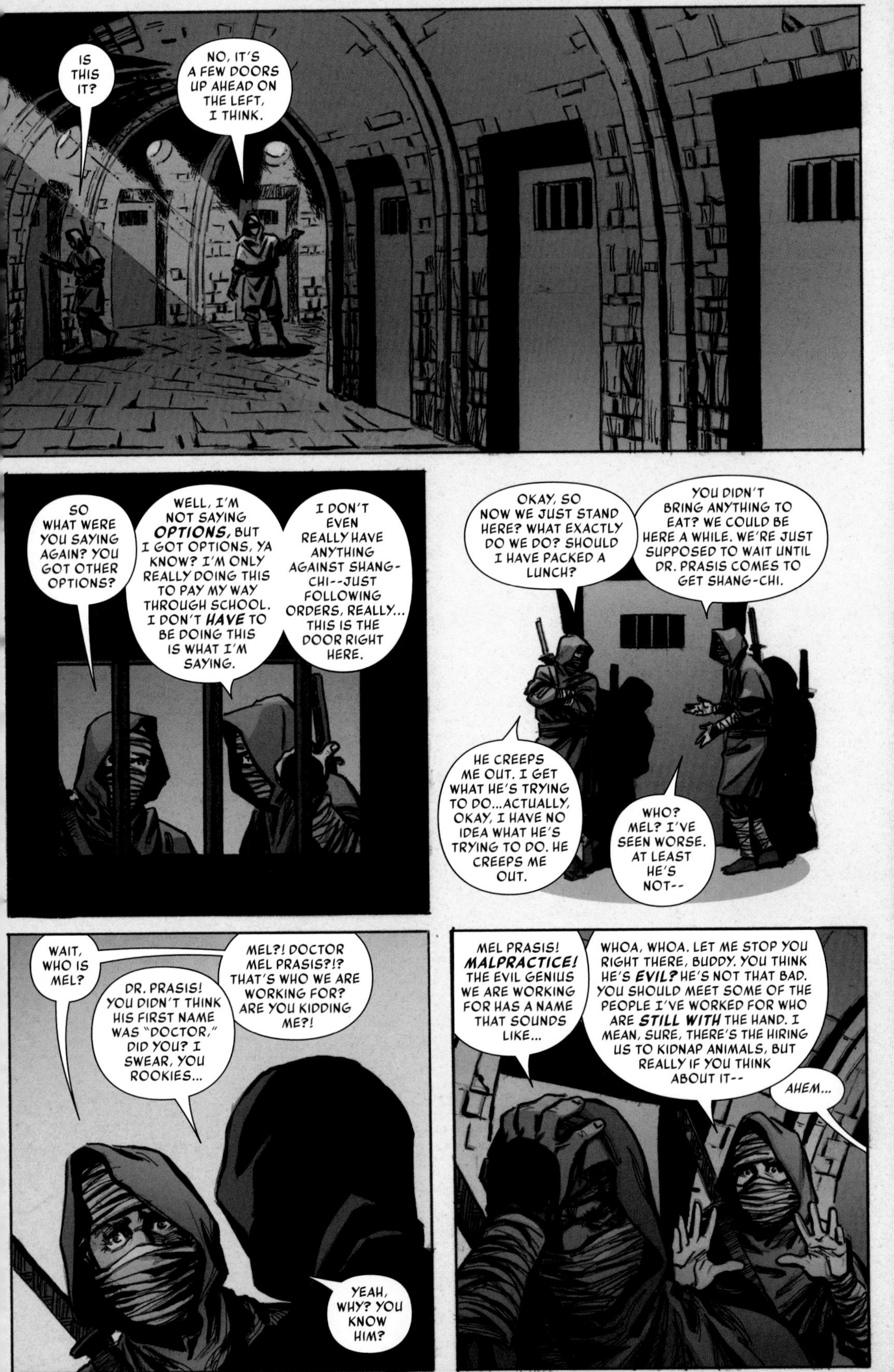

IS THIS IT?
NO, IT'S A FEW DOORS UP AHEAD ON THE LEFT, I THINK.
SO WHAT WERE YOU SAYING AGAIN? YOU GOT OTHER OPTIONS?
WELL, I'M NOT SAYING OPTIONS, BUT I GOT OPTIONS, YA KNOW? I'M ONLY REALLY DOING THIS TO PAY MY WAY THROUGH SCHOOL. I DON'T HAVE TO BE DOING THIS IS WHAT I'M SAYING.
I DON'T EVEN REALLY HAVE ANYTHING AGAINST SHANG-CHI--JUST FOLLOWING ORDERS, REALLY... THIS IS THE DOOR RIGHT HERE.
OKAY, SO NOW WE JUST STAND HERE? WHAT EXACTLY DO WE DO? SHOULD I HAVE PACKED A LUNCH?
YOU DIDN'T BRING ANYTHING TO EAT? WE COULD BE HERE A WHILE. WE'RE JUST SUPPOSED TO WAIT UNTIL DR. PRASIS COMES TO GET SHANG-CHI.
HE CREEPS ME OUT. I GET WHAT HE'S TRYING TO DO...ACTUALLY, OKAY, I HAVE NO IDEA WHAT HE'S TRYING TO DO. HE CREEPS ME OUT.
WHO? MEL? I'VE SEEN WORSE. AT LEAST HE'S NOT--
WAIT, WHO IS MEL?
DR. PRASIS! YOU DIDN'T THINK HIS FIRST NAME WAS "DOCTOR," DID YOU? I SWEAR, YOU ROOKIES...
MEL?! DOCTOR MEL PRASIS?!? THAT'S WHO WE ARE WORKING FOR? ARE YOU KIDDING ME?!
YEAH, WHY? YOU KNOW HIM?
MEL PRASIS! MALPRACTICE! THE EVIL GENIUS WE ARE WORKING FOR HAS A NAME THAT SOUNDS LIKE...
WHOA, WHOA. LET ME STOP YOU RIGHT THERE, BUDDY. YOU THINK HE'S EVIL? HE'S NOT THAT BAD. YOU SHOULD MEET SOME OF THE PEOPLE I'VE WORKED FOR WHO ARE STILL WITH THE HAND. I MEAN, SURE, THERE'S THE HIRING US TO KIDNAP ANIMALS, BUT REALLY IF YOU THINK ABOUT IT--
AHEM...

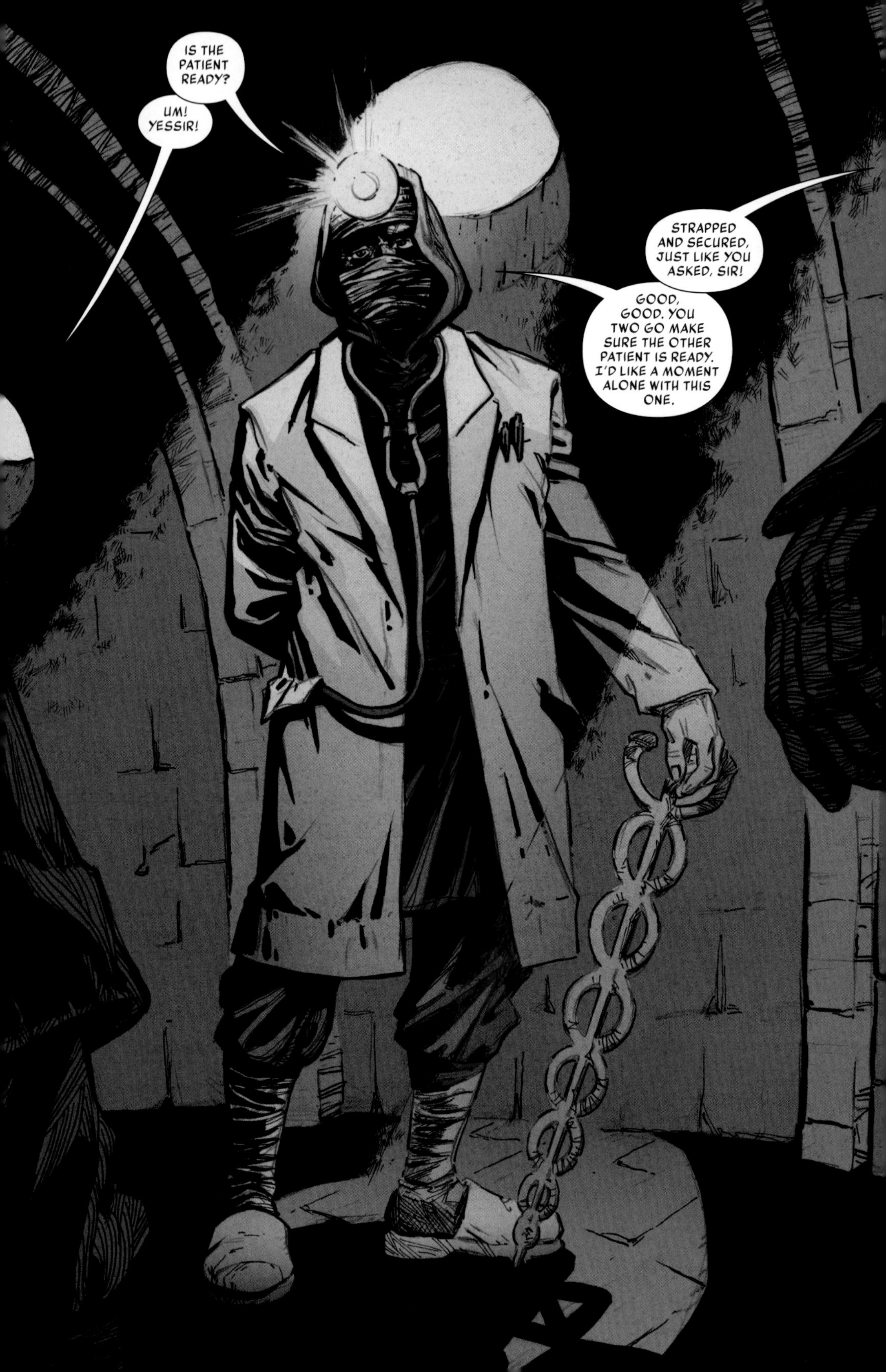
IS THE PATIENT READY?
UM! YESSIR!
STRAPPED AND SECURED, JUST LIKE YOU ASKED, SIR!
GOOD, GOOD. YOU TWO GO MAKE SURE THE OTHER PATIENT IS READY. I'D LIKE A MOMENT ALONE WITH THIS ONE.

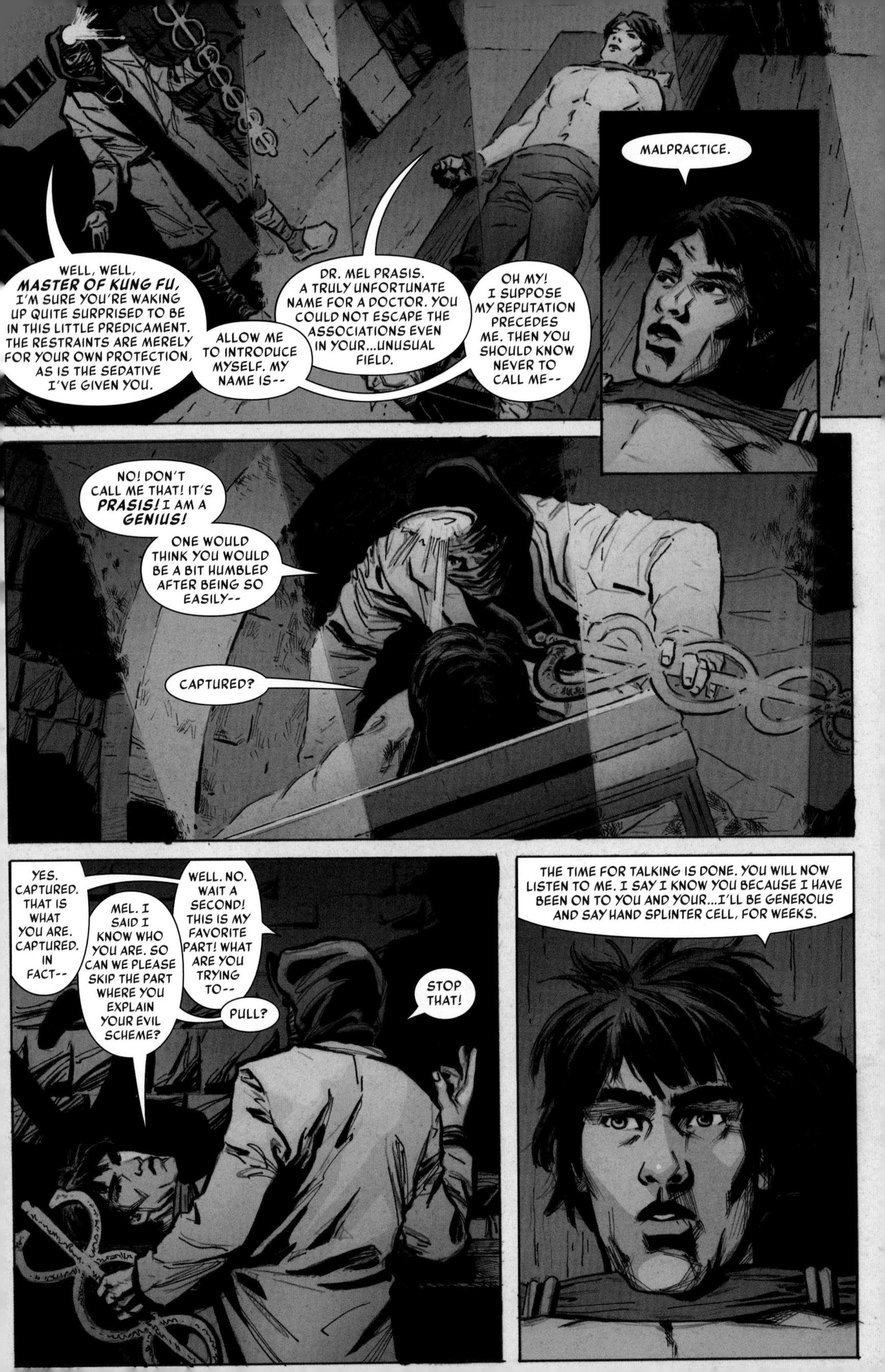
WELL, WELL, MASTER OF KUNG FU, I'M SURE YOU'RE WAKING UP QUITE SURPRISED TO BE IN THIS LITTLE PREDICAMENT. THE RESTRAINTS ARE MERELY FOR YOUR OWN PROTECTION, AS IS THE SEDATIVE I'VE GIVEN YOU.
ALLOW ME TO INTRODUCE MYSELF. MY NAME IS--
DR. MEL PRASIS. A TRULY UNFORTUNATE NAME FOR A DOCTOR. YOU COULD NOT ESCAPE THE ASSOCIATIONS EVEN IN YOUR...UNUSUAL FIELD.
OH MY! I SUPPOSE MY REPUTATION PRECEDES ME. THEN YOU SHOULD KNOW NEVER TO CALL ME--
MALPRACTICE.
NO! DON'T CALL ME THAT! IT'S PRASIS! I AM A GENIUS!
ONE WOULD THINK YOU WOULD BE A BIT HUMBLED AFTER BEING SO EASILY--
CAPTURED?
YES. CAPTURED. THAT IS WHAT YOU ARE. CAPTURED. IN FACT--
MEL. I SAID I KNOW WHO YOU ARE. SO CAN WE PLEASE SKIP THE PART WHERE YOU EXPLAIN YOUR EVIL SCHEME?
WELL. NO. WAIT A SECOND! THIS IS MY FAVORITE PART! WHAT ARE YOU TRYING TO--
PULL?
STOP THAT!
THE TIME FOR TALKING IS DONE. YOU WILL NOW LISTEN TO ME. I SAY I KNOW YOU BECAUSE I HAVE BEEN ON TO YOU AND YOUR...I'LL BE GENEROUS AND SAY HAND SPLINTER CELL, FOR WEEKS.

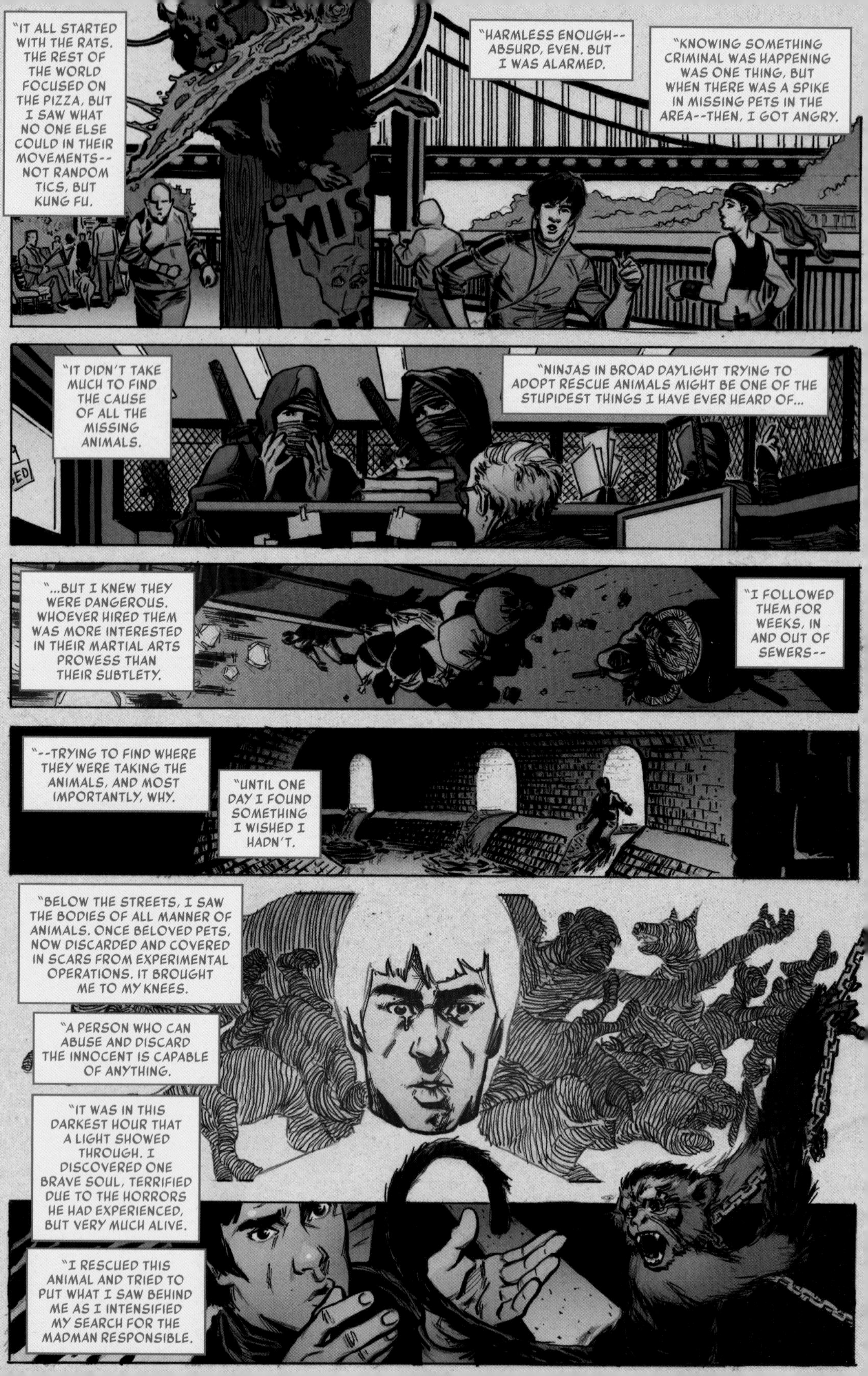
"IT ALL STARTED WITH THE RATS. THE REST OF THE WORLD FOCUSED ON THE PIZZA, BUT I SAW WHAT NO ONE ELSE COULD IN THEIR MOVEMENTS--NOT RANDOM TICS, BUT KUNG FU.
"HARMLESS ENOUGH--ABSURD, EVEN. BUT I WAS ALARMED.
"KNOWING SOMETHING CRIMINAL WAS HAPPENING WAS ONE THING, BUT WHEN THERE WAS A SPIKE IN MISSING PETS IN THE AREA--THEN, I GOT ANGRY.
"IT DIDN'T TAKE MUCH TO FIND THE CAUSE OF ALL THE MISSING ANIMALS.
"NINJAS IN BROAD DAYLIGHT TRYING TO ADOPT RESCUE ANIMALS MIGHT BE ONE OF THE STUPIDEST THINGS I HAVE EVER HEARD OF...
"...BUT I KNEW THEY WERE DANGEROUS. WHOEVER HIRED THEM WAS MORE INTERESTED IN THEIR MARTIAL ARTS PROWESS THAN THEIR SUBTLETY.
"I FOLLOWED THEM FOR WEEKS, IN AND OUT OF SEWERS--
"--TRYING TO FIND WHERE THEY WERE TAKING THE ANIMALS, AND MOST IMPORTANTLY, WHY.
"UNTIL ONE DAY I FOUND SOMETHING I WISHED I HADN'T.
"BELOW THE STREETS, I SAW THE BODIES OF ALL MANNER OF ANIMALS. ONCE BELOVED PETS, NOW DISCARDED AND COVERED IN SCARS FROM EXPERIMENTAL OPERATIONS. IT BROUGHT ME TO MY KNEES.
"A PERSON WHO CAN ABUSE AND DISCARD THE INNOCENT IS CAPABLE OF ANYTHING.
"IT WAS IN THIS DARKEST HOUR THAT A LIGHT SHOWED THROUGH. I DISCOVERED ONE BRAVE SOUL, TERRIFIED DUE TO THE HORRORS HE HAD EXPERIENCED, BUT VERY MUCH ALIVE.
"I RESCUED THIS ANIMAL AND TRIED TO PUT WHAT I SAW BEHIND ME AS I INTENSIFIED MY SEARCH FOR THE MADMAN RESPONSIBLE.

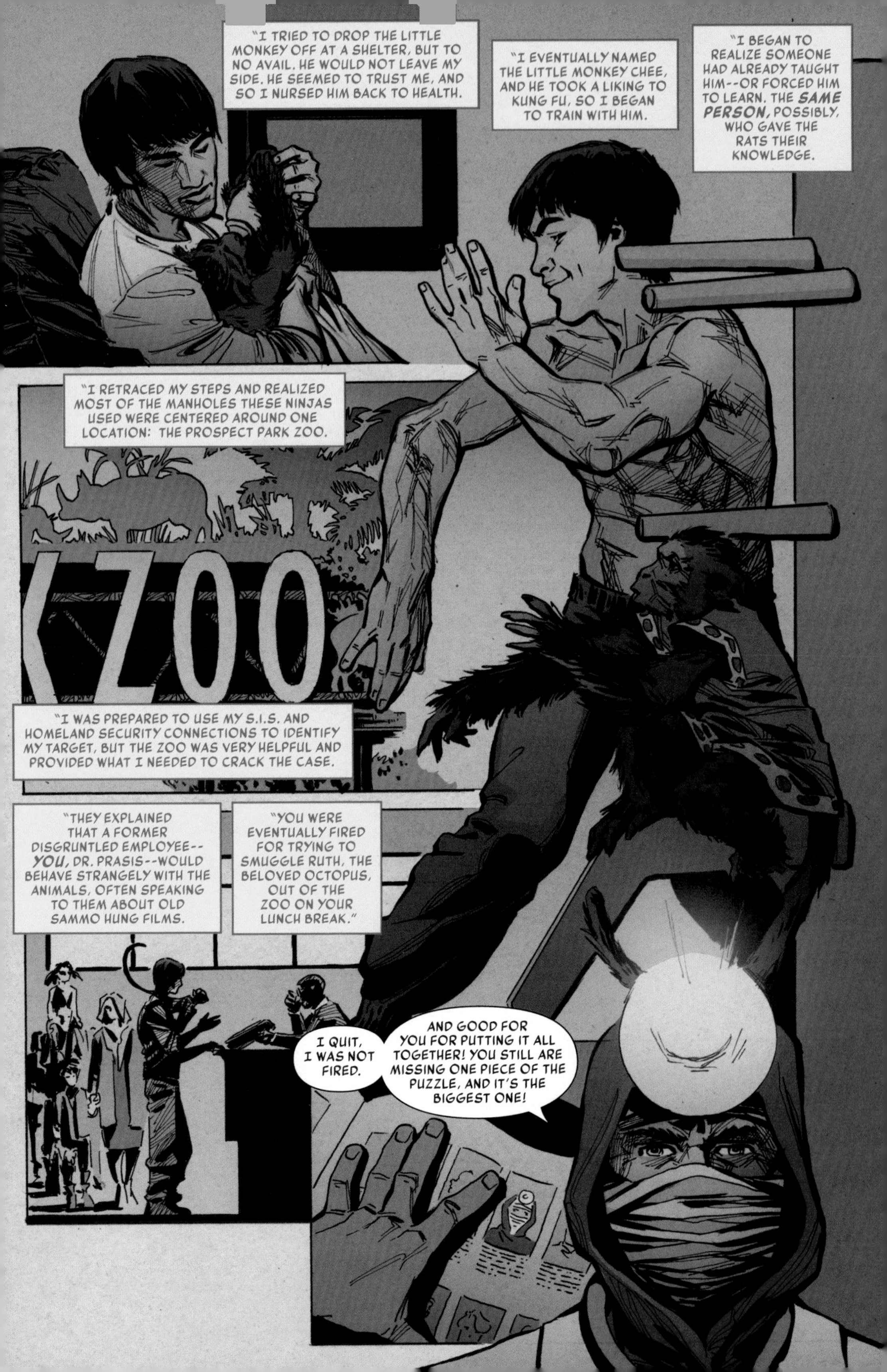
"I TRIED TO DROP THE LITTLE MONKEY OFF AT A SHELTER, BUT TO NO AVAIL. HE WOULD NOT LEAVE MY SIDE. HE SEEMED TO TRUST ME, AND SO I NURSED HIM BACK TO HEALTH.
"I EVENTUALLY NAMED THE LITTLE MONKEY CHEE, AND HE TOOK A LIKING TO KUNG FU, SO I BEGAN TO TRAIN WITH HIM.
"I BEGAN TO REALIZE SOMEONE HAD ALREADY TAUGHT HIM--OR FORCED HIM TO LEARN. THE SAME PERSON, POSSIBLY, WHO GAVE THE RATS THEIR KNOWLEDGE.
"I RETRACED MY STEPS AND REALIZED MOST OF THE MANHOLES THESE NINJAS USED WERE CENTERED AROUND ONE LOCATION: THE PROSPECT PARK ZOO.
ZOO
"I WAS PREPARED TO USE MY S.I.S. AND HOMELAND SECURITY CONNECTIONS TO IDENTIFY MY TARGET, BUT THE ZOO WAS VERY HELPFUL AND PROVIDED WHAT I NEEDED TO CRACK THE CASE.
"THEY EXPLAINED THAT A FORMER DISGRUNTLED EMPLOYEE--YOU, DR. PRASIS--WOULD BEHAVE STRANGELY WITH THE ANIMALS, OFTEN SPEAKING TO THEM ABOUT OLD SAMMO HUNG FILMS.
"YOU WERE EVENTUALLY FIRED FOR TRYING TO SMUGGLE RUTH, THE BELOVED OCTOPUS, OUT OF THE ZOO ON YOUR LUNCH BREAK."
I QUIT, I WAS NOT FIRED.
AND GOOD FOR YOU FOR PUTTING IT ALL TOGETHER! YOU STILL ARE MISSING ONE PIECE OF THE PUZZLE, AND IT'S THE BIGGEST ONE!

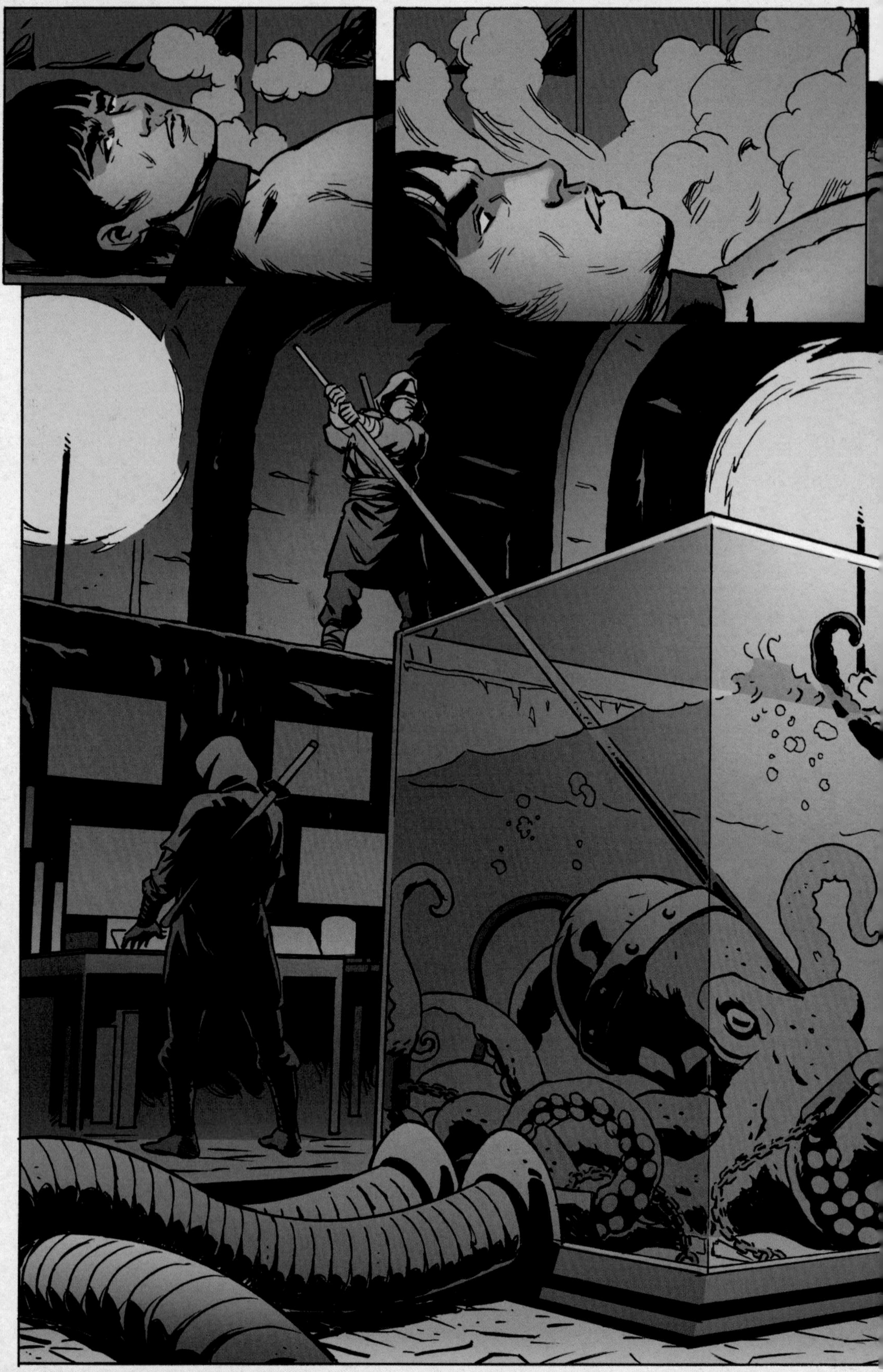

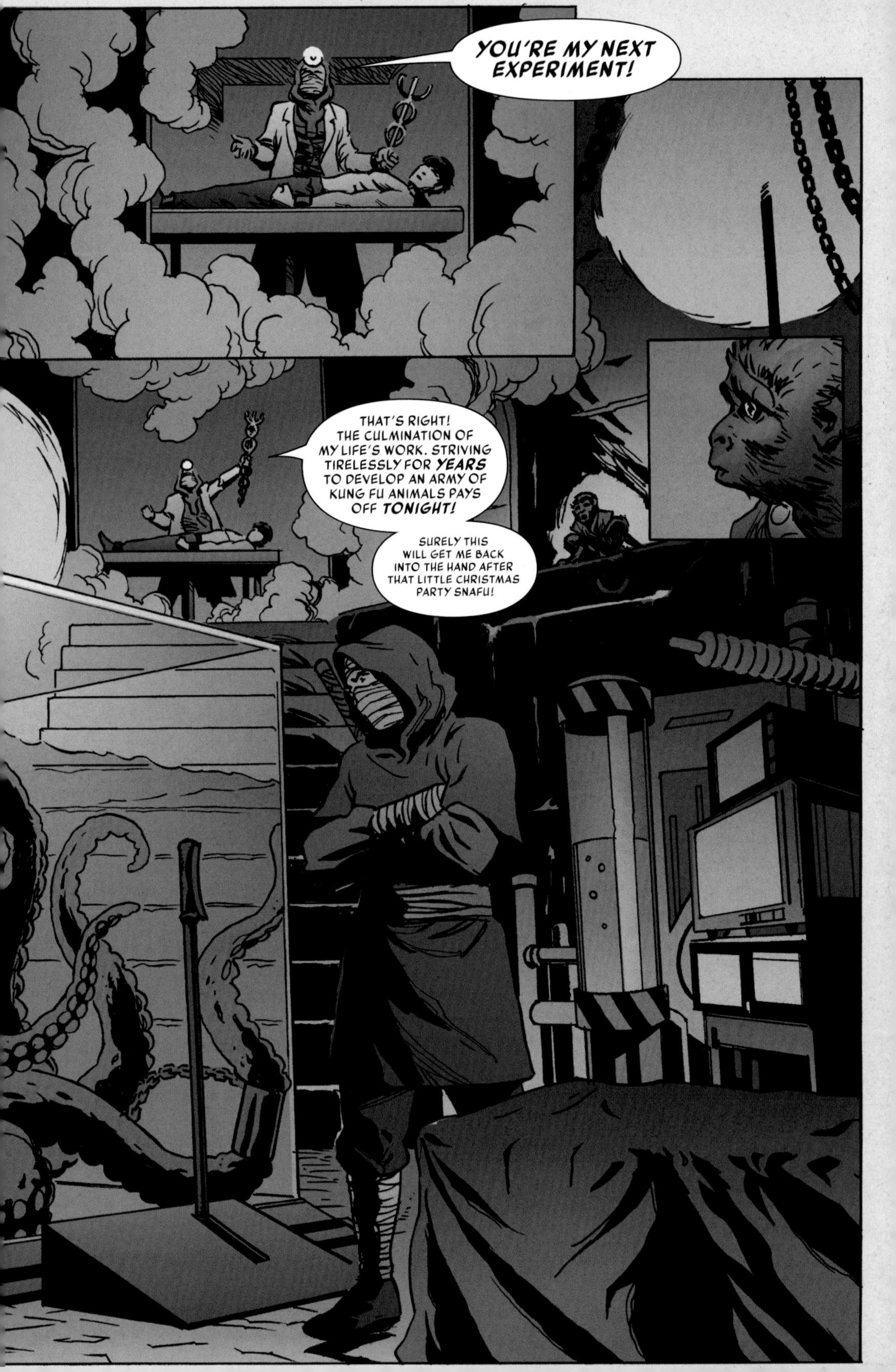
YOU'RE MY NEXT EXPERIMENT!
THAT'S RIGHT! THE CULMINATION OF MY LIFE'S WORK. STRIVING TIRELESSLY FOR YEARS TO DEVELOP AN ARMY OF KUNG FU ANIMALS PAYS OFF TONIGHT!
SURELY THIS WILL GET ME BACK INTO THE HAND AFTER THAT LITTLE CHRISTMAS PARTY SNAFU!

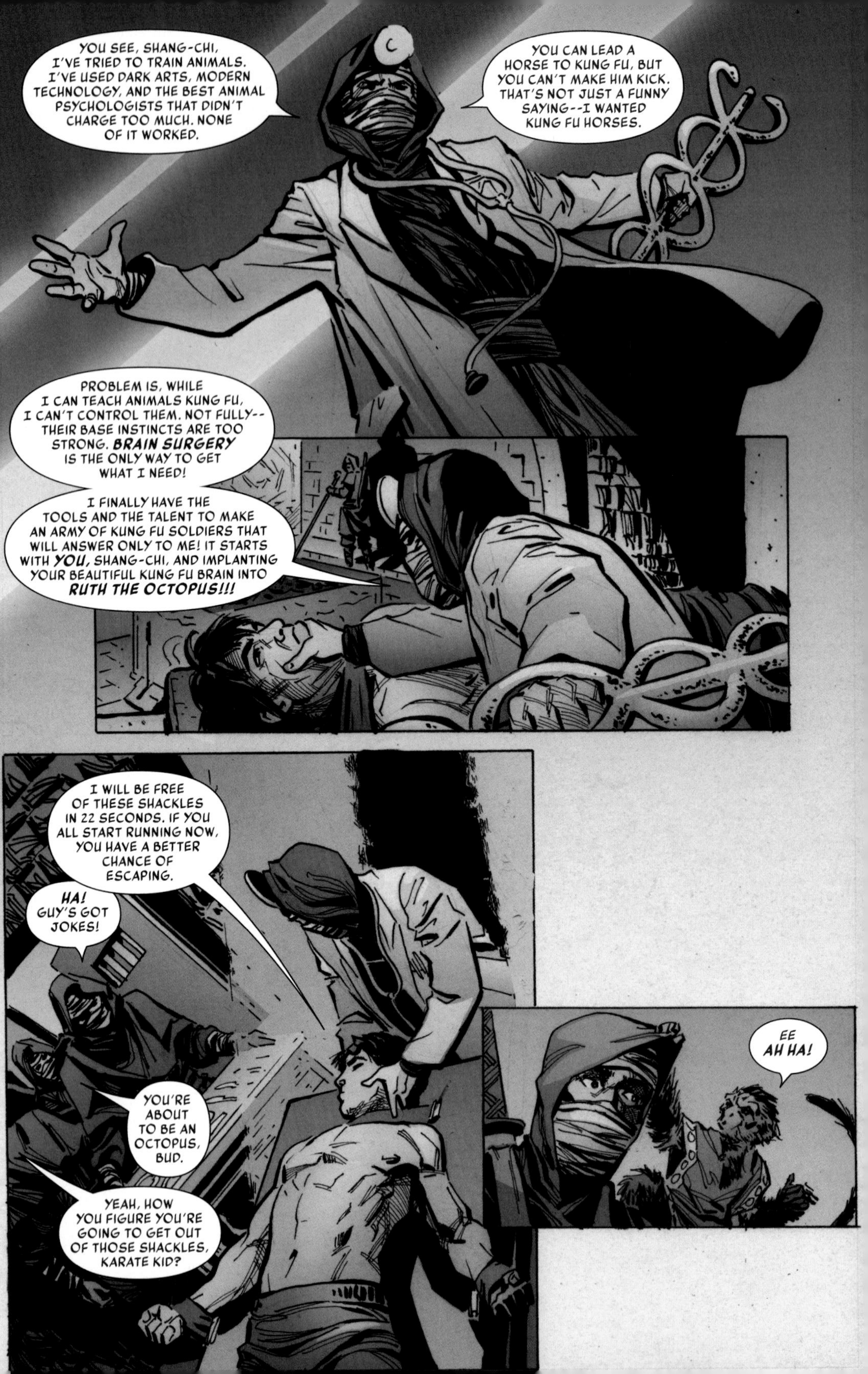
YOU SEE, SHANG-CHI, I'VE TRIED TO TRAIN ANIMALS. I'VE USED DARK ARTS, MODERN TECHNOLOGY, AND THE BEST ANIMAL PSYCHOLOGISTS THAT DIDN'T CHARGE TOO MUCH. NONE OF IT WORKED.
YOU CAN LEAD A HORSE TO KUNG FU, BUT YOU CAN'T MAKE HIM KICK. THAT'S NOT JUST A FUNNY SAYING--I WANTED KUNG FU HORSES.
PROBLEM IS, WHILE I CAN TEACH ANIMALS KUNG FU, I CAN'T CONTROL THEM. NOT FULLY--THEIR BASE INSTINCTS ARE TOO STRONG. ***BRAIN SURGERY*** IS THE ONLY WAY TO GET WHAT I NEED!
I FINALLY HAVE THE TOOLS AND THE TALENT TO MAKE AN ARMY OF KUNG FU SOLDIERS THAT WILL ANSWER ONLY TO ME! IT STARTS WITH ***YOU,*** SHANG-CHI, AND IMPLANTING YOUR BEAUTIFUL KUNG FU BRAIN INTO ***RUTH THE OCTOPUS!!!***
I WILL BE FREE OF THESE SHACKLES IN 22 SECONDS. IF YOU ALL START RUNNING NOW, YOU HAVE A BETTER CHANCE OF ESCAPING.
HA! GUY'S GOT JOKES!
YOU'RE ABOUT TO BE AN OCTOPUS, BUD.
YEAH, HOW YOU FIGURE YOU'RE GOING TO GET OUT OF THOSE SHACKLES, KARATE KID?
EE ***AH HA!***

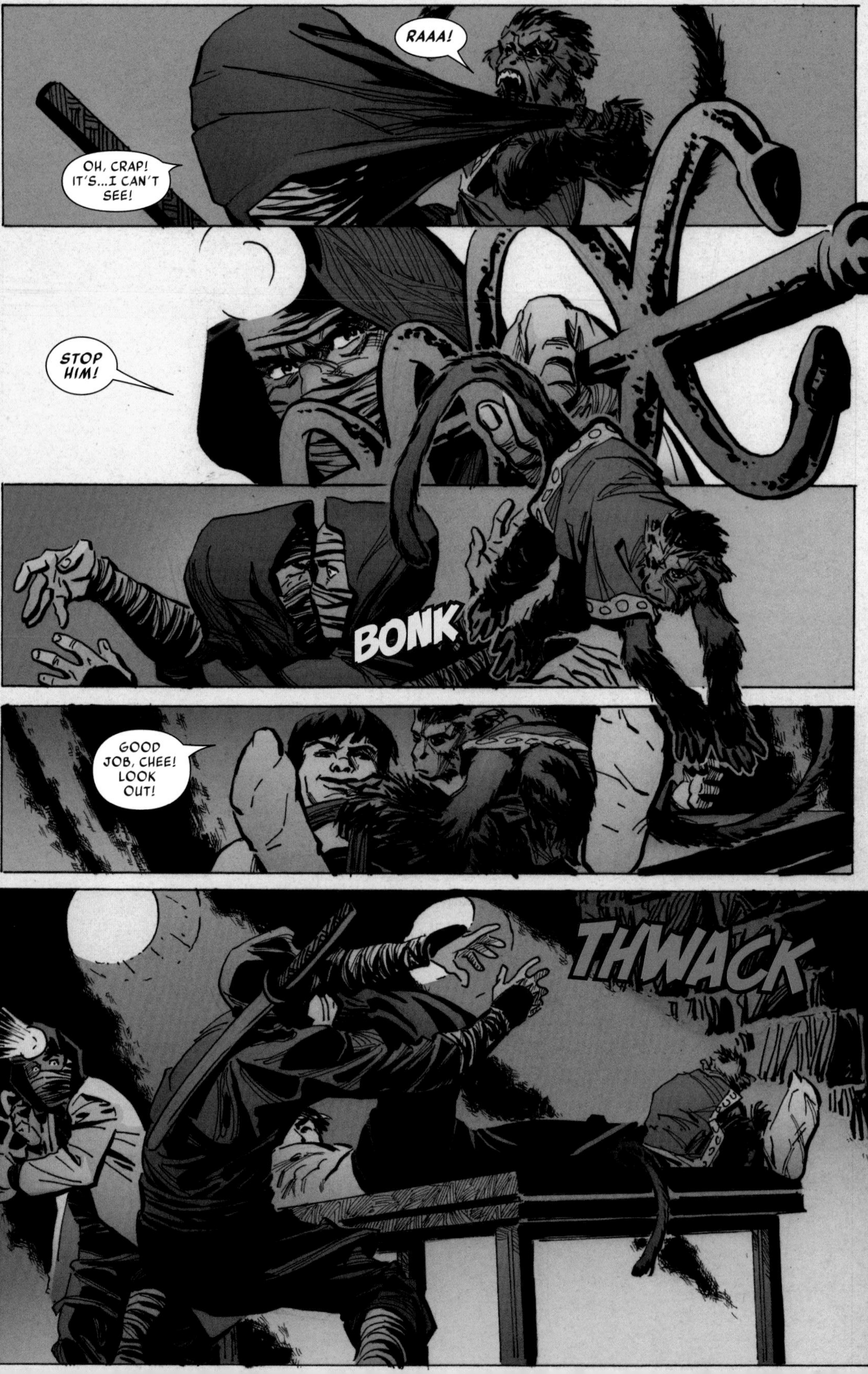
RAAA!
OH, CRAP! IT'S...I CAN'T SEE!
STOP HIM!
BONK
GOOD JOB, CHEE! LOOK OUT!
THWACK

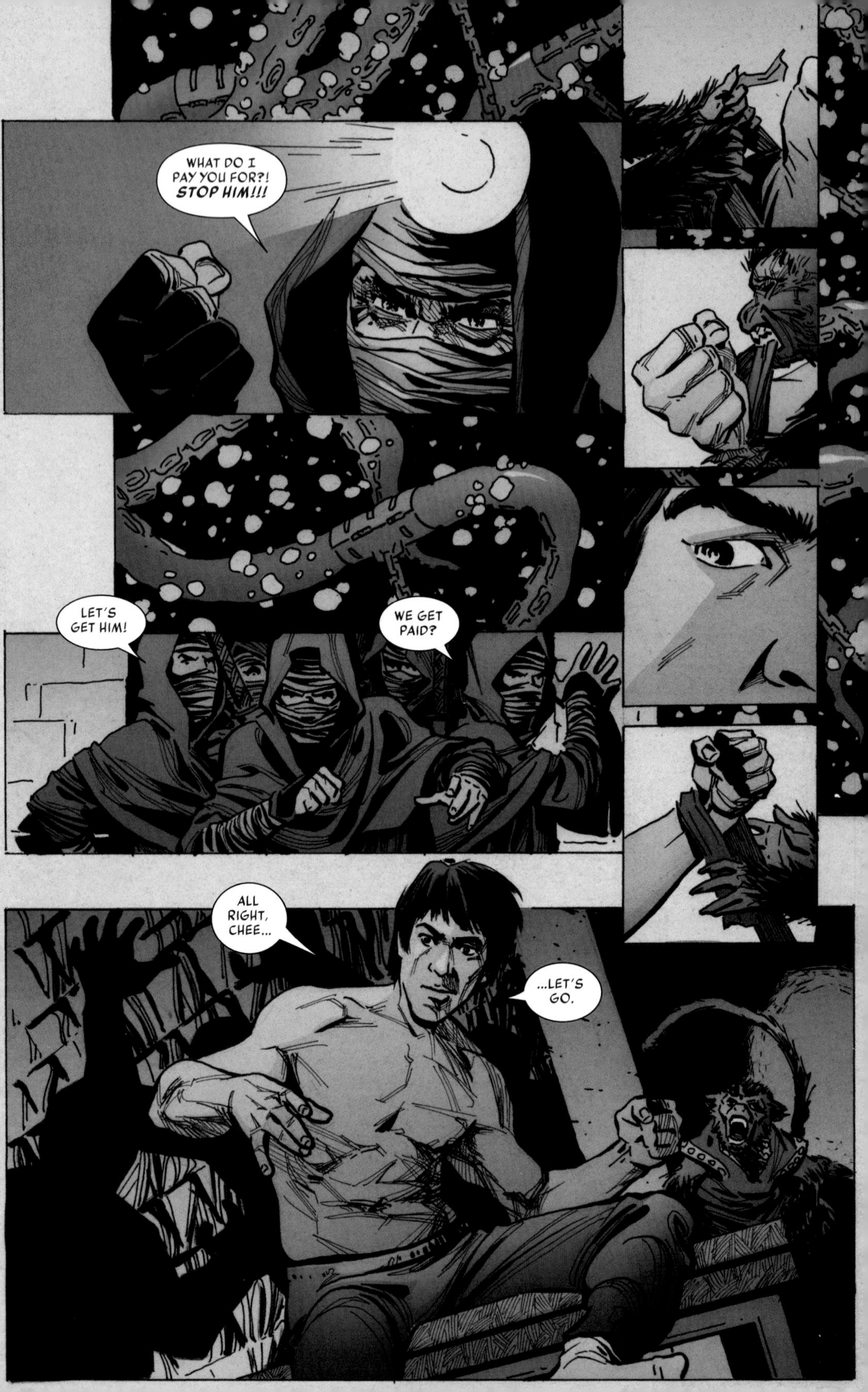
WHAT DO I PAY YOU FOR?! STOP HIM!!!
LET'S GET HIM!
WE GET PAID?
ALL RIGHT, CHEE...
...LET'S GO.

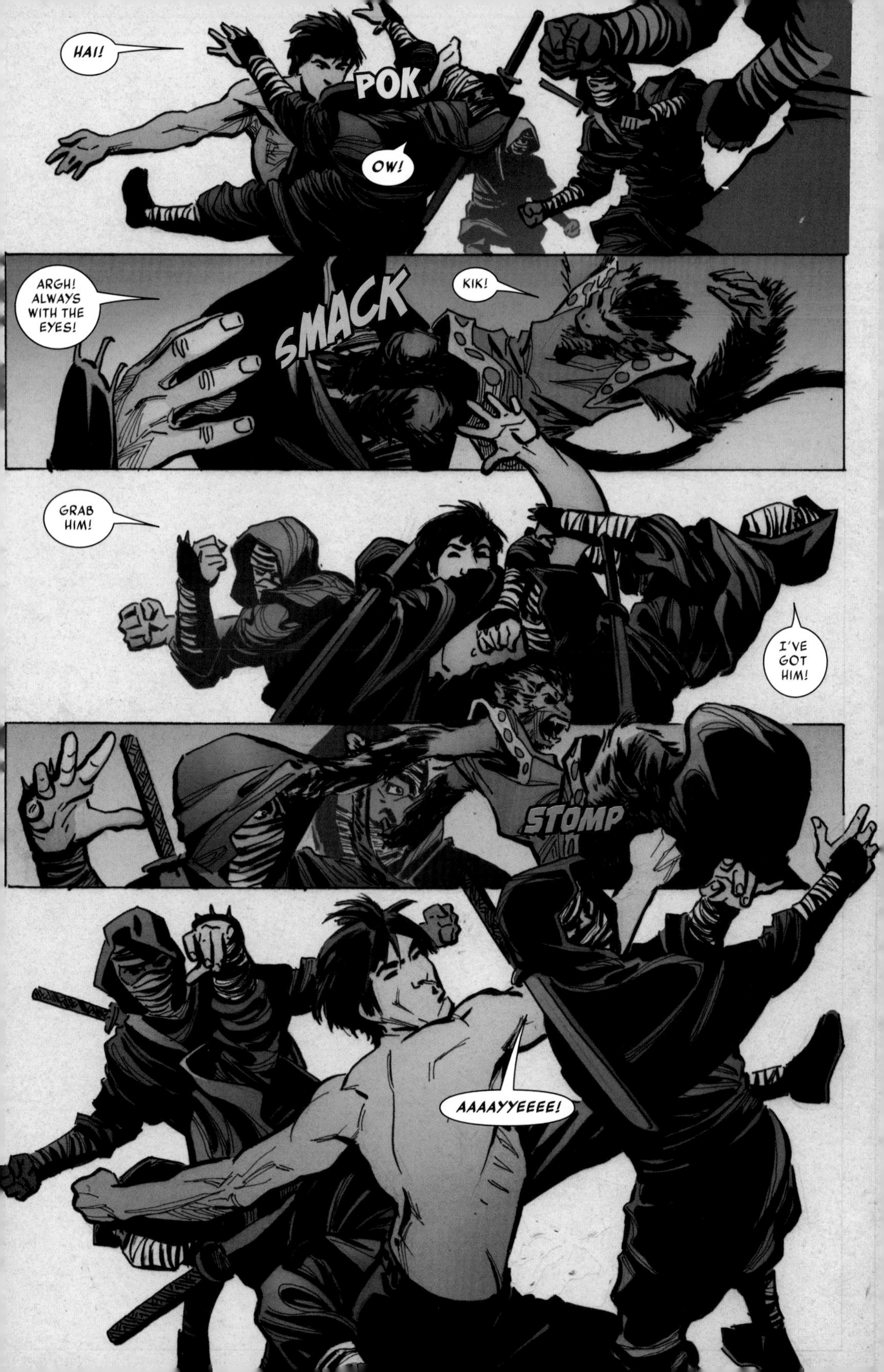
HAI!
POK
OW!
ARGH! ALWAYS WITH THE EYES!
SMACK
KIK!
GRAB HIM!
I'VE GOT HIM!
STOMP
AAAAYYEEEE!

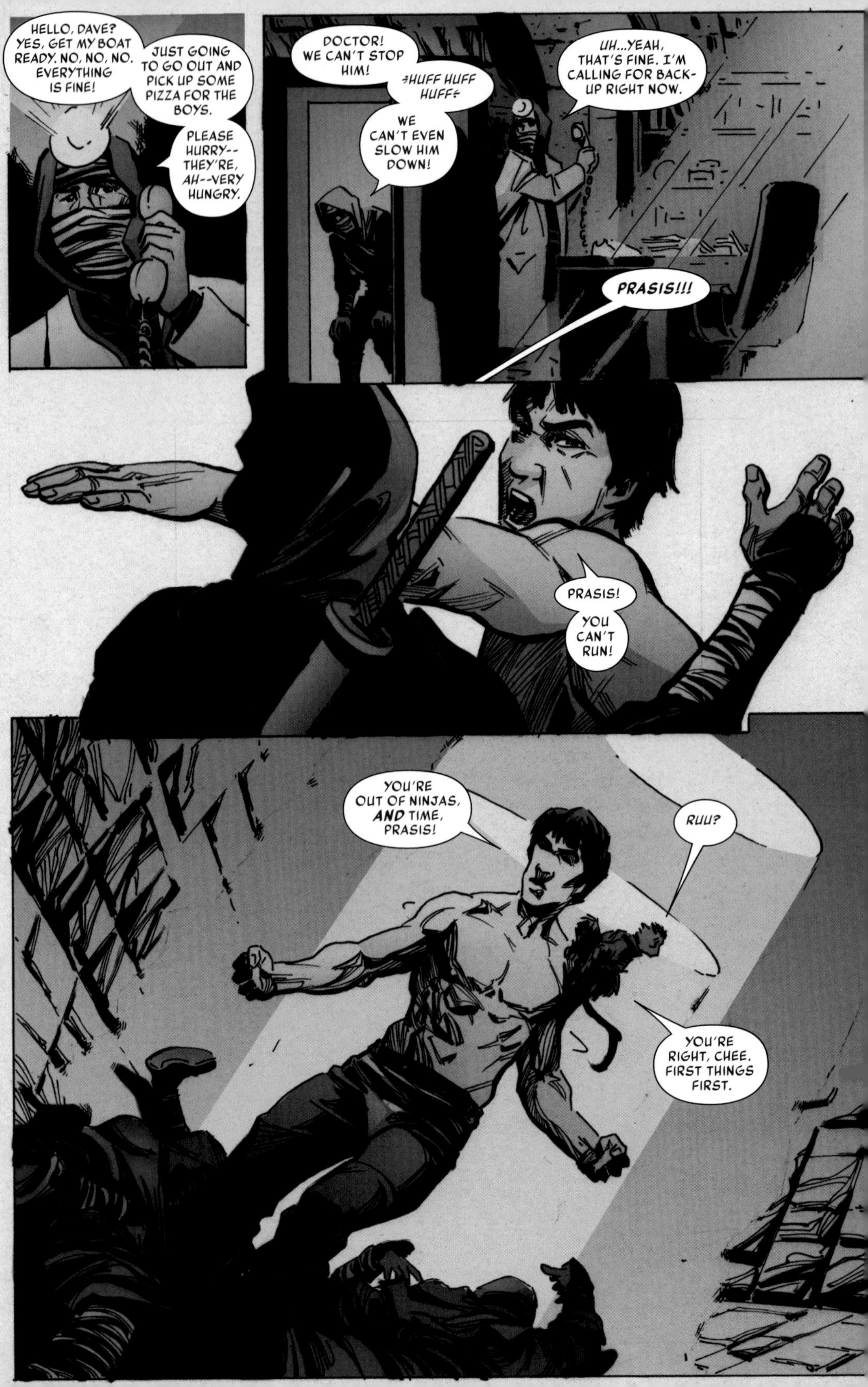
HELLO, DAVE? YES, GET MY BOAT READY. NO, NO, NO. EVERYTHING IS FINE!
JUST GOING TO GO OUT AND PICK UP SOME PIZZA FOR THE BOYS.
PLEASE HURRY-- THEY'RE, AH--VERY HUNGRY.
DOCTOR! WE CAN'T STOP HIM!
HUFF HUFF HUFF
WE CAN'T EVEN SLOW HIM DOWN!
UH...YEAH, THAT'S FINE. I'M CALLING FOR BACK-UP RIGHT NOW.
PRASIS!!!
PRASIS!
YOU CAN'T RUN!
YOU'RE OUT OF NINJAS, AND TIME, PRASIS!
RUU?
YOU'RE RIGHT, CHEE. FIRST THINGS FIRST.

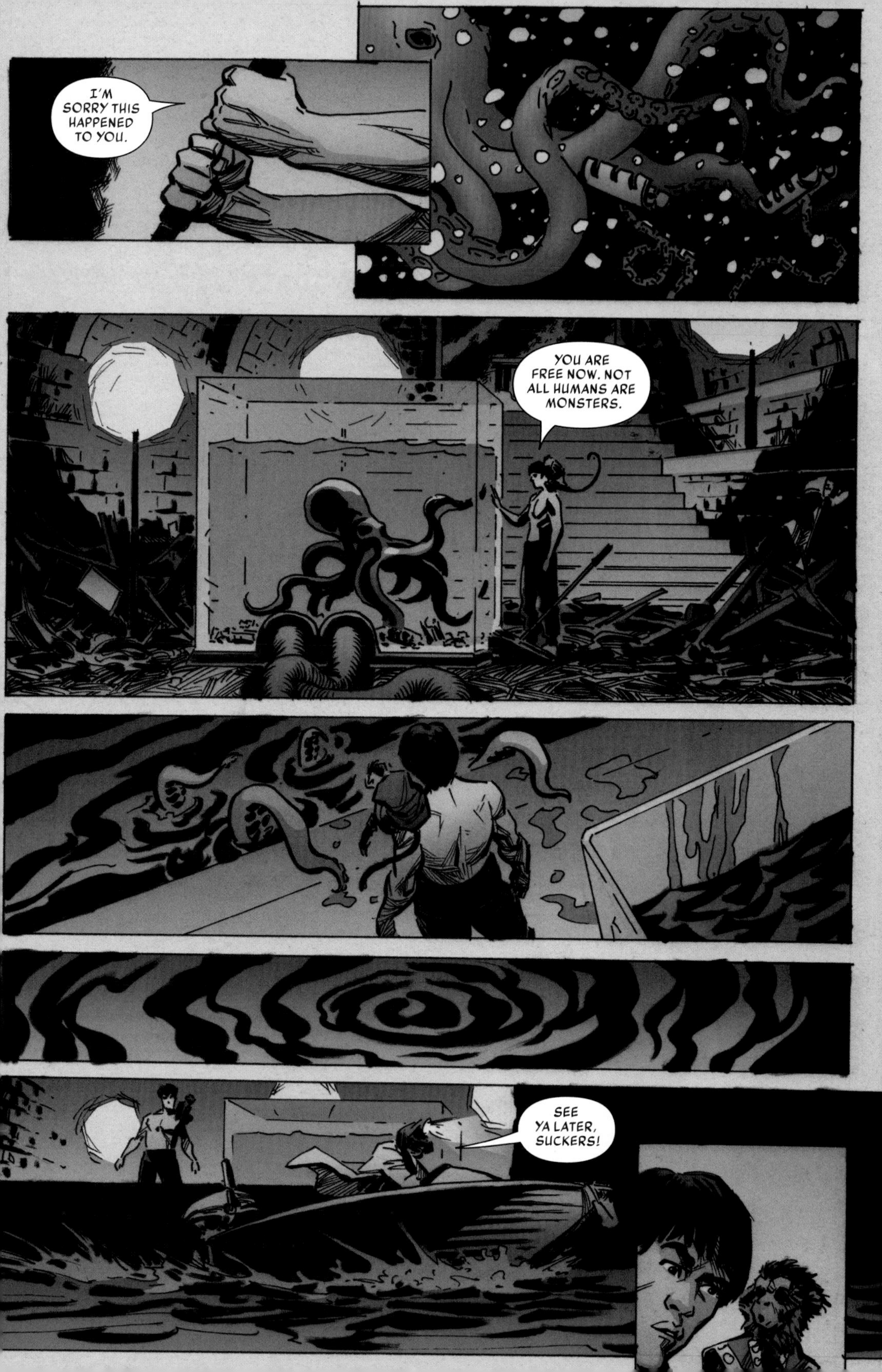
I'M SORRY THIS HAPPENED TO YOU.
YOU ARE FREE NOW. NOT ALL HUMANS ARE MONSTERS.
SEE YA LATER, SUCKERS!

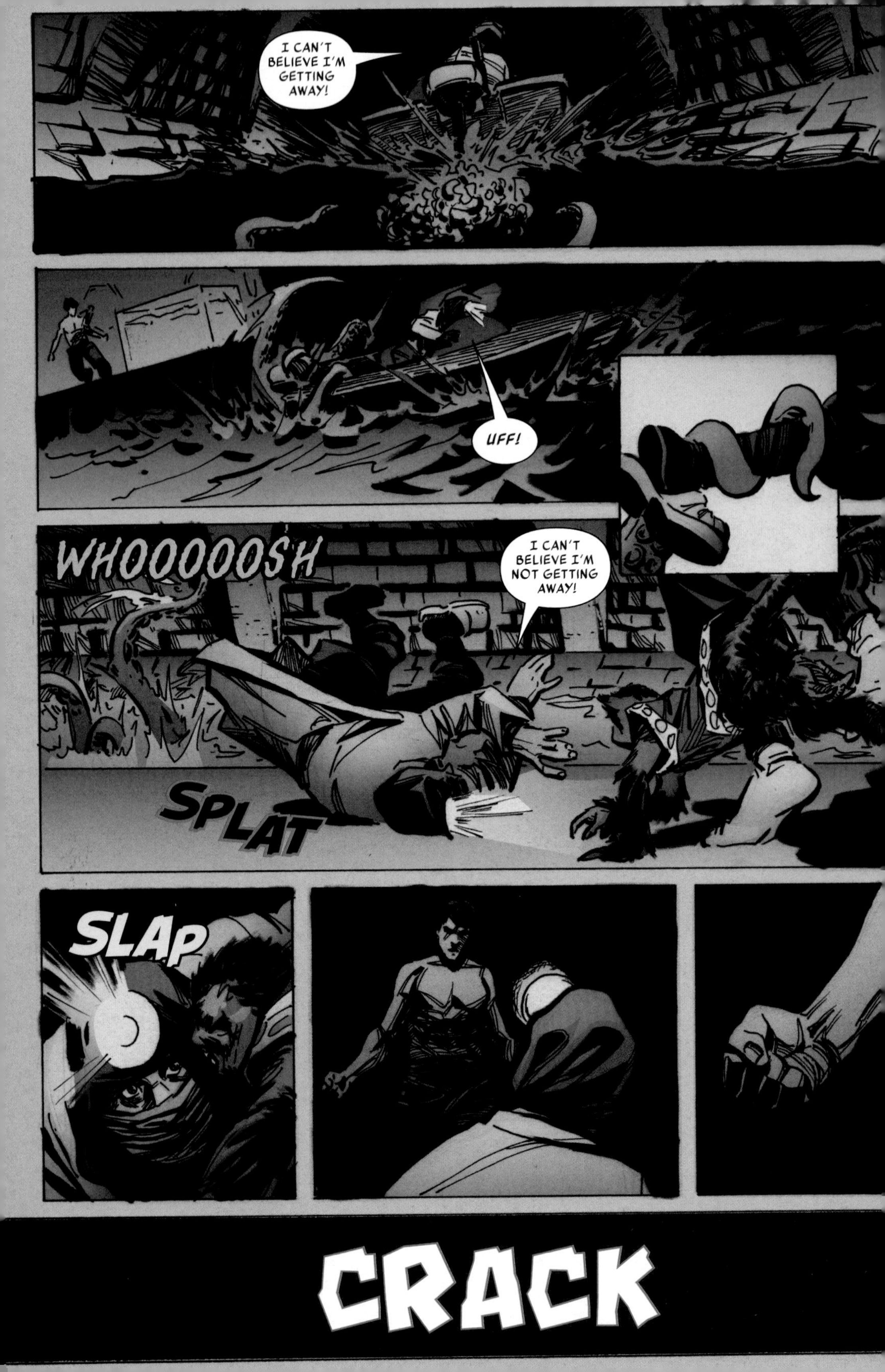
I CAN'T BELIEVE I'M GETTING AWAY!
UFF!
WHOOOOOOSH
I CAN'T BELIEVE I'M NOT GETTING AWAY!
SPLAT
SLAP
CRACK

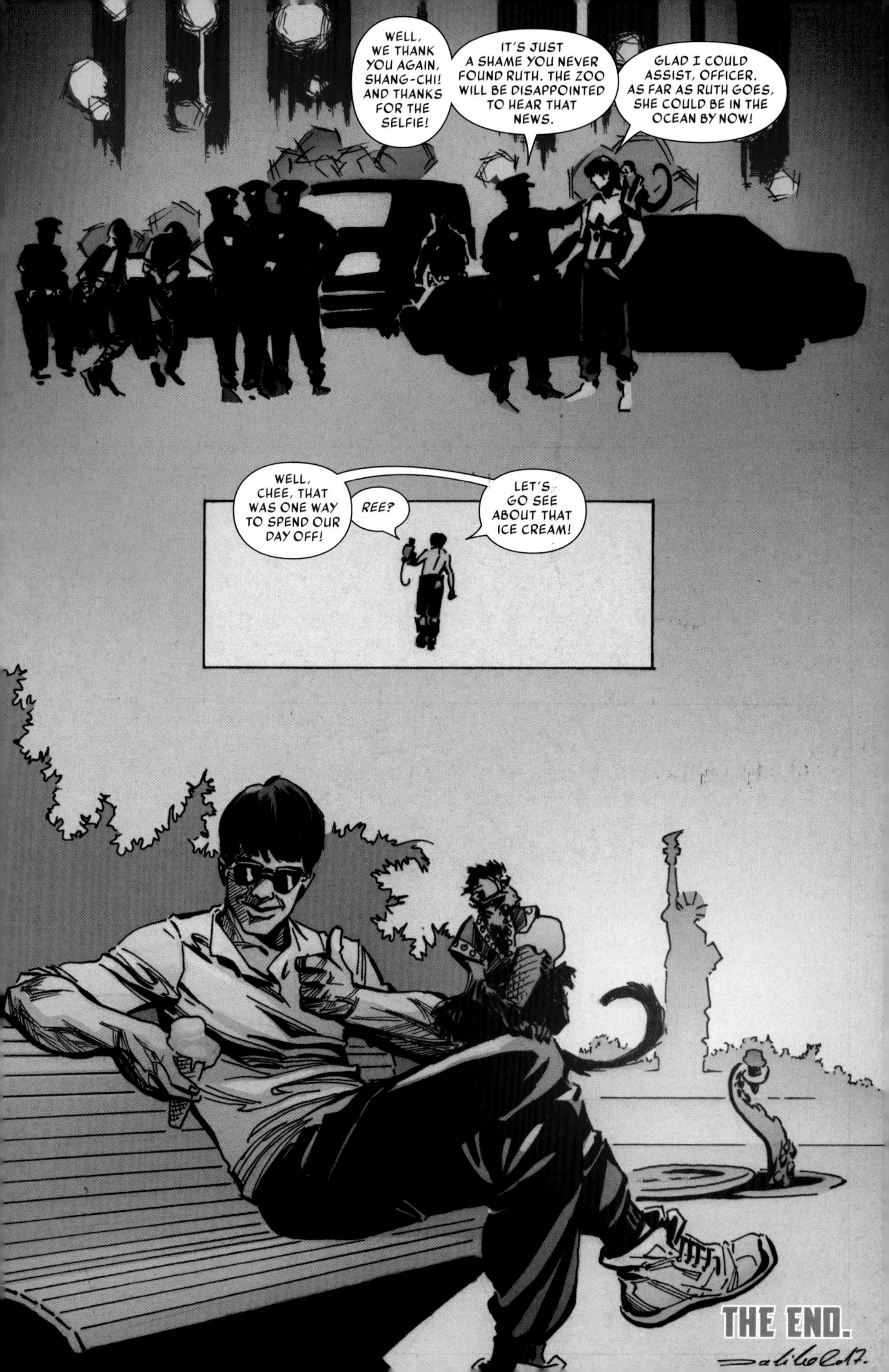
WELL, WE THANK YOU AGAIN, SHANG-CHI! AND THANKS FOR THE SELFIE!
IT'S JUST A SHAME YOU NEVER FOUND RUTH. THE ZOO WILL BE DISAPPOINTED TO HEAR THAT NEWS.
GLAD I COULD ASSIST, OFFICER. AS FAR AS RUTH GOES, SHE COULD BE IN THE OCEAN BY NOW!
WELL, CHEE, THAT WAS ONE WAY TO SPEND OUR DAY OFF!
REE?
LET'S GO SEE ABOUT THAT ICE CREAM!
THE END.

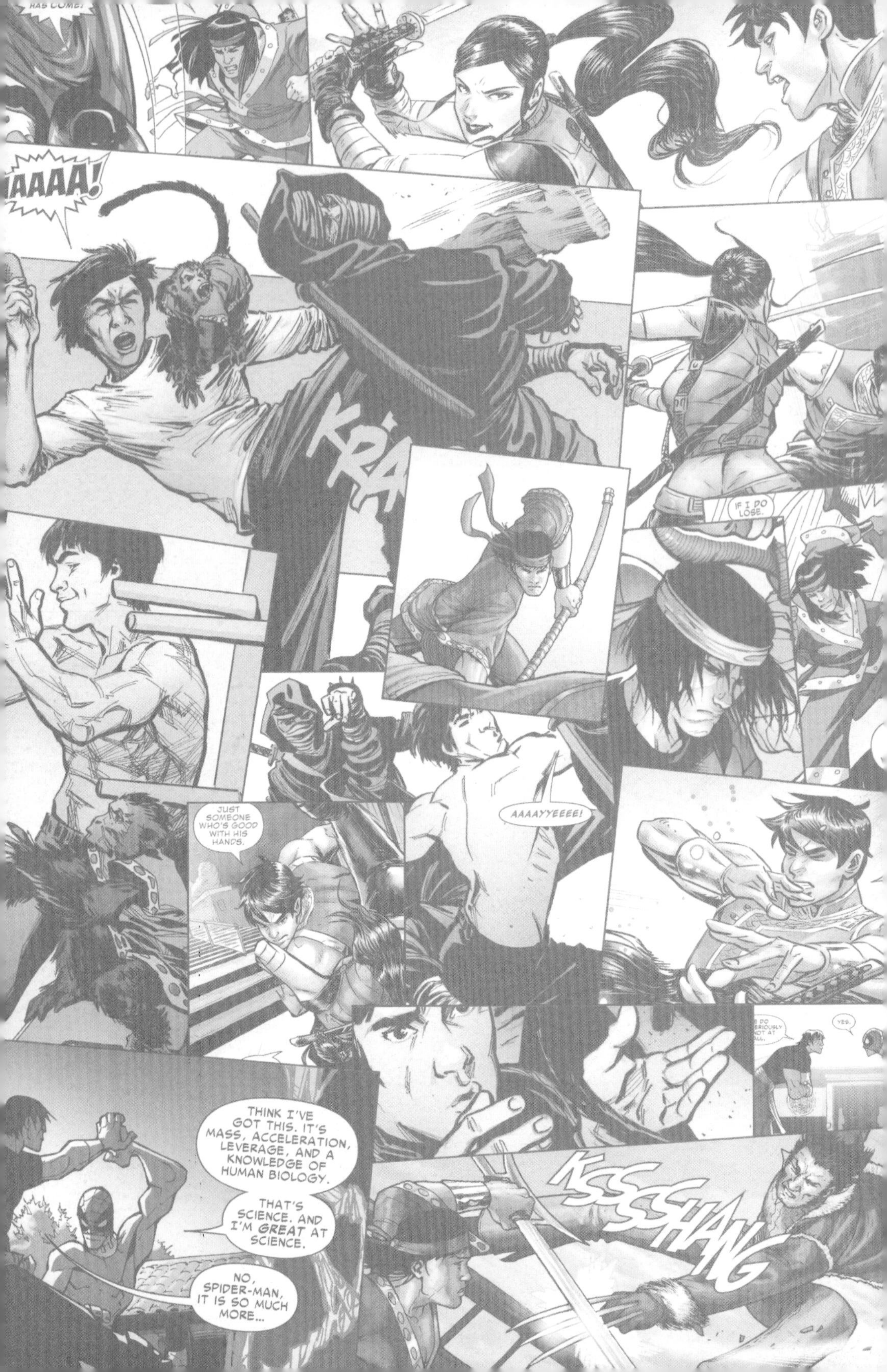
HAS COME!
AAAA!
KRA
IF I DO LOSE.
JUST SOMEONE WHO'S GOOD WITH HIS HANDS.
AAAAYYEEEE!
YES.
THINK I'VE GOT THIS. IT'S MASS, ACCELERATION, LEVERAGE, AND A KNOWLEDGE OF HUMAN BIOLOGY.
THAT'S SCIENCE. AND I'M GREAT AT SCIENCE.
NO, SPIDER-MAN, IT IS SO MUCH MORE...
KSSSHANG

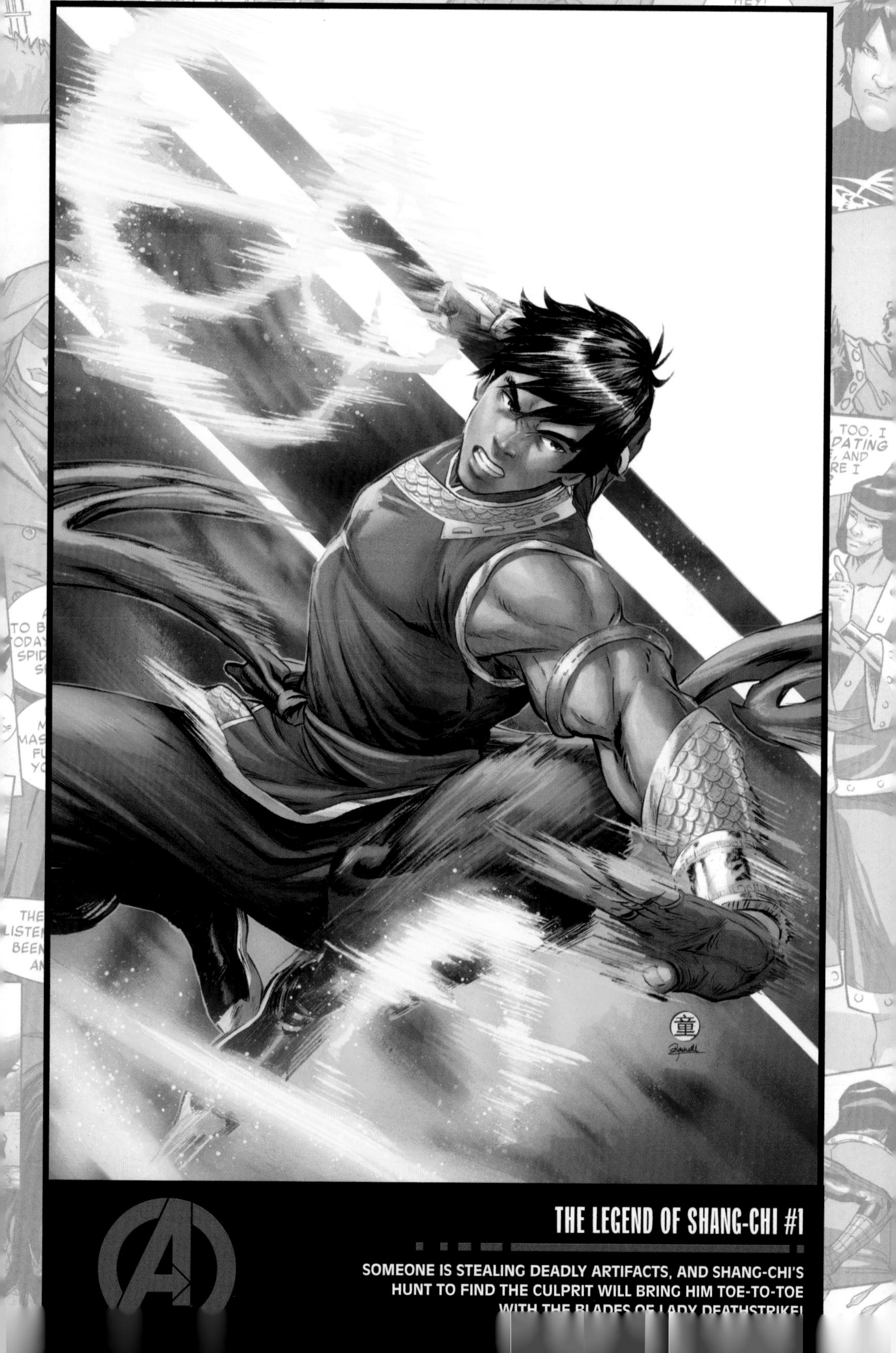

THE LEGEND OF SHANG-CHI #1

SOMEONE IS STEALING DEADLY ARTIFACTS, AND SHANG-CHI'S HUNT TO FIND THE CULPRIT WILL BRING HIM TOE-TO-TOE WITH THE BLADES OF LADY DEATHSTRIKE!

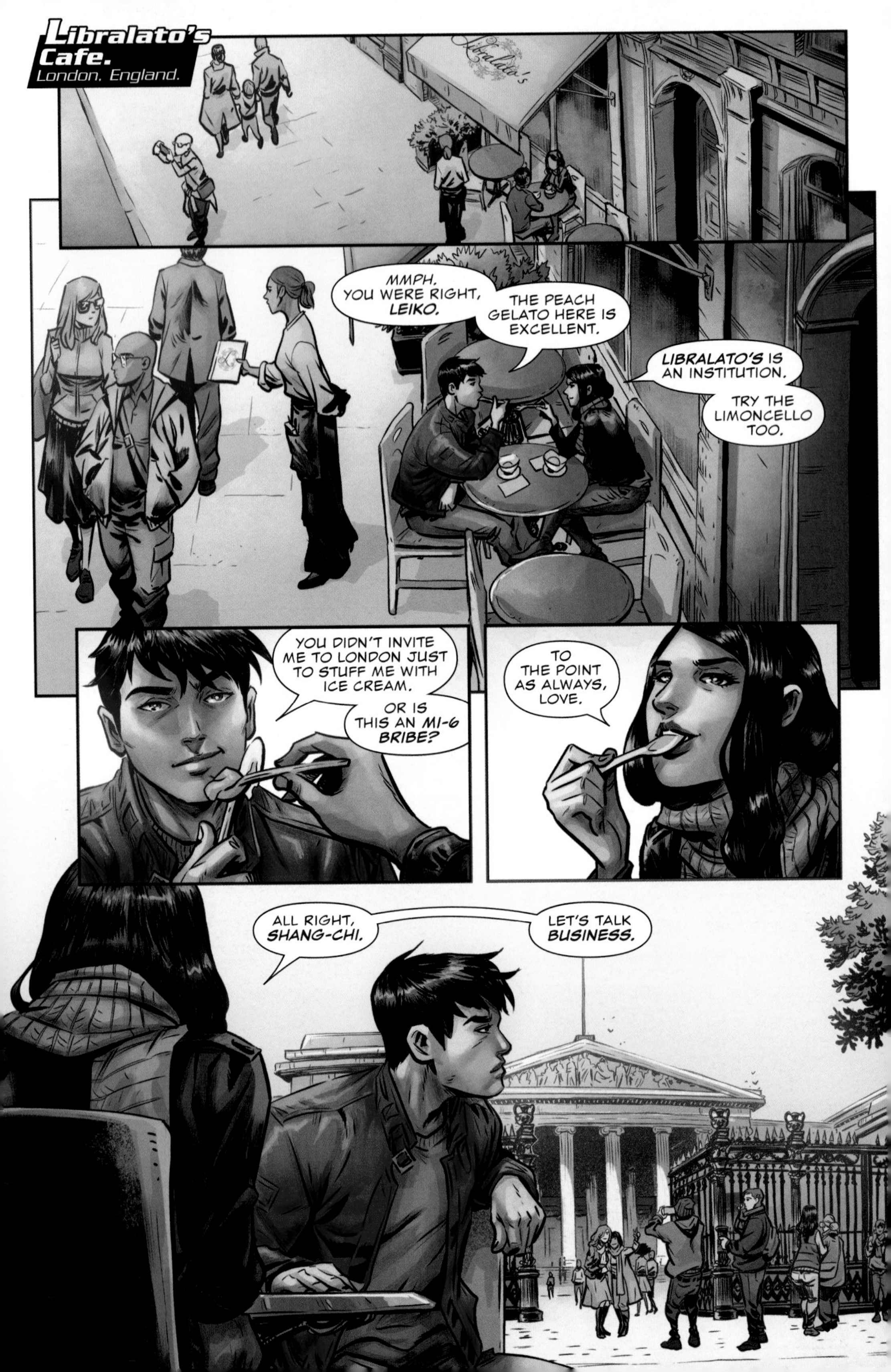
Libralato's Cafe.
London, England.
MMPH. YOU WERE RIGHT, LEIKO.
THE PEACH GELATO HERE IS EXCELLENT.
LIBRALATO'S IS AN INSTITUTION.
TRY THE LIMONCELLO TOO.
YOU DIDN'T INVITE ME TO LONDON JUST TO STUFF ME WITH ICE CREAM.
OR IS THIS AN MI-6 BRIBE?
TO THE POINT AS ALWAYS, LOVE.
ALL RIGHT, SHANG-CHI.
LET'S TALK BUSINESS.

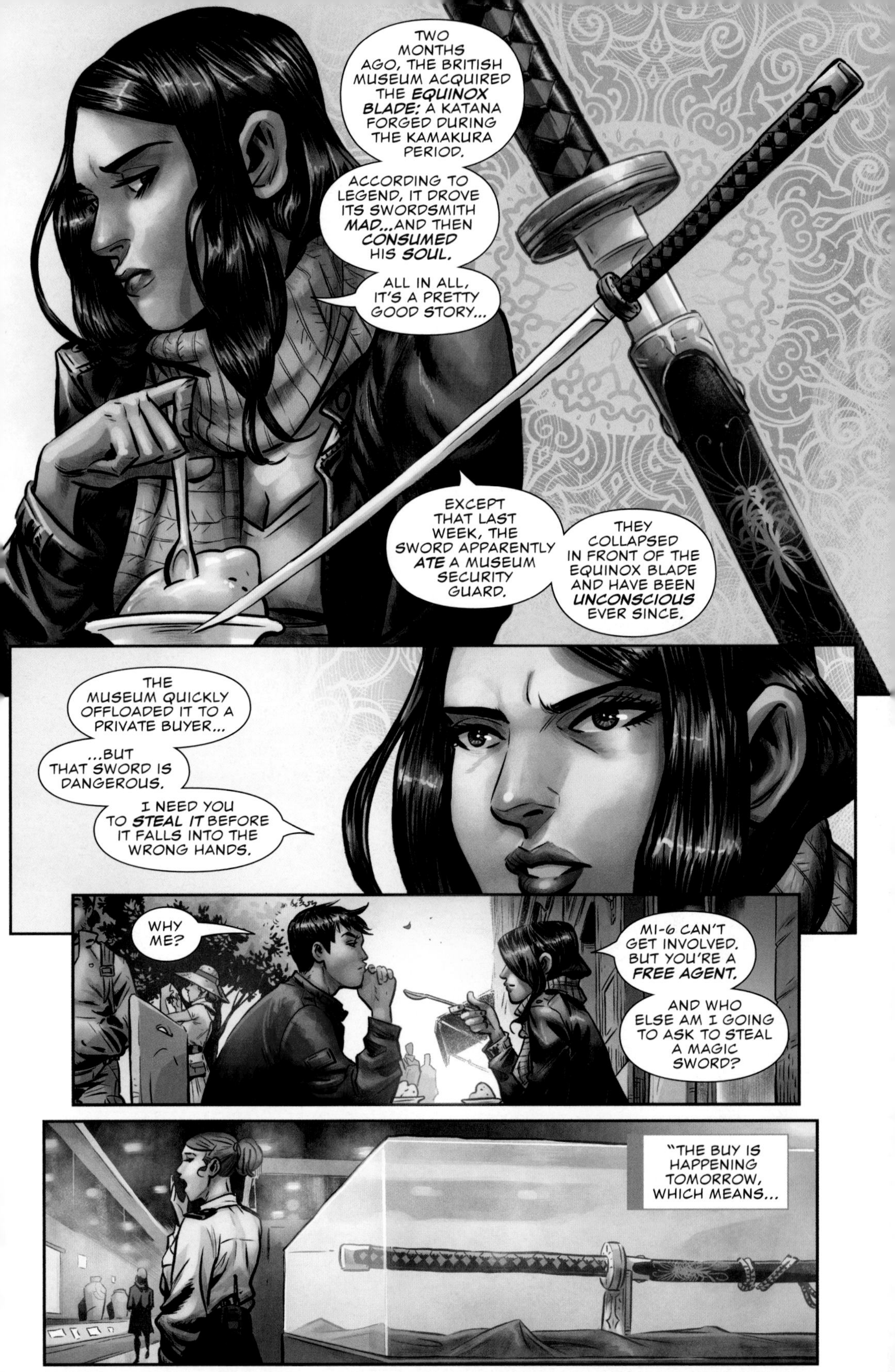
TWO MONTHS AGO, THE BRITISH MUSEUM ACQUIRED THE EQUINOX BLADE: A KATANA FORGED DURING THE KAMAKURA PERIOD.
ACCORDING TO LEGEND, IT DROVE ITS SWORDSMITH MAD...AND THEN CONSUMED HIS SOUL.
ALL IN ALL, IT'S A PRETTY GOOD STORY...
EXCEPT THAT LAST WEEK, THE SWORD APPARENTLY ATE A MUSEUM SECURITY GUARD.
THEY COLLAPSED IN FRONT OF THE EQUINOX BLADE AND HAVE BEEN UNCONSCIOUS EVER SINCE.
THE MUSEUM QUICKLY OFFLOADED IT TO A PRIVATE BUYER...
...BUT THAT SWORD IS DANGEROUS.
I NEED YOU TO STEAL IT BEFORE IT FALLS INTO THE WRONG HANDS.
WHY ME?
MI-6 CAN'T GET INVOLVED. BUT YOU'RE A FREE AGENT.
AND WHO ELSE AM I GOING TO ASK TO STEAL A MAGIC SWORD?
"THE BUY IS HAPPENING TOMORROW, WHICH MEANS...

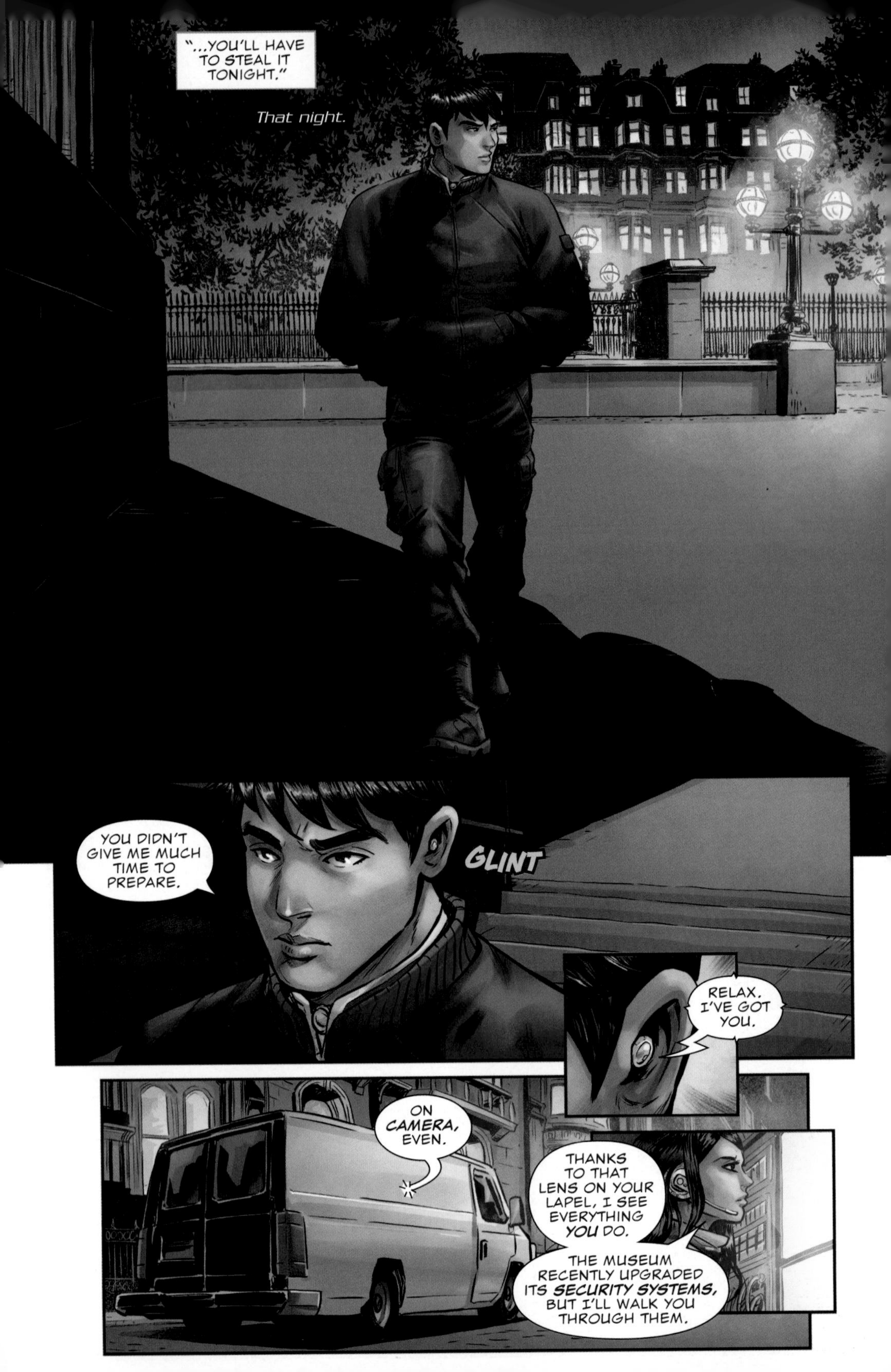
"...YOU'LL HAVE TO STEAL IT TONIGHT."
That night.
YOU DIDN'T GIVE ME MUCH TIME TO PREPARE.
GLINT
RELAX. I'VE GOT YOU.
ON CAMERA, EVEN.
THANKS TO THAT LENS ON YOUR LAPEL, I SEE EVERYTHING YOU DO.
THE MUSEUM RECENTLY UPGRADED ITS SECURITY SYSTEMS, BUT I'LL WALK YOU THROUGH THEM.

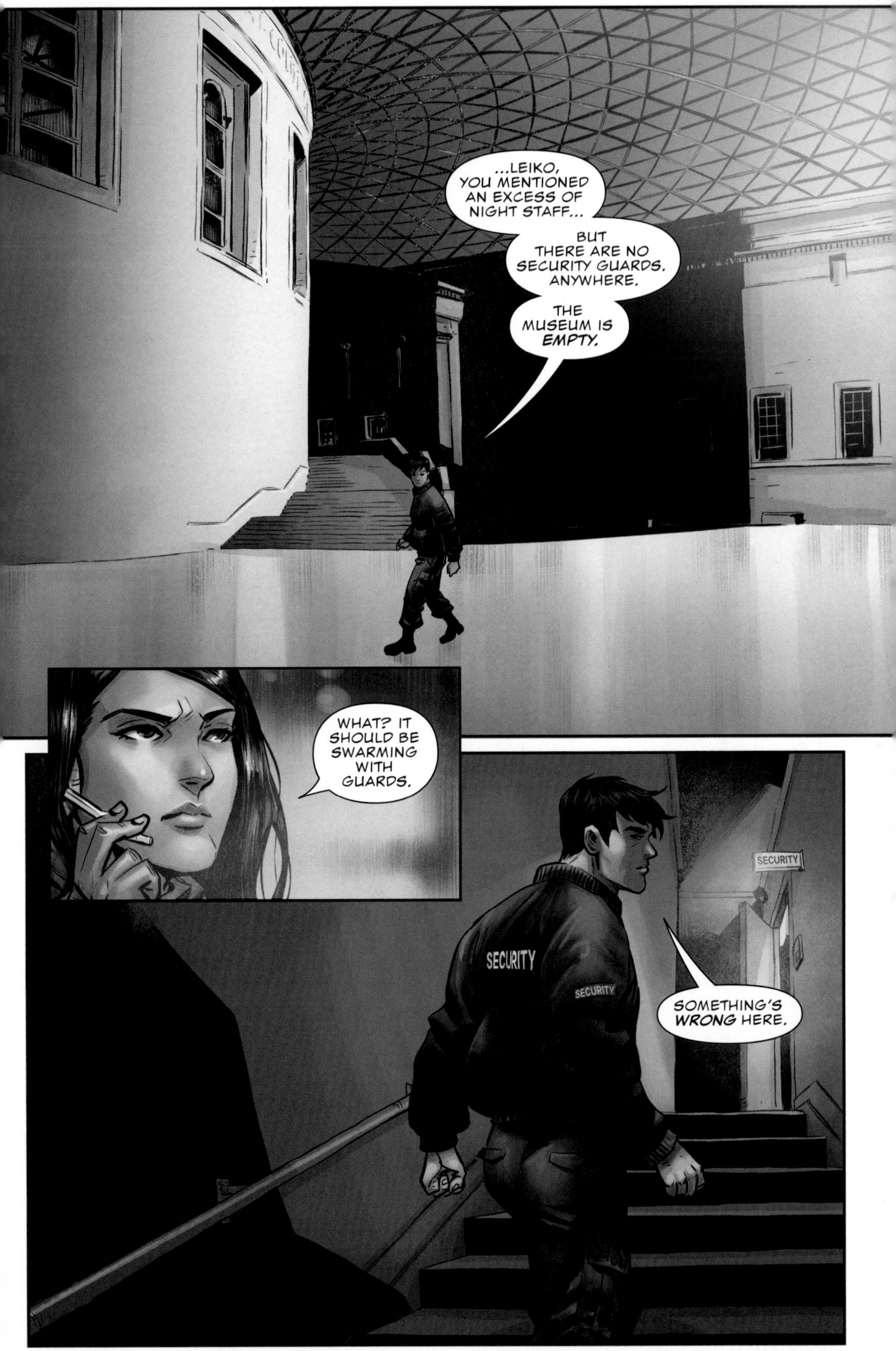
...LEIKO, YOU MENTIONED AN EXCESS OF NIGHT STAFF...
BUT THERE ARE NO SECURITY GUARDS. ANYWHERE.
THE MUSEUM IS *EMPTY.*
WHAT? IT SHOULD BE SWARMING WITH GUARDS.
SECURITY
SECURITY
SECURITY
SOMETHING'S *WRONG* HERE.

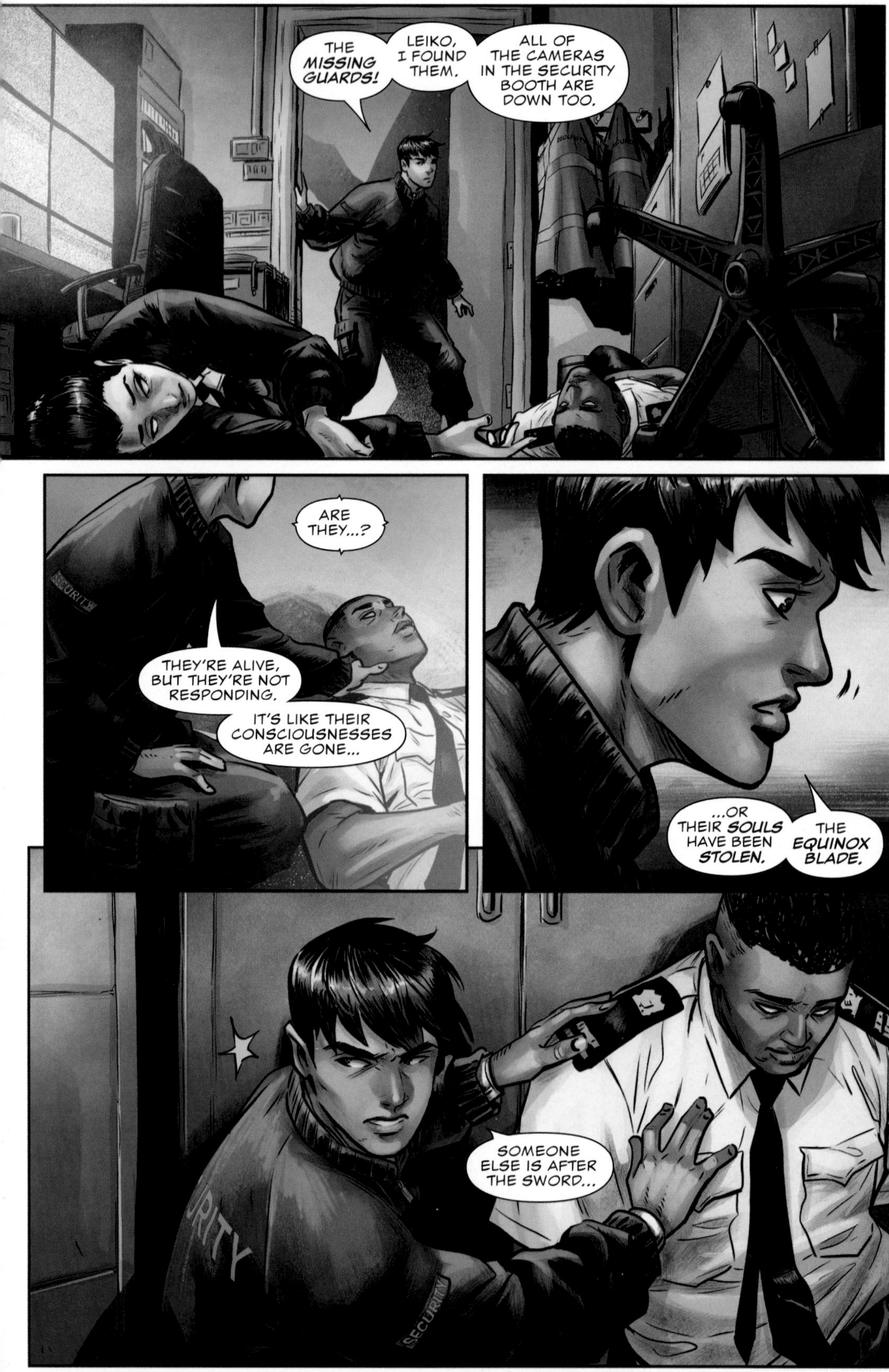
THE MISSING GUARDS!
LEIKO, I FOUND THEM.
ALL OF THE CAMERAS IN THE SECURITY BOOTH ARE DOWN TOO.
ARE THEY...?
THEY'RE ALIVE, BUT THEY'RE NOT RESPONDING.
IT'S LIKE THEIR CONSCIOUSNESSES ARE GONE...
...OR THEIR SOULS HAVE BEEN STOLEN.
THE EQUINOX BLADE.
SOMEONE ELSE IS AFTER THE SWORD...

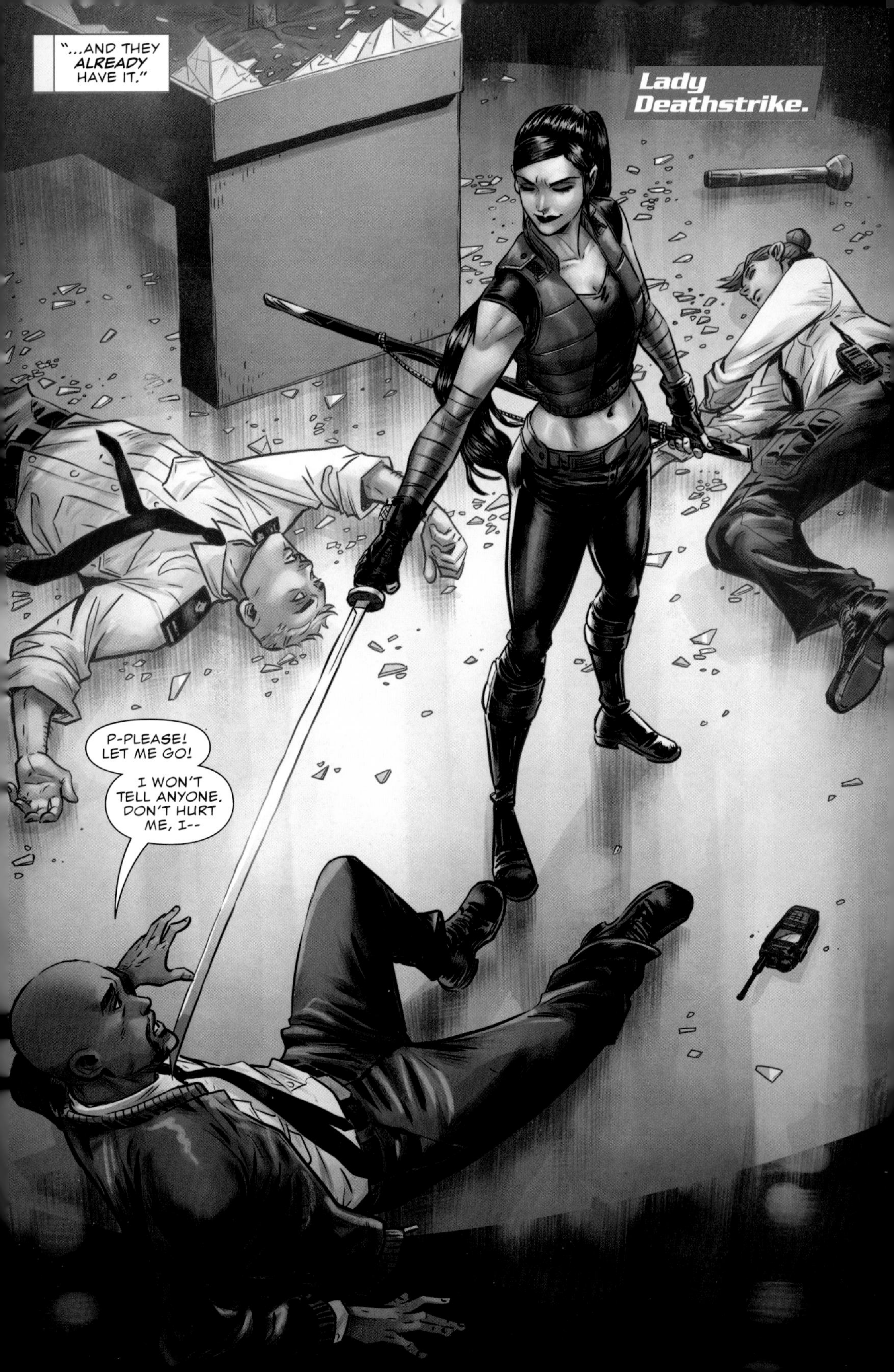
"...AND THEY ALREADY HAVE IT."
Lady Deathstrike.
P-PLEASE! LET ME GO!
I WON'T TELL ANYONE. DON'T HURT ME, I--

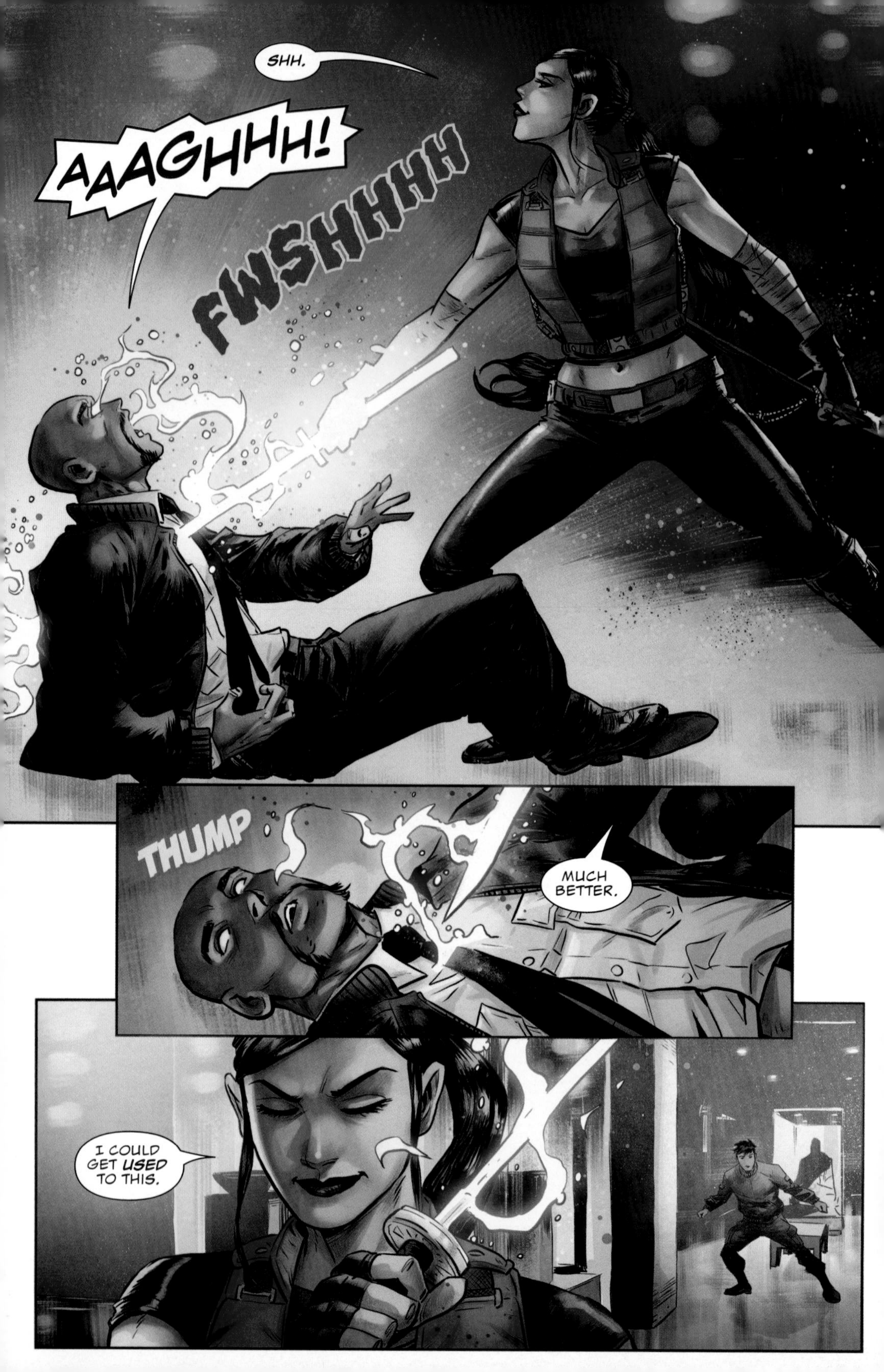
SHH.
AAAGHHH!
FWSHHHH
THUMP
MUCH BETTER.
I COULD GET USED TO THIS.

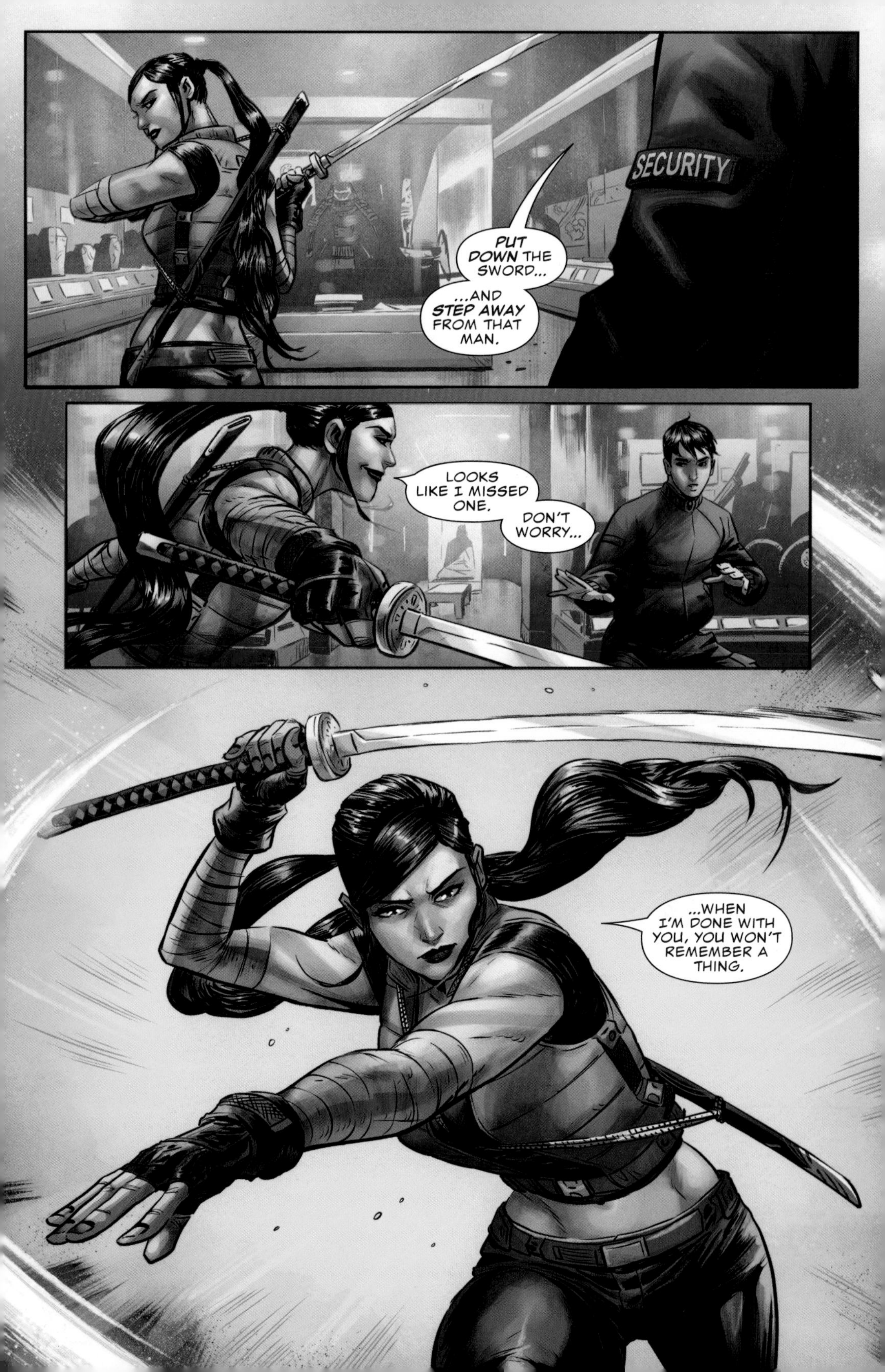
SECURITY
PUT DOWN THE SWORD...
...AND STEP AWAY FROM THAT MAN.
LOOKS LIKE I MISSED ONE.
DON'T WORRY...
...WHEN I'M DONE WITH YOU, YOU WON'T REMEMBER A THING.

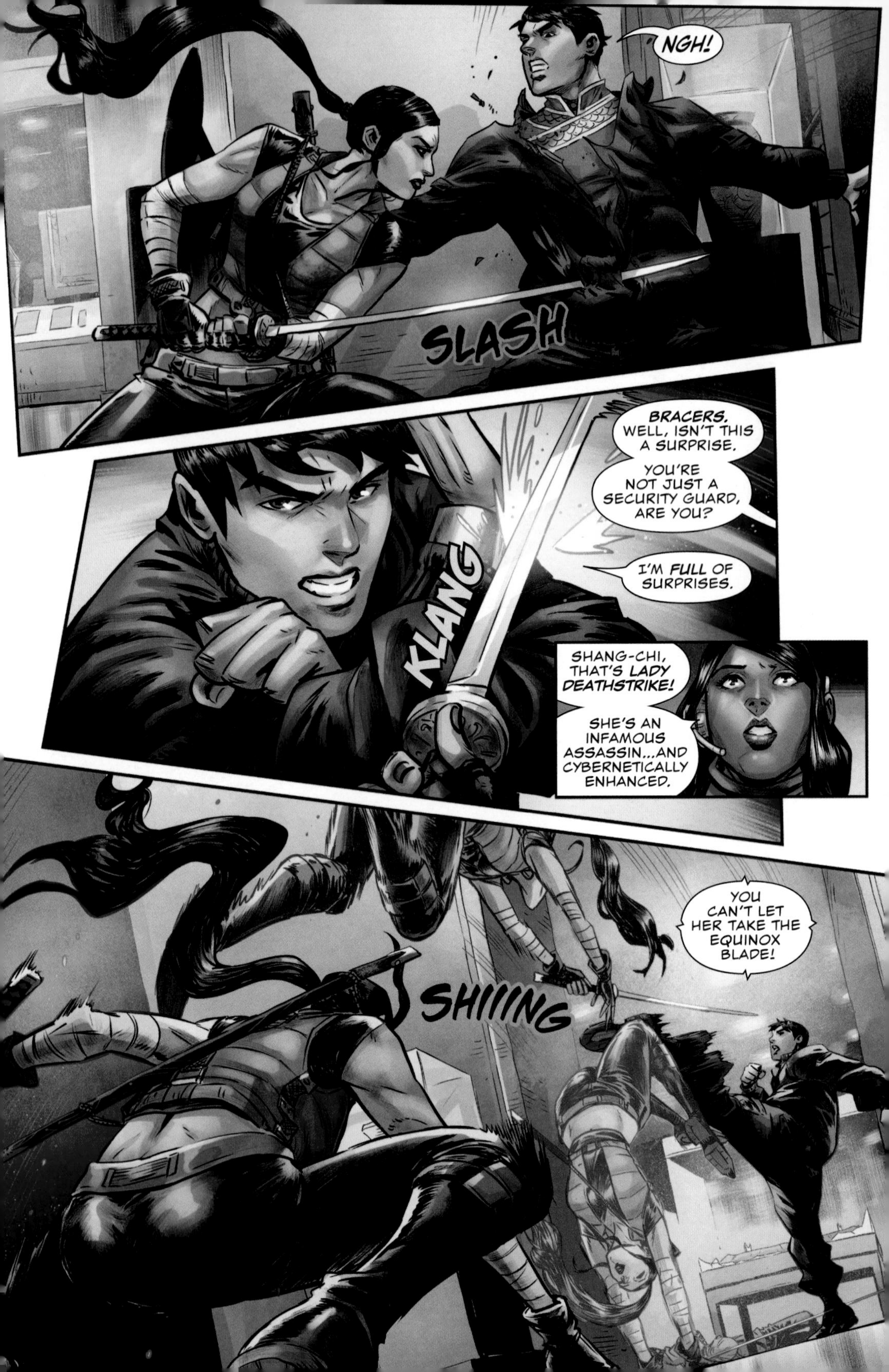
NGH!
SLASH
BRACERS. WELL, ISN'T THIS A SURPRISE.
YOU'RE NOT JUST A SECURITY GUARD, ARE YOU?
I'M FULL OF SURPRISES.
KLANG
SHANG-CHI, THAT'S LADY DEATHSTRIKE!
SHE'S AN INFAMOUS ASSASSIN...AND CYBERNETICALLY ENHANCED.
YOU CAN'T LET HER TAKE THE EQUINOX BLADE!
SHIIING

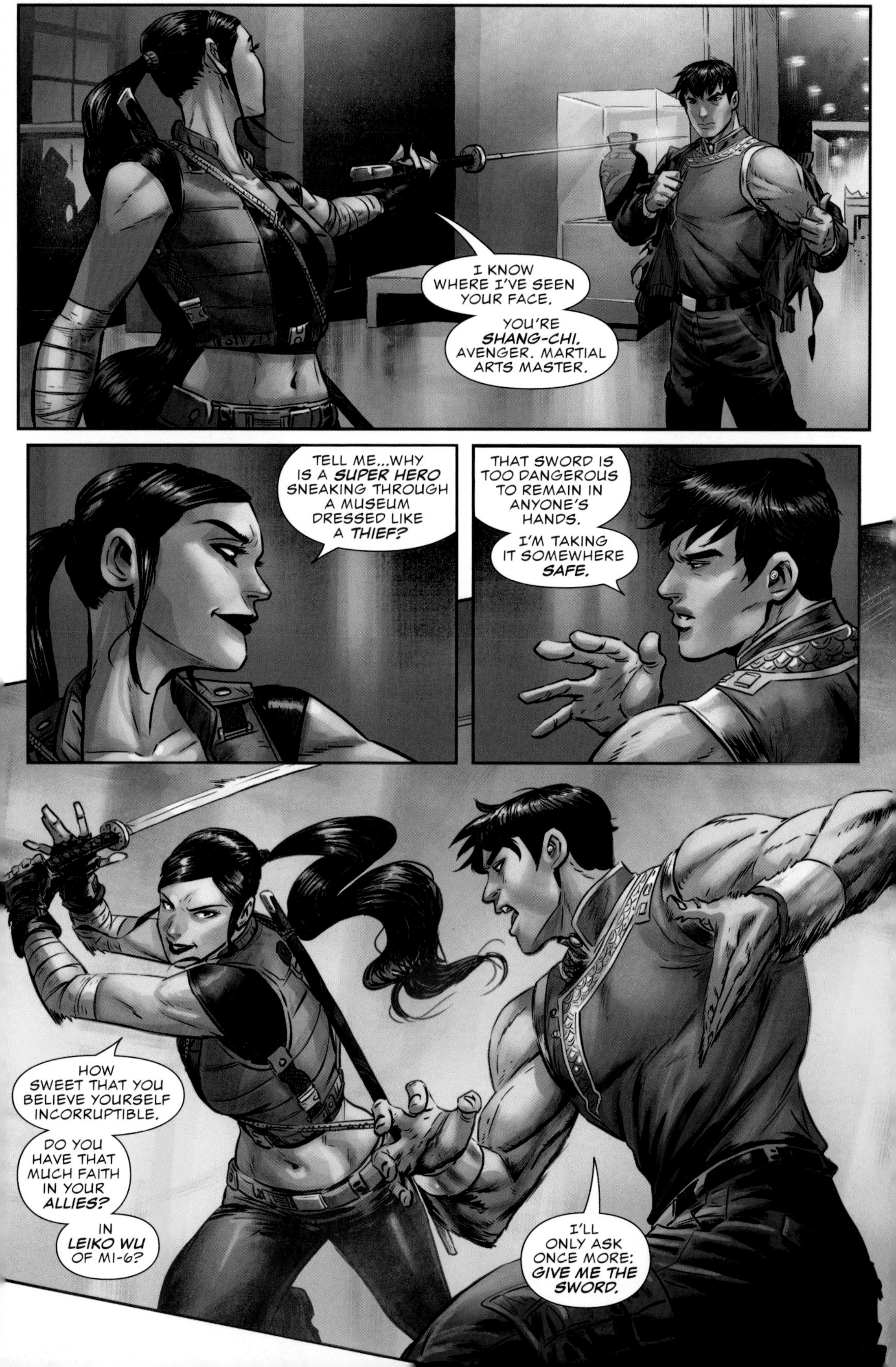
I KNOW WHERE I'VE SEEN YOUR FACE.
YOU'RE SHANG-CHI. AVENGER. MARTIAL ARTS MASTER.
TELL ME...WHY IS A SUPER HERO SNEAKING THROUGH A MUSEUM DRESSED LIKE A THIEF?
THAT SWORD IS TOO DANGEROUS TO REMAIN IN ANYONE'S HANDS.
I'M TAKING IT SOMEWHERE SAFE.
HOW SWEET THAT YOU BELIEVE YOURSELF INCORRUPTIBLE.
DO YOU HAVE THAT MUCH FAITH IN YOUR ALLIES?
IN LEIKO WU OF MI-6?
I'LL ONLY ASK ONCE MORE: GIVE ME THE SWORD.

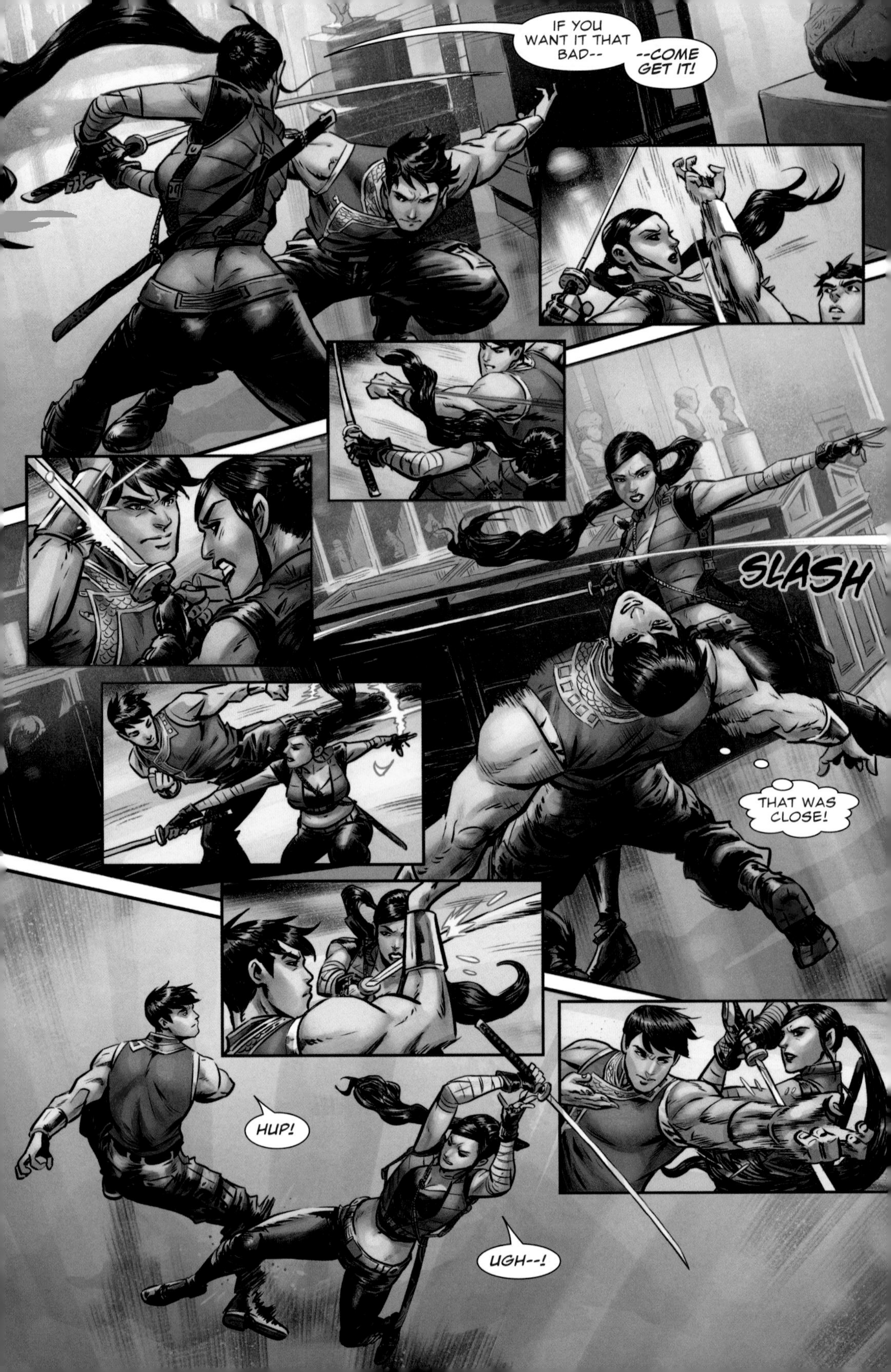
IF YOU WANT IT THAT BAD--
--COME GET IT!
SLASH
THAT WAS CLOSE!
HUP!
UGH--!

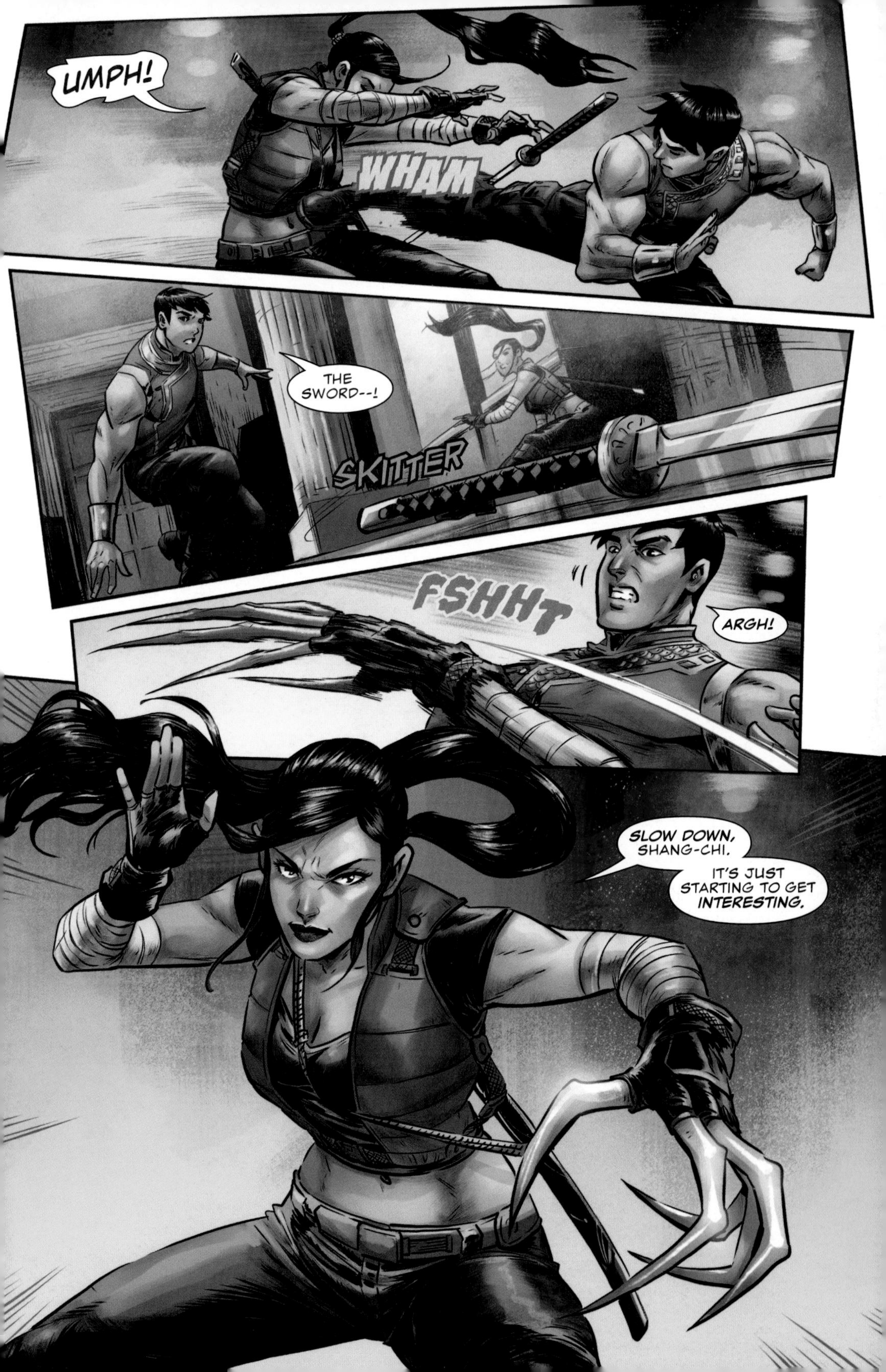
UMPH!
WHAM
THE SWORD--!
SKITTER
FSHHT
ARGH!
SLOW DOWN, SHANG-CHI.
IT'S JUST STARTING TO GET INTERESTING.

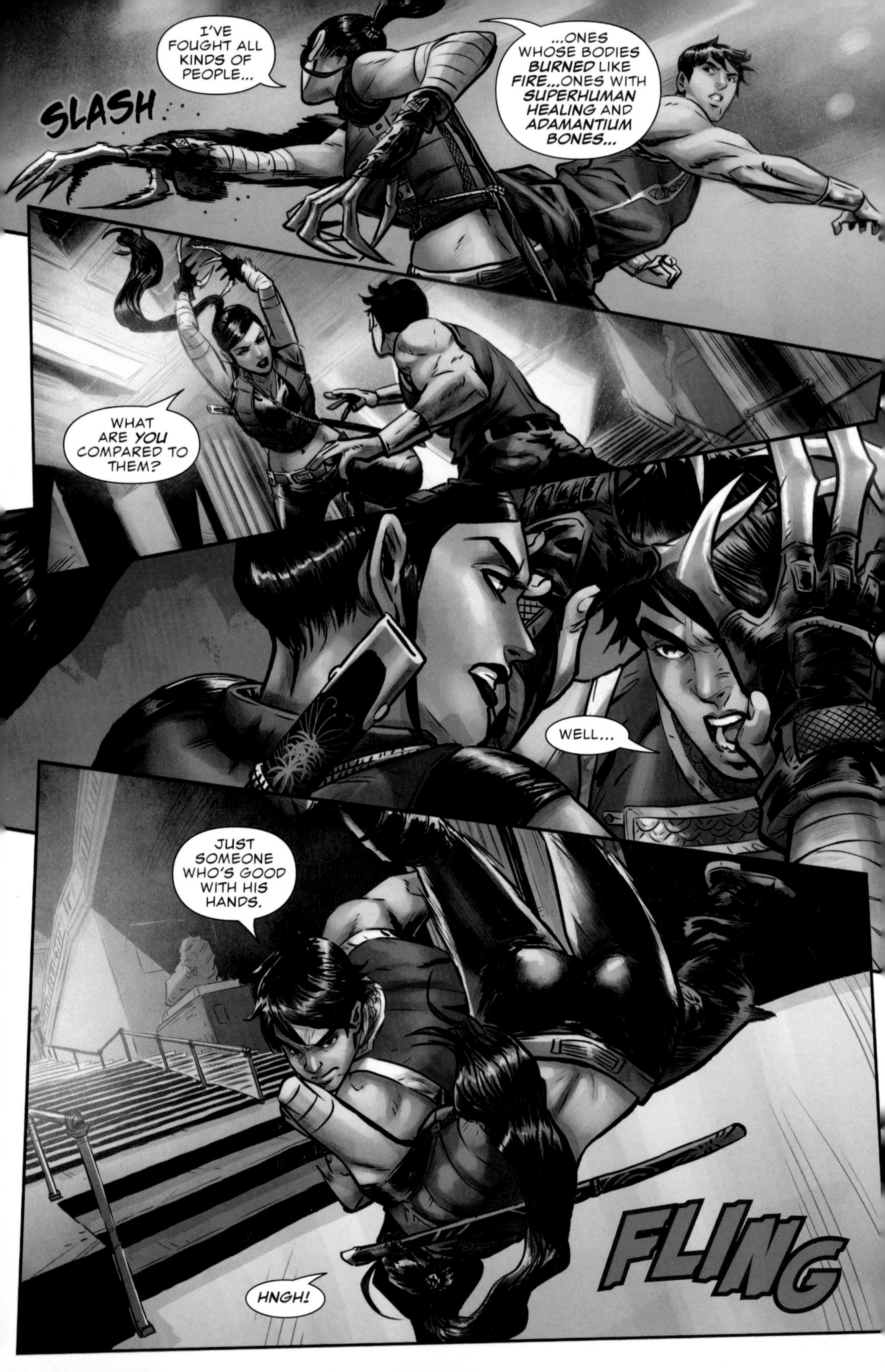
I'VE FOUGHT ALL KINDS OF PEOPLE...
SLASH
...ONES WHOSE BODIES BURNED LIKE FIRE...ONES WITH SUPERHUMAN HEALING AND ADAMANTIUM BONES...
WHAT ARE YOU COMPARED TO THEM?
WELL...
JUST SOMEONE WHO'S GOOD WITH HIS HANDS.
FLING
HNGH!

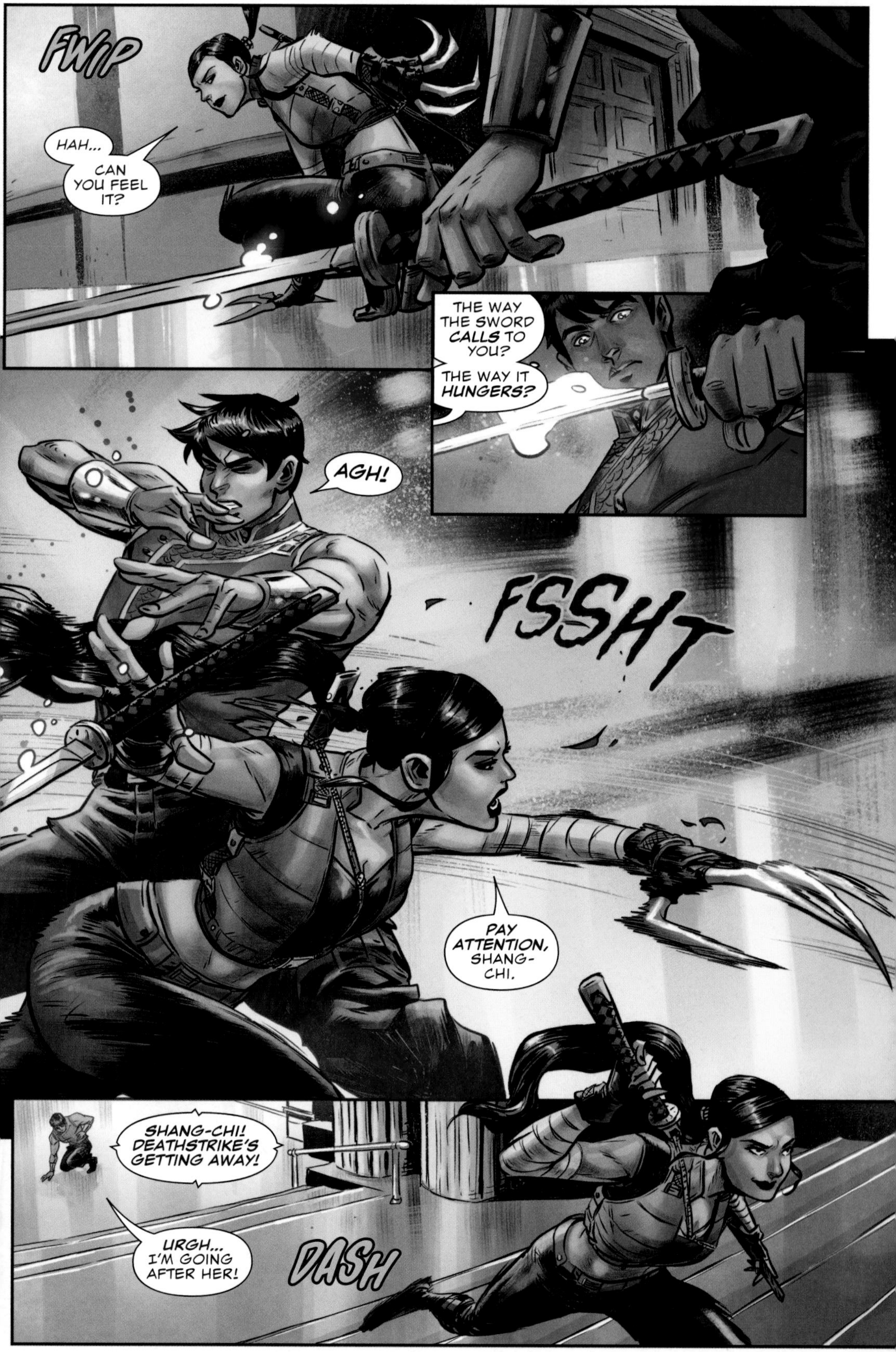
FWIP
HAH... CAN YOU FEEL IT?
THE WAY THE SWORD CALLS TO YOU?
THE WAY IT HUNGERS?
AGH!
FSSHT
PAY ATTENTION, SHANG-CHI.
SHANG-CHI! DEATHSTRIKE'S GETTING AWAY!
URGH... I'M GOING AFTER HER!
DASH

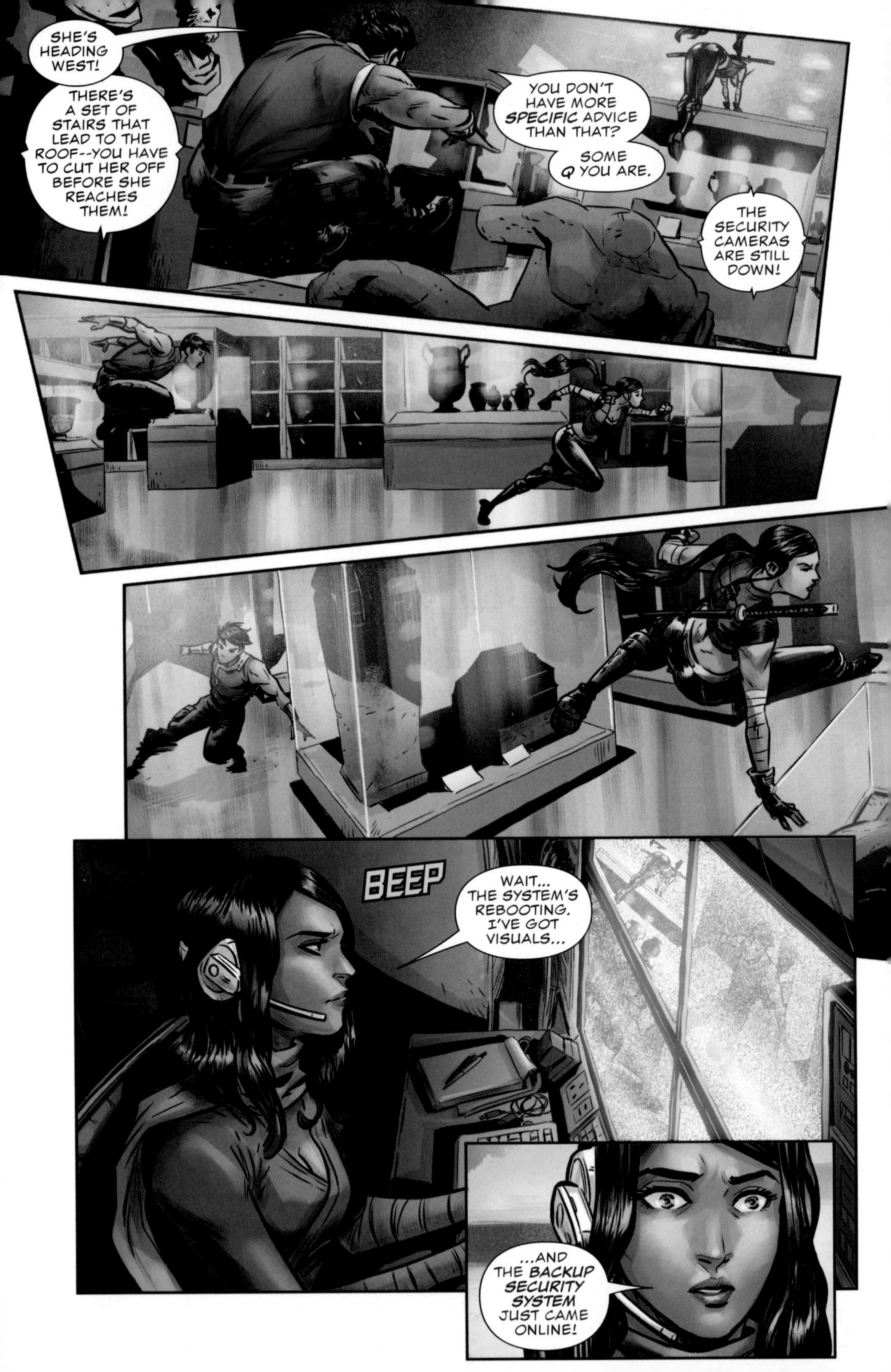
SHE'S HEADING WEST!
THERE'S A SET OF STAIRS THAT LEAD TO THE ROOF--YOU HAVE TO CUT HER OFF BEFORE SHE REACHES THEM!
YOU DON'T HAVE MORE SPECIFIC ADVICE THAN THAT?
SOME Q YOU ARE.
THE SECURITY CAMERAS ARE STILL DOWN!
BEEP
WAIT... THE SYSTEM'S REBOOTING. I'VE GOT VISUALS...
...AND THE BACKUP SECURITY SYSTEM JUST CAME ONLINE!

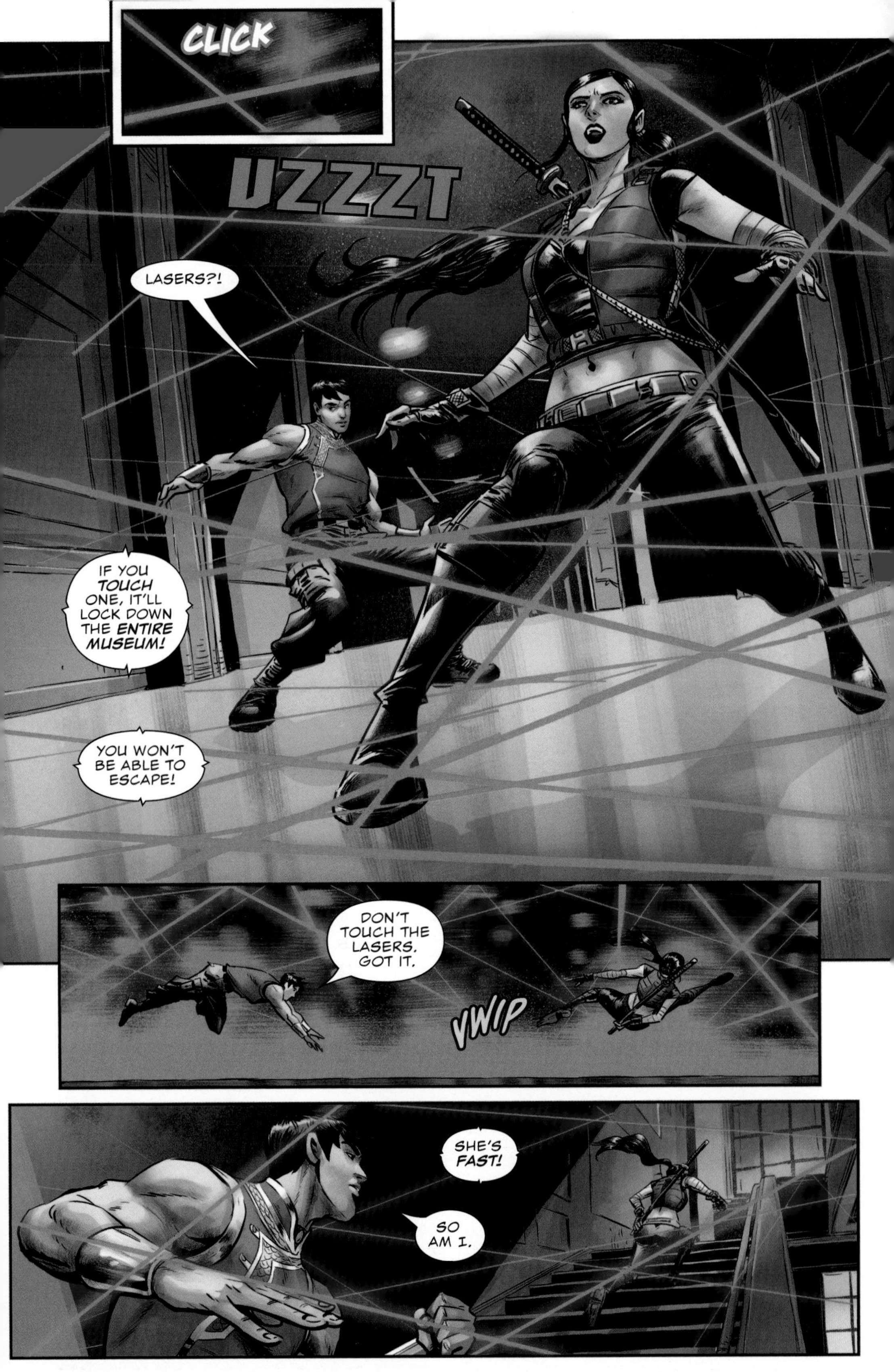
CLICK
UZZZT
LASERS?!
IF YOU TOUCH ONE, IT'LL LOCK DOWN THE ENTIRE MUSEUM!
YOU WON'T BE ABLE TO ESCAPE!
DON'T TOUCH THE LASERS. GOT IT.
VWIP
SHE'S FAST!
SO AM I.

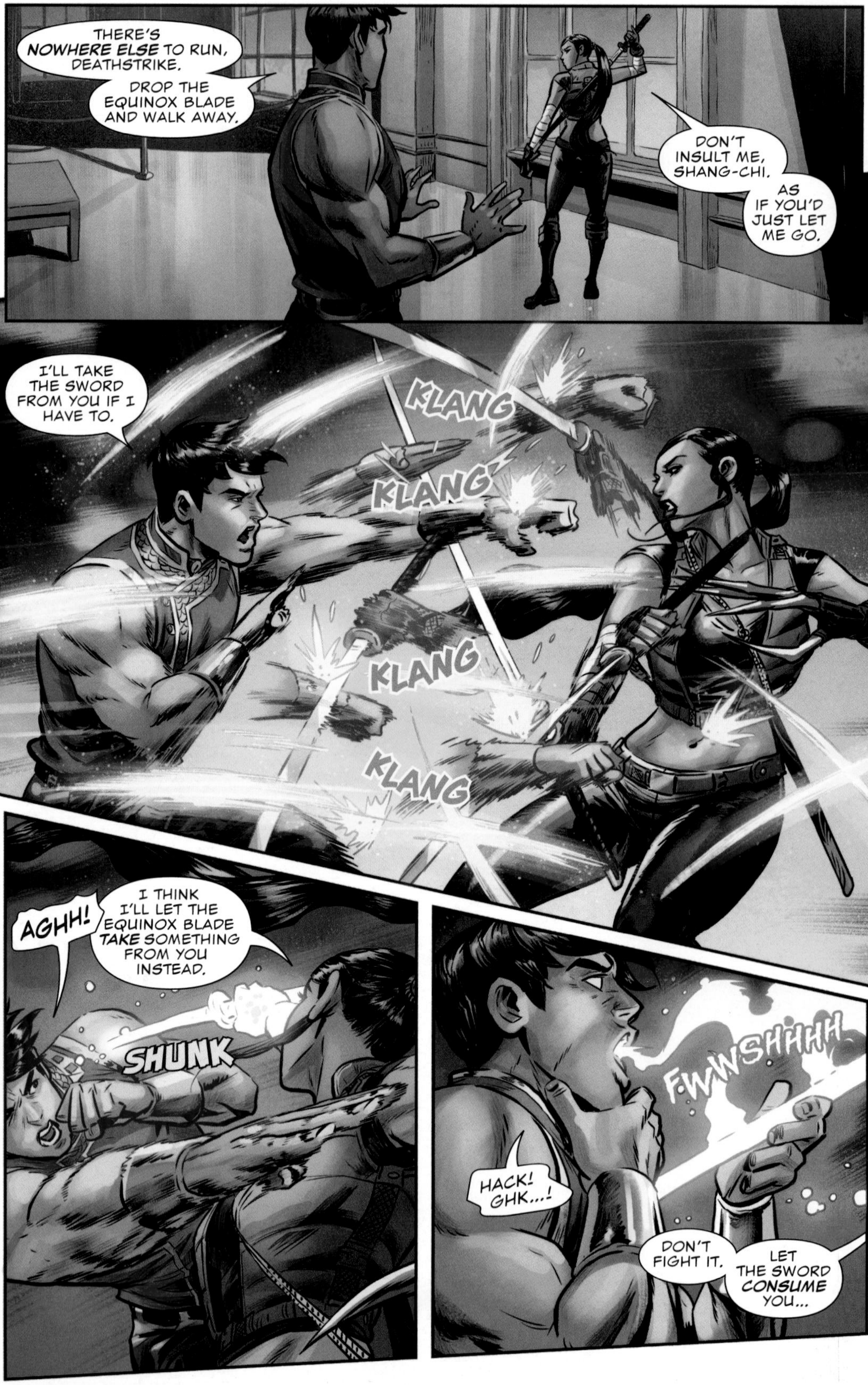
THERE'S NOWHERE ELSE TO RUN, DEATHSTRIKE.
DROP THE EQUINOX BLADE AND WALK AWAY.
DON'T INSULT ME, SHANG-CHI.
AS IF YOU'D JUST LET ME GO.
I'LL TAKE THE SWORD FROM YOU IF I HAVE TO.
KLANG
KLANG
KLANG
KLANG
AGHH!
I THINK I'LL LET THE EQUINOX BLADE TAKE SOMETHING FROM YOU INSTEAD.
SHUNK
FWWSHHHH
HACK! GHK...!
DON'T FIGHT IT.
LET THE SWORD CONSUME YOU...

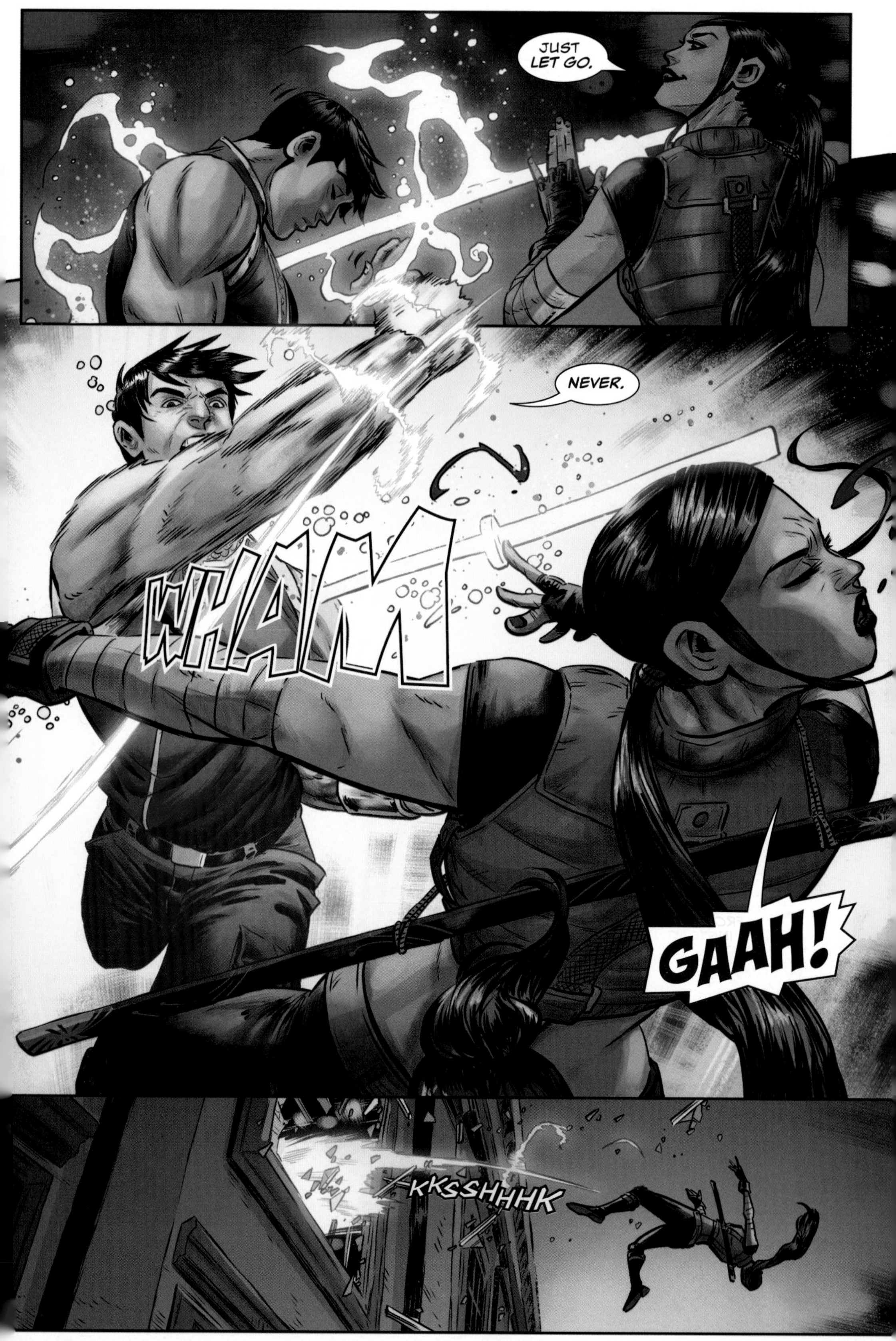
JUST LET GO.
NEVER.
WHAM
GAAH!
KKSSHHHK

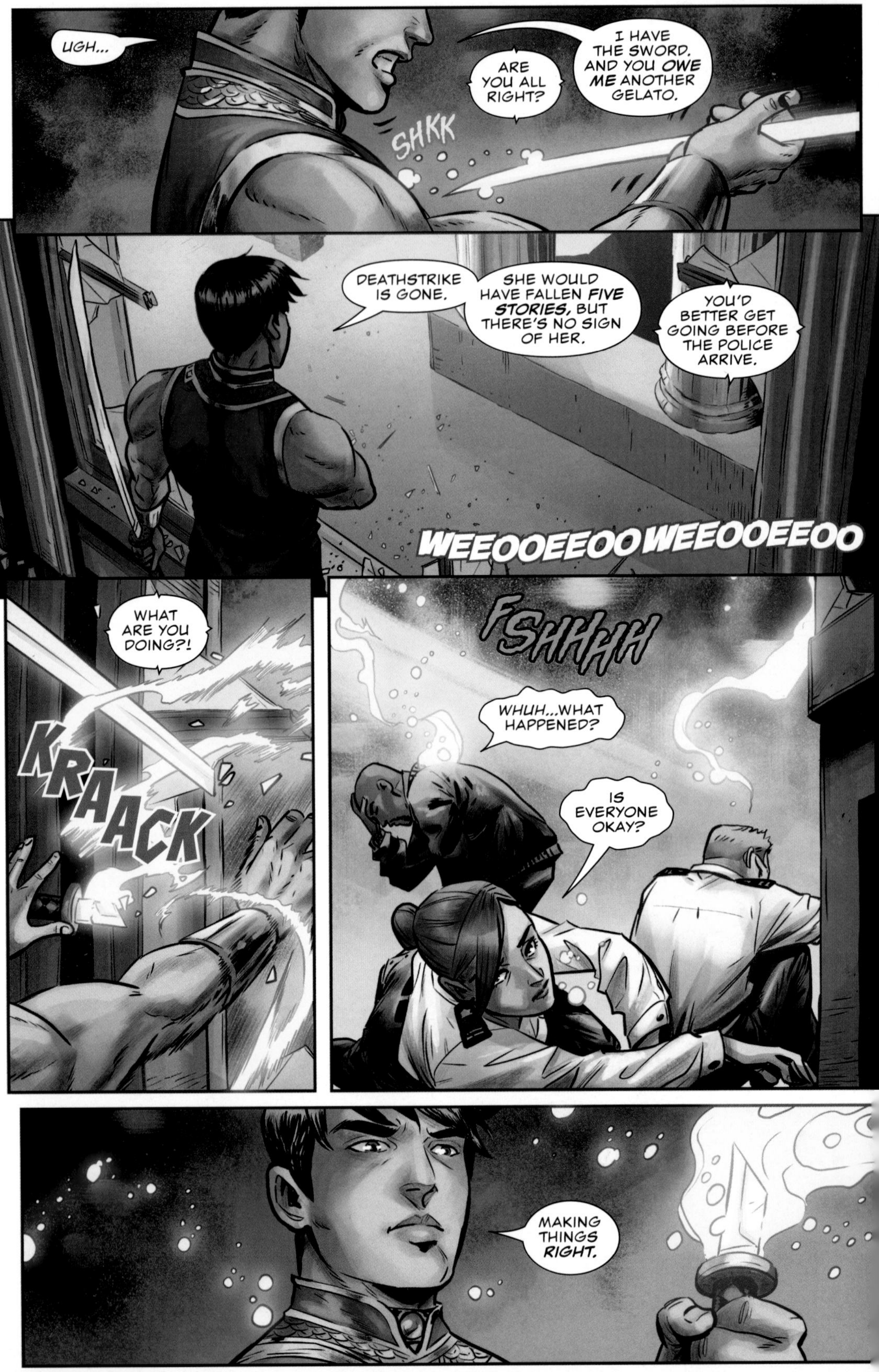
UGH...
ARE YOU ALL RIGHT?
I HAVE THE SWORD. AND YOU OWE ME ANOTHER GELATO.
SHKK
DEATHSTRIKE IS GONE.
SHE WOULD HAVE FALLEN FIVE STORIES, BUT THERE'S NO SIGN OF HER.
YOU'D BETTER GET GOING BEFORE THE POLICE ARRIVE.
WEEOOEEOO WEEOOEEOO
WHAT ARE YOU DOING?!
KRAACK
FSHHHH
WHUH...WHAT HAPPENED?
IS EVERYONE OKAY?
MAKING THINGS RIGHT.

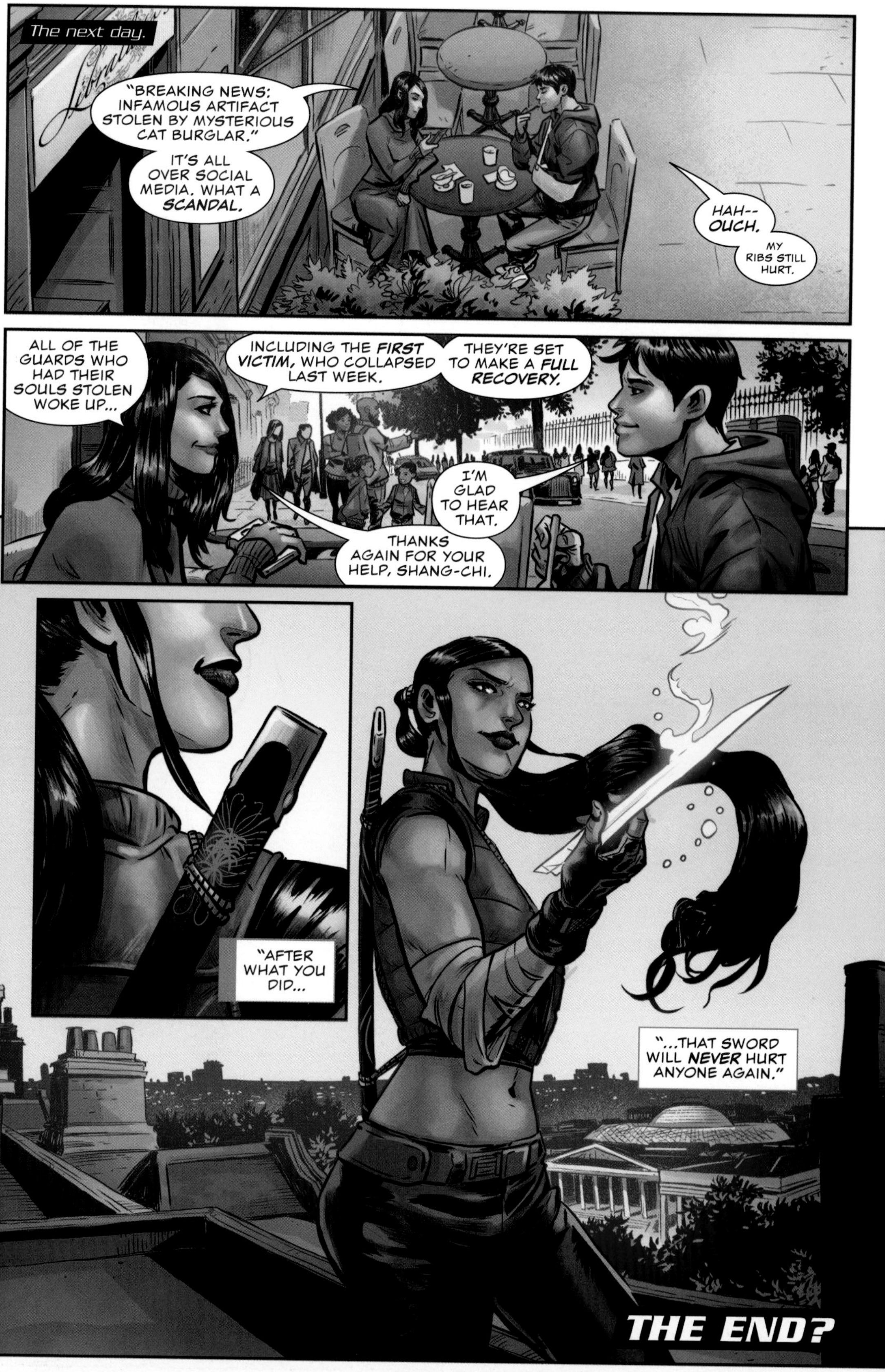
The next day.
"BREAKING NEWS: INFAMOUS ARTIFACT STOLEN BY MYSTERIOUS CAT BURGLAR."
IT'S ALL OVER SOCIAL MEDIA. WHAT A SCANDAL.
HAH-- OUCH.
MY RIBS STILL HURT.
ALL OF THE GUARDS WHO HAD THEIR SOULS STOLEN WOKE UP...
INCLUDING THE FIRST VICTIM, WHO COLLAPSED LAST WEEK.
THEY'RE SET TO MAKE A FULL RECOVERY.
I'M GLAD TO HEAR THAT.
THANKS AGAIN FOR YOUR HELP, SHANG-CHI.
"AFTER WHAT YOU DID...
"...THAT SWORD WILL NEVER HURT ANYONE AGAIN."
THE END?

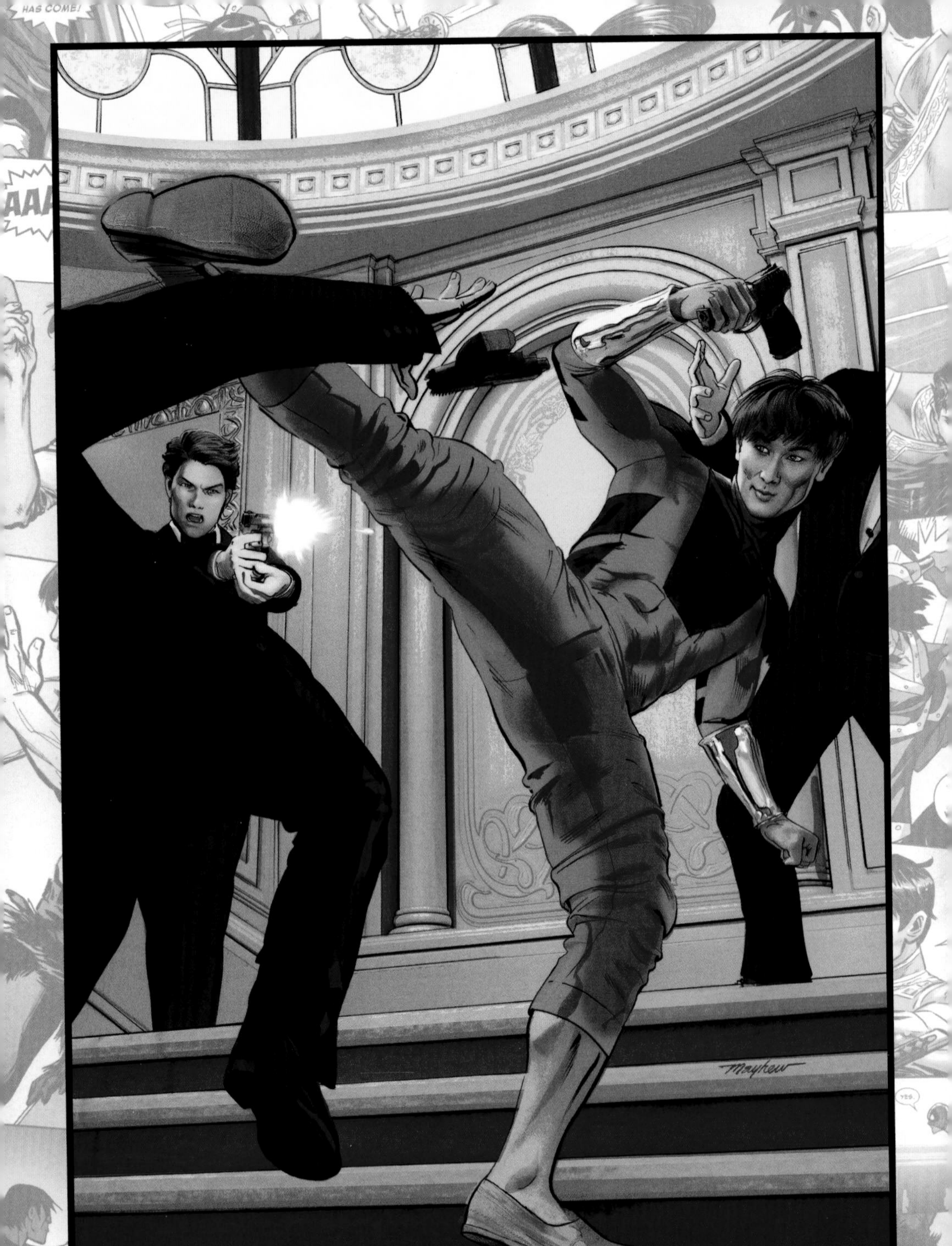
HAS COME!
AAA
YES.
mayhew